AWAKENING

BY

JENNIFER LEIGH PEZZANO

Front cover image by. Germancreative
Book formatting by. Jillian Michaels
First printing edition 2020.

www.jenniferleighpezzano.com

ACKNOWLEDGMENTS

To all those that have helped me on this journey.
To my ever-patient partner who has tirelessly supported me.
To my daughter who is my biggest cheerleader.
To my close friends and family who have celebrated and held space.
And to all my wonderful writing partners who have helped this story grow and flourish.
Thank you for being the vibrant color in the landscape of my life.

EMBRACE

PART 1

Rockport, Maine: 2015

CHAPTER ONE

My footsteps pounded against the wet sand as ragged breath pulled at my lungs, my heart a violent pulse in my ears. Every muscle within me screamed to stop, but I kept going, pushing myself beyond my threshold. The cool mist from the ocean slapped against my face as I ran along the beach, the crash of the waves drowning out my tumbling thoughts until there was nothing left but blissful, empty silence. As always, my legs eventually betrayed me, buckling under the burden of my exhaustion, and forcing me to a halt.

I clasped my hands against my knees, gasping for air as the wind pulled at the loose strands of my hair, tossing them wildly about. I gazed out into the reckless turbulent water as the tall figure of a man in a suit approached from the shoreline. His attire was rather peculiar, like a misplaced apparition among the jagged landscape of rock and water. The wind whipped against his dark hair as he came closer, walking at a brisk pace with a look of deep contemplation etched across his face. He greeted me with a nod as he passed, his eyes flickering over me for a brief moment. The unexpected intensity of his gaze caused my skin to prickle with heat before he continued down the long stretch of empty beach; the fog curling around him like a shroud.

An abstract feeling of yearning overcame me as my eyes followed his outline until he faded from view, and I was once again the centerpiece of my solitude, alone on the beach. The breeze chilled my damp skin, and I wrapped my arms around myself, staring out into the water as if the depths held the answers to the unyielding weight of all my reflections.

With shaky legs, I turned and trudged through the sand, making my way across the parking lot and toward the quiet of downtown. The crash of the waves in the distance soothed me. I loved these moments, the encapsulated hush of early mornings before the bustle of the day descended upon the streets. The seclusion filled me with a deep sense of serenity that pulled at the threads of my restlessness.

Arriving at my office, I slipped my key into the lock. November had found its way in, creeping through the cracks of the windows. It was chilly and dim as the morning sun struggled to pierce through the fog outside, bathing the room in a muted tone of gray. I flicked on the heat and retreated to the bathroom where I turned on the utility shower, shedding my sweat-soaked clothing upon the floor. The warmth of the water cascaded down the length of my body in rivulets, washing away the residue of another night riddled with unsettled sleep, tangled in dreams that slithered their way beneath my sheets, uninvited and full of questions.

* * *

After changing into a fresh pair of clothes from a bag I kept in the back of the storeroom, I nestled my feet next to the old radiator beside my desk while I dried my hair with a towel. The comforting rhythm of the heater ticked like a metronome below me as I ran a comb through my long, tangled strands, enjoying the stillness which filtered through the unadorned white walls and sat with me like a familiar friend.

I leaned back in my chair, looking out at the quaint shops that lined the sidewalks across the street, optimistically displaying various trinkets and beach souvenirs within their front windows in the hope of luring meandering tourists. It was the unpretentious air and welcoming sincerity of the locals which first drew me to this small town years ago as I fled from the stifling cacophony of the city. The quiet here stilled the persistent racing of my heart, while the expansive horizon spoke to me of potential and new beginnings, as if the endless churning waves could wash away the ties that bound me to my past.

My musings were interrupted by the sound of the door opening, and the familiar, pale blue uniform of our local mailman came into my peripheral view.

"Good morning, Jezebel." His chipper tone filled with an enthusiasm I struggled to reciprocate.

I looked up at him with a wane smile. "Hi, Jonathan."

Shuffling slowly through his stack of envelopes, he placed a small pile on my desk. His eager gaze fell on me, appearing to search for an opening to conversation. "So, do you have any plans for this weekend?" He flashed me a wide grin. With his deep brown eyes and sun-kissed hair, he was nice to look at, and I knew he was used to attention from women; all my employees fawned over him. I figured he viewed my reserve as some sort of challenge.

I shook my head. "Nope, no plans. I'm just looking forward to some quiet."

Jonathan had been persistently dancing around me for years, dropping hints with casual invites out to lunch and drinks after work. But the idea of going out on a date with him and his impatient excitement, saturated with forced witty banter and vague innuendos, filled me with exhaustion.

A harsh ring pierced my thoughts. Jonathan's eyes flickered over me while I sifted through the papers that littered my desk, throwing him a polite but dismissive wave goodbye as I found my phone.

"Jezebel's cleaning. How may I help you?"

Jonathan nodded, a twinge of rejection hovering in his gaze before he softly closed the door behind him.

After a long pause, a deep male voice filled the receiver. "Is this Jezebel?"

"Yes, this is she. How may I help you?" I tapped my pen impatiently against the faded grain of the desk, the week's shift sheet spread out before me as I glanced out the side window. The view of the New England coastline engulfed in early morning mist always had a way of helping me find my center.

"I am seeking a house cleaning service."

"And what type of cleaning are you looking for?"

"I am not entirely sure."

Something about the rich, formal tone of his voice drew me in; his words tinted with the hint of an Italian accent.

"Okay, that's fine. If you'd like, I can swing by your place to appraise the scope of work and then draw up a price bid. I happen to be free this afternoon. Are you available at twelve-thirty?"

"Yes, I am. My house is the one upon the bluff. You will not be able to miss it. I look forward to meeting you, Jezebel." There was a sudden click, then the line went dead.

I stared at the phone in my hand for a moment. The old colonial house, which sat perched atop the bluff overlooking the ocean, had been boarded up and unoccupied for the last hundred years, if not more. According to local lore, nobody knew who owned it, but every decade or so, workers would arrive and meticulously restore the house. I had always found it beautiful, filled with silence and rich secrets, as if it were some beacon keeping sentinel over the water. My mind brimmed with curiosity at the prospect of finally getting a chance to see inside the place.

* * *

That afternoon, I drove past the sleepy storefronts of the main street tof the outer edge of town, past the docks, and toward the jetty where the sea caressed the cliffs. The slate gray sky framed the stormy ocean as icy fog snaked its way along the rocks jutting sharply out of the water. I flipped on the classical station, the deep mournful tone of the cello which always seemed to fill me with an undefined longing, spilled from my speakers, matching the mood of the sky.

I turned from the main road onto a narrow, winding driveway. As I pulled up to the house, I saw a man on the balcony, looking out toward the watery horizon. His hands were tucked into the pockets of what appeared to be an expensive suit as the wind swept through his dark hair, his eyes fixed on the water. My pulse quickened with surprise as I realized this was the person that I had seen on the beach during my morning run.

The strong breeze pulled at my clothes as I stepped from the car, pushing the unruly strands of my hair away from the grasp of the wind. As I approached the front door, the man turned in my direction, his eyes locking with mine from above.

I shot a friendly wave up at him, calling above the roar of the surf. "Hi, I'm Jezebel."

After nodding in greeting, he disappeared from my line of sight. A moment later, the door swung open, and he stood before me. "August. It is a pleasure to meet you." His firm handshake engulfed my fingers in his warmth, and a small current passed through me as our skin touched. It was a feeling unfamiliar and a bit jarring, causing an indistinct stirring within me. His eyes were a deep blue gray, reminiscent of the ocean, a startling contrast against his dark features and faint olive complexion.

"Welcome, Jezebel. Please come in."

I followed him into the house, my eyes glancing over the tall windows covered in heavy burgundy drapes which framed the walls of the interior.

"Let me give you some light." He stepped past me and drew the curtains open. The room flooded with a pale overcast glare.

"You know, I think I saw you out on the beach this morning," I said as I threaded my fingers through the tangled curls of my hair.

August turned from the window. "Yes. You were running."

"I was."

He regarded me with a look of curiosity. "Do you always run like that?"

I furrowed my brow at him. "Like what?"

A small smiled slipped past his lips. "Like someone is chasing you."

I chuckled awkwardly and shrugged. "Yeah, I guess I do."

I stepped closer to the window, taking in the expansive view that stretched before me like an endless sea of deep blue. "This place is so beautiful. I've never understood why it's been empty for so long. Did you just buy it?"

"No."

"Oh. Renting, then?"

"Something akin to that." As he spoke, he glanced out the window, seeming to be lost momentarily in thought.

The long pause that ensued made it clear he was not going to offer any more information. I tentatively retrieved my notepad from my purse, my eyes flickering in his direction. "So, I'm just going to do a little assessment of the house, if that's okay with you?"

August nodded, watching me in silence as I took in the surrounding room, the directness of his gaze rattling my composure. The house had the familiar damp and musky smell from years of the ocean's spray, which battered the foundation and seeped in through the cracks. The windows held an opaque film of salt that I knew from experience no amount of cleaning would remove.

Thick canvas cloth covered the furniture, antique paintings framed in embossed gold designs lined the walls, and a grand piano stood in the far corner.

Intrigued, I stepped closer to one of the oil renditions, a Rembrandt that depicted the tragic story of Lucretia. I was familiar with the woman who sat with a gold cord held in one hand and a dagger in the other, a faint line of blood running down the middle of her dress, her life slowly draining away. The visceral expression of sorrow and betrayal portrayed within the depths of her eyes had always haunted me; it was as if she was staring into my soul, pleading for redemption.

"I take it you recognize one of those pieces?"

I turned to find August close enough that I could detect the faint but rich aroma of earth and pine on him, reminding me of the forest. He regarded me with an intensity that made my heart race. I was unaccustomed to the potency in which he looked at me, and a warmth rose to my cheeks.

"I do. Was the previous owner a collector?"

"Perhaps he was." A hint of secrecy played in his voice, sparking my interest as he turned and strode toward the dining room. "Please come with me. I will show you the rest of the house."

I followed him into the warmth of the kitchen. A beckoning

aroma of spices drifted through the air and my eyes glanced down to a pot simmering on the stove.

"Minestra di ceci," August said as he leaned against the doorway, watching me. "It is an Italian dish consisting of chickpeas."

"Well, it smells delicious."

He nodded with a faint smile and then motioned for me to follow him up a flight of stairs. We came to a large room lined with floor-to-ceiling windows, and a sliding glass door that led to the balcony.

In the corner of the expansive master bedroom stood an old wooden desk. Papers lay askew and stacked in precarious piles on the worn mahogany wood. A sizable, ornate four-poster bed, draped in a lush, silk-like fabric of muted brown tones, imposed itself against the far wall. If I were to lie down upon it, the view would surround me.

August stood quietly by the window, tousled hair falling lightly against his brows. He had a rugged masculine beauty to him, tinged with something sensual and vaguely ethereal. It was a striking combination I found captivating.

He glanced over at me with an expression of faint amusement, as if he had stumbled into my thoughts for a moment, causing heat to surge through my body. I cleared my throat nervously, and with my notepad in hand, I slipped back into the comfort of my professional persona. Scanning the room, I calculated formulas of space and cost on the white-lined paper, all the while trying to ignore his lingering gaze.

"So, it looks to me like you will need a move-in restoration, followed by weekly upkeep? Depending on your living arrangements, of course."

"If you insist. You are the professional."

I turned to him. Although the light streaming in behind him illuminated his silhouette and gently obscured his face, I could detect the slight hint of a smile.

"All right, then. I will prepare a work order and have one of my cleaners come out as early as next week. What day works best for you?"

"If you do not mind, I would prefer it if you were the one to come every week."

His request was a bit odd, and I struggled with my response. *Why did he want me in particular?*

"Well, these days I generally manage the administrative details."

"I will gladly pay double."

I ran my fingers along his mahogany desk, picking up a thick line of dust. I took a moment to study an antique vase of leaded crystal, which held an array of fountain pens, each tip etched in gold.

The years I spent being shuffled around from one foster home to another during my youth were lonely and painful, but they had given me keen instincts. I had learned to trust my senses and the acute feelings that enabled me to gauge a person's intentions. It was these same instincts that had kept me safe on more than one occasion. This man radiated complexity. But underneath his slightly brusque exterior, I could detect a gentleness there, and I felt no risk with him, only a deep, probing intrigue.

Aware that my business could use the extra money, I considered his proposal. Each year the flood of vacationers served as the lifeblood of our tiny company. But once they retreated to the city at the end of the season, leaving a hush to settle over the town, winter closed in with its icy grip and customers slowed to a crawl.

"Well, I suppose I can make some accommodations."

"Good, I will walk you out," he said as he slipped past me and headed silently back down the stairs.

The chill of the wind mixed with salty mist struck my face as August walked me to my car. Dark clouds hovered ominously above the angry sea, obscuring the horizon in gray.

"Looks like a storm is coming."

He simply nodded in reply, his expression unreadable as he watched me fumble around in my purse, looking for my keys. I glanced up at him, flustered by the potency of his eyes, which made me feel as if I were a butterfly pinned beneath cloth. It filled me with a conflicting mixture of reluctance and curiosity.

"Can I ask you something? Why is it you want me specifically for this job?"

My pulse quickened as August leaned in close, almost as if he were about to whisper a secret into my ear, the strands of his dark hair touching my face like a soft caress. I shivered against the eager wind and took a small step back, alarmed by his sudden proximity.

"If you must know, I feel very drawn to you. You have a receptive mind, and I know that you can be trusted."

The openness that hovered in his eyes coupled with his candid words seized my breath for a moment; it was unexpected and a bit eccentric, causing my voice to waver in reply. "And how would you know that?"

August's gaze held mine as if he were peering into my soul, stripping away at the residue, and leaving nothing behind but the exposed marrow. No man had ever looked at me this way before. It was unnerving, but at the same time, deeply enthralling.

"Just a feeling I have." His words were like a slow and silky caress. "Will next Monday evening around six work for you?"

I tucked away a strand of hair that had blown into my face, caught off guard by his request. "Oh, I'm sorry, but any time after five is outside business hours, I'm afraid."

"Well, I suppose it will have to be five, then." A small smile stretched across his face, his gaze warm and open as he leaned past me and opened the car door. "It was very nice meeting you, *Jezebel.*"

There was something in the way he said my name, a soft undercurrent of such concentrated intimacy it caused a flutter inside me.

"You, too," I said as I slipped into the driver's seat, surprised to find my limbs shaky. August stood there and watched me while I started the engine, his clothes dancing wildly with the wind. I took a deep breath, putting the car into reverse, filled with an undefined sensation that coiled around me like electricity. When I looked back out the window, he had retreated from view.

CHAPTER TWO

Monday night arrived. Within the silence of my apartment, I swept my hair back into a tight bun and glanced at my reflection in the mirror with a discontented sigh. Though I rarely was concerned with my appearance, I suddenly wished I had something more intriguing to wear besides the bland, muted tones of my oversized work shirt.

I loaded my supplies into the trunk of my car and drove through the soft blanket of early evening and up the steep driveway to August's house. I reflected on the tiny bundle of nerves that had settled in the pit of my stomach. The mere thought of seeing him again filled me with a strange sense of anticipation. There was something about him that captivated me with a reckless curiosity.

I parked and made my way to the door, lugging the heavy cleaning bag over my shoulder. A faint light shone through one of the kitchen windows. Before I had a chance to knock, I heard the soft tone of August's voice from inside.

"Please, come in, Jezebel."

Turning the handle, I stepped tentatively into the shadowy warmth of the house. August stood facing the window with the curtains drawn open; the pale shimmer of the setting sun engulfing him. Through the glass, I could make out the waves dancing with the warm tones of reflected light.

Lost in the depths of his thoughts, August did not turn to greet me. An awkward silence hung thick in the air, punctuated only by the rhythmic tick of a mantle clock sitting above the fireplace.

"Hey there. Would you mind if I turned on a few more lights?" I asked, my voice breaking the silence. "It's pretty dark in here."

August moved from the window and flipped a switch on the wall, illuminating the house in a warm glow. "Is that better?" His dark hair fell in disheveled waves against his face and lightly brushed the shoulders of his indigo suit as he walked toward me with a smile. "I do apologize. I enjoy the view unobscured by artificial light."

The concentrated burn of his gaze caused my heart to accelerate while I adjusted to the brightness. I smiled nervously, unaccustomed to this awkward version of myself. "Yes, this is much better. Thanks."

"Let me know if you need anything, Jezebel. I will be upstairs, working."

After a quick nod, I moved to retrieve the cleaning supplies I had left near the door. When I looked back, he was already retreating up the stairs. As I listened to his footsteps creaking softly above me, I wondered what kind of world he dove into, with his stacks of papers and gold-plated fountain pens.

* * *

I spent the next hour eradicating the thick dust from the living room. The canvas cloth had been removed, and judging from the paintings on the walls, I had expected the furniture and décor to be antique as well. I liked the idea that this house stood untouched with its secrets frozen in time, but everything was surprisingly modern. Only the grand piano that loomed in the far corner with its ebony wood slightly faded, whispered of times long ago.

I had always loved the piano, with its smooth, smoky tones that sparked a sense of nostalgia, and evoked memories of late winter nights curled up by the fireplace as a child, with Bach playing softly in the background as the hushed voices of my parents filtered in from the kitchen.

Running my cloth across the surface, I rested my fingers over the ivory, pressing gently upon a key and eliciting a single, mournful note which resonated throughout the room.

"I see you have met Abigail."

Startled, I turned to find him standing beside me. His hands were clasped in a graceful sweep behind his back that reminded me of an old painting.

13

"You named your piano?" I found that fact somewhat charming as I shot him a playful smile. "I take it you play, then?"

He nodded as warmth danced in his eyes, softening his expression.

"I've always wanted to learn how to play," I said with a sigh.

"Why don't you then?" he asked.

"I haven't had the time, I guess."

"Ah, time." His voice trailed off as he glanced out the window, appearing to be momentarily lost in his thoughts again. "I would give you some of mine if I could."

A tired smile flickered across his face, and suddenly I saw a lonely man. A man weighed down by something heavy.

"I would really love to hear you play sometime," I said, hoping my words would prompt him.

He looked at me curiously, as if trying to gauge my interest. "Would you?"

"Yes, I would."

He moved past me and sat on the bench. For a moment, his hands lay still upon the keys, hovering in the silence that filled the space between us. When he began to play, the music that flowed from his fingers started slow and haunting, then developed into a rich melody. I stood there beside the piano, overcome with a yearning and an abrupt pang of sadness that caught in my throat. Entranced and held captive by this intimacy he was unexpectedly sharing, I could not hold back the sudden emotion that pooled within me.

As he closed with a soft finish, I realized I had been holding my breath. I let it out in one long sigh. "Wow... that was really beautiful."

August looked up at me, noticing my tears.

I smiled and went to wipe them away, letting out an uncomfortable laugh. "Well, I guess you made me cry."

He took me in with his cobalt gaze, soft and filled with sincerity. "Well, I am honored to have moved you."

My fingers absentmindedly ran across the top of the piano. "Did you write that yourself?"

A hint of sadness flickered across his face. "Yes, I wrote that for my late wife." His voice was full of melancholy as his eyes trailed to the window, seeking out the ocean through the darkness.

I had a sudden longing to reach out and touch him. I recognized his sorrow, like a palpable weight around him. The feeling was familiar, for I carried my own pain pressed tightly against my chest. "I'm so sorry for your loss."

August nodded and rose from the bench. He brushed past me as he strode into the kitchen, leaving me alone with the fragmented feelings his music provoked. For a moment I stared at the loneliness that curled around me like a relentless shadow, the gaping hole in my heart that pulsed like a wound that would not heal. *Would I ever find my happiness? Did I even know what happiness felt like?* As I struggled to regain my composure, August came up from behind and slipped a cool glass of water into my hand, his arm brushing against mine as he lingered over my shoulder.

"Thank you for sharing that with me," I said as I took the glass to my lips, realizing how thirsty I was and grateful for the cool liquid which slid down and quenched my dry throat.

"You know, it takes a certain type of person to listen honestly and feel the story behind the music," he said, his voice like a warm whisper teasing my neck, and causing a faint tingle of goosebumps to run down my back. "Thank you for listening."

I turned to him. Our proximity filled me with a sudden rush of adrenaline, and I grew dizzy, my breath momentarily caught as I fell into the depths of his gaze; completely untethered by the intensity of his eyes, which swirled in a palette of blue tones. *Who was this man? And why did I feel so overcome by him?*

August withdrew from my side with a nod, and retreated up the stairs, abruptly leaving me devoid of warmth.

I managed to retrieve my senses and went back into the living room to resume cleaning. My fingers trailed over the books lined neatly on a shelf beside the couch, my eye falling to one in particular; tucked conspicuously in between the laminated spines of reference and history.

When I pulled out the faded leather-bound book, it rested large and heavy in my hands. Inside, held paper made from the soft parchment of linen, with cursive script in a language I could not decipher scrawled upon the pages. There was something ancient and mysterious that pulled at me as my fingers traced over the text, noticing faint smudges left from the ink that had bled and blurred the words. The creak of footsteps upstairs startled me, and realizing I was snooping, I quickly closed the book, placing it delicately back on the shelf.

The hush of evening had gathered around the house like a heavy cloak when I realized it was almost seven. I picked up my pace a little, working my way through the dining room and into the kitchen before heading upstairs.

"Hello?" I called out, expecting to find August there, but the room was empty. As my eyes fell on the bed, veiled in partial shadow, something about it pulled forth an obscure longing that I could not define. Feeling flushed, I turned and opened the sliding glass door, stepping out onto the deck. The cool breeze ruffled my hair and brushed across my skin like a whisper. I gazed out into the darkness of the landscape, perplexed as to where August had disappeared to, when I saw the faint outline of a man below me.

August stood atop the cliffs, gazing pensively out to sea as if he were searching for something. Mesmerized by his stillness, I watched him like a voyeur, one that had slipped quietly and unannounced into his private moment. I took a step back to give him his privacy, turning to close the door behind me, only to find he had disappeared into the darkness.

Silence encompassed the room, filled with a heavy energy that pulled at me as I began to clean. Throughout my years of being in other people's homes, I was always left with an impression, as if the room itself retained an essence, memories and emotions that etched themselves upon the walls like an invisible narrative. I ran my fingers down the length of his bedspread, the silk cool to the touch, and I wondered what lives had been lived here. For within this room I sensed a deep undercurrent of love and sorrow.

* * *

As I finished up and gathered my supplies, making my way downstairs, August emerged in the hallway.

"Let me help you with that."

He carried my oversized duffle bag out to the car while I followed. After I loaded up the trunk, he pressed an envelope into my palm, eliciting a small electrical current that made my skin tingle as his hand brushed against mine. When I looked up to thank him, his eyes lingered on mine, the darkness faintly illuminated by the dome light of my open door.

"I hope to see you next week, Jezebel."

His tone was somber, causing me to reply in an overly cheerful inflection, "That was the arrangement, once a week, right?"

"We shall see."

I stared at him, trying to gauge what his obscure remark implied as I gave him a nod and slipped into my car. My eyes glanced into the rearview mirror, watching him fade into the shadows as I drove down the dark road toward home.

* * *

It wasn't until the next morning, as I sat at my table with a cup of coffee and the week's balance sheets before me, that I opened his envelope. Inside, I found a large check and a note. I unfolded the paper and read the flowing cursive script.

Ego diu tangere te.

The words looked familiar, and I realized it was the same vernacular I had seen scribbled within the pages of the leather book I had found on his shelf the night before. I quickly did a search on my phone for the translation. My heart skipped a beat, and a warm flush surged through my body. It was in Latin and translated to, "I long to touch you."

CHAPTER THREE

I sat in my kitchen as the late autumn sunlight bathed the room in a dusty glow, my hands lost in the deep, cool richness of the clay, sculpting life into an image that had been haunting me in a recurring dream. The raven stared back at me with wild commanding eyes, perched next to a heart that lay in fragments. Most of my work was dark and brooding, the physical manifestations of my soul grappling with itself. The clay had a way of pulling out my demons and laying them bare before me. It was healing and stilled the persistent racing of my battered heart.

The various pieces I had created over the years sat on the shelves above me. Many people had told me that my work was beautiful, that it invoked emotion, but I couldn't bring myself to show my art to the public. The idea of exposing the raw filament of myself filled me with discomfort. It was as if, by showing my sculptures, all my carefully constructed masks would crumble, leaving nothing behind but brittle bone.

I ran my fingers through the clay, sculpting the feathers on the bird, which seemed to beckon me with a visceral hunger. My mind wandered back to August. All week I had been pondering his seductive message. His note had suddenly shifted the dynamics between us, and a clandestine thrill rushed through me as I took in the possibilities. Excitement and hesitancy collided within me as I considered the implications of returning.

What was it that he wanted? Was he testing me in some way? These questions loomed over me, sharp and encompassing. This man was an entrancing enigma I could not decipher, and his invitation was cloaked with obscurity, as if he were taunting me to open a door to the unknown.

There was a passion and intensity that seemed to emanate off him, but also a tenderness and warmth I was intrinsically drawn to, and it enthralled me. The thought of his hands on my body consumed me with a longing I had not felt before, as if he could strip away the residue, and leave something whole behind. All these tumbling feelings were out of character and foreign. I had grown used to the neat compartments of my life, and August filled me with a discomforting confusion that I no longer wanted to sit with.

Standing from the table, I grabbed my phone, my fingers trailing down the list of my employees I had taped to the refrigerator door.

Sydney picked up on the first ring. "Hey there, Jezebel. What's going on?"

I paced the length of the kitchen. "I'm so sorry to be calling you like this on a weekend, but I need a favor."

"No problem, what is it?" She chirped optimistically.

I took a deep breath. "We have a new client, and he needs an evening clean tomorrow. But something has come up, and I won't be able to go out there. Can you cover for me?"

I clenched my jaw, waiting in anticipation for her answer.

"Sure thing, I'll be there tomorrow."

I let out a sigh of relief. "Thanks so much, Sydney. I really appreciate it."

After hanging up the phone, the tight band of indecision that had wrapped around me lifted slightly, only to be replaced by a voice inside, trying to claw its way to the surface.

Had I become so used to pushing away possibilities, that I didn't even know what they looked like anymore?

My shoes hit the wet sand, pounding out my thoughts as the morning fog hovered low over the water. Everything was gray and cold, and the perspiration that clung to my skin felt like ice. I didn't see him at first; an outcropping of tall rocks that hugged the shoreline concealed him.

"Jezebel."

The sound of my name brought me to a jerking halt. I whipped around to find August standing behind me. My heart flipped, and hot prickles rushed over me as my hand flew up to my chest.

"*Jesus*, August. You startled me."

"My apologies." With his hands thrust in the pockets of his coat, he regarded me with curiosity, lifting one eyebrow up in mild amusement. "Fancy meeting you here."

"Yes." My words tumbled out breathlessly, and despite my reservations, I could not help the smile that crept across my face. His mere presence incited a giddiness within me.

"I must admit, I was a bit disappointed not to see you the other day."

I fiddled with my hair, pulling the elastic tighter around my bun. "I know, I'm sorry. Something came up, I should have called."

August stepped closer, his eyes piercing through me like vibrant sparks of energy. "You do not have to apologize for any discomfort my note may have caused you. I understand that it was a bold statement."

My face flushed with warmth. "Are you always this straightforward with people?"

He nodded with a faint smile. "Yes, Jezebel, I am."

I kicked my shoes around in the sand, watching the waves as they curled around us.

"I'm not exactly sure what you want from me."

I looked up to find the strength of his gaze pulling me into his depths, leaving me exposed.

"I want to provide you an opportunity to let your walls down, to experience a part of yourself that you have been repressing."

I stared at him. The explicit force of his words felt like a challenge, and it caught me off guard. Grappling with a response, my silence filled the space between us as I struggled with emotions that left me unmoored and disorientated.

"It is clear to me, though, that I have made you uncomfortable, and I apologize for overstepping. I will let you get back to your run, but I do hope you will reconsider continuing our work arrangement."

August's eyes met mine, a flicker of heat passing between us before he turned with a somber nod and strolled down the beach, his form gently slipping into the morning fog, leaving me standing there speechless and filled with emotions undefined.

The following Monday, as the shadows of late afternoon cast wavering light upon the walls, I found myself pacing around my apartment. August's words on the beach had consumed me for days, slowly chipping away at my resolve. I had not made prior arrangements for another cleaner, and this choice had opened a door, allowing me to stand tentatively at the threshold. The mirror in the bathroom caught my reflection as I released my hair from its restrictive coiled hold. My dark curls fell against the dress I had brazenly slipped on, one I had not had an occasion to wear until now. It was silky, black, and easily shed, and it spoke loudly of intentions intrepid and completely unrelated to cleaning.

The idea of offering myself to this man felt erotic and enticing. I had never done this before. I was not accustomed to acting spontaneously. In the past, all my intimate encounters had been orchestrated by a series of carefully thought-out steps. Impulsivity was not in my nature. I was stepping out of my comfort zone, and it was an alluring rush that left me strangely empowered.

My fingers ran along the edges of August's note, which still lay on my kitchen counter. *Should I really do this? Should I go to him?* Filled with a sudden burst of confidence, I grabbed my coat and headed out into the growing chill of dusk.

As I drove up to his house, I mused over my past. It had been many years since I had felt the touch of another. Most of my experiences with men had left me empty. My litany of lovers were like faded paper, their memories dull and lifeless, leaving no lasting impression upon my mind. After moving to this tiny town nestled against the sea, I had thrown myself into my business with ferocity, consumed with responsibility, and reluctant to dive into yet another disappointment. I appreciated the peace that my solitude brought and the predictability of my days, but I wondered at times; was I broken in a way that could not be repaired? Had the trauma of my past grown thorns, enclosing me in a thicket of self-preservation? Nevertheless, here I was, driving to a man I didn't know, as if some force beyond my control was pushing me recklessly toward him, with my own indiscretion sitting in the front seat, daring me forward.

Pulling up the driveway, I took in the large house. The lights that glowed from inside shone like a beacon, and my heart fluttered like a nervous bird within the walls of my chest. *What am I doing?* The question pressed itself around me, but my practical mind was nowhere to be found.

The gravel crunched beneath my feet as I walked to the house on unsteady legs. I knocked, but only silence echoed back. I stood there, staring at the closed door as if it were a sign that I should get in my car and drive home, back to the safe expectations of my life. But before I could turn to leave, I felt August behind me like a beckoning force that wrapped itself around my skin.

"Jezebel?" A look of surprise flickered across his face as I turned to him, his eyes seeking me out in the hovering darkness. "I was not expecting to see you here again."

"I wasn't either," I replied, my words wavering with hesitation.

"So, what made you come back...If you do not mind me asking?"

August's voice was soft and seductive as he hovered in the doorway, studying me with a look that sent my heart racing. Now that I was here, captive under the enigmatic spell of his presence, I was unsure of what to say. I fumbled nervously with the thin fabric of my coat, aware that my cleaning supplies still sat inside my car. We both knew I was not here to clean. I was here to offer myself to him, though the boundaries of what that entailed were blurred and undefined.

As this reality coursed through me, I began to tremble, not in fear, but excitement. It was as if I were about to plunge into something deep with this man, and once I did, there would be no ladder with which to climb back up.

"I don't really know. I guess...I found your boldness compelling after all." My words came out halting and breathless.

A soft gentleness swam in the depths of his gaze as he looked at me. "Please, come inside. You're shivering, Jezebel."

"I'm okay..."

His eyes grazed across my body and then fell to where my dress peeked beneath my coat. "Are you sure? If you are at all uncomfortable being here right now, just tell me."

I nodded my head, my words like sticky honey in my mouth. "Yes, I am sure."

August opened the door for me, shutting it quietly behind us. The sound of the ocean retreated, and my thoughts stilled as a tense, but supple silence filled the room.

"I've never done this, you know."

He turned to me and tenderly brushed a wisp of hair away from my shoulder. "And what would you like this to be for you?"

I stared at him, unable to formulate an answer, realizing no man had ever asked me that before.

"I don't know."

"I think you do." August's hands softly fell to my arms as he slid them slowly up my shoulders, removing my coat from around me and hanging it on a hook by the door.

"Beneath the layers of your mind, there is a language that only your body speaks. What is it saying right now?"

I closed my eyes for a moment, breathing in the richness of his question. "I want you to make me feel beautiful."

When I opened my eyes again, a rush of dizziness engulfed me under the deep burn of his gaze. "Do you believe that you are not beautiful, Jezebel?"

He reached up to cup my face. His large, calloused fingers left a surprisingly featherlight caress across my temples. With the back of his hand, he traced along my cheekbone before slipping down to my neck. His palm cupped the tender place where my pulse lay, and my racing heart thrummed against his touch.

August leaned close to me. "Because I can assure you that you are." His lips fell upon my neck in a soft kiss that caused me to suck in my breath. "Very... Beautiful." Each drawn-out word became a burst of pleasure upon my skin as his hand slipped down past my neck and to the swell of my breasts. A moan escaped my lips as his thumb brushed over the fabric of my dress, sending a ripple of longing that washed over me. His eyes grew heavy, devouring me with an intensity that left me woozy as if I were drunk.

"Is this all right with you?" He asked in a low, husky whisper. "Do you want me to stop?"

"No. Don't stop." My voice quivered as I reached out to pull him closer, desire springing from me with sudden urgency as my hands ran down the firm slope of his back. His mouth was deliciously close to mine when he suddenly released me, his eyes filled with a simmering heat.

"Would you like to join me upstairs?"

I nodded, my legs growing weak, trembling with an ache that emanated from deep within my core. He smiled, took my hand, and guided me up the stairs to the dark, lush contours of his bed.

CHAPTER FOUR

"**M**ay I take off your dress, Jezebel? I would like to see all of you." He stood behind me in the dark, his breath a sensual whisper against my neck.

"Yes."

The heat of his hands on my back sent shivers of desire coursing through me. He slipped off my dress, letting the fabric slide down my body and onto the floor.

"Lie down."

His tone was tender but firm. Aroused by his gentle, yet commanding control, I found myself yielding to his request. I could feel his eyes on me as I lay back on his bed, the sheets a cool satin against my skin. The familiar insecurity that gripped me whenever I presented my body to a man was strangely nowhere to be found. The scars I hid, the extra flesh I so cunningly concealed, my anxious need to adhere to the vacuous expectations of beauty; they all seemed to vanish as I lay there, naked before him like an offering. The heat of his eyes moved over the abundant curves of my body like a silent, hungry caress as he drew closer, kneeling on the floor beside the bed. My pulse quickened as his hands slid up my legs. His fingers stopped momentarily before slowly tracing the length of the scars which trailed along my thighs. I drew in a shaky breath, overwhelmed by the searing desire this man elicited in me.

He continued his leisurely exploration of my body, teasing me with a light brush over the folds of my sex; already tender and wet, before moving up to my breasts. My nipples ached with sensation as he ran his thumb against them in slow circular strokes. I grasped at his arms, trying to pull myself closer, shocked at how the simplest touch from him could provoke such a strong response. *How could this feel so good?* His hands were like ecstasy, sending ripples of pleasure through me.

"Oh my God, what are you doing to me?" I gasped, my words spilling out into the darkness, breathless and alive as August slid his finger gradually down the soft curve of my belly and found the heat of my center.

Overwhelmed by sensation, a sharp gasp escaped me as I arched against his hand, desperately trying to draw his fingers in deeper. But his touch remained tantalizingly slow. My body trembled with a powerful need for release, and I could feel myself slipping over the precipice of an orgasm when he abruptly stopped.

"No...no...no, don't stop," I begged him. "Please...." Whimpering against the sheets, I clutched them in my fists. This was torture of a kind I had never felt before. Every part of my body hungered for his touch.

He moved across the bed with a silent grace and gathered me into his arms. His fingers grazed over my lips, the faint taste of my desire lingering on them as his eyes met mine. I reached out and guided his mouth closer to me. There was a moment of hesitation from him, a flicker in his gaze before his lips touched mine. I grasped at the fabric of his shirt while his hands slipped into my hair. His lips were soft, his tongue dancing delicately with mine in a slow sensual waltz.

My center throbbed impatiently with longing as his breath fell across my skin, his kiss leaving a long, aching trail down to my neck. His name rushed out of me in a tangled moan when all of a sudden, a prick like the tip of a blade pressed against my skin.

It took all my strength to pull away from him, confused by the unexpected sensation. Reeling and woozy from his touch, I tried to gather myself, wondering if I had stumbled into some sort of bizarre role play.

"What... the hell was that?"

My question pierced the stillness in the room as I looked up at him with widened eyes. My heart hammered out a heavy rhythm against my chest as I grappled with the jagged blow of disbelief. His teeth were now faintly visible, protruding below the succulent curve of his lips, and my breath tangled in my throat. *Who was this man?*

The loudest part of me, the one that held all my fears, instinctively recoiled in horror, while a tiny voice inside me, the one that diligently tended to the garden of logic in my mind; wondered if this was all some strangely lucid, erotic dream.

August pulled back and ran his tongue lightly along the points of his teeth, and like the sweep of a magician's curtain, they vanished. The blue of his eyes simmered as he regarded me with a steady look of inquiry. "Do I frighten you, Jezebel?"

"I don't know... should I be frightened?" I began to shiver, sliding myself further against the headboard in an attempt to put more distance between us as the boundaries of my logical mind struggled to make sense of what was going on.

"No, I would never hurt you. I want you to understand that. And I do apologize for startling you." August moved to wrap a sheet around my body, his eyes sober again.

Confusion swam in murky puddles, but at the same time, I felt no danger from him. His gaze spoke of sincerity, and the energy that radiated off him was soft, and full of a gentleness. "Is this really happening right now? Were you really just about to-"

He shook his head, stilling my words before I could finish. "No, Jezebel. What you felt was only a polite invitation. I would never Embrace you without your permission."

"Embrace me?"

"Yes. An Embrace is an intimate, consensual act between two people."

My throat felt dry as I struggled to understand what he was saying to me. "And what exactly does this Embrace involve?"

"Technically, I would be drinking your blood." August's fingertips grazed my arm as he spoke, eliciting a current of electricity that cascaded through me. "But there is much more to it than that. Within your blood lies an essence that you would be sharing with me. It is sacred and immensely powerful."

I stared at him incredulously. "Are you for real right now?"

He nodded. "Yes, I can assure you. I am very real."

Despite my shock, a deep fascination bloomed, awakening within me the fragments of myself that longed to explore the depths. To connect with a yearning more carnal in nature which had been hidden and bound by society, screaming to be let out. This part of me stepped forward, telling me this was real, that this was actually happening, and that all the other aspects of myself had no place here in this room with this terrifyingly alluring man.

My words came out tentative, caught between the pull of curiosity and the push of apprehension. "Does it hurt?"

August smiled. "No. My Embrace would only bring you extreme pleasure."

"And then... what happens after?" My pulse had slowed its frantic pace, fading to a softer hum as my hands released their grip on the sheets. His voice was soothing and stilled the clawing of my unease.

He reached out to brush a strand of hair away from my face, his fingers lingering on my cheek as he spoke. "You may feel a bit lightheaded at first, and you would long for sleep. Though what I would take from you is no more than what one would give at a blood bank. Your body will easily replenish it."

I found myself strangely titillated by his seductive proposal, but beneath the lust he had stirred to the surface, lay a myriad of conflicting feelings. This confusion held me captive in a state of strange, emotional suspension.

"How is this even possible?"

The blue of August's eyes pierced into me. "There is so much to this reality that you can only begin to grasp, Jezebel."

I ran my fingers through my hair, trying to grasp at my tangled thoughts. "I'm not quite sure what you are trying to say here? What are you...some kind of vampire?" I couldn't help the mocking tone in my voice.

He shook his head, an amused smile playing across his face. "Oh, the *vampire*. Such an entertaining fairy tale embellished over centuries, rooted in fear and false propaganda. No, I am not a vampire, at least not in the way you think a vampire to be. What I am is a descendant of an ancient bloodline. I call myself De Sanguine, which roughly translates to *Of Sacred Blood*."

My head spun with a feeling of surrealism that was hard to compartmentalize. The world I had carefully molded around myself had collapsed, spinning me recklessly toward a reality unknown to me. Trepidation clung to me like a shield while the faint rush of excitement bubbled within. It was as if I had stumbled upon a treasure, a beautiful, elusive truth, hidden from me until now, and it beckoned to me, enhanced by the deep pull of my fascination.

"So, all the stories?"

"That is all they are, just stories. Though I do prefer the night, as it is much more peaceful."

"But you need blood to survive?"

"To thrive and stay healthy, yes. Though only about once a week or so."

"And why is that?" I was held captive by intrigue, and these unguarded questions spilled from my mouth with an urgency.

August ran his fingers lazily down my arm. "I am the ancient manifestation of a primal life force; a life force that everyone encompasses within them, best accessed through tantric energy. It is the sharing of this life force that sustains me."

His words hung in the air, like a sensual promise to finish what he started. But the enticing magnetism that had drawn me to him like a seductive cloak suddenly fell away, leaving a sharp clarity behind.

"Wait a minute." I stared at him as a flicker of distrust slipped in, demanding answers. "So all of this was just a lure? Did you hypnotize me or something?"

August shook his head slowly as a hint of something akin to sadness flashed briefly in his eyes. "No. Like I said before, this was only an invitation. I would never manipulate your mind. You have free will here, and you can leave if you want." The warmth of his hand fell on mine for a moment. "I know these are only words to you right now, Jezebel. But I want you to know that you are safe with me. What I am offering you is an experience of pleasure in exchange for energy."

A silence settled around us as I absorbed the reality of who this man was and what he was proposing. It was bizarre and unexpected, and there was no neat compartment in my mind for any of it. But at the same time, something about all this felt mystical and profound, and the depths of possibility beckoned to me. I was filled with an irrepressible yearning to explore this world that he was inviting me into.

"Okay," I found myself whispering into the darkness of the room.

August looked at me with a heavy gravity. "Is that a yes, Jezebel?"

I nodded as a rush of breathlessness overcame me.

"Are you absolutely sure?"

"Yes."

In the darkness of the room, he moved closer to me, laying me back down on the sheets as his hands gently caressed my face. His lips touched mine as his fingers coiled themselves in my hair. The overpowering and seductive pull of him rekindled the embers of my desire, and my pulse beat in a rapid flutter, whether from excitement or fearful anticipation, I could not tell.

"If you want me to stop at any time, just say so."

His voice drifted above me while his mouth moved to my neck, his lips softly brushing against my skin. My body quickened as a strong rush of pleasure consumed me. Then I felt it once more, that pinprick of sensation. He hovered there for a moment, waiting for my permission.

"Yes." I breathed into the thick softness of his hair, which smelled of the ocean. I clutched my hands around his arms as his teeth slowly sank deep into my neck.

He let out a sudden deep groan as he began to draw from me, and an instantaneous climax washed over my body. It pulled me under its intense grip and did not let go. Wave after wave of ecstasy fell upon me in a never-ending onslaught, and there was no shore. Every pull of his mouth triggered another explosion inside. It was too much, and I struggled for air, almost as if I had forgotten how to breathe.

"Stop!" I gasped against him. He released me.

I lay there, my hands grasping the sheets while I waited for the last orgasm to subside. My body throbbed and rippled with a piercing euphoria I had never experienced before. As I gradually came back to myself, I could see him sitting beside me, dark hair falling across his eyes, which seemed to shimmer a brighter shade of blue than before.

"What.... was... that?" My words spilled out in short, breathless pants.

He smiled and bent down to press a soft kiss on my forehead. "I tend to forget. The first time is always the most intense. Your body will adjust to me, though."

I hesitantly reached for my neck to feel for whatever marks he had left, but there were none.

"Do not worry, you will find nothing there, Jezebel."

"But how?" I shot him a questioning look.

"Regeneration." He reached over to take my hand, turning it over until he located a small slice on my thumb, one that I had cut with a pair of scissors the day before. "Let me show you."

He pressed his fingers lightly against the cut and then released, revealing smooth skin beneath.

I let out a gasp. "You're a healer."

"I am many things."

"But how is this possible?"

August gently stroked his thumb against my lips, stilling the words that yearned to tumble out in frantic succession. "I know that this is a lot for you to take in right now, and you have many questions, but your body should rest right now."

As if on cue, a sudden wave of drowsiness overcame me, and my eyelids grew heavy, longing to close. I nodded to him as the thick weight of sleep lured me into a deep oblivion, and August's voice became a faraway whisper in my ear.

"I will be back soon, Jezebel."

* * *

I awoke to a blurry confusion. Disorientated, it took me a moment to remember where I was. The silky feel of sheets against my skin and the sound of footsteps coming up the stairs stirred me from my dreamlike state. August entered the room and sat next to me on the bed, brushing his hand across my back.

"How do you feel?"

I stretched my limbs, muscles humming deep within. "Very relaxed."

"Good." He nodded as he placed an envelope beside me.

"What is this?"

"Your payment."

"But I didn't clean." I looked up at him with confusion.

"No, you did not, but you provided me with a service. One which I intend to compensate you for."

"Really?" The sharp sting of insult rose within me. "What if I don't want to take your money?"

"I would prefer it if you did, Jezebel."

I sat up in bed, pulling the sheets around me as the familiar feeling of self-consciousness crashed against me. "So, I'm just a whore to you, then?" Bitterness swirled on my tongue.

August shook his head. "No. It is not like that. There will be no intercourse between us. What you are is a Giver." His eyes searched mine in the dim light of the room. "I apologize if you find this offensive in any way, for that is not my intention. But it is important that we do not confuse things. I require a service from you, and if you agree to it, I will pay you adequately."

Though August's tone was tender, his words fell on me like a slap. He had taken an extremely intimate, sensual experience and turned it into a business transaction. I felt deflated. Here I was, thinking he had chosen me out of desire; not a mere necessity he had to fulfill.

"So, you felt nothing with me?"

"I feel many things with you, Jezebel. You are an incredibly beautiful woman with a very bright spark inside you." August reached over, taking my hand in his. "It is a passion I have not seen in a very long time. I believe that is what draws me to you. You possess an innate ability to connect to energy on a deeper level."

He looked at me with compassion, the gentleness in his gaze chipping away at my walls. August's capacity to see something deeper, softened me. It was rare to meet anyone who could reach beyond the façade I presented to the world.

"Does that surprise you?" He asked as his hand reached up to cup my face delicately. "The person you think you are, up here in your mind, is just a tiny fragment of the potential hidden within you."

My heart fluttered from his touch and the slow, sweet honey of his words. And I felt myself sinking headfirst into the depths of his eyes.

He hovered above me for a moment; his lips tantalizingly close to mine before abruptly drawing away. "It is getting late. You should get dressed. I will meet you downstairs."

Confliction swirled around me as I slipped my dress back on and retrieved my boots from beside the bed. I knew I should not subject myself to a transaction like this, but at the same time his magnetism stirred something inside me; a freedom I wanted to feel more of. It was as if he was able to reach beyond the layers I had erected around myself, touching a place that was beautiful, alive and filled with promise.

I met him in the hallway, tentatively clutching the envelope in my hand. August regarded me with a look of somber intensity as he spoke.

"Think about what we discussed. I understand that this is a great deal for you to process. But If you would like to continue with this arrangement, I will be waiting for you. Same time, next week." He moved to open the door for me, and a rush of cold air hit my face like a shock to my system. Suddenly I was leaving his reality and re-entering my own.

"I will think about it," I said, glancing at him pensively as I tried to shake off the dream-like state he had woven around me.

August reached out and brushed his hand down my arm for a moment, his eyes filled with a softness. "Thank you for sharing yourself with me tonight, Jezebel."

I nodded, pulling the thin fabric of my coat around me, which did nothing to ward off the bite of the wind, or the clawing of my emotions which swirled wildly within me from the surreal and overwhelming events of the evening.

Dazed, I stepped out into the darkness and headed toward the comforting familiarity of my car.

CHAPTER FIVE

As the week went by, August lingered in my thoughts. My long morning runs along the beach were filled with a desperate attempt to outpace the feverish desire he had awoken within me, but I could not seem to shake my yearning. Nights were filled with lucid dreams of his hands on my body. And when the silence of my apartment grew suffocating, my hands would slip down to the deep hidden place within myself, desperately trying to still the persistent ache inside, but I could not find release. It was as if August had kidnapped my pleasure, and it lay concealed and bound to him alone. Despite all my hesitations, I was hopelessly entangled in his current.

* * *

Midafternoon sun bloomed tentatively through the narrow windows of the public library as I furiously flipped through worn pages that smelled of mildew and dust, scouring old books in search of something that would give me more clarity as to who and what August was. The internet had turned up nothing, and all I was able to find tucked away in the occult section so far were old legends of blood-sucking beasts who slept in coffins and cast no shadow. Ancient myths of terrifying winged creatures from the Babylonians of Mesopotamia, which dated back four thousand years, but nothing about *Sacred Blood* or *De Sanguine*. Whoever he was, his secrets were locked up tight and could not be found within the archives of accessible information.

I leaned against my chair, stretching out the cramp in my lower back. It was moments like this that I was acutely reminded of my self-imposed solitude. So many years spent encased within myself, searching for slivers of peace among the rubble of my past. I had no one to confide in. But even if I did, would they believe me? The few friends I had were void of any substance, just a collection of surface-level exchanges through social media and the occasional text message on holidays. I had allowed the pain of my past to become my defining identity. But it was a burden too heavy to share with others, and so I had built an island around myself, unanchored and adrift in an endless sea of confliction.

The night I had made the drive down the bluff from his house, I toiled with the thought of returning. Years ago, I had established a set of rules that ensured a sense of restraint in my relationships. I never ventured too far from myself. Encapsulated within the safety of my walls, I always kept one foot out the door. But up until now, there had never been anyone who tempted my self-control. Therefore, it had always been easy for me to live on the surface of my emotions, to stand in the shallow waters and never yearn to dive deeper. However, the hungry serpent of my longing coiled within, wanting more; so, I would dream, and run, and dig my hands deep into clay, hoping to pull out the hunger.

August was a dangerous desire, one that challenged me. It was terrifying and thrilling at the same time, shackling me with the weight of indecision.

Monday night came again, and the hour of his request stared at me like an insidious taunt. Memories of the week before flooded me, consuming my rationality, and filling me with a restless longing. Ignoring all reason, I grabbed my keys and headed out the door. *Just one more time,* I attempted to convince myself while I drove out through the dark to him. *One more time to get him out of my system, and then I will be able to stay away.*

When I pulled up to the house, the sound of the piano drifted from inside. As I made my way to the front door, the notes grew with intensity; a staccato that was wild and unhinged, like a madman dancing in the night. The old brass handle was unlocked, so I let myself in quietly, drawn toward the music but not wanting to disturb his reverie.

The melodious sound drew me to the living room where August sat facing me, a silhouette of moonlight and ocean behind him; his eyes closed as if completely lost in the movement of his composition. He was so hauntingly beautiful, filled with a refined fluidity and grace that transfixed me. I stood in silence as his music moved to a crescendo and then faded to a soft finish.

He opened his eyes and smiled at me. "Jezebel. I am so glad you decided to return."

My instinct was to play coy with him as I had grown accustomed to doing with men, but I knew that he would see right through me. So, I spoke with an honesty that stripped away at my walls and left me with a feeling of lightness that I found to be quite liberating.

"To be honest, I wasn't planning to, but I haven't been able to stop thinking about you."

"Is that so?" There was a tenderness in his voice as he got up from where he sat at the piano and crossed the room to me.

I ran my hand slowly along his arm as I shot him a playful smile. "Yes, I think I may be a little infatuated right now. Are you sure you didn't put me under a spell or something?"

He faintly chuckled and reached up to press his thumb against my lips in a soft tease. His intimate gesture elicited a surge of desire, causing my limbs to grow weak.

"No, I assure you, you are not under any spell. All I have done is open a door which has long been closed."

"And what kind of door is that?" I asked, trying to regain my composure as his thumb gently swept across my cheek before pulling away.

August regarded me with a quiet reflection in his eyes. "The door to what lies beneath your mind. Your soul has been longing to be free, Jezebel. I noticed it the very first moment I saw you, that morning out on the beach."

My heart began to beat rapidly in my chest as slumbering emotions rose to the surface. "What do you mean?"

"What I mean is, I saw a woman withholding herself. When you experienced my Embrace, it allowed you to access the energy within that you have been suppressing. Lust, desire, sexual release. It is all just the energy of your soul trying to transmute itself into something deeper and more profound."

"So, I'm transmuting right now?"

August gave me a small smile. "In a sense, yes. You are feeling certain things more intensely then before. You see, an Embrace is immensely beneficial for the both of us."

I took in his words, musing over his meaning. So many years I had spent precariously clinging to the walls I had built around myself, and meeting August felt like a delicious gift washed upon the shore of my solitude.

"But I did realize what an impolite host I had been when you came to me last week. In all honesty, I was a bit rushed in my haste to Embrace you." He motioned toward the living room. "Please make yourself comfortable. Would you like something to drink? I have wine, beer, or I could make you some tea if you would prefer?"

"Wine would be nice, thank you."

I followed him to where a small fire danced in the hearth. Below the stone fireplace on the floor lay a soft animal skin rug with pillows placed upon it like a thoughtful invitation. He disappeared into the kitchen, his retreat barely making a sound, while I settled myself on the floor. The heat of the flames flickered across my skin as I rested my back on the cushions. Relaxation washed over me as I soaked in the delicious warmth, which wrapped itself around me like a blanket.

August reappeared, the firelight glinting against two glasses of wine. He handed one to me and raised his own, clinking the delicate crystal softly against my glass. I returned the silent toast with a small smile and took a long sip. "Does alcohol have the same effect on you?" I asked.

August smiled over the rim of his glass. "Yes. I eat, drink and sleep, just like you." He set his glass down and moved closer to me. Taking my feet, he unzipped my boots, slipped them off, and began to slowly knead the tender flesh underneath. His touch felt exquisite and intimate as his hands worked through the muscles, sending shivers of delight to course up my spine.

"And how long have you been playing the piano?"

"A long time. I dabbled for many years, but it wasn't until my wife..." He trailed off for a moment, seeming to lose his composure before returning to his thought. "The piano, for me, is an outlet. A way to turn pain into beauty."

"Are all of your songs about her?" Sympathy percolated in my chest. The drive to transfer pain into something of beauty was a concept I was all too familiar with.

August looked at me with a soft expression. "All of my songs are about life, Jezebel. The delicate strands that bind us to one another. The heart's insistent need to keep beating."

"What would we do without art?" I smiled up at him, feeling a subtle shift as his eyes locked with mine; a small undercurrent of understanding passing between us.

"Was she like you? Your wife?"

August nodded as his hands continued to gently massage my feet. "Yes, she was. You share her name, you know."

I glanced up at him in surprise.

He gazed off into the flames for a moment. "Yes, her name was Jezebel as well."

I stared at him quizzically, wondering why he hadn't mentioned this before. "Well, that's a little interesting, don't you think?"

August turned to me, his eyes reflecting deep pools of amber light as he gave me a wane smile. "Yes. Life is remarkably interesting, Jezebel."

"And why are you just telling me this now, August?"

He sighed as a hesitancy crept over his face. "I suppose I did not want you to feel as if I was projecting onto you."

"Are you?"

August pierced me with his gaze. "No. Though I will admit your name is what initially prompted me to reach out to your business, it *is* an unusual one to see. This fact is most likely derived from the heavy stigma attached to it."

I rolled my eyes. "Yeah, I'm pretty familiar with that one."

"It was only created by men who were uncomfortable with a woman connected to her sexual power." August's voice grew soft. "Sexuality and power are tightly woven together. This truth threatens those that cling to a patriarchal society."

I glanced into the fire, watching as the flames leapt against each other. "I wonder if that will ever change?"

"It will. But only when people learn the difference between power and control."

A comfortable silence washed over us. The relaxing feel of his strong but gentle grip drew out all my tension. With the warm fire at my back, the wine leisurely creeping through my veins, and August's hands at my feet, I became enveloped in a deliciously comfortable cocoon. Whatever reserve I had with him melted away into a puddle beneath me. I longed to crawl into his fascinating mind, to bathe in his complexities and sift through his many layers. I wanted to know everything about this man.

"I was born in Rome, Jezebel."

I looked at him steadily. "You can read my mind, can't you?"

He nodded. "Though out of respect for others' privacy, I generally tend not to." He slid his hands slowly up my legs. "But you, my dear, are very loud." A faint seductive smile played upon his lips as his fingers lightly teased the space in-between my thighs. "I do apologize for slipping in."

I let out a breathless laugh as he continued to stroke along my thighs in slow, circling motions through the fabric of my dress; causing my entire body to flush with longing. "Yes. I suppose my mind can be a bit loud at times."

"A mind that is loud only longs to be heard."

"Really?" I smiled at him. "And what do you think my mind is trying to say to me?"

He regarded me with an inquisitive look. "That is for you to find out."

I sighed and glanced over to the painting of Lucretia on the wall. Her eyes full of questions as she stared down at me from her gilded frame. "I have to admit, I did do some research on you the other day."

August chuckled, amusement flickering in his eyes. "Is that so? And what did you find?"

"Absolutely nothing."

He nodded. "Yes, we do tend to prefer our privacy."

"So, there's more like you?"

"Yes. Though we are sparse and scattered throughout the world." His voice was silk and velvet as he spoke, and I could feel myself growing wet as his fingers found the warmth between my legs, brushing lightly against the cloth before inching my dress up, and exposing my skin to the firelight. "Shall we dispose of this now?"

"Yes." My voice came out in a tremble, and I become like clay, once again caught, and molded within the enchanting hold of him.

August removed my clothes like a slow unveiling. His hands leisurely trailed up my legs, consuming my skin with the potency of his touch. A low moan rose from deep within me as he placed his lips against my skin, slowly trailing across my breasts and down to my stomach. The heat of his mouth ignited me, and I opened my legs up to him like an invitation; a deep burning ache to feel more.

August hovered over me; his composure suddenly replaced by something feverish as he took me in. With a groan, he dipped down and placed a soft kiss between the folds of my sex. I arched my back as a rush of delicious pleasure shot through me. His kiss suddenly grew deeper as his hands gripped my thighs, his tongue hitting all the right places inside as if he knew them by heart. I quickly lost myself, tumbling over the edge, my fingers tangled in his hair. His name spilled from my mouth, loud and frantic as I crashed beneath him.

I heard him murmur something in Latin as he nuzzled against me for a moment, breathing in the rich scent of my desire before he rose himself above me. In the light of the fire, the thick gloss of his hair shone like wet oil paint as he traced his finger lazily along my jawline.

We locked eyes in a stillness that felt suspended, and I was overcome by a longing to pry inside his depths, to break down his walls and uncover the wildness of what lay below.

"What are you thinking about, August?"

His finger leisurely descended to my neck, "I'm thinking about how beautiful you are."

My hands reached up to his shirt where I grasped the buttons between my fingers, slowly unhooking them. I needed to see him beneath all his clothes and silky seduction, to feel the heat of his skin on mine. Even though he was giving me more ecstasy than I ever thought possible, I wanted more.

"What are you doing?" His question came out soft and hesitant as his body stiffened above me for a moment.

"I want to see you." My words came out delicate and pleading. "Let me touch you."

He did not respond, only watched me silently, allowing me to slide his shirt down the length of his arms, my hands trailing over the smooth, tight muscles of his chest. His skin felt like silk and glowed like a liquid amber in the light of the flames. A flash of longing crept to the surface of his gaze as my fingers lightly brushed across his nipples, his eyes flickering with a momentary vulnerability.

A rush of excitement coursed through me and I brazenly slipped lower, pulling down on the waistline of his pants when he grabbed my hand.

"Jezebel. This is not about *my* desire. This is about yours. You are already giving me more than you know."

"But I want you."

His eyes caught mine in the light of the fire. "I would prefer it if we do not complicate this arrangement between us."

His words felt like a draft of cold air against my skin, and I pulled my body up to a sitting position. The acute sting of rejection reminded me why I had told myself I would not return to him in the first place.

"I think I should go."

"Jezebel." August placed his hand on my thigh, his voice soft and almost pleading. "Please do not take this as a rebuff. This has nothing to do with my attraction to you. Although you may not be able to fully understand my reasoning behind this arrangement between us, I do hope you can at least try."

I shook my head, grabbing for my clothes. "Are you always used to getting your way? Because I have a really hard time with one-way streets."

August regarded me with a look of sadness, as if the weight of his own loneliness had encapsulated him. "No, Jezebel. This is not a one-way street for me. This is an exchange. But at the same time, I do not want you to feel uncomfortable in any way, so I completely understand if you do not wish to continue."

Silence settled around us for a moment, my hands nervously twining themselves in my lap. My emotions vacillated between the urge to leave and the longing to stay. "This is all new to me. I am not used to feeling so out of control."

"May I ask, what about this makes you feel out of control?"

I glanced over at the fire, watching as the flames leaped and curled around themselves. Though I was frustrated with his unwillingness to reciprocate intimacy, I knew it went deeper than that. What he stirred within me felt untamed and raw, and the power of that terrified me.

"My desire."

August's hand rested lightly on my arm. "Desire is a gift. It is what pushes us beyond our self-imposed limitations. It is what forces us to create a richer life. Why would you want to stifle that?"

The firelight played with the shadows upon his face as he watched me with a gentle openness. The tenderness of his words touched the softness behind my walls, slowly chipping away at my resolve.

"I don't know."

Despite the small voice combatting within, all I did know was that I wanted him, regardless of what he could not give back to me in return.

"I want you to know that you are safe with me, Jezebel."

Though I did not quite know what he meant by that, my name on his lips was a rich persuasion and I pulled him to me with a reckless urgency. Running my hands down his back, I pressed my mouth against his, seeking out the one thing he *would* share with me. His skin was hot from the warmth of the fire, and a tingle spread through me as he returned my kiss, deep and deliberate, a languid caress of lips and tongue that made me light-headed. His mouth slid down to the pulse of my neck, arousing me as his teeth delicately grazed my skin.

My voice came out in a stifled moan. "I'm ready for you."

"Are you sure?" He hovered over my neck, the sharpness of his teeth producing goosebumps while he waited once more for my consent. I arched back and wrapped my arms around him, my breath held in anticipation.

"*Yes.*"

He gently plunged into me, drawing me slowly down onto the furs as I sank into an endless and overwhelming well of pleasure that rocked me back and forth. The ecstasy came slower and softer this time, cradling me. I didn't want it to end. I hungrily rode the waves of his Embrace and cried out against him. But almost as soon as he began, he pulled himself away from me with a muffled groan. I lay there, my body pulsing as August's fingers lightly brushed against my neck, healing the skin.

"That's enough for now." The rich gravel of his voice was warm and breathless in my ear.

"Oh my God, how does that feel *so* good?" I rolled over to lay my head on his chest, listening to the slow, steady rhythm of his heart, like an ancient drumbeat.

"I am accessing a powerful force within you. It is called *Vita Navitas*, or life energy. It is the very essence of creation, from which all life originated. While you are only able to draw out tiny fragments of it at a time through a release, I have the ability to prolong it for you." His hand moved up to my hair, faintly stroking the strands between his fingers.

"So, what does it feel like for you?"

"It is a rush, akin to adrenaline. The pleasure of heightened sensation. When I experience the essence of another, it aligns me once more."

"And is this what keeps you immortal?"

"Immortality is a concept created by man. There is an end to everything. I too will grow old and die; I just happen to exist in a realm where time flows on a different trajectory than yours. I age much slower. A lifetime for others is only a handful of years for me."

"So, how old are you, then?"

"I am *old*, Jezebel." August looked down at me with a faint smile. "I was born in the year 1302."

I tried to calculate all this in my head as my mind wrapped itself around what he was telling me. I found myself able to accept this information with unusual ease. And I grew excited by the heavy significance of it all. I wondered what I would do if given the ability to live so many lifetimes encapsulated in one body. I suppose in a way, I had always felt that the veil of this reality was thinly drawn, that if I were to only reach out my hand, it would part before me, revealing a world much more complex than I ever could imagine.

"Wow. You have seen so much."

He sighed, running his fingers along my back. "I have seen too much. Time is a substantial weight to carry. There is a lightness and beauty about people, whether they feel it or not. They are unfettered by the freedom of impermanence."

"Well, I think you are incredibly beautiful, August."

He smiled and kissed the top of my head, his lips lingering in my hair. "You should get some rest now." His hands moved against my back once more in slow, languid circles, the effects of his Embrace lulling me into compliance as I sunk headfirst into the deep, dreamless oblivion of sleep.

* * *

When I awoke, the fire had burned down to deep-red coals, and August was gone. I could feel his absence; it left a heavy silence that filled the house. Beside me, like a note of finality, lay a white envelope.

CHAPTER SIX

For days afterward, I threw myself into work. I spent hours at the office, calculating numbers and reorganizing files, trying to push August out of my mind. Nights were consumed with my hands in clay, molding and pressing out the longing to return to him once more.

But no matter how much I tried, I could not resist the pull, and so I found myself slipping into a quiet, dream-like rhythm with him. My weeks orbited around our evenings. Those singular nights when I would come to him, open and aching, and he would fill me with pleasure; fill me with his words, like delicate strands of poetry, but I was always left wanting more. I longed for the parts of him he would not show, what lay hidden behind his eyes. But August remained a book full of secrets, bound and locked before me.

* * *

Early winter sunlight flirted with the ground beneath my feet. The wind had a deceptive warmth to it as I made my way down the sidewalk from the hardware store, my arms loaded with supplies for the office. My mind was elsewhere as I approached the curb, distracted by the ethereal glare of the sun against a vibrant blue sky.

Suddenly, a hand grabbed my waist from behind, pulling my body close. The blur of a car rushed past my vision as a familiar voice spoke softly in my ear.

"Careful now."

August's breath against my neck was like a jolt of electricity surging through me, and my heart began to pound as I realized how close I had just come to stepping out into oncoming traffic. I spun around to find August's eyes on me, concern sweeping briefly across his face before concealing it behind a playful smile.

"Please tell me that this is not a habit of yours?" As he spoke, something shifted in his eyes, and his hand reached out to touch my cheek gently. "I would hate for anything to happen to you, Jezebel."

Letting out a nervous laugh, I shifted the bags in my arms. "No, I promise you, it's not. Apparently, my mind has just been somewhere else today."

August nodded as he took the bags from me. "Where are we going with these?"

"To my office." Brushing the hair from my face, I motioned across the street for him to follow. "Thanks. So, what are you doing here in town?"

"Well, I was heading to the market. That was, of course, before I saw you attempting to wander into traffic." August winked at me, his hand falling gently upon my lower back as he led me across the street.

My heart had not ceased its incessant pattering as we matched our pace down the sidewalk together. This unexpected run-in with him had startled me; it felt so strange to see him out of the tranquil element of his house. With his neatly pressed suit and tailored jacket, he reminded me of an expensive piece of china standing out among the clutter of a secondhand store.

"So, I guess you just saved my life back there," I said with a teasing glance.

August stopped at the doorway to my office. The sun glinted off the dark tendrils of his hair and I had a sudden overwhelming urge to kiss him as he stood there, watching me with a look of mild amusement on his face. "Well, I suppose you owe me then."

A slow, flirtatious smile crept across my face. "And what do I owe you?"

August moved to open the door for me, crossing the room to place the bags upon my desk. "How about we go for coffee?"

"Coffee?"

"Yes, Jezebel. I drink coffee, and I would love to have some with you."

* * *

48

We sat together at the tiny coffee shop down the street from my office, the comforting aroma of roasted beans wafting around us. I noticed the people in the room, women in particular, stealing quick glances over at August as he sat across from me, his hands curled around a mug of coffee.

I leaned in close to him, lowering my voice. "You do know that you stand out around here?" I fingered the cuff of his jacket. "And what is it with you and these fancy suits, anyway?"

Smiling languidly at me, he reclined back in his chair. "Force of habit, I suppose."

A woman brushed past August, blond hair pulled into a messy bun, her eyes catching his for a moment; a deep blush creeping across her face as the striking blue of his gaze met hers full on.

I bumped his leg with mine from underneath the table. "Something tells me you like the attention."

He shot me a lighthearted smirk and leaned in close, his breath hovering against my ear. "No, I was only politely acknowledging her desire to be noticed."

"Oh, come on. You're telling me that if I wasn't here right now, you wouldn't be trying to... oh I don't know, take her back to your place for an Embrace?"

August shook his head. "No, I would not Embrace that woman."

"Why not? Don't you find her attractive?"

"Physical attraction is just a small part of the equation, Jezebel. You see, most women are unable to handle what I offer them."

"What do you mean?"

He slowly raised an eyebrow. "How do you think the average woman would have reacted when I revealed myself in the way I did?"

My mind trickled back to our first night together, the shock followed by the quick acceptance of who he was. "Well, I guess they would probably have run out and never looked back."

"Exactly. But *your* mind was open to me." August's voice grew quiet. "There is an inherent strength within you, Jezebel. This is what drew me to you, and what allowed you to so easily come to terms with who I was. There lies a myriad of possibilities that exist within this realm of life that we all share, things that exist way beyond our self-perceived notions of the world around us; and you have an acute ability to tap into that." He motioned toward the woman who had now seated herself at a table across the room from us, her eyes flickering between August and her cup of coffee. "That woman over there, for example, is too nervous. She carries a plethora of fears that keep her from being in-tune with herself. She lives in an enclosed state of mind, therefore, she would be unable to accept that there is a much larger reality at play."

"But how do you know this? Where you were reading her thoughts just now?"

"No. I was reading her energy. Thoughts are only transitory, while energy is infinite, and it speaks much deeper than our mind."

I shifted in my seat. "So, you can do that as well?"

August took a sip from his mug, before quietly placing it back down upon the table. "We all have the ability to read people's energy, Jezebel. I know you can; you happen to be *very* good at it, in fact."

Twirling my cup slowly around on the table, I took in his comment. "And how do you know that?"

He smiled softly at me. "If you were not connected to that deeper aspect of yourself, the part that allows you to observe the subtle undercurrents of energy; you would never have come back to the house after you received my invitation."

"Well, I didn't at first, remember?"

"Yes, but that had nothing to do with your ability to read my intentions."

"And how do you know that?" With a small smile, I leaned across the table in a playful challenge.

"You said it yourself, Jezebel. You feared your own desire."

I glanced into the depths of his eyes, filled with a knowledge I found so deeply alluring. "I'm curious. What is it exactly that you see when you read me?"

August regarded me for a moment, his voice growing tender as sunlight streamed in from the window behind us, bathing the room in a haze of fragmented light. "I see a woman who wears her skin like armor. Whose heart is crying out for a place to run free. I see a soul that is intricately delicate, yet profoundly strong."

The tenderness that shimmered within the intensity of his gaze caused a gentle flutter inside me. His eyes sparkled as he broke out into a wide grin, gently tapping my hand with his. "Now it is your turn. What do you see?"

I studied him for a long moment, the silence hovering in the air between us. Despite all his sensual confidence, there was a mask of pain there, and I knew he was hiding from his own vulnerabilities. "I see a man who is running from something."

August grew pensive as he looked at me. Leaning across the table, his hand reached out for mine, giving it a tight squeeze. "*That,* you may be right about, Jezebel."

Standing suddenly, he whisked away my empty coffee cup. "Come with me. There is something I want to show you."

* * *

We stood together on a precarious outcropping of rocks, the calm waters of the bay stretching out before us. August leaned in close to me, his breath warm against my cheek. "Look." He pointed out to a large dark figure moving slowly below the rippling surface of the ocean.

A gasp spilled from me as the whale suddenly breached in a breathtaking display, showering the air with a cascading spray of water which shimmered against the sunlight.

"Oh, my god!" I gripped August's arm in excitement as the great power of the creature descended back beneath the sea.

"Do you see the calf with her?" As he spoke, I could see a small shadow swimming in circles around the mother. "I discovered them the other day on one of my walks. She will stay here to nurse her young until it is strong enough to make the migration."

I watched the gentle gliding dance between mother and child as they hovered together above the surface before dipping back down to the depths.

"Beautiful, aren't they?"

"Yes." I looked up to find his gaze was resting on me, full of a tenderness that made my pulse quicken. "Thank you for sharing this with me."

The breeze picked up, eliciting a chill upon my skin. Removing his jacket, August draped it over my shoulders, enveloping me in his sharp pine scent. The coat wrapped me up in the soothing remnants of his warmth as he pulled me close to him.

"You know, I always wanted to go whale watching. But I could never stomach the tourism aspect of it. This is so much better."

"Yes, it is." August reached out his hand to smooth the windblown hair out of my face. "When you monetize the beauty of nature, it can lose its effect upon the soul."

We stood together in silence, allowing the tender moment between us to whisper of possibilities. Filled with a euphoric lightness that his presence always seemed to evoke, I sank into the feel of his arms as the wild and graceful movements of the whales slipped beneath the waves, speaking in a language that only the ocean could understand.

"What is it that haunts you, Jezebel?"

Monday night had come, and August lay beside me on the bed. His head propped against the palm of his hand; the depth of his gaze fixed on me while his fingers lightly ran down the length of my scars.

My body lay delightfully relaxed after his Embrace, teetering on the edge of pleasure and sleep, and his question stirred the stillness within me. "You want to know about my scars?"

"Yes. I do."

"They are from a car accident, a long time ago."

"They are beautiful, you know." He watched me with languid eyes as he continued to explore the puckered flesh of my trauma. "They tell a story of survival and strength. There is nothing I find more stunning than a woman who has experienced the many layers of life."

Attempting to push down the memories that rushed at me like urgent whispers, my silence filled the space between us, and August did not press any further. We both had our secrets that curled around us. I had come to terms with this, and no longer did I fault him for his reluctance to reveal his depths, for I knew I was guilty of the same discretion.

August finally broke the stillness, running his fingers softly through my hair as he spoke. "When I was a child, I used to play with these older boys from my village. I wanted to impress them, so one day I told them I could climb to the very top of the tallest tree in the forest." August's eyes looked wistful as he recalled his memory. "They didn't believe me, of course, but being the headstrong child that I was, I did manage to climb to the top, before promptly falling to the ground and breaking both my arms."

Cringing from the visual, my hand moved to rest on his bare chest. "*Oh, geez.*"

"That was the day I learned that my parents were different from others. My mother sat me down and healed the fractures, telling me to not speak of this to anyone; that one day when I was older, she would explain everything to me, but her power was not as strong as it could have been. Years of hiding from herself had weakened her, and she could only do so much."

August revealed the insides of his arms. Thin faint scars which I had never noticed before, threaded across his skin.

"And you haven't been able to heal those?"

He shook his head. "No, I cannot heal scars. When I began to come into my own power as a young man, too much time had elapsed. These are fixed to me now, holding within them the memories of a fragmented family; one which I suppose I am still learning to make peace with. You see, whether you can see them or not, we all have scars, Jezebel. Some just happen to speak louder than others."

My fingers lightly traced the lines on his arms. "Well, I wish mine weren't so loud."

August brushed his hand across my cheek. "They don't have to be if you only listen to the memories they long to tell. The body speaks a language much like the earth. Though coated in layers of sediment, underneath the crust lies a multitude of hidden beauty. But true beauty is a shy creature. It will only show itself when the waters of the soul are calm."

Sighing, I wrapped my arms around him, pulling him closer, feeling the enticing sensation of his skin against mine and the unusual warmth that always seemed to radiate off him. The sudden closeness that had begun to grow between us stirred me. I rolled August over onto his back, breathing in the earthy scent of him.

"And how is it that you always smell so good?"

He let out a deep chuckle as I hovered over his neck. Bending down, I kissed the delicate space beneath his jaw, brushing my lips along the salt of his skin. The sudden sharp inhale from August and the press of his arousal against my leg sent warmth flooding through me. I traveled down to his chest, my tongue lightly running over his nipple. He let out a low groan and grabbed my arms. I had not kissed him like this before. He had never let me. My fingers lightly traced over the seam of his pants, finding the heat of his erection, and cupping it boldly in my hands. A hot ache began to throb within as I reveled in the power he had suddenly relinquished to me. This intimacy filled me with an intense longing as August shuddered beneath my touch, my name coming out of his mouth, breathless and broken.

"*Jezebel.*"

My mouth continued to run across his chest and down the length of his stomach, his soft hairs tickling my skin while I slowly stroked him through the fabric. He gripped me tighter and moaned before abruptly pulling me up to meet his gaze, his eyes filled with lust and confusion as he rolled me onto my back.

"*Please do not tempt me,*" His voice was a gruff plea in my ear.

"Why?" I looked up at him hovering above me. "Weren't you the one who said desire is not to be stifled?" My words were a challenge that I was curious to see if he would meet.

He ran his hand through my hair. "Yes. But I was speaking about the desire of the soul, which is not to be confused with one's own self-indulgence."

Something flashed across his eyes as he spoke, like a silent battle raging within. August abruptly sat up and pulled the covers around me, attempting to distill the mood with a playful smile. "I see that you are adapting to my Embrace quite well." He pressed his lips lightly against my forehead. "You're not sleepy at all, are you?"

Shaking my head, I ran my hand down his arm. "Would you like me to be?"

Grabbing his shirt from the bed, he quickly slipped it on. "No, but there are a few things I have to do tonight. You can let yourself out when you are ready." His fingers brushed my cheek. "Take your time."

He rose from the bed and strode across the room, disappearing down the stairs as if he were running from something, leaving me alone with the full weight of my unrequited yearning.

I laid there for a while, listening to the sound of his footsteps down below, and then the soft click of the front door shutting behind him.

CHAPTER SEVEN

An early December storm slammed the coastline while I sat in the office, catching up on paperwork. Rain drummed out a heavy rhythm of urgency on the roof above, while the wind lashed angrily at the windows, revealing nothing but a sea of darkness. I was restless and did not want to go back home to the emptiness of my apartment just yet. My solitude, always being a comfort to me in the past, now felt like loneliness. These feelings were harder to shake off since August had come into my life. They kept creeping up on me like mist, enveloping me in uncertainty. It was as if he had shattered my armor, allowing my past to slither in and demand my attention, its tendrils gripping me with a strength that I was powerless to stop.

Locking up the office, I stepped out into the rain, pulling my coat tight around my body. The streetlights cast an orange watery glow upon the sidewalk as I drew up my hood and made my way to the car. As I walked down the street, I had a sudden urge to grab a drink and found myself pulling open the large wooden door of the local pub. A blast of warm air hit me when I entered, and the thick odor of stale beer hung in the air as I slipped over to the bar and sat down. Only a few people were in the room; the interior illuminated by a garish green light while the soft buzz of voices filtered lightly around me.

Next to me sat Samuel, the well-known local historian in town. He had taken a fondness to me when I moved here five years before and helped generate my first clients through steady and consistent word of mouth. He was proud of his family's heritage, his ancestors being among the first of the pilgrims from Europe who settled along the coast centuries ago, content to carve out their family tree diligently beside the water.

Samuel nodded in my direction. "Good evening, Jezebel." The years had weathered him; his face craggy and worn from decades of fishing.

"Hey there, Sam. How are you holding up?"

He moved his beer over the deep stains of the wooden bar, his milky blue eyes fixed on the glass. "I'd be better if this damn storm would blow through already."

"Yeah, it's getting a bit depressing with all the rain." I shook off my coat and looked around for the bartender.

"How's business going these days?"

I shrugged. "This time of year is always the hardest. It's a struggle to keep my employees busy."

Samuel gave me a sympathetic grunt and leaned in, his eyes narrowing. "So, I've noticed you've been going to that old house out on the bluff a lot."

Nodding, I signaled for a beer as the bartender caught my eye from across the room. "Yeah, he's one of my new clients." The thought of *what* type of client August had become raised heat upon my cheeks, something I hoped the dimly lit room would conceal from Samuel.

"You know the story about that place, right?"

I smiled at him with amused interest. "What do you mean?"

He leaned in even closer. He smelled of the ocean, the pungent odor of fish mixed with the beer on his breath. "Well, a long time ago, there was a woman who lived there with her husband. She was a sorceress with inhuman powers, a witch with the mark of the devil on her." His words tumbled out in a low hiss as specks of spittle landed on my arm. I wiped it away and recoiled from his proximity.

"Really?" I rolled my eyes. "You don't actually believe that nonsense, do you?"

"It's true." He nodded to himself. "She was known to put the men who lived here under her spell." His hand sliced through the air for dramatic emphasis. "In fact, it was one of my very own family members who she had cursed. He went crazy shortly after. They hanged her for witchcraft right here in the town square."

He spoke with such brazen arrogance that I looked at him in horror as he stood, throwing some bills down on the counter. "I would stay away from that place if I were you, Jezebel... Cursed, I tell ya."

"It's just a house, Sam." I tried to hide the disdain in my voice.

He shook his head, gathering up his coat. "It's more than just a house."

Sam lumbered out the door and into the night, his exit leaving a gust of cold air which filtered through the room, giving me a momentary chill. I stared at the glass of beer in my hands, watching the condensation gather between my fingers. Samuel's dark words hovered like thick smoke as a sudden realization hit me. *Had that been August's wife?* A pull of sorrow snaked its way through my tangled thoughts, followed by a rush of anger over the historical ignorance and insanity of our culture. And I wondered, if I was right, what had possibly compelled August to come back to this place after all this time?

Monday night came, and I found myself driving with an impatient urgency to August. I sped through the dark, my foot pressing down hard on the accelerator. For some reason, I could not dispel the persistent feeling of dread in the pit of my stomach, the lingering thought that he would not be there when I arrived.

Relief flooded over me when I found him upstairs, looking out over the water from the bedroom window. He turned slowly toward me; the night casting shadows over his face. I crossed the room to where he stood and wrapped my arms around him. The intimacy pulsed between us as I nestled against this chest, breathing in the familiar earthy scent of him that I had grown to love so much. He spoke quietly into my hair with his hands upon my back, holding me tight, a faint hint of sorrow in his voice.

"This will be our last night together, Jezebel."

I pulled back from him in alarm. "What do you mean?"

He clasped my shoulders but couldn't seem to meet my eyes. "I leave tomorrow."

"But why?" A twinge of panic welled up as the sharp sting of desperation coiled around me.

August let out a long sigh. "Because it is time for me to go."

"But I'm not ready for you to go. I want you to stay." I found myself pleading with him like some frantic child as the sharp claws of disappointment rushed in. The idea of him no longer being in my life tore at me.

He spoke in a measured tone as he moved away from me. "This arrangement was only temporary. I deeply apologize if I did not make that clear to you before."

His words hit me like a sharp blow. So lost I had become in him, in the gentle connection we had been forging together. It never occurred to me that he would end it so abruptly. "I just thought... we would have more time together."

"I'm sorry. But it is best if we do not confuse things between us."

Frustration rose in my throat, thick and burning. "Damn it, August. You always talk about not wanting to confuse things, but I think the only person who is really confused here, is you!" I grew loud, suddenly finding his composure infuriating.

He watched me quietly as a deep yearning and sadness crept over his face. He shook his head, closing his eyes for a moment. "You are being irrational. What we share cannot go any further. It has already gone *too far*."

I stared at him as the hot rush of anger percolated through me. "What the hell does that even mean?"

The look he gave me was strained and filled with a heavy turmoil. "There are lines I should not have crossed with you, Jezebel."

"Bullshit! What lines? Show me these imaginary lines you have created." My arm furiously swept across the room as I stepped closer to him, daring him to let go of whatever walls he was clinging to. "Do you want to know what I think? I think you're just afraid."

"*Afraid?*" His eyes blazed with a sudden intensity.

"Yes! I think you're afraid of losing control. You know there is more between us then just a simple exchange. You're a hypocrite, August.

You always speak of the importance of freeing yourself from your own cage. But what about yours?" My words seemed to hit him like a slap in the face, and he stared at me in silence for a long moment.

"What exactly is it that you want from me, Jezebel?"

"I want *you,* dammit! All of you, not just the carefully thought out pieces you dole out. I want you to make love to me. I want you to lay beside me, naked and vulnerable, and show me what is behind all this armor of yours."

"Is that what you want?" His voice grew unexpectedly soft. "My vulnerability?"

"Yes." My voice came out a whisper as tears of longing and frustration threatened to surface.

August abruptly grabbed me, his lips meeting mine with a rough passion I had not experienced from him before. "Damn you, *Jezebel,*" he growled against my neck, slowly backing me up against the window. "Why do you have to make this *so* hard?" My breath was shaky as his mouth consumed mine with a fury that left me dizzy. He pulled away and took my face in his hands, his eyes full of liquid fire, his voice a labored whisper. "You have no idea how deeply I long to give all of myself to you."

"Then *give* yourself to me." My hands moved to his shirt as my trembling fingers gently undid the buttons. "Let me *see* you, August."

His eyes never left mine as he allowed me to shed his clothes upon the floor, revealing himself to me like something exquisite and sacred. My breath caught in my throat as I hungrily ran my hands along the warmth of his skin, trailing down his torso and hovering over the place he had kept so secret from me.

A feverish arousal coursed through me as I held him, firm and throbbing in the palm of my hand. He inhaled sharply as I began to run my finger down the length of him, his eyes burning into mine. He reached for me, and deftly removed my clothes, letting them fall in a puddle around my feet. With a soft moan, I pressed myself against him, my lips against his, drinking in this moment I had so desperately longed for. The sensation of his skin against mine was an electric shock to every nerve in my body, and I lost myself to the blinding rush.

The heat of his gaze followed me as I knelt to the floor. His hands gripped my shoulders in a feeble attempt to push me away, but I resisted and took him brazenly into my mouth; my desire to taste him overcoming all else. I wanted him to give himself over to me.

A loud groan spilled from deep within him as my tongue reverently drew circles across his skin. The pulse of his arousal thick and heavy as he relinquished his barriers.

"Jesus, *Jezebel*."

My name was a luscious exhale upon his lips as I took him in deeper, almost enclosing him completely. His hands slid into my hair and tugged hard as he shuddered against me. His sudden release was an overpowering heat that coursed through me as he filled the room with his impassioned cry, the warmth of him spilling into my mouth, thick and unexpectedly sweet, like honey. I marveled in his ability to lose himself with such abandon. It was erotic and wild, and it left me weak with longing.

"What are you doing to me?" he growled, abruptly lifting me into his arms and carrying me over to the bed. I wrapped my trembling legs tightly around his waist, filled with a heavy, aching desire as he placed me down onto the sheets, pinning me softly beneath him. He hovered above me for a moment, his eyes filled with heat, his voice breathless as his mouth found my neck. "*God, how you intoxicate me.*"

In one blissful motion, August slid himself inside me, letting out a deep moan and drawing me tight against him. The power of his arousal was surprisingly undiminished as his desire touched my depths. A simultaneous rush of pleasure and emotion coursed through my body, and I cried out in broken, fragmented gasps as I frantically clutched him against me.

The feel of him inside was a searing heat, filling me up in a way no man had before. Every thrust became a blinding current, and a sensation of something ancient and profound overcame me. Sheer ecstasy and euphoria, desperation, and sorrow. It was centuries of him violently coursing through every fiber of my being, rippling images like vivid projections on a screen, washing over all of me like a tidal wave. I clung tight to him, for fear it would carry me away. It was as if August was not only sharing his body with me, he was sharing the incredible depths of his soul, the intricacy of his story. It was intense and overwhelmingly beautiful.

"*Pulchra, dilectus, tu mihi tantum.*" He moaned against me in his haunting Latin dialect, his lips and hands devouring my skin. His eyes bore into mine, an inferno that eviscerated all my senses as he gently pinned my arms above my head, plunging himself in even deeper to the very core of me.

I began to dissolve, to lose all sense of who I was. So, this was what it felt like to be consumed, to be split apart by a connection so sharp it cut away at my walls, leaving the layers to crumble around me.

His breath became a tantalizing shiver against my ear as he chanted my name. His mouth moved down to the delicate pulse of my neck, and I arched myself back, knowing what he wanted even before he asked. Offering up every part of myself to him... he could have it all.

"*Yes.*"

"Oh, God!" he called out like a prayer upon my skin as his teeth sank fully into me. The feel of him inside while he drew out my pleasure with each pull of his mouth, brought me to such an astounding high that my vision began to blur. My mind shattered into fragments and my body coursed with an ecstasy so profound, I wondered if I would ever be able to come back. Through my blinding haze of pleasure, August shuddered against me, a visceral current of energy that washed over me as he released me from his Embrace, crying out so loudly in his own surrender that his voice echoed upon the walls.

A bliss spilled from me like an undulating river while August's labored breath fell upon my neck like a delicious dream, our bodies coming down from our tangled, elated high. His fingers went to brush his mark away, but I found myself stopping him, and he did not seem to object.

"That was *powerful*, Jezebel." August pulled me close, encircling his arms around me. "But then again, I suppose I always knew it would be that way between us." His lips rested lightly against my forehead. "You awaken things in me I have not felt in a very long time."

I suddenly knew that I had fallen headfirst over the divide, the one that separated my desire from an unattainable love that threatened to incinerate me. "And you make me feel whole again," I whispered against his skin as I gripped him tightly against me, not wanting this moment between us to end. A feeling welled up inside me and gave itself a name. *Happiness.* I had found the fragile and illusive strands of happiness, tucked away within myself, waiting for me to claim them.

August gazed down at me with a look of such tenderness it stilled my breath. "What is it about you, Jezebel? You move me so deeply." He reached out to sweep a strand of hair from my face. "There is such a passion inside you, it's breathtaking." His eyes trembled with an emotion I could not decipher. "You know, I have not been with a woman like this since my wife."

His words touched a delicate place inside, and a pause hovered in the air between us as I tried to grasp the depth of what this meant as Samuel's words at the bar rushed back to me.

August slipped quietly into my mind, plucking my thoughts from me. "You found out about her, didn't you?"

"So that *was* her?" A sadness washed over me as I hesitantly continued. "There was a man who was talking about this house the other day..."

A deep sigh moved through him as he slowly rolled away from me and sat on the edge of the bed. I reached out for him and trailed my hand across his back as the pale, wavering light of the moon cast shadows upon his skin.

"You don't have to talk about it."

Shaking his head, he leaned forward and rested his arms on his knees, slowly running his fingers through his hair. "Perhaps it is time that I do. You want to know what is behind my walls?" His eyes were filled with a wordless turmoil as he looked at me. "My wife." A deep sigh filtered through him as he continued. "Things were very different in America back then. The Salem witch trials were over, but people were still uneasy, and my wife had gotten a bit careless with her gifts. They did not understand her, and that misunderstanding led to fear. A dangerous combination."

"And so they accused her of witchcraft?"

He nodded slowly. "The night we were to leave, they came for her. I was powerless to stop it. I couldn't protect her, and I have never forgiven myself for that." August clenched his fists, his face furrowed in grief. "She was the one great love in my life, and our time together was too short. So much of me died with her."

His sorrow was a raw ache that filled the room with a heavy force. I moved to pull him close to me, resting my head against his back.

"I'm so sorry." I wanted to take it all away. The pain and torment he held within. I would carry it for him if I could. "So, why did you come back then?"

"This was the house that we built together. You see, I had so much anger and sorrow in my heart when I left, so many years spent living as a ghost. I knew I had to return, to say a proper goodbye to her. To try to lay to rest all the suffering within me, so that I could reclaim some semblance of myself once more."

It hit me with a sudden blow. All this time the house had been his, a mausoleum he had kept intact, paying tribute to her memory for all these years. His tender confession stirred me, and I took his hand, feeling him slip his warm fingers around mine.

"And have you?" I asked.

August turned to me, his eyes swimming with sentiment. "Yes, I believe I have. But I did not expect to find you." He stroked my open palm with his thumb, running over the curved lines. "Such a strange coincidence you are."

Reaching up, I traced his face with my fingertips, my touch lightly trailing across his forehead and down past the delicate sweep of his almond-shaped eyes. I memorized every detail of this moment, of what we just shared, to preserve it under the thick glass of my memory.

"You don't have to go," I whispered.

"*I'm sorry*, Jezebel." He leaned in close, placing a lingering kiss upon my lips. It was soft and gentle, and it spoke of a resolve I could not negotiate.

Sinking into his arms, I wrapped myself around him. He held me, his hands softly running through my hair while I melted into him. The warmth of his skin against mine was a comforting anchor as tears slipped out onto his chest. I knew I could not convince him to stay. He had unlocked a door, one that had been buried deep inside me. He had crept into my quiet little world, a world I could no longer comprehend without him, but one I knew I had to.

I began to feel the weight of Embrace's sleep wash over me. I struggled to stay awake, but I was unable to fight against the current. It slipped its tendrils around my mind, pulling me away from him, into the dark waters of dreams.

* * *

Morning's light gentle touch awoke me, and I opened my eyes to find myself once again alone. I did not call out for him, for I knew he was gone, slipped from me like an untamed bird.

I rolled over in bed to find the sheets void of any envelope beside me. What we had shared the night before had gone far beyond any agreed transaction between us, far beyond any intimacy I had ever experienced before. It felt like goodbye. His last words whispered to me through this simple gesture.

In a daze, I searched for my clothes upon the floor, only to find them neatly folded on the table beside the bed. My fingers ran over the creases made by him and my eyes pricked with sudden tears.

Willing my limbs to move, I reluctantly dressed and made my way downstairs, glancing over the furniture which was once again covered in thick white canvas cloth, erasing all evidence of him ever being here at all. Almost as if he had been nothing but a wild and delicious dream.

I stood in the living room for a moment, allowing this reality to settle around me. Gazing out the window, I took in the expanse of water laid out before me like an undulating blanket, billowing out until it softly touched the horizon. The silence that stood beside me was crushing, a heavy space that I knew August would no longer fill.

My legs were like weights, hesitant and plodding as I walked to the door. Reaching for the knob, my eye caught on a piece of paper. My hands shook as I pulled it down from the door and opened the carefully folded letter.

Jezebel,

My heart aches as I write this. You deserve so much more then pen against paper.

Leaving you is not easy. But I fear there is no place for us together.

I returned to this town with intentions to heal the wounds of my past... and discovered you in the process.

You are the spark of light in the vastness of my night.

For this, I will be forever grateful.

August.

My tears fell upon the paper, staining the flowing script of his name as a vastitude of sorrow gripped my chest. *He was really gone.* His note like a finality to a beautiful, breathtaking song.

CHAPTER EIGHT

The months tumbled by while I tried to reorganize myself. I didn't quite fit into my old life anymore. The edges of my reality had frayed and lay scattered around me, like a puzzle with missing pieces I could no longer arrange. August had obliterated me, releasing emotions which had lain dormant for so long it left my heart exposed; the delicate strands stretched and swollen.

August's last words to me burned in my mind like a mantra, the creases on his letter worn from all the times I had unfolded the paper, my fingers tracing over his script as if the very act could summon him back to me. I missed him with a sorrow that clawed fiercely at my skin, I missed his gentle words that made me feel full of possibility, the beautiful world of splendor and unbelievable pleasure he had shared with me. Being without him was like trying to come down off the precipice of the greatest high.

But beneath all this lay the raw pulse of anger. I was angry at August for leaving, for slipping away into the night. How could he have shared himself with me like that and then leave?

Sometimes, late at night, I would wake in a blind panic, scrambling around in the dark to locate my bearings. In these moments, it felt as if August had been nothing more than the creeping hallucinations of insanity, and I worried that I may have lost my mind completely. I would then find my way over to a mirror as if my image could provide a lifeline, but I struggled to recognize myself. It was as if he had stolen my skin when he left, leaving bone and tissue exposed. My russet eyes stared back at me with a haunted loneliness, tears leaked from the tangled depths and slipped down my cheeks while I traced the faint pink marks upon my neck. The only other remnant left of him, a definitive proof that was fragile and began to fade with time.

Spring arrived, and with it, the rush of tourists. I busied myself with clients and took on the role of cleaner again. I needed the kind of physical work that left my body sore and exhausted, so that when I came home to my apartment, I could walk past the heavy silence and succumb to sleep. Slipping into tangled dreams, I would find him waiting for me like a silent observer against the sky of my longing, and morning would always come to soon.

At times, I would find myself driving up to the bluff, in the fruitless hope that perhaps he had returned. But his house remained empty and locked. I would stand and watch the ocean angrily smash itself against the rocks. My yearning was like a silent call out to him from across the endless water, feeling alone and marooned on an island that no one else had access to. Who could I speak to? Who could I share this story with, without it sounding like the lovesick ravings of a lunatic?

The tail end of summer had slipped away, leaving autumn to court the trees again, blowing her flirtatious color around. The sun had begun to sink softly into the horizon, giving itself to evening as wispy trails of pink stretched across the sky like brush strokes. I had decided to take a walk out along the dock and noticed the familiar vibrant hue of a purple trailer, signaling that the tarot reader was back in town.

She always came during this time when the seasons shifted. She would park beside the wharf where the water lapped gently against the pier. The locals called her the crazy gypsy lady. Still, they would go to her when they thought no one was looking, slipping into her trailer to gaze into the future that was written upon their skin like indelible ink.

I found myself drawn to her door as it opened, and she stepped out, wearing a dress the deep color of the forest, her long gray hair blowing out around her like a halo.

"Oh, hello there. I'm just about to pack up for the night, but I think I have some time for a reading." Her bright green eyes fell on me while I stood there in silence. "That is what you came here for, right?"

I wasn't quite sure why I was there, but her smile was warm and inviting, and I found myself saying yes.

"Please come in."

She swept her arm in the direction of the open door, and I took a tentative step inside. Heavy incense burned from somewhere within the trailer, a pungent aroma of cedar and spice. My eyes scanned the intriguing items lining her shelves. Reaching out to touch one, my finger brushed over a statue of a woman holding a spear, ornate engravings etched deep into the wood.

"That's Hekla, an ancient priestess from Iceland. She is the remover of illusion." She motioned to the couch covered in a red velvet throw. "Please, take a seat."

I sat down, fidgeting with my hands. "I don't really know why I'm here."

"Ah, the great question we all ask ourselves." She gave me a playful smile, defining the intricate lines around her eyes. "You seem to be troubled by something."

She reached across the table between us and took my hands in hers, her grip cool and soft. "Would you like me to read your cards?"

I nodded, relief washing over me as I fell into the depths of her gaze, filled with such warmth and knowledge that I yearned to unburden myself to her. She took a deep breath and closed her eyes. "Let me read your energy first. There's so much truth hidden within you that the cards cannot always access."

Silence encompassed the room, with only the hush of the sea that crept between the space around us. I glanced over at the tarot deck sitting on the table beside us, worn and faded from years of shuffling. Suddenly, her eyes shot open, and she squeezed my hands hard. A look of wonder flickered over her features as she stared at me.

"You have met him."

I pulled away from her, a chill running through me. "What are you talking about?"

"De Sanguine. His energy is all over you, but it's not just that."

Her face crinkled in deep thought, then shifted to surprise. "He didn't only Embrace you, did he?"

My skin grew flushed as I recalled my last night with August, the powerful rush of him as he had shared himself with me. The overwhelming ache of emotion he had stirred within.

She shook her head slowly. "You know, his kind is not known to do that, to lay with us." She regarded me for a moment, her piercing green eyes seeming to shift through my layers. "There must be something incredibly special in you that he saw."

I stared at her. "How do you know about all this?"

She leaned forward, her eyes blazing with an intensity. "The sacred Truth Holders are an ancient group of beings, said to have descended from the stars." She raised her hands up like an invocation. "The only ones with direct access to the universal life energy that flows within all of us. They are here to help us heal the wounds of disconnect, and De Sanguine is one of the oldest left of the sacred blood. He is the keeper of all the secrets."

"De Sanguine... as in August?"

She smiled at me. "Yes, that is what we call him."

My mind scrambled around, trying to fit the pieces together, and a warm rush of something akin to excitement wash over me. "Wait... so you know him?"

She nodded. "I met him once, a long time ago."

"Did he Embrace you?" It shocked me to feel jealousy creep up at the thought of him with this woman. Of his caress on her, of him transporting her to such sublime heights of ecstasy.

As if she could sense my thoughts, she let out a laugh. "Oh no, nothing like that ever passed between us. I met him years ago in Syria in the ancient city of Damascus. This was long before the war broke out. I traveled there to witness the Custodiens Veritatem Gathering. I had connected with a woman while I was researching De Sanguine and those of his kind, and she was able to help me gain access. I had the honor of speaking with him."

She smiled at me with a wistfulness in her tone. "The most beautiful man I've ever met. He gave me my gift, you know. The gift of sight. Most Mystics and Clairvoyants of the world have been touched by him. Nostradamus, for example." She waved her hand in the air to highlight this fact, the tiny gold bracelets on her wrist softly tinkling against each other. "It is his way of creating an accessible lifeline of truth for us."

"Wait. He met Nostradamus?" I was familiar with the sixteenth-century French physician, having read one of his books of prophecies years ago. "How does he give people this gift?"

She tapped on her forehead. "He just places his hand here, like unlocking a little door within. We all have the capacity to be seers, most of us just don't have available access to that part of our brain. August does, and he is able to open it for us."

I shook my head, slowly taking in all she had just said. "I had no idea about any of this. He never told me. I mean, he told me a little, but we never got enough time together before he left."

"Oh, he probably never would have told you what I'm telling you right now. I think he feels weighed down by everything... overwhelmed at times. He is fallible. One of the tradeoffs of receiving our life energy. It makes him just as susceptible to fear and remorse as the rest of us. Perhaps he found in you a sweet escape from it all?" She paused a moment and looked at me reflectively. "I just can't believe he came back here after all this time."

A stillness settled over the trailer, and I quietly breathed in this knowledge around me. While we sat talking, the sun had sunk itself to a low orange ball that floated on the horizon. A dusky light filtered through the blinds, casting eerie trails throughout the room.

She leaned in close to me. "I'm sorry, but I don't think I ever got your name. I'm Raven."

I smiled at her. "Jezebel."

"Jezebel? You do know that was his wife's name, right?"

I nodded slowly.

"That's very interesting."

"Yes, it is, considering the fact that it is not even my real name."

"It's not?" Her green eyes searched mine with deep interest.

"No. My birth name is Sara. Jezebel was a name given to me in a dream."

"In a dream, really? What kind of dream?"

I adjusted myself on the couch, recalling the night the woman had come to me with her fiery red hair and piercing emerald eyes. "This was about twenty years ago, back when I was living in foster care. I was about fifteen or so at the time. Things were really hard for me then. My parents had been killed in an accident the year before."

My mind shifted uncomfortably around the memories that rushed in. The loud screech of tires against a wet road, the sickening crunch of metal. My parents' lifeless eyes. Weeks spent in the hospital among bright lights and blinking machines, my body trying to piece itself back together while my soul lay shattered. My hands fell to my lap, absent-mindedly tracing the thick scars that hid beneath the layers of my clothes.

"One night, I had this vivid dream. I was sitting in a meadow, on the edge of a forest. The sky was a deep purple, and this woman appeared in front of me. We spoke of many things as we sat together. In the dream, she had lost her family too. We seemed to share this similar sense of loss, and then as she was leaving, she gave me her name. Jezebel. She said it would give me strength."

Raven gaped at me. "Did you know that De Sanguine's wife was a dream traveler?"

I looked at her in confusion. "No, what is a dream traveler?"

Raven crossed the distance between us and joined me on the couch. Clutching my hands in hers, she spoke with growing excitement. "Every Truth Holder has a gift. A gift they are able to share with us. De Sanguine's is the gift of sight, but his wife Jezebel, well she had another gift." She squeezed my hand tightly. "One that had not been discovered yet. It was her ability to travel through dimensions of time and into people's dreams. It is quite possible that the woman in your dream could have been her, and in that case, it makes the connection you have with him potentially more powerful than either of you are aware of."

I sat there with my heart racing as I tried to digest all this information she was throwing at me; the gifts that those of his kind were able to instill in others, the potential connection I had to his wife. I realized I had stumbled into a world that was far more complex than I had originally thought.

"I apologize if this is a lot for you to take in. I have not met many who have experienced a truth holder's Embrace, let alone De Sanguine's. He tends to be extremely selective."

"What do you think it was that he saw in me?"

Raven stood up and moved across the room, her long dress swishing against the floor as she drew a box of matches from a drawer and struck one. She brought the flame to a large red candle sitting on the counter, illuminating the growing darkness with a warm glow.

"I'm afraid only he knows the answer to that, Jezebel." She blew out the match, and a thin line of smoke trailed upwards before disappearing. "How about we do that reading I promised you?"

Raven picked up the deck of cards that lay on the counter and joined me beside the couch. She shuffled them slowly and then fanned them out across the small coffee table in front of us. Her fingers lightly hovered over the cards before she pulled one out and placed it upon the table.

"Aw, the strength card. This is a good one, Jezebel," she said, tapping her finger upon the card which depicted a woman laying beside a lion, her fingers tangled in his mane. "It represents mastering raw emotions. This is the inner journey you are on right now."

Raven pulled another card slowly from the deck, her eyes lighting up. "The two of cups. I am not surprised to see this here."

"Why is that?" I asked, leaning closer to the card to inspect the image of a woman and man, their hands intertwined around two golden goblets.

"Look." Raven pointed to the face of the lion, rising above them like mist. "There's the lion again. This card represents the physical and spiritual intimacy between two people, there is a sacred journey here. When this card is pulled, it signifies a strong connection you share with another. A powerful partnership, affecting your past, present, and future."

"And the star." She looked up at me as she pulled the last card, placing it atop the others with a warm smile. "The star is all about reconnecting one's soul with the divine. Tapping into your exalted origins, and your attraction to a higher union." Her eyes were full of a soft wisdom as she spoke. "You possess a strength inside that I believe August has not encountered since the loss of his wife, and I see transformation, and healing for the both of you."

CHAPTER NINE

After my encounter with Raven, I was left with a buoyancy and awareness I hadn't felt since August left. I had found a tiny lifeline that connected me to him somehow, and in doing so, I also discovered a friend. For in the weeks after we first spoke, I went to Raven's trailer often, always at the closing of the day, when sunlight flickered against the waves. She joked about her inability to cook, so I brought her dinners; warm food wrapped in tinfoil that I made for her in my kitchen with my mother's worn cookbook propped up on the counter, dog-eared and dusted with flour.

We walked along the beach together one evening, our shoes cast aside on the dock, shrugging off the day around us as we dove into the mysterious world of occultism. She had an awareness and a knowledge of reality I was only beginning to grasp.

"I'm so glad I met you, Raven." I sat beside her on the sand, watching the waves softly lick at our feet.

She placed her hand gently on my knee. "And I as well. My lifestyle can get a bit lonely at times, being a gypsy and all," she said with a playful wink.

"You have no idea what it has been like for me, to not be able to share what happened between August and me. There were moments when I thought I was losing my mind... that he had just been some illusion."

Raven glanced at me, a small smile upon her face. "Well, everything around us is an illusion, really." She swept her hand across the beach. "This world that we exist in is only a tiny fragment of a much larger and more powerful force around us. We are just like these tiny ants scurrying about."

She pointed to the ground where some ants were searching for crumbs among the sand. "They have no idea what is up there above them, and so they never even think to look up."

I stared out over the water, feeling the push and pull of the tide around me like a magnet. "I have to see him again, Raven. I still don't fully understand why he left."

She nodded solemnly, gazing out to the ocean. "I think he still carries so much pain inside from the loss of his wife, and opening himself up to you was a visceral reminder of that." She looked at me, lazy sunlight glinting off her hair. "But I believe you will see him again, Jezebel. You know, I have wondered why he didn't clear you when he left?"

"Clear me?" I asked.

"Yes. After an Embrace, or in your case a series of them, we usually get cleared. A simple swipe above the temple and memories of the encounter become erased, so that we may resume our life without being consumed by the enormity of it all. It is clear to me that he didn't want to lose what you had together. Whatever the two of you shared, clearly went far beyond a simple Embrace, and I do not think this story is over between you two."

Raven's words hit me with a force. I had wondered so many times, in anger and sorrow, why? Why had he just left me like that? Left me to scramble around and pick up the broken pieces of myself. *But what if Raven was right?* What if I would see him again one day? Despite my tender heart, the idea filled me with a dangerous rush of joy. The thought of him returning was like the promise of a rare and wonderful gift.

I sighed, and cupped the soft sand in my hands, letting the warmth of it trickle down between my fingers as I allowed the familiar residency of my doubt to creep in. "Sometimes I wonder though, since I happen to share his wife's name... that maybe he was just trying to invoke her again by being with me?"

Raven shook her head. "No. He's not delusional. He knows his wife is gone. I think what you are to him is much deeper than being a simple replacement for her. I feel a very strong connection between you two."

We both shared a moment of stillness, watching as the waves gathered the last colors from the sky and spilled them onto the shore.

Raven turned to me, her eyes seeking mine in the growing dark. "Do you mind me asking what it felt like? To be with a man like August?"

My pulse quickened at the mere thought of him and his brightly burning intensity. How he had broken open parts of me I never even knew existed. "Words can't really describe it," I said. "It was mind-blowing and powerful. I felt things with him I have never experienced before."

"Wow." Raven seemed to capture my emotion within her eyes. "You have been deeply blessed, Jezebel."

Autumn had slowed her twirling dance to make room for winter's cold embrace, with crisp mornings and frost that clung like tiny crystals.

I stood on the pier, watching Raven as she packed up her trailer.

"I'm going to miss you," I said.

"And I shall miss you. I wish I could stay a bit longer, but my family awaits me down in the Catskills. It's time for some hibernation and soul renewal."

She placed the last of her bags in the front seat of her truck before turning to me and slipping a clear bottle of liquid into my hands.

"What's this?" I asked.

"It is Mead, made from an ancient fairy meadow."

"Seriously?" I stared her quizzically.

She laughed and threw me a playful wink. "No, silly. But it was made by some very lovely monks up at this beautiful monastery I visited in New Mexico last year." She then pressed a piece of paper into my hand. "This is my number. If you're ever feeling stir crazy up here this winter, give me a call."

"I will." I smiled at her. "I look forward to seeing you next summer."

"Yep. Same place, same time." Her bright eyes looked deep into mine, placing her hands on my shoulders. "I'm so glad I found you, Jezebel. I truly believe we were destined to meet."

I nodded and drew her into a long hug. "I know we were. Thank you so much for everything."

She hopped in her truck and started the engine. White clouds billowed out from the exhaust and into the frigid morning air. Rolling down the window, she called out to me as she pulled out onto the road. "Take care of yourself, okay?"

Her taillights slowly faded off into the distance, and I was left alone again, to sit with all this truth laid out before me. A truth that, for the first time in months, left me with a sense of hope. Like a tiny bud growing among the barren landscape of my loneliness, whispering of spring's dependable renewal.

Winter seemed particularly angry this year. The cold slap of the wind would hit me whenever I stepped outside. My runs along the beach became longer, in a feverish attempt to outpace my own solitude. I welcomed the bitter sting, for it redirected my thoughts, and hollowed out my longing.

The holidays crept by, and the town around me came alive with cheerful lights, optimistic greetings, and the persistent push for consumerism. While my employees took their vacation leave to visit family, I spent Christmas alone like I always did, with no one to distract me from the painful reminder of my own isolation.

It was in these moments that the absence of my parents would hit me with a brutal force, a wound I knew no amount of time could ever completely heal. Gathering a blanket, I would head down to the darkened beach with a bottle of wine in my hand, allowing the deep red liquid to tug out the sorrow that I had managed to keep tightly locked away for most of the year. There I would lay it out, trembling and exposed upon the sand, with nothing but the wind and the roaring sea as my witness.

Every morning when I awoke, my frantic heart clung to the possibility that today would be the day that he would return to me. But it never was. He never came, and I knew I had to find a way to move on.

* * *

As winter graciously handed itself over to warmer days, I realized that it had been over a year since August had disappeared from my life, and although the fever of him would still wash over me on occasion, the predictability of time had stepped in, allowing me to rebuild my foundation once more.

The pieces of myself were coming back to me, but this time they were more vibrant and alive, instead of the familiar shards of my own self-negation. It was as if something had awakened within me, a part that had lain dormant all my life. Like a hungry serpent, I was uncoiling myself; shedding my skin to reveal new growth among the verdant swell of spring, like a whisper of color among my palette of grey.

CHAPTER TEN

I sat finishing paperwork in my office late one Friday afternoon with the front door propped open to let in the warm spring air. The smell of sweet violets filtered in, thick and cloying around me.

My employee, Jules, had stopped by the office to pick up her paycheck. She casually leaned her tall, thin frame against the open doorway, "So, a bunch of us are meeting up tonight to check out the new bar that's opened down the street. I hear it is a notch above the local tavern."

"Uh-huh," I absentmindedly replied, while I sat at my desk finishing the week's invoices.

"You should come, Jezebel. My *brother* will be there." She shot me a mischievous smile, her brown eyes sparkling.

Jules had been hinting at us meeting for a while now. Apparently, he was a construction worker, staying in town for a few months on a job, and according to her, she thought we would really hit it off.

I looked up at her and sighed. "Jules."

"Oh, come on, please? Let's shake off some winter funk."

I let the idea settle around me. While I wasn't looking to *hit it off* with anybody these days, at the same time I wondered, could I dispel some of my longing in the arms of another man?

"I'll think about it, okay?" I threw a strained smile at her as she left the office.

"Great! I will see you at eight-thirty then," she called confidently over her shoulder, her short brown hair bouncing as she slipped out the door.

* * *

As I entered the bar, my skin prickled with heat as the press of bodies created a warm den-like atmosphere around me. Mahogany tables lay throughout the low-lit room, the interior accentuated by plastic ferns in a halfhearted attempt at providing a little class to the local drinking scene.

I spotted Jules and a few other people cloistered in the far corner. I weaved my way through the crowd, the red dress I had boldly slipped on that evening clinging to me like a bandage.

"Jezebel! You made it!" Jules called out enthusiastically, waving me over. The loud scraping of chairs filled my ears as everyone made room for me. "Hey, boss." She threw me a playful wink. "So glad you could come."

I smiled faintly and looked over at the attractive blond man who sat next to Jules, his face partially obscured by a well-trimmed beard with faint hues of red that caught the light.

"Jezebel, this is my brother, Patrick."

"It's so nice to finally meet you," he said, standing up and extending his hand out to me. "My sister has been talking a lot about you."

His smile was large, friendly, and welcoming. His brown eyes grazed over me like an easy invitation and in that moment, I wanted to take it.

The conversation flowed and the warmth from my drink began to wrap itself around me like a blanket. Patrick talked of his job and his adventures on the road with animated enthusiasm and effortless laughter, and I found myself enjoying his company. His presence stilled the noise in my mind.

As the night died down and everyone started to filter out of the bar, Patrick offered to walk me to my car. A surprisingly warm breeze blew against us as we walked through the dimly lit streets together.

"It was really nice talking with you, Jezebel. I had a great time tonight."

"Yeah?" I leaned against my car and pierced him with my steady gaze as the soft tone of the waves in the distance pummeled the shore. "Then why don't you come over to my place."

It wasn't a question; it was a challenge. I needed to feel consumed. Hollowed out. Obliterated. I wanted to try and erase the stain August had left on my skin.

Patrick looked at me in surprise. "You're bold. But I like it."

"Then get in," I said, motioning to the front seat.

* * *

His breath fell on my neck as I unlocked the door to my apartment, his hands gripping my waist tightly.

"*God,* you're so hot," he said into my hair.

Walking into the living room, I brazenly slipped off my dress, leaving it on the floor as I retreated into the bedroom. My insecurity replaced by a restless longing to lose myself. He followed behind me, his dark eyes flickering with heat as he watched me remove my underwear and bra and then lay myself on the bed, waiting for him to join me.

I watched him in mild amusement as he undressed. He fumbled with his clothes, his erection straining against his underwear. I realized he was nervous.

"Come here," I said, patting the bed next to me. The mattress shifted to accommodate his body next to mine, and I straddled his waist, rocking myself slowly against him. He moaned and grabbed my thighs while I leaned down to meet his lips, waiting for the warm rush of desire to spill over me, but as I kissed him with his rough beard that tickled my lips, nothing came. I kissed him harder, pushing myself deeper against him, frantically rubbing my tender flesh against his, waiting desperately for a spark to ignite within me.

"Oh, jeez. You're going to make me cum if you keep doing that."

Smiling, I rolled off him, reaching to grab a condom out of my drawer. I quickly slipped it over his length and pulled him on top of me. It took me a moment to guide him in, my body slow to respond. As Patrick began to move inside me, I hastily matched the rhythm of his movements, willing my desire to stir, my fingernails gripping his back.

"Harder," I said. His thrusts grew deeper and faster, and I could hear him panting on top of me. His face contorted into some version of his own private pleasure, while all I felt was empty. The depths I longed to fill inside me; this man could not begin to reach. Filled with an aching loneliness, tears fell silently down my cheeks as I heard him call out and shudder above me.

Patrick noticed my tears, and concern flashed across his face. "Are you all right?"

I rolled out from under him and sat up. "I'm fine," I said.

"You don't seem fine. Did I do something wrong?"

"No, Patrick. I just think it's time for you to go... I'm sorry."

"Are you sure I didn't hurt you? Was I too rough?" he asked, sliding over to me and placing his hand on my knee.

Sitting rigid on the edge of the bed, I stared down at my hands, which were clasped tightly in my lap. "No... you were fine. This has nothing to do with you, okay. I just need to be alone right now."

Patrick nodded and got up to grab his clothes, his quick retreat filling the room. The hasty rustle of fabric. The sound of the front door shutting behind him, and then the powerful silence that followed.

I slipped my body under the sheets as a myriad of emotions pulled at me. Sorrow, frustration, and shame all tangled together. I gripped my pillow as loud, choking sobs emanated from within me, slowly sinking into the yawning abyss of a deep penetrating sleep. One that carried me across the divide to him.

Laying upon the earth, the feel of moss was cool against my skin. A thick canopy of trees towered above me, partially obscuring the blue of the sky. The air was pungent with the aroma of pine. August always came to me in dreams this way, like Pan in the forest.

I whispered his name, and the wind blew it across the trees like a shiver. His hands brushed against my skin before he appeared before me, trailing slowly down to where my longing lay waiting for him. His face gradually materialized before me, dark blue eyes that stole into my depths. He never spoke in my dreams. Like the keys of his piano, it was his fingers that traced out a language upon my flesh. As he slipped them inside me, water began to pour out, a gushing river that flowed onto the ground and spread throughout the forest floor.

I awoke then, gasping with pleasure while the last few ripples of my orgasm gently subsided.

Standing beside my car, I took in the construction site around me. Framed buildings in various stages of completion dotted the surrounding cliffs like weeds. The late afternoon sun sparkled upon the churning sea below me as I spotted Patrick, walking to his truck with a sturdy gait, hard hat swinging in his hand.

"Patrick!" I called out, making my way toward him.

He spun around at the sound of his name, turning to me with a quizzical look.

"Jezebel, what are you doing here?"

"I just wanted to apologize for what happened the other night."

He ran his hand through his hair sheepishly, giving me a lopsided smile.

"I had a nice time with you, and I really didn't mean for you to feel..." I trailed off for a moment, nervously shoving my hands deep into the pockets of my sweater, trying to gather my thoughts. I realized I had not rehearsed this, having driven up here to his work site on a whim, hoping to dispel the gnawing feeling of guilt within me.

"Hey," Patrick placed his hand on my arm, and I looked up into his calm brown eyes. "It's okay, I understand. Well, I guess I don't really, but I would like to."

I sighed in relief as the wind off the ocean suddenly picked up around us, blowing my hair into my face.

"I honestly didn't expect to see you again. But I'm really glad that you showed up here, Jezebel. I would like to try... and maybe start over? There's this nice restaurant in town that I would love to take you to, if you're interested?"

Patrick's sweet invitation stirred something within me that I had a faint longing to explore. But at the same time, I felt reluctance. The memory of our night together still made me cringe with regret. I knew it had foolish of me to think that Patrick could eradicate my longing for August.

Seeming to sense my hesitation, he held his hands up in a playful gesture of innocence. "Strictly as friends if you'd like. No strings attached."

A warm smile crept across my face. "Okay, that sounds nice."

"Great." Patrick's face stretched into a wide grin as he fished his keys out of his pocket. "How does tomorrow at six sound? I could pick you up at your place?"

We sat across from each other. Wine glasses rested on starched white linen, nestled within a quiet corner of the restaurant as the expansive view of the ocean stretched out before us.

"So, my sister mentioned that you're not from around here. What was it that brought you to this sleepy little town?" Patrick asked, his lips hovering over his drink.

I twirled the stem of my wine glass as I spoke. "Well, I grew up in Brighton, where I spent too many years stuck in a dead-end job as a payroll clerk in Bio Tech. It was a great company, but... I was tired of living on other people's terms. I wanted to reinvent myself. So, I saved up enough money to jump start my own business. I guess I was looking for somewhere quiet, and I have always loved the ocean."

"Well," he said with a wink. "Looks like you have found plenty of both here."

The evening passed effortlessly between us. Patrick spoke of his past; he was a rough and tumble midwestern boy who had grown up on a ranch. He regaled me with stories of his and Jules' wholesome childhood, filled with the endless waving grass of the prairie and a family full of laughter.

There was a lightness and ease to him that I could see myself sinking into.

"So, you haven't settled down yet?" I asked, emptying out the remainder of the wine bottle between us, our plates of food cleared away long ago. Out the window, the last of the sunset lingered in the sky, faint wisps of color developing into a soft midnight blue.

"I guess I have yet to find someone worth settling down for." Patrick pinned me with a contemplative look, and I detected a faint hint of a question there; almost as if he were offering me up the challenge. I found myself averting my eyes, suddenly uncomfortable with the forwardness of his gaze.

"Your life does sound pretty exciting though." I shot him a teasing glance, attempting to lighten the moment between us. "I mean, you get to travel around and see the country, meet new people... sow your wild oats?"

"Hey now," Patrick said playfully, leaning across the table and placing his hand on mine, giving it a gentle squeeze. "I am a perfect gentleman. It was you that seduced me, remember?"

Heat rose to my cheeks, but I didn't pull away. The warmth from his touch was surprisingly soothing. "Yeah, I guess you're right. That was really out of character for me, by the way."

Patrick gave me a soft smile. "Yes, I gathered that."

* * *

Pulling up to my apartment, Patrick cut the engine and turned to me in the darkened interior of the car. "Shall I walk you in?"

I shook my head. "No, I'll be fine." I rested my hand on Patrick's knee for a moment. "Thank you for tonight. It was really nice."

"It was, wasn't it?" He grinned and leaned back in his seat. "So, I only have a few more months on this job. But I would really like to see you again."

A hesitancy seemed to fill up the space between us as I grappled with my response, unsure as to what compartment I could fit him into. My loneliness had become my constant companion and Patrick felt like a breath of fresh air, cleansing the heaviness away. *Was there room for him?*

"Can I ask you something?"

"Sure." Patrick's gaze grew serious as he looked at me.

"What is it exactly that you hope to get out of this?"

He sighed, running his fingers through his hair. "I don't expect anything from you, Jezebel. I just enjoy your company."

I smiled and found myself reaching over to brush away a strand that had fallen into his eyes. "You're sweet, you know that."

"Is there a but coming?" He regarded me with a look of uncertainty.

Despite my tender heart, and all my reserves, which tentatively curled against the edges of my mind, there was a comfort I felt with Patrick. He was like a warm blanket that I longed to slip around my shoulders. Shaking my head, I gave him a small smile. "No, there's not. I would like to see you again too."

CHAPTER ELEVEN

Patrick would often show up at my office after work, his clothes covered in sawdust and smelling of pine. He courted me slowly with flowers and a gentle hand at my back. Allowing me to ease into the idea of him. We would grab a drink at the bar down the street, our conversation blending into the murmur of the room around us. Oftentimes we would take long walks along the beach with Patrick's dog, Gusto, who he lovingly referred to as his neurotic traveling companion. He was an energetic Jack Russell Terrier who spent his time tirelessly running up and down the shore, frantically barking at seagulls.

I enjoyed these moments with him. Our talks stilled the noise in my mind. Patrick was carefree and charming, like an open book with colorful pages that invited me in. It was on one of these evenings that he showed up at my office, rapping softly upon the glass of the open door.

"You ready to head out of here for the day?" Patrick cocked his head in the direction of the pier. "Cause if you are, you should come with me."

I stood and stretched, before shuffling my papers off my desk and into the file cabinet. "Yeah, I think so." I glanced at him with a playful smile. "And where are you taking me, Patrick?"

The warmth of his eyes glinted as he shoved his hands in his pockets. "You'll find out."

* * *

The sun had sunk low, reflecting the light in a shimmering dance that played over the waves. We stood on the pier, watching the fishing boats come in, their rudders leaving a lapping trail behind them as they slipped beside the dock. Patrick sauntered over, his voice jovial as he addressed the men and then climbed aboard. After some

88

chuckling and back slapping between Patrick and the fishermen, he reemerged with two large lobsters dangling in his hands, and a boyish grin plastered on his face.

"Well, you seem to be very friendly with the locals."

"Yep, best place to get seafood in this town," Patrick said. "I try to come down here at least a few times a week."

"And what are we going to do with these guys?" I asked, warily eyeing the creatures which seemed to coil toward me with their tethered claws flailing at the air.

He winked at me. "We're going to eat them."

Patrick and I stood in my kitchen together, condensation gathering on the windows from the steam that rose from the boiling water on the stove. His eyes trailed over my sculptures, which had now begun to crowd my kitchen table, all in various forms of completion.

"These are really beautiful, Jezebel."

"Thanks. I'm looking into renting a studio, because as you can see, I'm starting to run out of table space." I pushed back the strands of hair that clung to my face while I reached up to grab some plates from the cupboard. "I like to think that one day I'll be ready to show my work."

Sitting on the living room floor of my apartment, we ate the steamed lobsters. The light of the sun hit the golden hue of Patrick's hair as he leaned in close to me, his fingers reaching out to lightly brush away some butter left on my chin. Then his lips were on mine, warm and salty, and I let him kiss me, enjoying the feel of his hands as they slowly ran down my back.

"Is this okay?" Patrick asked, his voice husky against my cheek as his hand lightly slipped underneath my shirt, teasing my skin.

I nodded and pulled him closer as I sank into his touch, drawing out a whisper of arousal. His lips were a soft contrast against the coarseness of his beard, and I let his mouth guide me to a place that wanted more. I closed my eyes, allowing my body to take over as a quiet wave of pleasure washed through me.

That evening we lay naked together in my bed, my head nestled comfortably in the crook of Patrick's arm, watching the setting sun throw shadows across the room. Patrick had been slow and gentle with me, his hands delicately exploring my body, his eyes full of tenderness. And while I did not reach ecstatic heights with him, there was no crushing disappointment either. I found myself grateful for the quiet he provided; there was no frantic emotion clawing at me. Being with him was peaceful and comforting, and I realized I needed this.

Our days blended together as spring made promises of summer. We fell into a routine that I knew was innately born from the mutual needs of two lonely people experimenting with our hearts. Keeping company, the possibility of more. Patrick began to stay over often, showing up at the apartment with his large warm smile and his dog in tow. These lazy evenings with him stretched around me like a soft blanket of comfort, reminding me of when I was a child, and I would play house with the children down the street. A game I enjoyed, but one I knew wasn't real. *How could it be?* What I felt with him was tender but also infused with confliction, for August still haunted me. He would coil into my dreams at night. Dreams which left me gasping and filled with longing as I lay in Patrick's arms, my gut churning with a feeling akin to guilt as I watched him sleep beside me; his face washed in the gentle tremble of shadows which played upon the walls. Blissfully unaware of the silent struggle within me.

* * *

We sat upon the cliffs by Patrick's job site, sharing sandwiches and beer as we watched the ocean swallow the sun, bathing the water in a gentle myriad of colors.

"Do you ever think of leaving this town, Jezebel?" Patrick turned to me, the last rays of light reflecting in his eyes.

I shrugged and wrapped up the remainder of my sandwich, placing it back in the cooler. "Not really, I mean my business is here. Plus, I don't know where I'd even go."

"You could go anywhere." Patrick shot me a warm smile and reached out to brush a strand of hair away from my face. "You know, I really think your spirit is too big for this place."

Slipping my hand in his, I gazed out across the water. His words were like an expensive gift I didn't feel I deserved, and I found myself trying to brush them away. "Oh, I don't know about that. I'm nothing special, Patrick."

"Yes, you are, Jezebel."

The look Patrick gave me was filled with so much tenderness, it gathered around me like a soft sigh. I leaned against him, resting my head on his shoulder. As the days between us grew shorter, I clung to the comfort of him that seemed to anchor me. I had been trying to slip on the idea of what we could be together, beyond the time we had left. I could see what a life with him would look like. Cheerful mornings filled with him whistling in the kitchen. The sweetness of his touch. Laughter spilling through the apartment. It made me smile. And I wondered, if August had never come into my life, would he have been the refuge I was looking for?

But being with Patrick felt like trying to squeeze into a pair of pretty shoes a size too small. I knew I wouldn't be able to walk in them for long. My heart yearned to run reckless and wild through tangled jungles, and the memory of August was like the heavy beat of a drum, incessantly calling out to me despite all my efforts to ignore it.

"What are you thinking about?" Reaching out, Patrick ran his fingers along my cheek, his eyes full of an openness and a longing that caused a bruised feeling of sorrow to suddenly overcome me. I knew that regardless of how much I wanted to, I couldn't return that look, not with the intensity that his gaze implied.

"Oh, I was just thinking about how much time we have left together."

Patrick pulled me close to him, his lips finding mine and drawing me into a deep kiss that seemed to speak of a hopeful promise I was afraid I couldn't fulfill. "We have as much *time* as you want."

I buried my face in his neck, breathing in the faint aroma of the ocean on his skin, my words locked up tight, reluctant to answer.

Gusto had now claimed his spot at the foot of my bed, curling himself up into a perfect circle. I rested my head against Patrick's shoulder as the blue flickering light of the movie we were watching played across our skin. His hands slowly roamed underneath my shirt, his voice hovering against my neck. "So, I have decided to stick around after the work crew leaves."

My body involuntarily stilled against him, my heart sinking in my chest. The silence that followed spoke volumes and Patrick removed his hands from me, sitting up on the edge of the bed. I picked up the remote and turned off the TV, moving closer to where he sat.

"Patrick." My voice constricted as my hand fell on his back. He stiffened and pulled away from me, shaking his head.

"I have been so fucking presumptuous, haven't I?" He turned to me, his eyes full of anger and pain. "Have I just been a plaything to you? An amusing pastime?"

"No, it's not like that," I pleaded as the hot prick of tears clouded my vision. "Being with you has been wonderful. I really like you, Patrick."

He stood up from the bed and grabbed his shoes. "Save me the pleasantries, Jezebel. I get it."

"Patrick, please..." I followed him out into the living room. "Don't leave like this, please talk to me."

Patrick hovered in the doorway, his jaw tightly clenched and his eyes dancing with tears that felt like a punch to my gut. "What is there to talk about? I thought we had something here..." He shrugged his shoulders, his voice gruff as he hastily wiped away a tear that had broken through the surface. "But I was clearly wrong about that."

"You weren't wrong, we do have something." My voice was a whisper as tears slipped down my cheeks. Had I been so selfish in my attempt to move on? How could I explain to him that despite it all, I still longed for August. That I had experienced such profound emotions with him, emotions that had managed to render all others down to a pale comparison. That no matter how hard I had tried; I couldn't shake him from me.

"But it's not fair to you if we continue this. Because I can't give *all* of myself to you, and you deserve someone who can. I really wanted to, Patrick, I have tried. You are *so much* of what I have been looking for... but I realize that there's this part of me that belongs to someone else."

Patrick softened for a moment as his hand reached up to gently stroke my hair. His brown eyes crowded with disappointment. "Well, whoever this man is, I hope he realizes how lucky he is."

His tender response released a flood of aching remorse within me, and I suddenly wondered if I was making a terrible mistake. I gripped his arms as a choking sob spilled out. "I'm so sorry."

"Me too." Patrick dropped his hand, taking a step back from me. "I really hope you find what you're looking for, Jezebel."

Through my haze of tears, I watched him close the door behind him, leaving me alone with the silence of my own entangled sorrow.

Summer slipped in like a rush. Now that Patrick was gone, I busied myself once more with clients and work, settling into a rhythm that no longer felt frantic. I had grown accustomed to the silence of my life again. Patrick had somehow managed to soften the blunt edges around myself. And the feel of August's memory had become a story I whispered to myself at night, the recollections of his touch no longer a burn upon my skin.

Every day, I would find myself glancing out my office window, hoping to see the familiar outline of Raven's purple trailer parked along the dock. We had kept in touch over the winter. Nights spent curled up on my couch with the phone pressed against my ear, her soothing words keeping me grounded. I looked forward to seeing her again, of relinquishing the burden of my thoughts to her warm, knowing gaze; cradled in a growing friendship I realized I had been seeking for years.

The sun made its descent upon the water, bathing the office in a hazy, pink light. The sound of the waves and children laughing filtered in through the open windows. Jules arranged an assortment of food platters and drinks on my desk, which was now covered with a crisp white tablecloth. Tonight, the office had been transformed into a cheerful art exhibit. Various flowers crowded in vases among the room, their alluring scent trailing through the air. My sculptures were displayed on little black stands I had found down the street at the hardware store. Jules had been the driving force behind this event, finally convincing me to show my work.

"Thank you so much for putting all this together," I said, taping price tags along the bottom of my pieces.

"Not a problem. It's been fun. I think I got the whole town to come out tonight." Jules looked flushed and excited as she spoke, her long silver earrings brushing against her neck. "It's just too bad Patrick had to leave town so quickly. I'm surprised he didn't want to stick around a bit longer. I thought you guys had a good thing going?"

"We did. But you know how it is. His lifestyle wasn't really conducive for a long-term relationship."

She furrowed her brow. "Well, the way he talked about you, I thought for sure he was going to make some adjustments."

Jules appeared to not know what had transpired between us, and I couldn't bring myself to tell her. The last night with Patrick, he had left with so much pain in his eyes. I had hurt him, and my gut still clenched whenever I thought about it. Love could be such a misguided and unrequited affair. Why couldn't the simple act of loving someone be enough to stir the heart of another?

I stopped at my largest piece, entitled *Embrace*, running my fingers along the smooth depiction of muscle and skin. I had spent almost a year working on this one. It portrayed a nude man and woman entwined; her head thrown back in ecstasy while his mouth feverishly fell upon her neck. I didn't really want to sell this piece, it had too much meaning behind it for me. Hours I had spent drawing August out through the clay, paying homage to what we shared together; something sacred and ephemeral. But Jules had insisted I display it. She called it my deliciously erotic magnum opus and said it would draw attention to my show. So, I threw an exorbitant amount on the tag, knowing no one would possibly buy it.

"You know, I wouldn't be surprised if this one sells tonight," Jules spoke from behind.

I turned around and rolled my eyes. "No one in their right mind is going to spend ten thousand dollars on my piece."

"Exactly my point," she said, poking my arm playfully. "There are a lot of kooks in this town."

* * *

At around seven, the bell on the office door came alive. People filed in quickly, and soon the room was packed with bodies. The low murmur of voices and the tinkling of ice in glasses filled my ears as I was shuffled around by Jules.

"You've already sold four pieces," she whispered in my ear. "People are loving your stuff." She pushed a glass of wine into my hand. "Relax and enjoy this." She smiled warmly. "You look amazing by the way."

Jules was referring to the low-cut cocktail dress she had loaned me. The dark green silk material hung against my curves and flirted with the floor as I walked, making me feel like some glamorous red-carpet attendee.

I moved to the front door to prop it open and let some air into the room, which had begun to grow quite stifling. The fresh evening breeze from the ocean rushed into the space, instantly cooling the flush upon my cheeks. I stood and sipped my wine, watching all the familiar faces of the locals and business owners move around me. I smiled and nodded in thanks while they offered up their praise of my work. A warm rush of happiness bubbled within me, a lightness of being I had not felt in a long time. I had no idea that exposure would feel so good. This evening had not just been about the liberation of my work, but the liberation of myself as well. I had released my demons from their encapsulating shell, and they no longer clung to me with such persuasion.

Jules approached me from across the room, jolting me from my ruminations. She wore an excited look on her face as she grabbed me by my arm and whispered dramatically into my ear, "Oh my God, Jezebel! I think someone wants to buy your big sculpture."

My heart sunk. The thought of something I had spent so long pouring my soul into suddenly being gone filled me with dread. I stared at Jules in shock.

"That extremely gorgeous man over there is very interested in your magnum opus." She pointed to a man in a black suit with his sleeves rolled up, standing in front of Embrace. His back was to me, and wavy dark hair brushed against the collar of his jacket. He turned around, and a familiar set of deep blue eyes met mine from across the room.

CHAPTER TWELVE

My pulse quickened, and all sound seemed to slip away, except for the frantic rush of my heartbeat in my ears. I gripped the doorframe to steady myself.

"You should go over and introduce yourself." Jules' voice sounded far away as she prattled on. "He said he would love to meet the artist."

She pulled me from the doorway and into the crowd, my legs suddenly heavy and uncooperative as the space between us grew smaller. I stared at August in a state of shock.

"August, this is Jezebel." The irony of Jules' introduction was not lost on me. I attempted to smile, but after being apart for so long, his presence overwhelmed me. I grew dizzy, and my stomach fluttered like the wings of frenzied butterflies dancing within.

"It's so nice to meet you." He gave me a playful wink, clearly amused by the situation.

"I'll let you two chat." Jules patted me on the shoulder before disappearing into the crowd.

"Jezebel." August's face suddenly grew serious and filled with tenderness as he took me in. "You look absolutely beautiful." He moved closer, speaking softly as his hands ran along the curves of the sculpture. "This piece is breathtaking."

His hands on the clay elicited a jolt of pleasure through my body as if it were me he was touching. "You never told me you were a sculptor."

"Well, you never asked." I said, my voice wavering in reply. "There is a lot that you don't know about me, August."

He regarded me with a look of sudden regret. "Yes, I suppose you are right."

"How long have you been back?"

"I only arrived today. I happened to see the flyer for your show and thought I would surprise you."

"Well, you did." My heart refused to slow its frantic pace as I stood beside him. Trying to appear calm, I drew my glass of wine up to my lips and realized my hands were shaking.

August's eyes searched mine imploringly and noticing the tremor, he reached for me, his fingers grazing the inside of my wrist. "Is there somewhere more private you would like to go for a moment?"

I nodded and signaled for him to follow me. Navigating us through the crowd, I slipped into the narrow hallway and opened the supply closet door, motioning him inside and shutting it behind us. I fumbled for the switch in the dark while his hand slipped to my waist, causing a jolt of electricity to spill through me as a stark light flooded the tiny room.

"God. How I have missed you." His voice was heavy with intensity as he traced the curve of my cheek with his thumb before sliding down to rest against my lips, his eyes full of longing. "I had to come back to you, Jezebel. I'm just sorry it took me so long."

My mind swam with thoughts I could not compartmentalize. Seeing him again was like taking a deep breath of air I had not realized I'd been holding until now. But at the same time, hesitation curled around me, and the buried anger I thought I had let go of threatened its way to the surface. I placed my hand on his chest to push him away, feeling his rapid heartbeat against my palm. "Do you think you can just waltz back into my life like this, without an explanation? And what makes you assume I'm even available anymore for whatever this is between us?"

A look of heavy remorse flashed within the depths of August's eyes. "Was it wrong of me to show up like this? Shall I leave?"

His gaze tore into me, a ferocious indigo and violet, which stretched my heart open despite the confliction which coursed through me. A longing mixed with the weight of all the sorrow his absence had fashioned to the sinew of myself coiled within. He had come back, and though the meaning of that was still unclear, hope fluttered against my chest; delicate and raw.

"*No.*" The word tumbled out of my mouth in a whisper as a rush of reckless heat overcame me, and I lost myself to the exhilarating drug of him that seemed to obliterate everything else. Gripping his arms tight, I found his mouth. I couldn't think, and I suddenly didn't want to. All I could do was devour his lips. I curled my fingers into his hair, which smelled of earth as he pressed me against the door, his hands sliding down my dress.

"Are you really here right now?" My voice came out breathless as his mouth began to trail down my neck.

"Yes. I am really here."

His lips beat softly upon my skin as he drew my body closer. Despite the tiny voice hissing within me, the feel of him after so long was inebriating. "I have waited... for you... every day," I gasped as I pressed the heat of myself against him, fumbling with the enclosure of his pants.

"Jezebel." His eyes were a deep burn on me as he gripped my hips to slow down the frantic pace of my desire. "How I long to savor every inch of you right now." His voice was husky as his gaze traveled across my skin. "But I would prefer it not to be up against a door in a supply closet."

A trembling exhale escaped my lips as he slowly pulled away from me. Straightening my dress, he ran his hands through the curls of my hair. "I would love nothing more than for you to join me at the house tonight."

I nodded and smiled languidly at him, taking a deep shuddering breath to compose myself.

I was dazed and shaky as August gently led me back into the room, my limbs weak from the overwhelming rush of him. The crowd had noticeably thinned, and Jules was clearing drinks and platters of food away. She caught my eye and winked, almost as if she knew what had transpired between August and me. My cheeks warmed as his hand fell on my waist.

* * *

I stood by the door while the last of the crowd dispersed, leaving a stillness that settled over the room. Jules breezed by me with her purse in hand.

"I'm going to head out." Jules nodded toward August with a smile. "Looks like you found a friend. Did he end up buying your piece?"

I shook my head. "It's complicated. We have some history together."

She raised her eyebrow. "Well, now I am intrigued."

I smiled at her, resting my hand on her arm. "Thanks again for tonight."

"You're very welcome. It was fun. People really liked your work." She blew me a kiss before slipping out the door, the sharp clip of her high-heels sounding on the pavement as she headed out into the night.

I turned back into the office and walked over to where August stood beside the sculpture of us, his hand trailing down the piece. "You have so much passion inside you, Jezebel." He turned around to face me, a look of awe in his eyes. "It at times, renders me speechless."

I reached out to him, my mouth falling against his lips; soft and warm, stirring me once more. My words came out in a whisper against him. "You know that sculpture is of us, right?"

August brushed his thumb across my cheek. "Yes. But I did not think it was possible to take what we have shared together and make it even more beautiful."

We drove in silence to his house. I had so many questions but didn't want to break the spell his presence had conjured. His hand found mine in the dark contours of the car, warm and enveloping. I closed my eyes, letting the road take me to the place that had shattered my reality and self-control so long ago. It had become the only place that made sense to me anymore.

* * *

The house was dark when we arrived. August drew me inside, where I noticed the table set for two.

"I know it may be presumptuous." His lips softly brushed my ear as he spoke. "But I wanted to share some dinner with you."

Drawing his arms around my waist, I leaned back against the sturdiness of his chest, absorbing this moment between us.

"Why don't you take a seat," he said, slowly leading me over to the dining room. I sat and watched him light the candles on the table, enveloping the room around us in a golden glow before he retreated into the kitchen. I glanced out the window which was open to the crashing sound of the ocean. A soft summer's breeze slipped in through the curtains, making the flames from the candles flicker and dance.

August returned, setting food warmed from the oven upon the table. "This is a bouche a la reine," he said, uncovering a dish that looked like pastries stuffed with chicken and an herbed cream sauce.

"Did you cook this for me?"

He nodded and smiled, taking a seat next to me and filling up my glass with a deep red wine. I took a sip, feeling the rich oak and berry run over my palette, the heavy warmth settling in my belly. My sensations, which always seemed to be heightened around him, swirled within me. The wine. The food. His eyes on me; all of it so exquisitely delicious.

"As I am sure you can imagine, I have had many years to perfect the craft," he said with a wink, handing me a plate of food. "I deeply enjoy cooking; I find it to be a form of art in a way, taking rudimentary ingredients and transforming them into something that evokes pleasure."

Affection washed over me as I envisioned him in the kitchen cooking. It was these simple domestic moments with him that I longed for.

August watched me as I began to eat, but the comfortable silence became punctuated by my thoughts as the euphoric haze of his presence abruptly lifted, leaving me with conflicting emotions that swirled around me like fire.

"August." I set down my fork, leveling him with my gaze. "I have to say, *this is* very presumptuous of you." I swept my hand across the table for emphasis. "All this. Do you think you can just woo me back into your arms with a little dinner?"

Leaning back in his chair, he ran his fingers through his hair. His casually confident demeanor replaced with a flicker of discomfort and uncertainty.

"Are you going to tell me where you've been all this time?"

He regarded me with an obscure look, cloaked in layers I could not uncover. "I've been many places, Jezebel. But I am back now."

"Are you really? What does that mean?" I asked, a stab of hot anger welling up inside me. "You were gone for over a year. How do I know you're not going to just disappear into the night again? Which, by the way, is something you seem to be very skilled at doing."

The pause between us felt heavy as August stared back at me in silence.

"Jesus Christ." I shook my head, my fists clenched tightly in my lap. "Almost two years you have been gone, August. I figured that would have given you enough time to at least have a speech prepared."

Abruptly rising from the table, I left him sitting there as the thick pulse of frustration coiled within me. Flinging the front door open, I made my way down the gravel driveway, the thunder of the waves engulfing the dissonance of my mind.

CHAPTER THIRTEEN

"Jezebel!" August's hands grabbed me, gripping my shoulders. "Where are you going?"

I yanked myself away from his grasp, my words spilling out into the wind. "I'm not a fucking toy that you can just pick up and play with when the mood suits you!"

His eyes shifted to a slate gray, filled with a heavy sorrow that tore into me. "You have never been a toy to me."

"Then what am I to you?" I stared at him intently as the wind crashed against us.

"*You* are more to me than I ever thought possible. I came back because the very idea of you fills me with such emotion that I am rendered helpless, and though I have tried... I am unable to stay away." August's voice cracked with a desperation I had never seen in him before. "But the truth is, *I need you*, Jezebel."

His words slammed into me with such force that my thoughts tumbled around in my mind. Staring out into the depths of the sea, I took a deep breath, searching for an anchor. "But you left me for so long, August. All your words can't change that."

"You are right, they cannot. I have been a fool, and a coward." The look he gave me was filled with a vehement emotion that threatened to devour me. "But I want nothing more than to be given the opportunity to redeem myself."

"I thought you said there was no place for us?"

He stepped closer, reaching out to run his fingers delicately across my cheek. "I no longer care about any of that. Life is meant to be lived, not compartmentalized."

His touch was like a bright spark of fire that warmed my skin, and I grew flushed, the anger slowly trickling away as I fell into the depths of his eyes.

"I never thought I would have the capacity to feel this way again, but I do, and I am so sorry that it took this long for me to come to terms with that." There was a power to his statement, like he was relinquishing something deep within himself and offering it up to me. August grasped my hips with an intensity as he drew me flush against him. "Do you know how deeply I feel for you? So many years I have spent dead inside until you came along and revived something within me. You have breathed color into my world once more." August reached up and lost his fingers in the tangle of my hair. "Do you not feel this connection between us? You must on some level? For it was my essence that I shared with you the last night that we were together."

The memory of August's energy slamming into me with such visceral power sucked the air out of my lungs, causing my voice to come out tangled and hushed. "Yes, I felt all of it."

August ran his thumb along my cheek, his voice a gruff whisper. "Please. Forgive me."

"*Damn you*, August. You know I can't think straight when I'm around you."

"Then stop thinking." He cupped my face in his hands as his eyes pulled me into the current of his concentrated fervor. "The mind can be a restless creature, born of insecurity and doubt. Believe me, I am all too aware of this reality, but what speaks beneath all that?"

My whole body hummed as I closed my eyes. The sound of the ocean crashed beneath us, sweeping all my doubts away and pulling forth the warm pulse of yearning, allowing the silent language of my heart to step forward.

"I need you to promise me that you're not going to run off again like that."

"I *promise* you, Jezebel. I am here, and I am not going anywhere."

My whole body shook as I pulled him tight against me. August's lips touched my skin, leaving a trail of thick pleasure which bloomed inside me, and I sunk into the heavy, frantic drug of his kiss. A breathless gasp spilled from my lips as he lifted me up effortlessly into his arms and carried me back into the house; enfolding me in his warmth as my mouth fell hungry and impatient against his.

* * *

Moonlight danced across our skin as we stood in his bedroom together. The intensity of August's gaze broke me open as he slowly slid the straps of my dress down my arms, allowing the fabric to fall at my feet, his hands slowly caressing the length of my back before moving to the soft swell of my breasts. My body trembled as he eviscerated me with his touch, while my fingers grasped at his clothes, fumbling with the cloth until I found his heat and held him firmly in my hand. August drew in a sharp breath and groaned, lifting me up and backing me against the wall as I wrapped my legs tightly around his waist.

A blinding rush so acute burst within as he entered me. I cried out, my body shuddering as he lay so still within me, his pulse throbbing in time with my heart. A visceral wave of emotions that were not mine washed over me with breathtaking clarity, colliding with my own desire.

"Do you *feel* me, Jezebel?"

"Yes." I gasped as he dove himself in deeper. "*I feel you.*" I clutched his back, my nails digging into his flesh, the entirety of my being falling away, until there was nothing left but our bodies wrapped so beautifully together like the silken threads of a cocoon.

"Meus amor. God, how I have missed you." His voice was a silken whisper in my ear as he continued his slow dance of ecstasy inside me. Every muscle violently contracted as a divine current of bliss ruptured within, and I exploded against him with abandon. August watched me with a heavy longing as I lost myself, my eyes tearing with overwhelming elation. He filled me so completely, it was almost too much to take.

He gently kissed my tears away and then gave them back, his mouth salty upon my lips. "You are so exquisite. *Dilectus meus pulcherrimus, quid tibi mecum tanturn.*" he moaned against my skin in disjointed Latin as his thrusts grew more fervent.

Crying out, I clutched his back as he engulfed me, hollowing me out and leaving nothing behind but the bright spark of a devotion I could barely define; delicate but consuming. Another wave cascaded through my body, and I crashed against him, tumbling blindly over the edge once more as I took August with me; the delicious warmth of him spilling inside.

* * *

Upon the bed, I lay tangled in August's arms, his hand tracing lazy circles across my back. I was lusciously spent as my emotions trickled out around me, tender, unguarded and alive.

I found his face in the darkness, my fingers brushing over his lips. "I wish I spoke Latin."

August smiled with a teasing look in his eyes. "So, you want to know what it is I say when I lose myself in you?"

"Yes, I do." My voice quivered as he drew his mouth against my ear, his hands slipping into my hair.

"*My beautiful beloved, how you enrapture me.*"

His words caressed me, and I began to ache from deep within as his lips traveled down my neck. "August, I want to be with you."

"You are, Jezebel." His tone was rich and sleepy.

"No. I mean, really be with you."

He guided my face to his, eyes flashing different shades of blue before me. "What are you asking?"

I didn't quite know what I was asking. All I knew was that I wanted to break down the barriers that separated us.

"Are you able to *change* me?"

August shook his head slowly. "No. I cannot do that."

"You can't, or you won't?"

He sighed. "I cannot. It does not work that way. I descended from a bloodline, and I am not equipped to alter that, nor would I ever wish to do so. I would never want to take this life from you. Time can be a heavy burden upon the soul."

"You've never talked about children." A pause shifted the air between us as he tenderly stroked my cheek with the pad of his thumb. "Did you and your wife choose not to have any?"

Sorrow flashed in August's eyes. "No. We did in fact want a child, and she became pregnant once. But we lost her too early. One day she came to me and said that becoming a mother was not meant to be. There was so much pain and resolve in her voice, that out of respect, I never mentioned it again."

Reality rushed in like a thick fog lifting. The intensity of what August and I shared together had pushed passed the boundaries of what sex was to me, and not once did the topic of protection come up. He met my eyes in the darkness, answering my question before it spilled from my mouth.

"No. I am unable to give you a child. You must have a link somewhere within the bloodline."

"What do you mean?"

"In order for you to conceive, you have to possess the abilities of my kind."

My fingers reached up and lost themselves in his hair. I wanted with such an acute longing to bathe in the thick richness of who he was, to forge a permanent connection. "You know, I would give up this life for you, if I could."

He looked unsettled as he took my words in. "Please do not say that."

"Why?"

Like flames igniting from the embers of a fire, his gaze suddenly grew ravenous as it shifted to my body, causing a flush of heat to spread across my skin as his hand slowly slid up my leg. Feverishly, I pressed myself against him as he began to stroke the slickness of my sex with his fingers.

"Because this life you have been given is a precious gift." His voice was a lustful rasp as his touch teased out my pleasure. "And you are absolute perfection just the way you are."

I gasped, trembling against him, raw and open. It did not take long for the surge to sweep over me like a blast of momentary mindlessness. He watched me quietly, desire and amusement flickering across his face. I rolled on top of him and pinned his arms against the mattress as the feel of his arousal pulsed underneath me.

"What was that for?" I asked playfully.

"Forgive me, but I cannot help myself. I love watching you." His hands pulled themselves from my grip and reached up to brush back my hair. "It is so beautiful when you let yourself go."

I arched my neck back like an addict, craving more of his engulfing pleasure.

"Then Embrace me," I whispered.

He looked up at me with a teasing smile. "You cannot get enough, can you?"

"*Never.*" I drew him closer.

He stopped me, his hand slipping down to my neck as his fingers gently caressed my pulse. "I want you to know, Jezebel, that an Embrace is only a temporary arrangement. If I were to take from you long term, it would permanently deplete your essence."

I looked at him with confusion. "What do you mean?"

August ran his hand down to my collarbone, tracing soft circles across my skin. "Your essence is the lifeline to your health. When there is an imbalance there, illness can occur."

"So... I could get sick?"

He regarded me somberly. "Yes, Jezebel. If I Embraced you consistently, you could develop health problems down the line."

"Well, what about just once in a while?"

"As part of an occasional shared intimate moment between us. Yes, of course."

I took in this information as the truth of what that meant coursed through me. "Wait, does that mean that you are going to go Embrace other women, then?"

"Would it bother you if I did?"

His eyes burned into me while I rolled off him and sat up on the bed. The thought of him touching another woman caused my gut to lurch abruptly.

"Jezebel." August drew his fingers slowly down my back. "I have Embraced thousands of women; Givers are very sacred to me. But not one of them has ever made me desire anything more until you. You are the first I have ever shared myself with like this."

I turned to him. "So, what are you saying?"

"I'm saying that even though an Embrace is an act of shared intimacy, it pales in comparison to what I feel with you."

My heart fumbled around in my chest, but despite my hesitation to accept this potential reality between us, I sighed, allowing August to pull me down next to him where I nestled my head against his shoulder, running my hand slowly down his torso.

"August?"

"Yes."

"Did you know that while you were gone, I met a seer who knows you, a woman named Raven. She said she met you once in Syria."

"Ah, yes, Raven. I remember her well. I am so glad you two were able to cross paths." He ran his fingers through my hair as he spoke. "A very wise woman she is."

I nodded as my hand trailed across his skin, brushing over the tangled patch of curls on his chest. "She helped me understand a lot, you know. You left me with all these heavy emotions, and I had no place to put them."

August lifted my chin to meet his eyes, placing a long kiss upon my lips. His voice was filled with a hushed fervency as his breath danced against my cheek. "*I am so sorry.* I know that it was incredibly unfair of me to leave you the way I did, and without clearing your mind first. I was going to..." he trailed off for a moment, confliction burning within the depths of his gaze. "But I found myself unable to do so."

I pulled him closer to me. "I'm not sorry. I would have never wanted you to, anyway."

Shaking his head, he tenderly cupped my face. "But I never gave you that choice, did I Jezebel? And for that I am deeply ashamed. I was a coward for leaving, and selfish for making you carry that weight with you for so long. I hope you can forgive me for that?"

I rested my forehead against his. Though the past two years had been painful for me, I realized I would not take them back even if I were given the chance. August had stripped away at my walls, leaving room for something much larger to take its place.

"*I do.* Because you came back to me."

"I suppose there was a part of me that always knew I would." August gently stroked his fingers down my cheek. "And I couldn't bear the thought of you forgetting me."

Our eyes sought out each other's light within the darkness of the room, shedding away the residue, until there was nothing left but the filaments of ourselves, reaching out among the muted sound of the waves crashing against the rocks below us.

CHAPTER FOURTEEN

The evening slowly slipped into the early stillness of morning. Wisps of delicate color spread across the sky, bathing our skin in pastel hues while we lay together, speaking of things not yet shared, the blanket of our own tightly woven stories unraveling between us like gentle confessions.

I talked of my past and the night of the accident which had changed everything; the fragments of my time in foster care and the lonely ache that followed me like a hungry shadow. August spoke of his voyage across the world, of growing up during the political unrest of the middle ages, the division of the church and the disintegration of Rome. Intricate strands of beauty, art, culture, and politics he wove for me into a tapestry of color and light, the vastness of his history, settling around me like fine silk.

His voice grew soft when he began to speak of his wife, their travels, and her gifts, and his years spent in anger and turmoil at not being able to save her.

"I suppose I have believed for so long, that I no longer deserved happiness."

The deep vibrato of August's voice was tinged with a hint of sadness as I lay against him, his hand playing through the coils of my hair. "Is that why you left?"

"Yes. You stirred something deep within me I believed I had no right to explore."

"So, what made you come back then?" My question was soft and hesitant but filled with hope. I wanted to know what had compelled him to return.

"The mind can only convince the heart of something for so long, I suppose."

I ran my hand slowly down his chest, reveling in the solid reality of him beside me again as my heart swelled with gratitude. "I'm so glad you came back to me."

He pulled me tight against him, placing a lingering kiss on my forehead. "Me, too, Jezebel."

"August."

"Mmmm." His voice had become soft and drowsy.

"There is something I need to tell you." I took a deep breath, my fingers fiddling with the sheets. "My birth name is Sara. The name Jezebel was actually given to me by a woman I met in a dream as a child."

August's hand stopped its movement against my hair. An overwhelming silence hung thick and pressing around me. Finally, he spoke, his voice full of revelation.

"That was *you?*"

I sat up to find his eyes filled with tears. "You know about this?"

August nodded slowly. "I knew about all her travels."

"Why do you think she came to me?"

A sigh escaped him. "She never seemed to have control over who she visited." His fingers absentmindedly trailed down my back. "But I remember that night, the night of the Gathering. It was the first time she traveled. She spoke of a young girl who had a story much like hers. She told me how she had given her a piece of herself, the power held within her name."

August reached over, pulling me close to him again, his hand softly cupping my cheek. "There lies such vibrant potential beyond our comprehension." His thumb brushed along the bottom of my lip. "Life is full of beautiful mystery, and this intrinsic connection we share may only be surfacing. Do you understand how profound this is, Jezebel."

I nodded, placing my hand on his chest. "I do. I feel it. I have *always* felt it between us."

* * *

We lay in a peaceful silence together, watching the blushing colors of the morning filter across the room. Our limbs entwined, hands delicately tracing over each other's skin, memorizing every detail as if it were written in braille.

August abruptly rose from the bed, turning to me. His dark hair fell messy and rumpled around his face, and his eyes shimmered with a joy I had not seen in him before. It gave him a youthful appearance, and I could suddenly picture what he must have looked like when he had been a child.

"I'm going to watch the sunrise. Would you care to join me?"

I nodded and grabbed a sheet from the bed, wrapped it around myself and followed him out to the deck. A cool breeze blew against me as we watched the water dance with the flush of the morning sky. From across the waves, seagulls called out to each other in their shrill mournful tone.

"God, you are so beautiful." August's hand moved to brush the tangle of my hair away from my shoulder, his lips falling on my neck. I closed my eyes as he wrapped his arms around my waist, his breath like a sensual shiver affixed upon my flesh. "The way the light hits you... reminds me of the Greek goddess, Eos."

"And who is Eos?" I asked with a smile, leaning against the warmth of his chest.

"She is the Goddess of the dawn, representing renewal."

"This has always been my favorite time of day," I said with a sigh. "Knowing that even the darkest of nights can be washed away into something beautiful."

August rested his chin on the top of my head and pulled me closer. "Yes, there is a profound stillness born from the space in-between darkness and light. It reminds me that there is always room for rebirth, you just have to be ready for it."

I reached up and ran my fingers through his hair. "I think I'm ready."

"Me too." August smiled and slid his hand underneath the sheet, pulling the fabric away and replacing it with his soft caress. I shivered in the cool morning air as drops of dew hovered on my skin. "You have helped me find my happiness again, Jezebel." His voice was a tender whisper against my ear as his fingers slipped down into my warmth, coaxing out my pleasure as he gently entered me from behind.

A drawn-out gasp escaped me, and my hands tightly gripped the railing as he moved within. The wave of my desire crested with such force while his mouth devoured the flesh of my neck like a burning flame. He held me up, firmly pressed against his chest, while the sky continued to shift her colors around us, welcoming the heat of the sun. I cried out to the ocean, to the vastness of the horizon, to the powerful beauty of him which spilled into my core, filling me up so completely.

August carried me back into the bedroom. I could feel sleep rushing in, its tentacles reaching to pull me down to the depths.

"I do believe I have worn you out."

"You are insatiable," I murmured as he lay me gently on the bed.

He let out a soft chuckle. His voice a warm, rich caress. "Yes, I am. But it takes two to dance, Jezebel."

I smiled as he spread the sheets over me, the air billowing out around my body for a moment like a cool touch upon my skin. My heart fluttered as a feeling I had not known since I was very young washed over me, one of home, and a love that felt unfettered. August brushed his hand tenderly across my forehead as he smoothed my hair back, and I tumbled into dreams.

* * *

I awoke to the afternoon sun, which had already begun her dance across the sky. Shadows and light flickered upon the bed as I sat up to find August lying beside me, asleep. I watched him with a quiet longing. His face lay serene against the pillows, his own humanity delicately exposed before me.

August opened his eyes, the force of his gaze piercing through me with a look of such concentrated passion that it caused my heart to flutter. I slid my body on top of his, tasting the fullness of his lips, his skin like a hot burn against mine.

"I never thought I would wake up to you beside me," I breathed softly into his ear.

He slowly ran his hands up my arms but did not answer; only rolled me over onto my back and entered me with a hushed intensity, his thrusts fervent and uninhibited. The emotions that spilled from him were sudden and extreme, and they slammed into me with a force that unraveled my senses; pulling forth a heavy potency that filled the room with a shivering silence.

We lay entangled in each other's arms, August's hands delicately tracing over the flush of my skin with a look of quiet introspection on his face. Through the blissful haze of the last twelve hours, my life had filtered down to August and this room. But reality rushed in once more, like an acute shock to my system.

"I just remembered that I need to go into the office for a few hours today."

He nodded quietly, a playful smile creeping across his face. "Yes, but how are you going to do that, my dear?" He rolled on top of me, gently nipping my neck and sending tantalizing shivers upon my skin. "For I was the one who drove you here, remember?"

"Oh, am I your prisoner, then?" I asked, my breath growing labored in arousal as his lips lazily traveled down my stomach. He stopped just above my sex, which was already aching for him again.

"Would you like to be?"

"Maybe." I arched myself toward him, longing for his mouth on me, but he suddenly drew himself back up to my neck.

"*God*, you are such a tease," I moaned.

He hovered over me, his eyes flashing with amusement. "You can take my car if you would like; the keys are on the kitchen counter." August sat up, his gaze abruptly growing distant as he glanced out the window. "There are some things that I need to take care of here at the house."

* * *

The sun slanted its lazy summer rays against the sidewalk as the ocean blew a warm breeze across my skin. I unlocked the door to the office and stepped inside, taking in the remnants of the night before. Emotions curled within me like a deep ache as I recalled the euphoric memories of his sudden return.

I spent the remainder of the afternoon cleaning up the office and carting the sculptures that did not sell back to my apartment. I left Embrace standing by the desk to keep me company while I reluctantly dove myself into the payroll; empty coffee cups and take out dispersed around me. I stood to stretch, my body humming in pleasure at the release of tension while I gazed out the window to see the sun setting upon the water.

After a quick shower and a change of clothes, I drove back out to the bluff. I enjoyed the sleek interior of August's car, the silence of the engine and soothing blue lights that lit up the dashboard. My mind settled around the reality of him in my life once more, the dance I had been accustomed to between us had shifted, the rhythm felt more fluid. August had returned to me with his hands suddenly full of availability like beautiful offerings, and the possibilities of that stirred me with an exhilaration that made my heart race.

Small glimmers of light off in the direction of the bluff danced across my vision as darkness settled in upon the water, enclosing itself among the lapping waves. I rounded the bend and up the steep incline to his house. I suddenly gasped when I realized that the lights were the flickers of fire, deep orange and yellow flames which engulfed the house like an angry torch in the night.

I raced up the driveway, accelerating hard. The wheels spun out on the loose gravel as my hands gripped the steering wheel, my heart hammering out a loud drumbeat within my chest.

Jumping out of the car, I ran in the direction of the flames, screaming his name over the deafening roar. The heat hit me with a powerful force, rippling against my skin in waves. So many thoughts tore through my mind, clawing at my insides as I scanned the perimeters of the inferno in a blind panic, searching for August. But all I could make out was fire, smoke, and ash, which fell around me like drifting snow.

Then I saw him. In the distance, he stood on the edge of the cliff; a dark figure obscured by the leaping shadows of the flames. I ran to him and grabbed his arm roughly as relief flooded through me.

"August! What happened?"

He turned to me, a look of deep stillness upon his face as he spoke in a tender whisper. "It is *alright,* Jezebel."

He took me in his arms where I collapsed against the shelter of him, my breath spilling out in a shaky sigh. My legs were weak and trembling as the adrenaline began to subside. "I didn't see you at first. I thought--."

August cut me off by drawing my face close to his. "I'm sorry I scared you." The reflection of the flames made his eyes dance wildly in the deep amber glow as his fingers traced my skin, sliding down my temples. "My wife, she came to me in a dream last night."

"She did?" Surprise caught me off guard as I struggled to connect the dots. "Has she visited you before?"

August shook his head. "No. I always hoped she would travel to me, but she never did, until now." His eyes swam with tears as he looked out to the darkness of the sea for a moment. "She had a message for me. It was time to let her go. This house was never really mine; it was hers."

I glanced back toward the flames in confusion, watching as the fire hungerly devoured the house. "Wait. You did this?"

He nodded slowly. "I apologize for the theatrical display, but I needed this cleansing. Fire holds a very ancient power. When one is open, it has the incredible ability to purify. This is my rebirth, Jezebel."

The sounds of sirens off in the distance drew near as August pulled me close to him, wrapping me up in the encompassing safety of his warmth. He bent down, his hair brushing across my neck as the heat of his lips fell upon my skin, his voice like a whispered vow. "I want to start a new life, and I would like it to be with you."

My heart burst open, ready to take in all that he was offering me. I entwined my fingers through his, squeezing tight as my head settled against his chest.

We watched the flames in silence as they danced violently against the night sky, mesmerized by the wild beauty of it. The crackle and hiss of life consuming itself as the fire twisted around the structure of the house, like two lovers locked in an embrace.

JEZEBEL

PART 2

Paris, France: 1720

CHAPTER ONE

Leaning against the cold brick wall of the church, I waited for the bell toll to signal the end of mass. *If there was a God, would he have cursed me?* Yet the only God that existed beside the realms of a church pew were the filaments of collective consciousness. These people, with their books of beliefs clutched frantically against their chests, what would they do if they knew that all their ideas and hopes were simply thin pieces of paper, held together by thread and glue? Something much larger was at play. Though what that was eluded even me. All I had was a deep yearning that stirred within my flesh, a reckless appetite to poke and stretch the fabric of this reality and find the deeper substance beneath.

My body detected the faint tremble against the bricks as the doors opened, and the heavy rush of people filed out into the pale chill of mid-afternoon sunshine. I approached a young man, his clothes neatly pressed and smelling like soap. I preferred churchgoers to the dark and desperate stench of men at the pubs.

"Good day, Monsieur," I flirtatiously curtsied as I passed him and inserted my boot into a crack in the cobblestone, feigning a sudden fall upon the hard ground.

"Mademoiselle!" He ran over to me and leaned down to grasp my waist as he lifted me to my feet. "Are you alright?"

"Oh my...." I attempted a step and then collapsed against him in a dramatic fashion. "Oh no, I do believe I may have sprained my ankle, Monsieur. I cannot seem to walk on it at all."

I looked up into his face, so young and fresh, filled with life's sturdy promise. Winter's lazy sunlight kissed a small scattering of freckles on his cheeks. His innocence and humanity radiated off him, like the tender growth of spring.

"Not to worry, Mademoiselle. Let me help you, S'il vous plaît." He guided me gently by the waist, stepping out into the street to hail a carriage. Helping me up the narrow step, he settled into the seat beside me. I could hear his heartbeat as it accelerated like a soft thumping in my ears. My proximity made him nervous, and I knew he did not have much experience with women.

I lay my hand gently on his knee, my words like a soothing anesthetic. "Thank you so much, Monsieur, for helping me. My name is Jezebel."

He smiled at me, starting to relax against my touch. "It is a pleasure to meet you. My name is Jacques."

"Jacques..." I drew his name out upon my lips in a slow, seductive sigh. His mind was so open and pliable; it did not take much effort at all to wrap him up in my deep, penetrating gaze. "Such a kind, good-hearted man you are, helping a lady in need."

"The pleasure is all mine, to be in the company of a lovely lady, such as yourself."

I smiled coyly as I traced soft circles upon his thigh. He faintly shuddered with desire, his trousers growing tight in response to my touch as my fingers continued their slow, mesmerizing dance against him. His eyes became glazed and his voice grew rough, trembling as he spoke.

"Where shall I take you, Jezebel?"

I pointed to a tall red brick hotel that came into view. "I'm staying at the La Pavilion De Lorraine, just around the corner."

Jacques told the coachman to stop. Gently taking my hand, he helped me down from the carriage and onto the street below. "Please, allow me to escort you inside?"

I flashed a bashful smile at him while I conjured up my limp once more. "I would be eternally grateful, Jacques."

He slowly led me into the lobby with one arm supporting me, then with a sudden flourish, I found myself being lifted into his arms. I smiled up at him playfully. "Oh, Jacques," I teased as he carried me up the flight of stairs with ease. "I do believe you have swept me off my feet."

He grinned back at me. "I cannot help myself. For you make quite a fetching damsel in distress."

When we arrived at my room, I slid from his hold and retrieved my key from within the pocket of my cloak. I turned to Jacques, my gaze pulling him back into my entrancing fold, deeper and more intense this time as I spoke. "Please come inside."

Without a sound, he obeyed me as I opened the door, his hands already eager and under my allure, his fingers grasping at the fabric of my skirt. "Why don't you make yourself comfortable?" I spoke to him as I entered the small room and removed my cloak. I heard the click of the door shut and the quick rustle of his jacket as it fell hastily upon the floor. I moved close to him and helped remove the rest of the garments from his body as he stared at me with enraptured longing, caught in the web of my seductive spell.

"Good boy," I whispered as I trailed my hands down the flushed skin of his torso, watching him as he succumbed to faint shudders and soft moans. "Why don't you lay down?"

He complied as my hypnotic gaze led him over to the white sheets. My lips grazed over his chest, moving slowly up toward his neck, where his pulse thrummed fervent and rapid.

He reached out to lift my skirts, but I slipped away from his touch.

"Who are you?" His voice came out breathless, and I could see a small sliver of fear, hidden within the depths of his desire.

"Do not worry, I am not going to hurt you. All you need to do is relax and allow me to give you pleasure unlike anything you have *ever* experienced before."

Leaning down, I pressed my mouth to his neck, teasing out his arousal with a gentle kiss as a deep moan escaped him. He wove his trembling fingers into my hair. "Oh, oui."

Answering his call, I plunged my teeth slowly into him as he shuddered against me, calling out in ecstasy underneath my hold. He grasped my back in fierce desperation as his seed spilled from him, sticky and warm while I drew forth his essence, feeling the exhilarating rush of adrenaline, the quickening pulse of quenched satisfaction. My body hummed with intensity, the heavy dullness washing away, as every color, sound and smell heightened itself to a blinding detail once more.

I released him, watching as he came back to himself, his eyes wild with ecstasy.

"What have you done to me?"

I smoothed his hair with the palm of my hand. "Hush now. You should rest."

He nodded; his eyelashes fluttering like the delicate wings of butterflies as he drifted into the depths of sleep. I brushed my fingers against the wound on his neck, erasing my mark upon him as the heavy breathing of a man lost in the inertia of slumber filled the room. I knew he would wake up confused, unsure as to why he was alone and naked in an unfamiliar room. But I was aware of the capacity of the human mind to use logic as an anchor, and by morning's light, he would most likely think of this as nothing but a strange, lucid dream.

Quickly gathering my meager belongings, I folded them into the inner lining of my cloak and closed the door gently behind me. I retreated down the narrow stairs and breezed by the lobby, slipping my room key against the shiny granite desk.

I stepped out into the cool air. Afternoon was giving way to evening. Long shadows leaned against the buildings as I made my way into the blur of the Parisian city streets.

CHAPTER TWO

Night crept in, steeling itself amongst the cracks of the city. I stood along the bustling docks of the Loire, my figure blending into the shadows while I watched the ebb and flow of the river beneath me, waiting for a woman; a seer who had agreed to meet with me.

For the past few years, I had been searching for a man known only as De Sanguine. Combing through Europe, I had met with almost every fortune teller, palm reader and mystic throughout Paris. Most of them had been charlatans, with no spark of the Gift emanating from them. I knew that those who truly had it most likely had been visited by him. If I could only find them, perhaps they would be able to provide me with a clue as to where he could be.

I knew he was in France somewhere, for it was a seer I had recently met in Marseille that had spoken of her encounter with him, but he was elusive and kept to himself. My need to find him was a burning drive that consumed me, for he held the key to the truth of what I was. Perhaps in finding him I would be able to find myself as well.

A small boat came into view. The light of a lantern reflected off the water in ripples. A tall woman wrapped in a bright blue cloak stood upon the deck. When she stepped onto the dock, her footsteps soundlessly found me as she pulled her hood back to reveal dark locks of auburn hair that tumbled around her shoulders.

"I'm Freya," she said. "I've been expecting you."

I nodded. "And I, you. Thank you for meeting me here."

She led me away from the docks and to a small path flanked by the tangle of willow trees, which bent their branches like a bow along the riverbank.

"What is it that you long to know by finding him?" she asked me. The gaze of her sepia eyes sparkled in the hushed light of the moon.

"The truth of who and what I am," I said. "I have been searching

125

for De Sanguine all over Europe, and I believe he may hold the answers I seek, if I could only find him." I held my hands out, palms facing upward. "Everything I know, I've had to teach myself."

I gazed out onto the open water, as it lay still and soundless around me while recollections of myself as a child spilled out. Me, running blindly through the forest, while my parents burned among a cheer of Protestants. I shook off the chill that always overtook me with memory's sharpened knife.

"There is still so much of myself I do not understand."

Freya nodded, her eyes somber. "Yes, I can see your story, Jezebel, and it is not a pretty one." Her hand lightly touched mine. "I cannot tell you where De Sanguine is, but I do know that he is here in France, and *he* will find you when the time is right."

"What do you mean?" I asked.

"You shall see." She smiled and gave my hand a tight squeeze before releasing her grip and turning to disappear back up the path and into the darkness of the city streets, leaving me to the noise of my trembling reflections.

The days wove seamlessly together as I walked the streets, hours consuming themselves as I soaked up other people's thoughts and emotions like the delicious undercurrents of wine; an amusing pastime, but one that would leave me dizzy and spent afterwards.

As winter drove itself in deeper and seemed to quarrel with the sky, the city began to shrink into itself. The icy bite of the wind crawled along the streets howling and snarling with ferocity as people hurried past; coiled in their garments, eyes fixed ahead, seeking the warmth of shelter, a fire and a home, while I prowled the edges like a hungry ghost.

As the days unfurled themselves, my attempts were foiled many times as I tried to get close enough to sneak my way into a man's gaze. I grew desperate as the sharp ache of my own weakness clawed at me, stinging my lips, and threatening the delicate strands of my self-control.

Evening swept over the streets, and with it, a light drizzle of rain which clung to my garments like mist. I managed to capture the attention of an inebriated man, who was stumbling home from one of the pubs. I rose to greet him, materializing from the darkness of the shadows.

"Why hello there, pretty lady." His words slurred as he swayed back and forth on his feet, the sour odor of sweat and stale beer permeating around him like a thick blanket. I choked down my disgust as I gasped him firmly and drew him against the brick wall of an alleyway.

"Oh, you like it rough, do you?" He sneered at me. "I have no money to pay you, whore." His head lolled against the wall; a slippery snake-like smile plastered on his face.

"Do not worry," I whispered as I took his chin in my hand, exposing his neck. This man was so far gone, I would not need to waste my powers of hypnosis on him. "It is not your money that I need."

I sunk my teeth into him, feeling his body tremble and crumple to the ground as a moan of pleasure rose from deep within his throat. I pulled him up against me as I drew his essence from him with a frantic hunger. Delicious warmth pooled into my veins once more. I knew that it was time to stop as he was beginning to grow limp against me, but I could not bring myself to release him. A ravenous animal-like instinct had overtaken my senses, and it compelled me to continue. Silence filled the alleyway as his moans had all but ceased to a stifled whimper, when a strong hand seized me from behind, wrenching me from my hold.

"Enough!"

An imposing, dark-haired man stood before me, his eyes piercing through the shadows. He took me by the shoulders and shook me, until my head cleared once more, and the adrenaline in my body subsided to a low hum.

He squatted down to examine the crumpled man on the ground.

His fingers softly grazed across the man's neck, regenerating the skin, then placed his palms upon his temples. A flicker of light pulsed briefly through his hands before he released them and rose to face me.

"He will live." A fleeting look of anger and distaste flashed within his eyes.

I opened my mouth to speak, but shame had stolen my words. Who was this man? And then it hit me, as I recalled what Freya had said to me on the dock, so many nights before. *He will find you, when the time is right.* But before I had a chance to say his name, he pulled me out of the alleyway and into a carriage that stood waiting out on the street. Thrusting me inside, he slammed the door shut; fixing me with a penetrating gaze that brought a bright flush of disgrace to my cheeks as the carriage begin to move beneath me.

The gentle clip of the horse's hooves on the stone streets was the only sound as he pinned me to the seat with his arresting stare. "You should know, we are to never take the lives of others."

Like a scolded child, I managed to wrench my eyes from him, seeking solace in the city going by out the window.

"I know." My voice came out in a whisper.

"How many have there been?"

I turned to him, my words choking in my throat. "Only a few. I do not mean to. It only happens when it has been a while."

He moved closer, filling up the space around me with his presence. When he spoke, his tone was gentler this time, almost tender.

"It is incredibly dangerous to Embrace when your energy is waning. Not only is it against our code of ethics to harm, but it puts our very existence at risk."

Frustration rose within me. So many years I had spent traveling from place to place, trying to unravel the complicated strands that bound me to this life.

"What code of ethics? I have had absolutely nobody to teach me! I have lived centuries alone with this curse."

His eyes grew soft and full of empathy. "Oh, my dear. What we are is not a curse. It is a gift." He reached out and touched my arm gently. "I am sorry that you had no one to teach you that."

I nodded as tears threatened their way to the surface. My gaze met his in the flickering glow of the lamp lights passing by the carriage windows.

"Who are you?" I asked him.

"My name is Augusto De Sanguine. But you may call me August."

"I am Jezebel." I reached out my hand to him. He brushed his lips against my fingers for a moment, pressing them softly against my gloves. The heat of his mouth through the fabric raised a faint and unfamiliar pulse within me.

"I have been searching for you," I said, my eyes glancing tentatively at him. "How did you manage to find me?'

August's gaze met mine. "I sensed you long before I found you, Jezebel. And I am glad I found you when I did."

A warm rush came over me, his powerful presence soothing my jangled nerves. I could not remember the last time I felt safe. Years spent running from place to place, from the overwhelming sensations I felt burdened with, running from myself. "May I ask what it was you did back there, when you placed your hands on that man's temples?"

August regarded me with a look of surprise. "You do not know?"

"No, I do not."

"I was clearing his mind, Jezebel." He leaned towards me, and for the first time, I noticed how blue his eyes were. They were a startling brightness against the dark interior, contrasting the deep ebony of his hair. "Would you care to go someplace where we are able to speak at length?"

I nodded. "Yes, I would like that very much."

Sliding open the window, August spoke to the driver in fluent French. The carriage picked up speed as the horses sprung to a trot, leaving behind the city streets. We glided across a bridge and into the lush undergrowth of the forest, bumping along a rutted, dirt road. Coming to a sudden stop in a clearing, August motioned for the driver to stay, as he helped me down from the carriage. My feet touched the ground and my pulse quickened for a moment as his fingers lightly grazed my wrist.

"Come with me."

I obeyed his soft-spoken command as his hand took mine, leading me down a shadowed path. Branches brushed past me in the dark as the sound of running water filtered in among the gentle hush of winter's icy breath that whispered through the trees. I could make out a clearing where a building nestled against a grove of aspen, strands of ivy trailing along the bricks. Beside it flowed a stream which snaked its way around the structure and fell with a delicate trickle into a deep pond below.

"What is this place?" I asked him as we stood together in the darkness.

"It is an old abbey I purchased years ago. I come here when I need the quiet."

He motioned for me to follow him, retrieving a key from his pocket, and working it into a lock on the faded wooden door. I turned to him in the doorway, seeking out his face among the shadows.

"August, there's so much I need to know about who I am."

He nodded as the door swung open to reveal a modest sitting room. "I know, Jezebel, and I will teach you."

CHAPTER THREE

The evening spread around us as we sat in the abbey talking. August's presence was a bright light, illuminating the darkness within me. I had been unable to grasp fully the depth of my loneliness until now. I spoke of my childhood and the years spent in a church orphanage. The alarming shifts that had begun to take place when I had turned fifteen and entered my time of change. With no one to guide me, I had been incapable of comprehending the meaning of what was happening, suddenly thrust into a world foreign and undefined.

"So, how old were you when you lost your family?" August sat across from me, the flickering firelight dancing against his face. He reminded me of a wild panther; beautiful, languid, and full of power.

"How did you know I lost my family?" I asked him.

He leaned forward, resting his arms on his knees, and clasping his hands together. "I'm a Seer, Jezebel. I possess the ability to look into the past and see into the future. I do apologize for prying, though. I do not usually explore the depths of another, unless asked."

I sighed, staring into the amber light of the fire. "I was eight. They were accused of being heretics and both burned at the stake."

August watched me, his face growing dark. "This is an unfortunate and tragic demise many of our kind experience. I am deeply sorry you lost your parents in such a way."

I gazed into the depths of the flames as a silence settled over us for a moment.

"When was your first Embrace, Jezebel?" August's voice broke the soft stillness between us.

I took a deep breath, gathering my thoughts. "It was my friend, Natacha. We had become very close over the years as we grew up together in the orphanage." The memories stirred themselves up like a heavy substance simmering inside of me. "We were out in the garden one day, giggling about something, when she kissed me. I kissed her back, and it was then that I felt my first stirring."

I recalled that day in vivid detail. The rich colors and sensations imprinted upon my memory like the thick stain of oil paint. She had leaned over me in the warm sunlight of a summer's afternoon, her golden hair sparkling with the fragments of the sun's rays as she pressed her mouth softly to mine. What overcame me was an irresistible thirst, an itch I longed to scratch. As our kiss grew deeper, I had found my lips at her neck, my teeth growing sharp against her flesh. I had expected an immediate struggle. A cry of pain perhaps, but she had remained complacent to the strange act of intimacy between us as the most profound sensation of life rushed through my body. Her energy pulsed like a beautiful flame as she moaned loudly against me in pleasure. When I released her, I reached out with my hand to inspect the damage; only to find it slowly vanishing from my touch.

"That was the day I learned that not only could I bring great pleasure, but I could heal as well."

He nodded as he rose from his chair, moving to address the embers of the fire next to me. The closeness of his body suddenly beside mine was strangely stimulating as his shirt brushed up against my bare arms. I found myself reaching out to touch the lapels of his jacket while I continued to speak.

"She was never frightened of who I was, and we were furtive lovers for many years, until she grew ill...." I trailed off, not wanting to relive the painful memories of her illness; the paleness of her skin and the light in her eyes that began to dwindle. I had been but a child in the knowledge of who I was, not knowing at the time that I was slowly depleting her. The relentless guilt of this never released its grip on me. I sucked in a deep breath, fighting back the tears that threatened to spill over. "I have not shared intimacy like that since Natacha."

August's eyes grew soft, and he moved to rest his hand over mine, gently circling over my skin with his thumb. "I am sorry you lost her, Jezebel."

I nodded, staring out into the flames until the silky murmur of his voice pulled me back to him.

"And I am sorry you have not experienced a connection like that since, for an Embrace is most potent when shared by a consensual desire for one another."

"What do you mean?" I asked.

"In order for you to receive the full benefits of an Embrace, you must give in to your own pleasure as well. Let me guess," August said. "You just pick someone off the street at random and hypnotize them with your gaze?"

I shrugged with discomfort, suddenly feeling exposed. "Yes. What other options do I have?"

He sighed deeply. "Oh, Jezebel. There is a limitless depth of power held within an Embrace, but only if you forge a connection with someone."

"And how am I to do that?"

August moved closer and trailed his fingers deliberately down my back. His magnetic touch elicited a strong rush of desire that gave me goosebumps, inviting the spark of my buried longing to slip out of its locked chest for a moment and hesitantly linger above me.

"Do you feel that?"

"Yes," I whispered.

"That exists within us for a reason. It is the thread that connects you to the life force. Do not try to suppress it, for it will only weaken you."

August's heavy gaze fell on me. His eyes were like fire, emitting sparks that could warm or consume. I felt as if he were challenging me, daring me to lose myself.

"I have never Embraced a woman that I have not desired on some level," August said. "Each person holds a unique essence within them, it is a sacred gift they are giving us. To honor that, you must surrender to your own vulnerabilities, for the very act of surrendering is what allows the door of transcendence to open."

The wisdom in his words stilled the noise in my mind, allowing the gentle breath of possibilities to filter through me.

"And have you ever lain with a woman that you have Embraced?"

"No," he replied, his tone suddenly firm.

"And why is that?"

"Jezebel, there is an infinite well of intimacy that can be shared without sexual intercourse."

"Yes," I agreed, "but why won't you?"

"It is too risky. If I were to enter a woman that I have Embraced, I would be sharing hundreds of years of my energy with her. I have yet to meet a Giver who I desire to share that with, nor one who I feel would be strong enough to handle it."

"A Giver?" I asked.

"Yes. Givers are those that are open to an Embrace."

I stared into the fire and watched the flames leap and tumble into each other as the weight of my isolation hovered around me. August's presence evoked a yearning, and I knew he was right. I had devoured so much of myself by stifling my own desires.

"I have never known anyone else like me," I spoke, breaking the silence between us. "I came across a fortuneteller in Rome last year. She had met you, and she told me that I must find you, that it was my destiny. I have been looking for you ever since."

August took my hands in his, his look full of such tenderness, it stirred something deep within me. "I believe it was not only your destiny, Jezebel, but mine as well. You possess an incredible reserve of inner strength. The fact that you have gone this far without our knowledge passed down to you, that you have not burned yourself out with your own flame, speaks volumes about your power. I would be honored to be your teacher."

I smiled at him as relief and elation flowed through me. I found myself reaching out to touch his face in in a gesture of gratitude, gently brushing my fingers down the length of his cheek. "Thank you, August."

His eyes flickered with a faint trace of desire before he stood, releasing himself from my touch. "Tonight was your first lesson."

"How so?" I asked.

He shot me a long, quiet look. "Patience. You are too hasty, and you do not allow the space for others to have an open mind. People hold a deeper depth of understanding than you may believe."

My heart quickened in sorrow and affection, as I recalled my brief but powerful relationship with Natacha.

"You must form a mutual connection with the Giver. You will find the effects of an Embrace last much longer and are more profound."

"So, I am not to use hypnosis?" I asked.

"Hypnosis should only be used under certain situations. You must never abuse this power. To force your will over someone else is lazy, and you are not honoring their essence."

My cheeks grew warm as a familiar rush of shame overcame me once more. When I had discovered my ability to gently manipulate the minds of others, I had assumed it was the only strategy for my survival.

"And how do you propose I do that?" I asked.

He stood and strolled across the room to retrieve something from within a large leather-bound book that lay tucked upon a shelf. He pressed a folded piece of paper into my hand.

"There are people who know about us, and there is a place where you can meet them. They provide a discreet service. You must respect that and give adequate payment in return." His eyes flashed in the dwindling light of the fire. "Do you understand?"

I nodded tentatively, glancing down at the ink of the flowing cursive script peeking through the paper.

"Good," he said as he went to gather up my cloak and hat. With his hand placed lightly upon the small of my back, he ushered me out the door and down the path into the faded light of the early morning. "My carriage will return you to your place in the city. We will meet here again next week; I will be waiting for you."

"Thank you for your wise counsel." I was filled with a sense of renewal that left me buoyant as the orange glow of dawn crested over the trees and fell upon us, bathing his features in delicate color.

"It has been my pleasure." His smile on me was like the sun, warming the shadowed places inside.

"And Jezebel, let go of your need for self-preservation. Like a shield, it protects you, but it also becomes too heavy a weight to carry forever."

I nodded as I turned to step into the waiting carriage. My head swam with the rich sweetness of the night's exchange. In my hand, I held the piece of paper August had given me. A piece of paper that would lead me into a world I could only begin to conceptualize. The jolt and creak of the wheels moved beneath me as I was carried back into the yawning repose of a city just beginning to awaken.

CHAPTER FOUR

My hand hovered over the blood-red grain of the wood before I knocked four times, as was instructed on the paper August had given me. The door inched open to reveal an older man, his thick mustache curled up into a high arc that skimmed over his cheekbones.

"Greetings, Jezebel."

"How is it that you know my name?" I tentatively asked.

He winked at me, the corners of his eyes wrinkling into a playful smile. "August told me I was to be expecting a scarlet-haired beauty." He motioned for me to step inside. "Please, come this way."

I allowed him to guide me down a dark hallway, through a maze of corridors, our footsteps resounding softly together.

"My name is William. I am the one who oversees the Voluptatem Lacum." He stopped and stood in front of a door, opening it with a flourish. "Welcome."

The space was opulent and warm, velvet drapes the color of deep burgundy lined the walls, accentuated by couches and pillows of a lush design. The lighting was muted as candles burned low in the corners, casting shadows which flickered throughout the room. On a table beside the door was a bowl of room keys and red-colored ribbons.

William gestured toward the table. "The Givers wear the ribbons, so they may be able to decipher who is who within the gathering room."

I scanned the space around me. Various men and women were clustered in small groups, speaking in hushed, intimate tones. A splattering of red ribbons could be seen throughout, while others wore none, indicating that some here were among my kind. A heavy sensuality flickered like electricity, permeating the room, and my pulse quickened in anticipation.

"The room keys," William explained, "are for privacy, of course.

Do enjoy yourself, Jezebel." He bowed to me formally as he retreated, disappearing down the long corridor.

I took in the bevy of possibilities which lay before me, watching as a tall bearded man with a ribbon approached me. "I could not help but notice that you are new to our gathering room."

"Is it that obvious?"

The deep auburn of his eyes twinkled warmly in the dimly lit space. "Well, you are quite striking. I must admit that I find myself very drawn to you."

I admired his boldness as a warm flush crept through me. "I am Jezebel."

He took my hand in his. They were cool and soft, like the hands of an artist. "John," he replied, bringing his lips to my skin. "It is a pleasure to meet you, Jezebel. Come with me, I will introduce you to the other Givers." With a smile, he leaned in close, his breath against my ear. "But first you must promise me a moment of your time tonight."

"Of course." I looked up at him as his hand found the small of my back and led me into the center of the room.

* * *

Time seemed to move slowly around the evening, as if suspended underwater. I took in this new world I had been invited into, drawn to the faces of my kind; women and men elegantly composed, who regarded me with friendly nods of acknowledgment. No longer did I feel so adrift. The isolated life I had built began to stretch and crack like skin that had grown too tight.

I scanned the room for the handsome man who had spoken to me when I first arrived. When a voice from behind caused me to turn around. "May I be so presumptuous, Mademoiselle?" John asked, winking at me as he dangled a key in his hand.

"You may, Monsieur." I smiled seductively, enjoying the flirtatious atmosphere between us.

He took my arm and led me to one of the many doors that lined the walls. I was not used to being chosen. The feeling left me with a slow burn that crept upwards from my center.

The room we entered was small and sparsely furnished. A bed lay in one corner, and next to it sat a table with a pitcher of water.

John turned toward me as he shut the door behind us. His body hovered close as his eyes met mine, his breath warm against my skin. "May I kiss you, Jezebel?"

I nodded as his mouth took charge, his hands slipping into my hair. His kiss was deep, and I found myself wanting to push him away for a moment, to regain some sort of control, but remembering August's words, I willed my instincts to relax.

He stirred against me. It was the arousal of a man desiring a woman of his own volition. Not the pliable mold of someone under my inky spell. This excited me, and my hands slipped underneath his shirt. The pulse of delicious energy which coursed through his veins injected a wild carnality within me.

John let out a long, rich moan against my ear. "I am ready for you."

I gently drew him over to the bed and helped him remove his clothes. I lifted my lips to taste the salt of his skin. My caress upon his body caused a tremble to pass through him as his pleasure became my own. Delicately, I brushed my mouth over his neck, and he arched back, offering himself up to me like a surrender.

John shuddered beneath me, groaning deeply as I drew from him. His labored breath fell against my ear as he grew lost in the ecstatic high of my Embrace. What I pulled from him was an energy I had not felt since Natacha. His essence was warm, rich and vibrant, and it filled me with exhilaration.

"Such heavenly creatures you are." John ran his hand lazily through my hair as I lay beside him on the sheets. His eyelids grew heavy as he gazed at me in a state of rapture, his body slowly beginning to sink into the weight of sleep. "I do hope to see you again, Jezebel," he whispered.

I rose from the bed and placed an envelope upon the nightstand, glancing over at the peaceful repose of John before quietly slipping myself out the door.

August's carriage arrived outside my hotel, just as he had promised. The driver soundlessly tipped his hat in greeting to me as I climbed in. As we drifted through the dark city streets toward August's abbey, I was filled with a childlike eagerness to see him again. I desperately longed to thank him for opening up a whole new world to me. The night at the Voluptatem Lacum had been intoxicating. The potent effects of the Embrace still lingered within me. I could not recall the last time I had felt so alive, so full of a power that was ancient and profound.

August stood outside of the abbey, waiting for me. He gently clasped his hand in mine as he led me down from the carriage. A small shiver ran through my core as our hands touched, his smile lighting up the depths within the dark.

"Good evening, Jezebel. You are looking positively radiant tonight." There was a twinkle in his eye as he spoke. "I take it your little foray into the Voluptatem Lacum was a success?"

"Yes. It was quite... illuminating. I had no idea eager participants existed."

"Oh, yes," he replied as he turned to lead me down the path. A cold mist had crept through the trees, shrouding his figure in grey. "The Givers are very special to us. They go through a highly intensive consultation process. That way we are able to ensure they are of sound mind and can be trusted."

As we arrived inside, August silently reached out to pull my cloak away from my body. It was a slow unveiling that felt intensely intimate. The depths of his eyes drew me in, his face was so close; I could smell the forest on him.

"Make yourself comfortable. I will be right back."

He disappeared into another room, leaving me to gather myself on the couch. The fire crackled beside me, its warmth removing the remnants of the chilly night air from my skin. Returning with a bottle and two glasses in his hand, August seated himself in a chair across from where I sat, leveling me with a serious gaze.

"I could spend many evenings with you, explaining the rich complexities of our power and what it means to be a Truth Holder, but I feel it would be better to show you instead." He gestured to the bottle, which sat on the table between us. "This is an ancient elixir. Its properties dispel the veil of the world around us, helping to see the deeper truth. If you are up to it, I can take you on this journey."

I stared at the bottle, its cork holding silent secrets inside, and a hesitancy flared within me, the vast possibilities of the unknown looming over me like a hungry apparition.

August reached over and touched my hand. "Do not be afraid, Jezebel. We must never fear the depths, for that is where we come from."

Pouring the thick amber liquid into the glasses, he handed one to me. "Here's to the journey back home," he said as he raised his glass and drank the contents down. He calmly set the empty glass upon the table, waiting for me to join him.

I tipped the elixir into my mouth. It was bittersweet against my tongue as it snaked its way through my veins. An odd surge coursed through me, then everything blurred and faded to black.

CHAPTER FIVE

I stood on the precipice of a heavy silence. Darkness swirled around me like a viscous liquid I could feel against my skin.

"August!" A flash of panic rose in my chest as my words spilled out into the abyss.

"I am here, Jezebel." I could not see him, but his voice was a soothing whisper close to me as his hand rested on my shoulder.

"Where are we?" Before he could answer, a blinding flare of light engulfed my vision. It looked like fire, and it beckoned me with a persuasive force as an overwhelming sensation of ecstasy consumed my body. I succumbed to the swirling flames, a fire that did not burn but enfolded me. As quickly as it had come, it vanished, and I was surrounded in a sea of stars; floating weightless, warm, and comforted, like a child in the womb.

"This is where all existence begins, Jezebel." August's voice spoke from inside my head, reaching in and exchanging my thoughts with his own rich words. *"We are the Truth Holders. The ones chosen to carry these memories of Creation within us. To reconnect the threads that were separated at birth, and the ones that have severed humanity so long ago. We have access to the very spark of energy that ignites the flame of life, which in turn enables us to heal others from their own disconnect and fear; bringing them back to remembrance, and to the inherent power that lies inside us all."*

Against the darkness, I hovered like a tiny vessel, buoyed by the sea of an infinite universe before me. The vastness of the stars swirled in colors that danced in the distance, moving closer until they brushed against my skin, shimmering pinpricks of light that pulled at me.

"You have a unique gift to give to the world, Jezebel. You must uncover it."

My feet touched solid ground, and all at once I found myself standing upon a snow-covered mountain. Wind whipped my hair against my face, but the cold did not touch me. Beneath me lay a wide valley. Its familiar beauty washed over me as light illuminated the rich colors below; the blues and greens of an infinite hue which stretched out before my eyes like a quilt.

I turned to August in awe. "This was the place I was born. How did you know to bring me here?"

He smiled, gazing out into the endless expanse of the Wicklow mountains while memories of my childhood flooded me with images that danced across my mind. My small hand clasped within the warmth of my father's, my mother's laughter like sunlight.

"I did not bring you here, Jezebel. You did. This is *your* journey, after all."

A pulsating ripple of energy built up from the ground beneath my feet, imbuing everything around me with a vibrant shimmer.

"That energy you see, you have access to. You just have to tap into it." August moved to stand beside me, his eyes calm and smiling. "Do you know what your gift is yet?"

I nodded, feeling the elusive tug of it like wings sprouting.

"Yes." I spoke with a voice I did not recognize, infused with a knowledge I had yet to understand. "I am a Traveler."

* * *

The room spun around me. The cool wood of the floor anchored my body as August's form slowly came into focus. He knelt beside me and placed his warm hand on my forehead, his touch instantly stilling the light-headedness within me.

"Welcome back, Jezebel."

I blinked, trying to dispel the heaviness of the tonic from my mind, but it was strong, affixing my limbs to the floor.

Running his fingers softly through my hair, he gently tucked a strand behind my ear, his voice soft as he spoke. "It will take a while for the potency of the elixir to clear from your system. Let me help you into the bedroom so that you may get some rest."

August lifted me up, his arms encircling my waist as he carried me to the bedroom. I tried to speak, but my mouth would not move. He gently placed me upon the bed. Velvet covers enclosed me like a lullaby of sensation as I drifted off into a thick dreamless sleep.

* * *

When I opened my eyes again, soft light spilled through the window. Its delicate rays shot glimmering fragments across the room. August sat in a chair next to the bed, quietly watching me.

"How long have I been asleep?"

"A few hours." He leaned forward and rested his hand against mine. "How do you feel?"

I shook my head as I attempted to sort out the past evening's events. "I'm not quite sure, honestly."

He nodded. "The experience of the elixir can be profound. It may take some time to process what you were shown."

"Where exactly did I go?"

He leaned forward in his chair, clasping his hands together. "In a sense, you went back to conception, Jezebel. The moment your spark of life began. In doing this you are able to reconnect with the power that was granted to you at birth, and to harness the gift you have been given."

I moved to sit up when an unexpected arousal coursed through me. I gasped, clutching the sheets as I looked at August in confusion.

"Just one of the side effects," he said gently. "You have tapped into the divine climax, so to speak. What we all run around trying to grasp tiny pieces of." His eyes twinkled playfully at me. "You are still transmitting. It will soon pass."

I stretched my shaky limbs, a surge of energy flowing through them. August helped me from the bed, his hands sliding down the curve of my waist to adjust my rumpled skirts. I let him tend to me, enjoying the feel of his touch and suddenly wishing there was no clothing between us. I found myself longing to release my ties, to shrug off the heavy ribcage of my bodice. I wanted to feel his hands on my skin, his lips against the places hidden by fabric.

August's eyes fell on me like a searing challenge as his fingers rested briefly upon my waist. The intensity of him close to me was so visceral, I grew dizzy and turned away from his gripping gaze. I realized I was afraid of him, terrified of what he could unleash within me, for I had never truly been with a man before.

"Thank you." My voice trembled.

He nodded, releasing me and retreating down the hall. I stood there for a moment, willing my self-composure to return before following August into the living room.

"Jezebel, I will be leaving next week for the gathering of Truth Holders in Syria."

"Syria?"

"Yes," he said, as he moved to wrap my cloak around my shoulders. His gaze descended on me like a slow burn. "Would you like to come with me?"

My heart fluttered within my chest. His invitation was a seductive lure I could not resist. "Yes, I would very much love to accompany you, August."

"Good. The ship leaves at dawn in five days. There will be a carriage awaiting you. I will meet you at Le Havre on the docks."

That week, as I prepared for my journey across the ocean, I was filled with a sense of anticipation. The events of my evening with August had left me with a feeling of calm that filtered deep within my being. The culmination of knowledge he had shown me was slowly revealing itself day by day. And though the words from the elixir had spilled from my mouth, significant and awash with power, I had yet to understand what being a Traveler meant.

I stood among the dusty city streets of La Havre as my carriage faded from view. Picking up my bag, I made my way over to the docks, the shrieks of seagulls filling the morning air.

The sun was just beginning to rise behind me, bathing the watery horizon in a pale sliver of shimmering gold when a hand fell on my shoulder. I turned around to find August beside me, the rolling sea reflected in the deep blue of his eyes.

"Are you ready?" he asked. I nodded as he led me over to an impressive, Spanish-style looking ship anchored at the edge of port. Crafted from smooth polished oak, it gently bobbed among the lapping waters of the harbor. "Behold the Virgo Veritatis. Depending on the weather, our journey will take roughly two to three weeks."

I looked at him. Seeming to sense my concern, August smiled. "Do not worry, there will be Givers on my ship. They will let you know who they are."

"Your ship?"

He nodded silently, taking in the ship's bulk. "She has been with me for over two hundred years. Come, allow me to show you to your private cabin."

He gathered up my suitcase and gestured to a young boy who had been standing next to him.

"Pierre, please take this to Mademoiselle's quarters."

August placed his hand gently on my back as we followed the young boy up the plank and onto the swaying deck, traversing down a long narrow hallway to a set of rooms. Pierre opened the first door and set my belongings down, bowing to me with a flourish. He looked to be no more than thirteen years of age. Rusty blond hair peeked out from his oversized sailor's cap. I nodded and smiled at him before he scurried down the hallway and out of sight.

I glanced around the cabin. Two large windows overlooked the water, while a canopy bed sat in the corner. Beside it was a sitting area with a writing table and a small stove. "Is this all for me?"

"Yes, I am staying in the room next to you." August gestured out into the hall. "Make yourself comfortable, Jezebel. I have some business to attend to. I will find you later this evening." With a nod of his head, he slipped out the door, his coattails gently swishing behind him, leaving me to my thoughts.

I walked out onto the deck, the briny scent of the sea engulfing my senses. The sunshine was a bright glare upon the grain of the wood railings. I took in the activity buzzing around me; the clanging of bells signaling departure, shipments being stacked hastily below, and the ebb and flow of bodies as they slid past me. The captain called out, and a sudden lurch shook the floorboards, creaking beneath my feet as the ship began to ease herself forward, pushing against the water; to begin her undulating journey to the sunbaked sands of Syria.

CHAPTER SIX

August found me in my cabin that evening. His presence was like a faint stirring within me before I heard his soft rap upon the door.

"How are you settling in?" He stood in the doorway; hair untied and falling to his shoulders in tousled waves that I had a sudden longing to run my fingers through.

"Very well," I said. "These are the nicest accommodations I have ever enjoyed on a ship." I recalled my last few voyages by sea, hunkered among the cramped dark quarters of steerage, the stench of sweat and sickness around me. "I feel like a queen."

August moved closer, bridging the space between us as his hand tenderly brushed against my cheek. "I want to thank you for accompanying me on this journey. It means so much to me that you are here."

A flash of desire rippled through me as his hands trailed into my hair. The sudden silence that washed over us was palpable with an unspoken, heavy sentiment. The only sound was the creaking of the ship beneath our feet as it gently swayed against the water. My body grew hot as I lost myself in his gaze. My longing was so acute, it sucked the air out of me. I stepped back from him, breaking the spell between us, and willing my breath to return to me.

"Jezebel." His voice came out in a whisper. "What is it about your own desire that frightens you so?"

I shook my head as the words caught in my throat, dry and brittle. "I do not know."

He extended his arm to me. "Come, let us take a walk."

My limbs felt warm and thick like syrup, my body humming as I slid my arm through his.

Walking along the deck, the chill of the wind whipped against my hair and cooled the flush upon my skin. Moonlight coiled its way through the water as it sparkled and danced upon the surface. Except for the gentle murmur of the watchmen on deck, the ship had grown quiet as the hushed lull of sleep fell among the cabins.

"August." I had stopped to lean against the bow, watching the sea lap softly against the edges of the ship. "That night, when I took the elixir, I had said I was a Traveler. What do you suppose that means?"

"Well, it is hard to say. Sometimes, our gifts can be elusive and take a certain amount of discovery to understand them, only showing themselves to you when you are ready. Others are more clear."

"Like yours?" I asked.

He nodded, joining me where I stood up against the bow, his body deliciously close to mine; his woodsy scent entangled around me. "Yes. I give the gift of sight to others, but you..." He studied me for a moment in silence. "You are a beautiful enigma, Jezebel. I believe there may be a power within you not yet discovered."

* * *

We passed the night talking. Stories of our past filtered out like ghosts as the moon made its slow dance across the sky.

"Tell me. Why have you spent so much of your time running from place to place?" August was gazing out at the water. "What is it that you fear will happen if you stand still?"

I took a deep breath as emotions that his presence alone seemed to pull out collided against the fragile spaces within my mind. "I suppose I am afraid that my loneliness will consume me."

He turned to me, a shadow against the blackened sky. "Loneliness is only an illusion, born from the idea that we are incomplete." He placed his hand upon my arm, squeezing it lightly. "There is an infinite reserve of serenity that lies within you. A power that longs to awaken itself."

"You have never been lonely, August?"

"I am deeply familiar with the feeling of loneliness. It was my constant companion as a child."

"How so?" I drew closer to him, his radiating warmth like a soothing blanket.

"When you are young, you believe that your parents hold all the keys to who you are. You spend your youth looking up at them, trying to find the reflection of yourself in their eyes. My parents had their eyes closed, therefore I had to find my own reflection."

There was a trace of sorrow in his words that I wanted to sift my fingers through, to feel the visceral depth of who August was. A man of power and knowledge, but also a man of tribulation.

"Don't you see? Loss can wear many masks, but the purpose of it remains the same. It is here to become a catalyst for something much greater to come into our lives."

I looked at him, my brow furrowing in thought as I recalled the beggars among the streets of Europe, their eyes full of destitution. "But not everyone is given the gift of betterment, you know."

August nodded. "That is true. But life provides endless opportunities for growth, though you must long to reach for it. It is a choice like any other."

The wind picked up, whipping at my clothes while I gripped the railing of the ship. August's hand reached up to cup my cheek, turning my face to his. The look he gave me was one full of a reverence that startled me. "Do you know how incredibly beautiful you are?"

My breath contracted, and the floor seemed to shift beneath me as his fingers stroked my cheek. "Do not run from the vastness of your own potential."

* * *

As the faint glow of morning brushed the horizon, August walked me back to my cabin. Standing in the doorway, he drew my hand up for a kiss, his lips soft and delicate against my skin, causing a gentle flutter within me. "Goodnight, Jezebel." The tantalizing whisper of his voice hovered over me before he slipped away and retreated to his room.

I paced my cabin, hoping to quell the deep ache inside that consumed me. The evening's rich conversation wrapped itself around me, while August's question from earlier still held itself suspended in my mind. *Why was I so afraid of my own desire?* Why did I resist this yearning that pulled me to him? I undressed and lay upon the bed, but I was restless and could not sleep; the beating of my heart like the wings of a caged bird, longing to escape.

Days passed and the air around us grew warm as we drew closer to the equator and the glassy blue waters of the Mediterranean Sea.

"So, you never really told me what this mysterious gathering is all about, August. Is it meant to be a secret?"

We were down below in the mess hall together, my hands deep in bread dough. The kitchen was filled with the rich aroma of stew, which slowly simmered on the large cast-iron stove beside us. I was helping him prepare dinner for the men onboard that night. August seemed to prefer to work alongside the paid crew. Every day I would either find him up on deck, helping with the adjustment of the riggings and the navigational charts, or down below in the bowels of the kitchen. He said good food helped the morale of sailors at sea.

"Not so much a secret," he said. "But more of a sacred congregation. Every fifty years or so, we gather to make new connections and reestablish old ones."

He turned to me and brushed back the loose strands of hair that clung to my face from the humidity of the kitchen. "I do believe you will enjoy yourself." August said with a smile as he reached over to take the dough from my hands, gently placing it into a pan and setting it aside to rise. "You need to find your power, and the Gathering can provide a deep connection for that."

"My power?" I picked up a cloth to wipe my hands of the remaining dough. "Isn't that what *you* are helping me to find?"

He shook his head. "No. I cannot help you with that. You have to find that on your own."

I sighed. "What do you think I have been trying to do?"

August looked at me seriously as a heavy sorrow flashed through his eyes. "You have been hiding, Jezebel. Somebody took your power from you long ago. It is time to take it back."

His words hit me like a sharp blow as a faded and stifled memory rushed to the surface demanding air. Thirteen years old. A marketplace. A man. A dark alleyway. A woman hurrying by, averting her eyes to my cries. Pain and disgrace that burned my flesh like hot oil.

"How did you know?" My question came out breathless as images which had been shrouded for so long suddenly uncovered themselves.

August pulled me from the kitchen and into the dim stairway. The voices from the mess hall grew muffled as we stood together in the enclosed space. "You forget that I am a seer?" His breath fell against my skin like a warm caress, blanketing my nerves. "What happened to you as a child brings me such sorrow." His eyes danced with fervency as he spoke. "No one should ever steal another's power from them. To me, it is the ultimate sin. But underneath all your trauma lies an endless well of strength, and you must reclaim it."

My voice trembled as the words fell from my mouth. "And how am I to do that?"

August's gaze grew tender and soft, enveloping me in his knowledge that had become my anchor. "There is a reason our Embrace brings such ecstasy. It is the thread that connects us to one another, it is also the thread that enables us to heal. There is a tremendous power that lies within your own pleasure. Once you reclaim that power, you will then be able to truly repair your wounds."

His words drew forth a rush of boldness. "What if I want you to help me with that?"

"Oh, Jezebel." August whispered as he leaned in and cupped my face tenderly, his thumb brushing against my lips. "I desire you very deeply." His touch sent tantalizing shivers through me, and my skin grew flushed as his fingers delicately traced along my jaw. "And how I long to explore the potency of what we could be together. But I feel that you are not ready for me quite yet."

My heart pounded in my chest, limbs growing weak. Men for me had always been but a vessel for an Embrace, until now, and my yearning for August was a feeling I did not know what to do with. I longed to reach for him, to feel his lips on mine, but my body would not move. August stepped away from me and retreated to the kitchen, leaving me alone, and reeling from his words.

* * *

The evening had folded around me as I sat in my cabin, my thoughts swirling like liquid when a sudden knock at the door startled me. I opened it to find a small plump woman standing there, blonde curls tied up into a messy bun.

"Good evening, mademoiselle. Master De Sanguine sent me. He wanted to know if you would like to have a bath drawn tonight?"

"Yes, I would love that," I said to her as she breezed in, her brisk energy filling the room.

I sat upon the bed and watched her scurry about the cabin with an efficient silence, bringing in pots of water to warm on the fire and pouring them into a metal basin. An aroma of English Rose and lavender wafted throughout the room.

When she had finished, she bowed to me. "Do enjoy, Mademoiselle." She shut the door quietly behind her, her quick footsteps retreating down the hall.

Shedding my clothes, I slipped into the warm gift of the water. Steam rose from my skin like strands of thin silk as I soaked in the heat, allowing it to penetrate deep into my muscles. August's declarations had stirred something within me, a tiny spark ignited. His voice swirled in my head. *You must heal yourself.*

I allowed my hands to slip to my thighs. Trailing upward, I found the soft bud hidden beneath the coarse coils of my hair. I had never touched myself before, never felt the pulse of my own climax; my desire locked up tight until now. Slowly, my fingers explored the folds of my sex, tender strokes that awakened my senses, soon growing quick and desperate as heat built up from within, demanding release.

I closed my eyes as I rocked myself in the buoyant water, my body rippling with an overwhelming pleasure that consumed me. Envisioning August's hands in place of my own, I gripped the edge of the basin and exploded against myself in a violent shuddering orgasm which spilled out of me like waves of brilliant light, causing me to cry out to the empty room.

CHAPTER SEVEN

The sun began her slow descent into the water as I stood on deck and took in the pink blush of the sky. The days since our conversation in the kitchen had altered me profoundly. My memory of the marketplace had been buried so deep until August had yanked it from my depths, unearthing the trauma I had carried around like a hushed, forgotten secret for so many years. This unveiling permitted the light to filter slowly through, illuminating the cracks and allowing me to peel the layers back, exposing the delicate but persistent bloom of healing.

"Beautiful, isn't it?" August's voice caressed me from behind, stirring me from my thoughts. I turned to him and saw the colors of the sunset reflected in his eyes.

"Yes." My answer was a sigh in the gathering dusk as August moved to stand beside me.

"The time between dreams." He looked out to the ocean as he spoke, the wind ruffling his hair. "The ones we chase and the ones we weave."

My hand reached for his, and he grasped me tightly in his warm grip. We stood there together, allowing a placid silence to settle over us as we watched the sun slowly slip beneath the waves. August's thumb began to gently stroke the inside of my palm, alighting my nerves with a sweet fire. I allowed this sensation to wash over me, no longer feeling the frantic need to stifle my longing, to shrink away from desire. This vibrant pulse of life stirred within me. The tangled thorns of my past, which had kept me inert and ensnared in my own fear, had begun to wither to a soft pulp that I found I was able to brush away with ease.

"We are five days from Syria." His words broke the stillness between us. "I have a villa on the outskirts of the city. We will stay there during the Gathering."

I nodded. Though I had grown accustomed to the bob and sway

of the ocean underneath my feet, I looked forward to touching solid ground once more.

August squeezed my hand tightly before releasing it. "I am in need of an Embrace tonight. Would you care to join me, Jezebel?"

His invitation brought a flush of heat to my cheeks, and my limbs grew languid. The thought of sharing intimacy with him was like a sensual quiver that curled around me. "Yes. I would love to."

I followed August down beneath the ship, past the mess hall and through a narrow passageway where he stopped in front of a closed door. His eyes fell on me with a sweltering intensity before he turned the handle, opening to a small room.

Inside sat a woman. Her long blonde hair tumbled down her shoulders and caught the light of the fire that burned in the stove beside her. She was flushed, and I could sense her excitement as she rose from the couch to greet us, her bright green eyes flickering over me as she spoke.

"You did not tell me how beautiful she is, August."

August turned to me, his eyes twinkling. "Marie, this is Jezebel."

Marie bowed deeply. "It is a pleasure to meet you, Jezebel."

I returned her greeting with a soft smile.

Marie moved toward me, reaching up to run a finger through my hair. "I have never seen hair this color before." Her gaze penetrated me as she spoke in a breathy tone. "Like a rich wine." Her finger trailed seductively down to my neck. "I want you first."

Marie began to unlace her bodice, her eyes never leaving mine as her dress fell at her feet, revealing skin the color of cream. Memories of Natacha flooded me, bittersweet and reverent, and I found myself reaching for her and drawing her tight against my chest. Slipping my mouth against hers, I tasted the smokey notes of whisky on her tongue. She moaned against me as my hands slid over the familiar softness and up to her breasts, her nipples firm between my fingers. It had been so long since I had experienced the potent essence of a woman, and her energy wrapped around me with the sweetness of honey.

The heat of August's gaze simmered on me as I guided Marie over to the couch, settling her down against the cushions. Her legs opened as I slowly ran my hand up her thigh. A mottled blush spread across her chest as I dipped my finger inside her, feeling the silken liquid of her desire upon my fingers.

"Oh, God," she whimpered as she trembled beneath my touch. "I am ready for you."

I rose up, my lips teasing the flesh of her neck as August spoke from behind me, his voice a tantalizing whisper in my ear.

"Do not take too much, Jezebel."

August's hands slowly slid down my waist, eliciting an erotic charge that cascaded through me as I sunk gently into Marie. Her cries muffled in my hair as she shuddered beneath me.

I released her with a gasp, my body pulsating with the sweetness of her essence as August bent down to place his lips softly upon the flesh of her breasts, his hands traveling up the length of her back. My own arousal built within me as I watched him pull her into his deep Embrace, her screams of pleasure reverberating throughout the room as she clung to him.

"You two are so beautiful." Marie giggled as if drunk. Her head lolled to the side as she watched me, her expression one of a satiated cat's. August gently placed her against the pillows and spread a blanket over her.

"Promise me you will come back soon." She twirled her fingers in his hair.

He whispered something in her ear, and she smiled, closing her eyes.

August shut the door quietly behind us. In the dim, flickering light of the hallway we stood there staring at each other, the heated silence between us laden with sexual tension like static electricity as August's eyes penetrated me like a slow burn.

Overcome with a desire I no longer wanted to contain, I pushed him against the door, gripping the lapels of his jacket in my hands and fell upon his mouth; hungry and frantic. A warm rush spread throughout my entire body as he returned my kiss with equal passion. He grabbed my waist, his urgency pressing hard against me as his lips moved down to my neck.

"*Oh God, Jezebel.*" His voice was a low growl against my skin. "I do not think I can be gentle with you right now." His eyes blazed with intensity as he clasped my arms and took a step back, breathing heavily.

"I do not want you to be." I reached out and pulled him close to me again. I didn't want gentle, I wanted him and all his fire to consume me.

My hands traveled down to his trousers, unbuttoning them in a frenzy where I found the thick heat of his pulse. My touch caused August to draw in a sharp hiss of breath as he spun me around, pinning me to the wall. He tore at the fabric of my dress, releasing my breasts as his mouth fell on them in a burst of heat that sent waves of pleasure rippling through me. I moaned, my fingers lost in his hair, desperately longing to feel more of him, to feel his desire deep inside me.

Tipping my head back, I gasped as his eager hands sifted through the layers of my petticoats and found my center, warm and wet.

"*Oh, deus meus.*" His words were silk and honey while his fingers traced slow, aching circles within me.

"*Please, August.*" I panted as I gripped his arms, my legs trembling and weak. "I need to feel you inside me."

His eyes flashing with lust, he released me with a deep groan. "Not here, Jezebel."

August nimbly adjusted our clothes and then took me by the hand, quickly leading me down the swaying hallway. I stumbled, my head swimming while he grasped me around the waist, steadying my body and guiding me up the stairs toward our quarters.

As we rounded the corner, the same plump woman who had drawn me a bath the other night came bustling toward us. "Good Evening, Monsieur." She stopped to address August with a curtsy. "Are you retiring to your quarters early? Shall I light the lamps for you?"

"No need, Claudia. Thank you."

Her eyes trailed to me with a look of prying amusement as she took in the disheveled appearance of my dress. She nodded silently before slipping past us and continuing her steady march down the hall.

August led me into his room. A pale sliver of moon shone through the porthole, bathing the dark interiors of the cabin with a faint indigo light. I could faintly make out the outline of his face as he softly closed the door behind him, enclosing us within the delicate hush of darkness.

CHAPTER EIGHT

All I could see was August's silhouette within the shadows of the room as he stepped closer to me. The space between us pulsing with a concentrated energy. The sound of our labored breath mingled together as he unlaced the ties of my corset with quick fingers, allowing my dress to slip slowly down, the fabric rustling as it fell to the floor.

"You are so beautiful." His words hovered against my neck as he pulled me tight against him. His hands on my skin were an arousing heat that set my whole body ablaze, and I slipped into the dizzying abyss of his touch. All that came out was a soft moan that filled his mouth as he drew me into the deep well of his appetite.

My hands shook as I ran them up his chest, feeling for the buttons on his shirt. Moving to assist me, he shed the fabric in one fluid motion while he unbuttoned the waistband of his trousers. His longing teased against my skin as we collided together in the darkness.

"Make love to me, August." My voice came out in a strangled gasp.

My body surged with desire as he suddenly grabbed my thighs and lifted me up into the strength of his arms. Backing me gently against the door, he slid himself inside me. I cried out as something bright and hot burst within. My legs wrapped around him tightly, fingers digging into his back, my nails raking across the length of his flesh as an overwhelming sensation of bliss spilled out from my center, obliterating my senses.

"Oh, *Jezebel*." His mouth was fiery and frantic against my skin as he held me up and began to move within, gripping my hips and plunging in slow and deep. Speaking my name as if he had claimed me for his own. The idea of being claimed by him brought me to such a high that I suddenly exploded, calling out to him in the dark.

He grew still for a moment as I shuddered against him, lost to this ecstasy he had awakened within. "*Do not stop.*" I moaned, "*Do not ever stop.*"

I was intoxicated by his breath on my skin, the feel of him which filled me so completely. Another wave of heat slammed into me as he began to move once more, deeper this time. His thrusts enfolded me in the most intense pleasure, cresting with such force that I writhed violently in his arms as he cried out; the beautiful rush of him spilling inside me as we both clung trembling against each other.

* * *

I lay upon the sheets and watched August as he breathed life into the embers of the fire, illuminating the room in an ochre glow which danced across his skin like liquid. My body had become a soft, supple animal, languid and humming with a rich elation. August crossed the room to join me on the bed, running his hand along the delicate curve of my waist.

"God, you are so exquisite." His voice was a husky whisper as he held me within the hunger of his gaze.

I sat up and pulled him to me, his muscles contracting as I slid my hand down his back and over to his thigh, my fingers tracing up the length of his desire which lay ready for me once more.

"I want to savor you this time, Jezebel." He knelt on the floor beside me and brought his mouth to my breasts, his breath enticing my skin as his lips swept a teasing trail down my stomach and to my inner thighs.

A bright spark ignited me as his tongue dipped into the hidden place within, drawing out my longing. I clutched his arms as a delicious surge of pleasure consumed me, and I arched my back, rocking desperately against him. "*More...I need more of you,*" I pleaded as my fingers reached up to tangle themselves in the strands of his hair. My insatiable hunger for him was like an aching thirst I had to quench.

"So impatient you are." August playfully growled against me, his lips stretching into a sensual smile as he moved above me, gripping my hands, and gently pinning me to the bed.

With a groan, he slipped himself inside me, diving so deep and slow that my eyes rolled back in abandonment as I lost myself in the powerful current between us.

"Jezebel." August's voice was a warm caress from far away, pulling me back to him. *"Look at me."*

His gaze was like fire and it burned me with intensity as he plunged deeper, obliterating my senses, and breaking down whatever was left of my walls. Exposed and shaking, I burst apart beneath him as the visceral energy of his release flowed into me once more, colliding up against mine in a beautiful, breathless dance.

We became interwoven, the last few days slipping past us and merging with the lapping waves. My mind fell into a state of reverie as I eagerly awaited the blush of evening when August would come to me like a fever dream, all hands, mouth, and urgency. He was something I had never felt before. While my love affair with Natacha had been sweet and delicate, like ripe fruit, being with August was profound and extreme. I craved him constantly.

Moonlight bathed the cabin in silver shadows that fell upon our skin as we lay in bed together, the ship gently swaying beneath us. August rested his head on my chest, listening while I recounted my childhood with my parents before they were ripped from me. The bits and pieces of bittersweet memories which floated silently within a box I had kept locked until now. A summer's garden, my mother's fiery red hair glowing in the light, her hands streaked with wet earth. My own tiny hand cupping a seed. My father's smile, large and filled with life, laughter dancing in the depths of his brown eyes. Then the time of darkness, which rushed in with bared teeth. Accusations of heresy spreading like wildfire among the village.

I played with the thick coils of his hair that fell upon me as I unleashed my past, until all that was left was a soft pause which filled the space between us. "You have not spoken much of your family, August. What is their story?"

He sighed against me. "My family's legacy is not the happiest of stories either. What do you want to know?" He positioned himself on the bed so that he was looking at me.

"Well, I am sure it had to have been happier than mine," I replied.

He furrowed his brow, his eyes growing troubled. "Not all of us are good people. Misery is a veiled creature that comes in many forms."

"What do you mean?"

"My father, he was a weak man. He carried his anger around like a dagger and shield." August slowly ran his hand down my stomach, causing goosebumps to form along my skin. "And my mother, she hid from herself. There was no love within my family. I was born an only child, but I left when I was fourteen, right before I began to shift. It was my uncle who took me in and taught me all that I know."

As August spoke of his past, the pale light of the moon fell over his face, obscuring his eyes.

"Are they still alive, your family?"

"Honestly, I do not know. For I have not spoken to my family since I was a young man, and my uncle unfortunately passed away many years ago. Shipwrecked and lost at sea." His hand rose and rested against my cheek before absentmindedly trailing down to my neck and placing his fingers upon my steady pulse. "We may be immune to sickness and the quickening of time, but we are not immune to accidents."

The day we reached Syria; the sun was hot against our skin. A salty breeze teased us as we stood out on the deck and felt the ship drop anchor.

"Welcome to Damascus, the city of ancient truth." August's touch was firm on my back as he led me down the plank, eliciting a giddy rush as my unsteady feet stepped onto solid ground for the first time in weeks.

"This is the oldest city in the world, Jezebel." His voice was soft and full of reverence.

"It is beautiful." I squinted against the glare of the bright blue water which lapped lazily against the shore. Palm trees scattered the hot white sand and beyond me stood the ornate rounded domes and marbled columns of the city, laid out like an endless treasure among the desert.

August's villa was nestled in the outskirts of the city. We traveled slowly by camel across the sands, the undulating sway of the animal lulling me into a trance. The sun began its descent, casting long shadows against the rust colored, sunbaked hills that seemed to bend and ripple in the heat.

"We are here," August said, his voice cutting through the silence of the desert.

I gazed out into the expanse of a sprawling courtyard. In the center stood a large fountain. Clear water flowed from the top and trickled in a melodic cascade down the mosaic tiles and into a deep cerulean pool of blue. Trees and exotic flowers encompassed the space around us, enveloping my senses in the rich fragrance of hyacinth, cedar, and hibiscus.

"Welcome to my little desert Oasis," August winked at me as his hands slipped to my waist and helped me dismount from the camel.

A warm smile spilled across my face as I took in the lush surroundings, which beckoned me like a cool drink of water. "How enchanting."

I marveled at the ease of his lifestyle. While I had been living as a vagabond, bound to nothing, over two hundred years of merchant trade had served him well. August wore the life of a wealthy man with a humble poise that I found captivating.

The door suddenly opened to a flurry of activity which spilled out around the courtyard. The villa's caretakers enthusiastically greeted us with a flourish and carefully whisked our belongings off the camels and into the house.

August led me inside behind the procession and ushered me down a long hallway of carved stone. Our footsteps reverberated off the walls as cool air slipped around us in the dusky twilight. August's hand rested upon my back as he leaned in close to me.

"Let us get some rest; the Gathering is tomorrow."

Awakening my desire with nothing more than the silky whisper of his voice in my ear, he opened the door and quickly led me to a bed in which we fell into like thirsty travelers. So transfixed we had become with each other, that it wasn't until the faint light of morning crept across the walls, splashing us with its golden radiance, did we surrender ourselves to sleep.

The heat of the afternoon sun found my skin, coiling its warmth across the sheets. I turned to find the space next to me empty. Rising from the bed, I threw on a robe and wandered down the long hallway, the white marbled floor cold against my bare feet. I stepped out into the brightness of the courtyard, a humid breeze sweeping across my skin as I sat down upon the smooth tile of the fountain. Dipping my fingers into the cool spray of the water, I ran the droplets down my arms, awakening my senses.

From behind me, August pressed his lips against my neck. "You are awake."

I looked up as the shimmering azure of the sky bathed him in a halo, exposing the tenderness of his beauty, which made my heart swell with longing.

"Why did you not wake me sooner?"

He smiled, his eyes flashing as he sat beside me. "You looked far too exquisite laying there among the sheets to rouse." His fingers reached out to brush away a strand of my hair. "We are to leave for the Gathering in an hour."

* * *

When we arrived at the city of Damascus, the sun had sunk her sultry rays beneath the dunes, bathing the city in a warm pink blaze. As we traveled through the marketplace, I took in the rich fragrance of bergamot, cinnamon, and myrrh. The local merchants moved hastily around our camels, packing up their wares for the day; cotton and silks folded into woven baskets. The vibrant, jewel toned robes they wore rippled against them in the cooling breeze.

We descended a rocky slope to the edge of the city where a large domed temple ascended over us, flanked by guardians at either side of the entrance, their dark clothes billowing out around them, matching the dusk of the sky. We dismounted as they bowed low to us, addressing August in their throaty Arabic tongue.

"Masa' alkhayr, Hakim."

He nodded wordlessly to them and took my hand, walking through the substantial double doors, each adorned with intricate designs upon the ebony wood as we became enclosed in a dimly lit silence. The aroma of earth and stone permeated around me. It was the scent of time, and an ancient power that pulled at my core. August stopped at a red painted door and turned to me; his eyes met mine with a heavy, meaningful intensity.

"Are you ready, Jezebel?"

CHAPTER NINE

I nodded as August leaned down and planted a deep, lingering kiss upon my lips. "Go take a seat, I will find you later."

Opening the door to a large room filled with silent seated figures, he moved from my side and walked up the marbled isle, his footsteps echoing against the stone. Everyone began to move like rippling water and a reverberating tone rang out in greeting; hundreds of voices speaking as one.

As I drifted toward the back, I watched his presence take up the whole room, resembling some beautiful God-like creature. I knew he was powerful, but I had no idea he was praised like this. Kneeling upon the floor, I joined the others.

"Welcome to the Gathering of the Truth Holders," he began, his voice rich and commanding amongst the hushed crowd. "Today we gather as one family."

The gentle resonance of everyone's breath was like the lulling tide of the ocean. My eyes took in the motifs that were ornately carved into the walls and trailed their way up to the high-domed ceiling above me. The immense space made me feel minute and reverent.

"We are here to celebrate the intricate pattern of life, to pay homage to the connections that fulfill us, and to awaken a deeper connection within ourselves. The one that binds us all to each other."

I sat quietly listening to him speak, I had never seen this side of him before and it filled me with wonder. His words brushed across the room with a gentle, unpretentious authority, and my affection for him swelled. I felt so blessed to have found this man, to lay beside all his wisdom while he cried out for me in the profound richness of our mutual desire. My thoughts sent a hum of elation to course through me as his eyes sought out mine, locking on with an intensity that produced a rush of warmth throughout my body. He continued as if he were speaking directly to me.

"There is such magnificent beauty to be found within ourselves and others, within the thread that unites all existence. Let this gathering reflect your intention to honor this connection, to honor your own power and to hold in reverence the vastness of truth that life sustains for us." He motioned to the group, and they rose like a gentle wave. "Enjoy," he said, as a soft murmur filled the room.

Two doors at the far end of the great hall opened with a flourish, leading out to darkened passageways lined with candles. The press of bodies was comforting as I took in the crowd, buoyed by the radiant faces of *my* people, their energy hovering around me like a spark of fire.

Following the stream of movement into the hallway, I could hear the soft droning notes of a sitar in the distance. The smoky aroma of incense clung in the air, hints of sandalwood filling my senses as I came into an expansive atrium. Glass lined the walls and rounded ceiling, and I looked up to find the inky night of the sky sprinkled with stars.

"Are you enjoying yourself?"

August ran his hand along my back, eliciting a shiver upon my skin.

"Yes. I had no idea you were worshipped like that."

He chuckled. "No. It is not me that they worship, it is what I provide for them. My speech was just a formality, a ringing of the bell, so to speak. When I started this Gathering, we were all isolated, scattered across the world. Many of us lost like you were." He lifted my chin, tenderly grazing my cheek with his thumb. "I wanted to bring us all together, to help awaken and strengthen our individual power, and to provide a sense of home for us all." His eyes enveloped me as he took my hand in his. "Come, there are others I would like for you to meet." August led me over to a group standing behind us. "Jezebel, please meet some of my very close allies."

"Welcome, Jezebel." A tall woman reached out and clasped her hand in mine. "I'm Klyda." She had an elegant haunting beauty to her, long ebony black hair against pale skin. "And this is my friend Sasha, and Elias."

She motioned towards the two others, who regarded me with

warm, open smiles. August's hand fell to my waist, leaning in close. "Please excuse me for a moment," he spoke before disappearing into the crowd, leaving me standing there hesitant, and unsure of what to do, my solitude like a caged animal suddenly thrust into the wild.

"Is this your first gathering?" Elias addressed me first, his thick, dark beard accentuating the warmth of his brown eyes, the color of rich cocoa.

I nodded. "Yes, I had no idea all this existed for me until now."

"So, did you come here with August?" Sasha asked. Her coiled chestnut hair bounced against her face in ringlets as she regarded me with a look of indistinct provocation, her full lips pursed, gauging me.

"I did. I met him in Paris."

"Oh, how nice." Sasha gave me a faint smile, like a covetous cat.

Klyda chuckled next to me. "Oh, do not be jealous Sasha, it is so unattractive. You had your turn with him."

Ignoring the look Sasha shot her, Klyda leaned in close, the musky scent of her amber coiling around me as her black hair brushed softly against my cheek. "I take it you must be his newest lover?"

Her words unnerved me. While I knew August had many lovers, as he always stressed the importance of erotic energy, I was not prepared to meet one of them standing before me. I nodded tensely as I looked around the room, suddenly feeling exposed and a bit cheapened as a hesitant question washed over me. *Could August be off with someone right now? Have I only been his latest enjoyment, to be disposed of when something more intriguing comes along?* I realized we never had the discussion of exclusivity.

Klyda's hand fell on my arm as she smiled down at me warmly. "Relax, August is not like that."

"Like what?" I asked, trying to stifle my discomfort from the sudden knowledge that she had slipped into my thoughts.

"He never strays from the bond until that bond has run its course. You need not worry, Jezebel. He will remain faithful to your connection."

A sense of relief washed over me, and I shook my head. "Honestly, all of this has been a little overwhelming for me. I have been a drifter all my life. When August found me, I did not expect it to go any further than his teachings."

"Jezebel." Klyda pulled me into her gaze. The rich warmth of her amber eyes caused the rest of the room to fall away. "There is something very special about you, I cannot put my finger on it, but I can feel it. Like a magnetic field." She fluttered her hands around me, smiling with a silky softness. "It is no surprise August is drawn to you. The way he looks at you, well..." she trailed off, turning to Sasha. "Have you ever been looked at that way by him, Sasha?"

"No. I have not." Sasha remained stone faced, clearly not amused by Klyda's goading.

Klyda placed her warm hand on the small of my back. "Jezebel, welcome. We are deeply honored to have you join our fold."

* * *

Wandering through the halls, I tasted the lavish food and wine while various musicians played throughout the rooms, the deep melodious stringed resonance of the Oud enticing my senses.

I still had not found August as the night deepened and the energy of the Gathering slowly began to shift around me. Bodies pressed closer together, lips became entangled and a carnal hush filled the rooms. Everywhere I looked, candlelight danced upon bare skin as couples entwined against each other. I slipped past a pair in the throes of an orgasm, the woman's eyes locked onto mine, almost beckoning me to join her as she cried out in ecstasy. The visual thrill of this unrestrained lust aroused me, and I ached for August's touch as I searched for the tall, dark figure of him among the crowd.

"*A Desiderio Celebrationem.*" August's breath in my ear caused a sudden and delicious spark of pleasure to run through me. "The celebration of desire." I leaned my back against his chest as his hands slid down my body, awakening me. "I have been looking for you, Jezebel."

"And I, you." I sighed as the feel of him wrapped me in warmth.

"You move with such sensuality, it hypnotizes me." His lips languidly traced my collarbone, his words falling upon my skin like a sensual whisper.

"You hypnotize *me*, August." My breath came out in a shudder.

I closed my eyes. The chorus of soft moans surrounded me as I fell into the spell of the room, which was so erotically charged it crackled like an electrical current.

His hands found their way to the ties of my dress. With one hand, he slowly pulled the fabric down, and slipped his fingers into me with the other, tenderly drawing circles against my sex. Desire washed over me, my legs buckling beneath the weight of my eagerness.

August's breath was a hungry whisper on my skin as he walked me forward and pressed my body against a marble column. My hands grasped the smooth stone, cool against the heat of my skin. From behind I heard the rustle of his clothes as he shed them upon the floor, and teased me with his length, sliding himself slowly inside and then pulling out. I hungrily pushed myself against him as sharp, frantic moans escaped from my mouth, intermingling with the unrestrained cries around me.

As my pleasure mounted within, a sudden sensation of tiny needles ran across my limbs, prickling my skin. A shrill tone filled my ears, followed by an overwhelming rush of dizziness that cascaded through me, violently lifting me from my body as my vision grew fuzzy, then faded to a silent darkness.

* * *

I found myself standing in a vast open field. Grass tickled my bare feet and I ached in the places where August had been inside only moments before. But he was no longer with me. I was alone.

I waited for the fear and confusion to wash over me, but there was none. All I felt within was a calmness and a deep sense of understanding, for I knew what was happening. I had traveled. But to where, I did not know.

CHAPTER TEN

A warm, gentle breeze moved around me. My hands trailed down and caught loose fabric, touching the soft material draped over my body; it was almost translucent, and it shimmered against my fingers like the gossamer wings of a butterfly. I stood in a field, encircled by dense forest. The sky above me reminiscent of a dream, a rich purple the color of amethyst.

A flock of birds alighted from the trees, startling the stillness. My feet were soundless as I glided along the ground, almost as if I were floating. As I drew closer to the center of the field, I could make out a soft silhouette of a young woman sitting amongst the waving grass.

"Hello," I called out to her.

She turned around, her piercing amber eyes meeting mine. A heavy blanket of sadness swam within her depths.

"Where did you come from?" she asked, standing up. Dark curls cascaded down her back, her mouth pulled into a tight frown. She wore her clothing in an unusual style, like that of a man's, with coarse blue pants and a shirt of strange bright patterns.

"A place far from here." I smiled warmly at her. "I am sorry if I disturbed you."

She shook her head, staring up at the purple sky. "You didn't. I think I was waiting for someone."

I sat down upon the grass, motioning for her to join me. She looked to be no older than fifteen. The flush of youth bloomed radiantly upon her skin, but she carried the weight of life as if she were someone much older than her years.

"What is your name?" I asked.

"Sara." She slowly sat down beside me.

"It is a pleasure to meet you, Sara. My name is Jezebel."

I did not know why I was here, or who this girl was. But I was compelled to reach out to her, for her sorrow was palpable, and it hovered in the air between us. I placed my hand gently upon her knee.

"What is it that troubles you?"

Words tumbled from Sara's mouth like a river as she spoke to me of her pain and loneliness. The sudden loss of her family, and the thick scars that traversed her thighs like a road map. And I in turn revealed my own pain of childhood and the isolation that had followed me around like a hungry animal, clawing at my insides.

"It's so terrible at the foster center I'm at." Sara's fingers brushed across her thighs, silently tracing the trauma that lay hidden beneath. "The other day, some girls cornered me in the shower, calling me a freak, and saying that no one would ever want to touch me. And now apparently that's my new name in the center." Sara balled her hands into fists; her jaw tightly clenched as tears flowed down her cheeks. "I need to get out of that place."

"And you will," I said, gently placing my hand on hers, feeling her body relax against my touch. "You just have to remember that your circumstance is only temporary, and one day soon you will be given your wings, and you will fly."

Sara curled her knees tightly up against her chest, rocking slowly. "I just miss them so much."

"I know you do, and you always will. Not a day goes by that I do not think of my family. But in time, it will not hurt as much." I looked up at the sky and noticed the purple fading to a soft pink. "We each have a story, Sara. One that we carry within our own compartment of pain. But hidden beneath the sorrow lies such raw beauty. One day when you begin to unravel your own story, you will see this, and you will understand why these trials were handed to you."

Sara moved to wipe away her tears, looking into my eyes. "But I am so alone."

I took her hands in mine, feeling a connection that seemed to go far beyond our shared sorrow. A tethered chord pulled at me, and words spilled from my lips as if plucked from the depths of a knowledge undiscovered until now. "As long as you honor yourself, every broken part, and hold it with tenderness, you will never truly be alone. Remember that. For a heart that bleeds also has a profound ability to transform into something greater than you could ever imagine."

I wanted to help her, to give her something she could carry with her until the very end of her days, when I suddenly felt the tingle upon my skin, and somehow intrinsically knew that my moment with her was ending. "I believe that it is time for me to go, Sara."

"Please don't go," she pleaded, her eyes growing wide.

The ringing in my ears grew louder.

"I must." I stood up, a rush washing over my body. "Sara." I gripped her arms. "I want to give you something. Something that will provide you strength and a compass in life."

Like some divine tug guiding my words, my name spilled out of me. "My own mother blessed this name when she gave it to me, she had the power of intention. This name is very sacred, for it represents the ability to push past boundaries and live without fear. I now want to give this power to you. I want you to take my name."

"Jezebel?"

"Yes." My vision began to ripple and blur around me before I faded away from her completely and tumbled back into the darkness.

* * *

"Jezebel! Jezebel!"

I heard August's anxious voice in my ear. His hands stroking my hair. The feel of a cool, wet cloth against my forehead as my eyelids fluttered open. I was lying on a couch with a blanket wrapped around me. August's face came into focus, his eyes full of worry and something else I had never seen in him before. A faint trace of fear.

"What happened?" he asked me.

I tried to sit up, but my body betrayed me. My limbs lay weak and trembling. August gathered me into his arms, cradling me like a small child.

"You went someplace, didn't you, Jezebel?"

I could only nod. My tongue felt thick in my mouth.

August held me tight against his chest as he rushed me through the halls of the temple, past bodies consumed within the music of their erotic dance and out into the cool night air. Stars bathed us in a blue light as August helped me up onto one of the camels that stood harnessed and waiting for us. Hitching the other one to the saddle, he slid up behind me, enfolding his arms around my waist. With a click of his tongue, he guided the camels into a fast trot as we advanced across the desert.

* * *

When we arrived back at the Villa, my strength had returned, and I was able to walk again. I sat up on the bed in the wavering candlelight while August fussed around me, his eyes full of concern as he gently arranged me against the pillows. I was unaccustomed to seeing him in this state. He always had a fluid composure to him, but tonight he looked fragile.

"How do you feel?" he asked.

"Better." I smiled and reached out to pull him close to me, breathing in his familiar scent of earth and pine. His arms wrapped around me as my body habitually responded to the proximity of him.

"I'm sorry," I said as I drew lazy circles along his back. "We never got to finish what we started at the Gathering."

August pulled away from me, shaking his head as his fingers nervously slid through his hair.

Reaching out, I ran my hand across his brow. "I frightened you, didn't I?"

"Yes, Jezebel. You did." Apprehension pooled in his eyes. "You were gone. Your eyes were open, but nothing was there. It was as if the essence of you was no longer in your body. You went completely limp, with barely a beating heart." His voice shifted to a whisper. "*I thought I had lost you.* What happened?"

"I traveled somewhere. I am not entirely sure where, but it was as if I was in somebody else's dream. I was in a beautiful field surrounded by a forest, and there was a young girl in a meadow."

August sat upon the bed next to me. "And what was the sensation you had while traveling?"

"I was calm, and I felt very drawn to this girl, as if I were meant to be there, to help her somehow." I took a deep breath; my palms open upon my lap as if invisible offerings lay within them. "I wanted to give her a strength that would carry her forward in life. So, I gave her my name."

August nodded; his face filled with marvel. "This is fascinating, and completely new territory," he said as he got up from the bed and began to pace the room, energy radiating off him like electricity. "Though I suppose it is possible, I have never heard of one having the ability to travel through dimensions and into dreams before, until now." He stopped pacing and stared at me. "A Desiderio Celebrationem. It is a very powerful ceremony that takes place among the Gathering. It allows one to harness vast amounts of energy through erotic transference. I believe this erotic energy most likely was what triggered your travel."

"It could have been," I said, smiling up at him seductively. "You definitely bring it out of me."

August suddenly chuckled, a playful smile on his face. "You know, this could potentially put a hindrance on our love life."

I got up from the bed and pulled him close to me, trailing my fingers down his chest. "*Nothing* can put a hindrance on the way you make me feel, August."

His eyes fixed me with a look of reverence. "You must find a way to harness this power. I just wish I had more to offer you in terms of guidance."

My hands reached up to unbutton his shirt. "Well, I suppose this will be an unknown road we will travel together."

"I suppose it will be."

Pulling him down upon the bed, we shed our clothes, curling ourselves around each other. My experience at the Gathering had left me exhausted, and I drifted into a haze as August held me. The feel of his skin against mine, and the smooth rhythm of his heart pulsing in my ear, lulled me into a state of surrender. Enveloped within the safety of his arms, I sunk into dreams.

* * *

Early morning light gathered low in the sky as I awoke. August lay beside me sleeping, his hair fanned across the pillow, the shadows of dawn flickering against his bronzed skin. My fingers delicately traced the curve of his lips, awakening him.

"You are so beautiful," I breathed.

The deep burn of his gaze penetrated me as he pulled me into his arms. "Love is a mirror, *Jezebel*."

The word *love* had always been something intangible and hard for me to define until now. My heart swelled as I ran my hands through his hair, kissing the tender skin below his jawbone.

August let out a slow breath, gripping my back. "Oh, what you do to me," he murmured.

I rose and trailed my lips down his chest to where I found him, trembling and erect underneath the sheets. Longing to worship him with a reckless abandon, I took him deep into my mouth. He shuddered beneath me, a loud groan rushing out of him as my tongue danced against his desire.

August gripped my shoulders, pulling me up to meet his gaze, which was wild and full of heat. "*I need you.*"

"How bad do you need me?" I asked in a sultry whisper as I slid myself on top of him and teased the slickness of my sex against his length.

"So bad it *consumes me*, Jezebel." Grabbing me with a sudden intensity, August rolled me onto my back and thrust himself inside.

A deep primal moan spilled from my lips as I succumbed to the ecstasy of him, and an emotion so sharp washed over me with a force I could barely define. I had spent my entire life living on the precipice of myself, running from my own loss, and August was like coming home to a place I never wanted to leave. I felt whole for the first time, and the gravity of this hit me like a tidal wave, causing tears long overdue to spring from within. I openly wept against him, overcome by the strong current of passion that he so effortlessly pulled from me.

August caught my tears with his fingertips, his mouth engulfing mine in a heavy kiss that spoke of something sacred, tender, and mutual. Our energy collided in a slow but feverish rhythm as we lost ourselves, spiraling together into the depths.

"August." We lay against the sheets, skin slick with heat. I leaned over him and coiled my fingers into his tangled hair. "I never thought anyone could make me feel this way."

"Me neither." Reaching for me, he grasped my face tenderly in his hands. "*I love you,* Jezebel." Tears trembled in his eyes, causing the delicate strands of my heart to unravel. "Do you know how terrified I was when I felt you leave your body, not knowing if you were going to return to me? No longer do I care to imagine a life without you in it."

He moved my hand to where his heart lay, beating stridently within his chest. His voice was a whisper as his eyes burned into me with a fierce passion that stilled my breath. "Nobody has ever moved me the way you do. I have spent hundreds of years searching for a connection like this. I want you here beside me always. *I want you to be my wife.*"

The salt of my tears slipped down my cheeks once more, overcome with the power of his confession, so inherently parallel to my own. I wrapped my arms around him, my breath in his ear. "There is nothing I want more in this world than to be your wife, August."

CHAPTER ELEVEN

We never returned to France. Instead, we traveled further East, into India. A rich land of spices and color. My heart was like a wide-open ocean, churning with euphoria, and I dove headfirst into the endless depths of this new life we were forging together.

Standing on the banks of the sacred Triveni Sangam, we took in the confluence of three rivers that joined as one. Wooden fishing boats drifted by against the backdrop of the setting sun, while bathers in the river, obscured in shadows, purified themselves.

"This river is holy." August entwined his fingers with mine. "It represents the three points of life; the past, the present and the future. When the three rivers connect, they become one."

He looked at me with soft adoration in his eyes. "This is what I believe marriage to be, Jezebel. The joining of what we carry with us, who we are, and what we will become together."

I leaned against him, taking in the colors of the sunset, streaks of red and pink that merged and rippled through the current of the river. "Then let us have the marriage ceremony here."

The ceremony of marriage would consist of an Embrace between the two of us. August had explained to me the sacredness of exchanging blood, how in doing so we would be linked through the intrinsic flow of energy. Our spirits bound together as one. I had expressed concerns about my traveling during the ceremony, knowing how intense an Embrace could be, but August reassured me that I must never deny the opportunity to explore my power; that I must always remain open and available when my gift presented itself.

* * *

We walked among the marketplace of Allahabad, past the spice souks with their aromatic beckoning trail of curry, cinnamon and clove intermingling with the opulent scents of frankincense, jasmine and musk which hung in the thick humid air around us. We were searching for a man named Mahatma, a truth holder who lived in the city, known to officiate the unions between our kind.

We came to a red door, nestled between two large buildings within the marketplace. August rapped upon the entry in a series of sharp knocks. There was a pause and then the door swung open to reveal a small man in a robe, spectacles perched low upon his nose.

"Namaste." He bowed to us. "I have been expecting you." He turned to August, placing his hand softly on his arm. "De Sanguine, it is such a great honor to meet you at last." He shuffled down a long, dark hallway, sweeping his arm out in a motion for us to follow.

Mahatma seated himself at his desk. Large engraved statues loomed above him on a tall wooden shelf; Vishnu, Ganesh and Shiva looking down at us with painted tranquility.

"So. You are seeking an officiate for your marriage ceremony?" His eyes danced with a joyful kindness.

"Yes, Mahatma," August began, sliding his arm around me. "We wish to have the ceremony at the banks of the Triveni Sangam."

"Ah, yes. The Triveni Sangam. A very sacred place, that is." Mahatma smiled, his hands resting in a fold of prayer as he spoke. "I have officiated many Ceremonies among our kind, but never have I had the honor of preforming one there."

Mahatma rose from his seat and crossed the room to where we stood. "Such a privilege this will be for me. For there is such divine radiance between you two." Placing a gentle hand upon my shoulder, Mahatma drew me into the depths of his warm brown eyes. "And you, my dear. I see all the many people you will touch with your gift."

On the evening of the Ceremony, I draped myself in silk, the color of red wine. The fabric moved against my skin, fluid and soft like a sensual caress. I had shed the restrictive garments of the European fashion I was accustomed to and delighted in the new feel of my body, loose and free within the flowing cloth.

I stared at myself in the mirror. My green eyes reflecting the myriad of exhilarated emotions that swirled inside me. Tonight, I would be uniting myself with August, the threads that connected us would be forever bound. The thought of spending the rest of our years together brought me to a profound state of elation. Years which stretched before my mind like the thick pages of a book, with all the beautiful possibilities and rich secrets of our story tucked away within the whisperings of ink.

Trembling with anticipation, I proceeded down the path to where August awaited me at the river's edge. The night sky flickered above me as the hushed chorus of crickets filled the balmy air. As I drew close to the river, the soft glow of hundreds of candles illuminated the shore in a large ring. In the center of the circle stood August. My breath caught in my throat as I stepped over the flames and joined him within the flickers of fire.

He moved close to me, clasping his hands tightly in mine. The shadows of the light cast a shimmered reflection upon his skin, bathing his eyes in an ochre glow as he gazed at me with adoration. "You look so *magnificent*, Jezebel."

Mahatma stepped forward from the darkness in a flowing gold robe that trailed across the sand, joining us within the circle. For such a small man, the energy that flowed from him was exceedingly large and commanding. But his presence radiated warmth, and an ancient wisdom which he carried with a humble poise.

"I am here to witness the union between two souls. No longer shall you walk alone. For it is your love that unites, illuminates, and sanctifies this powerful journey of existence. Together you will transcend the fragmented pieces of yourselves, for when something is shared, it becomes whole once more, and where there is love, there is life."

Mahatma spoke with a measured tone of reverence as I lost myself in the moment, in the feel of August's hands in mine, his eyes gazing at me with so much devotion it caused warm tears to slip down my face in a trail of joy I surrendered myself to completely.

"You are no longer separate. You have become one. You may now Embrace." Mahatma quietly stepped back into the shadows, leaving us alone within the soft light of the flames that danced between us.

August lowered me onto the sand. His lips brushed away my tears and slipped down to my mouth. I encircled my arms around him as the drug of his kiss pulled me into a state of heightened desire. His urgency pressed against me as my hands reached underneath his shirt, connecting with the warmth of his skin.

Releasing his mouth from mine, August smoothed my hair back with the palm of his hand; his eyes ablaze. "Would you like to go first?"

I nodded and rolled onto him, straddling his waist while I ran my lips down his neck, teasing him with my tongue. He drew in a sharp breath as my teeth lightly grazed over his skin. "Are you ready for me?"

August pulled me tight against him, his voice husky as he moaned into my ear. "Yes, *my love*. I am always ready for you."

A tremendous rush spilled into me as I sunk my teeth into him. August shuddered and cried out beneath me, his hands gripping my back as the essence of him flowed through my veins. I felt everything. His fears, his strengths, his love for me. It was a euphony of his emotions and thoughts, all vibrantly pouring into my body.

I released him with a gasp, my head spinning with a blissful high. August's eyes locked onto mine with a simmering passion as he pulled me against him and kissed me deeply.

"You will always be able to feel me now." His voice filtered into my thoughts like liquid, delicately touching the spaces inside my mind as he ran his hands down the silk of my dress and found my center, wet and throbbing against his fingers.

"Oh, God. You are so glorious." He moaned upon my neck. "The places you take me, *Jezebel*."

His touch sent ripples of pleasure that slammed into me, and I leaned my head back and gasped. The night sky swirling above, millions of stars dying and being born before my eyes.

"And now I want to feel you." August spoke with a whisper, his teeth sharp against me. "Are you ready for me?"

"Yes." I moaned, closing my eyes, and awaiting the sweet gift of his bite.

An overwhelming explosion of euphoria overcame me as he drew me into his Embrace. It was unlike any pleasure I had ever experienced before, a continuous cascade of ecstasy so acute and eviscerating it shattered me. My hands clawed frantically at his back, and I cried out until there seemed to be nothing left but trembling fragments of myself laid out upon the earth.

August slowly released himself from me, intertwining our fingers tightly amongst the sand.

"So, this is what an Embrace feels like." My words came out breathless as I gradually returned to myself, gravity pulling me back down into my body with its solid, predictable weight. I smiled up at him languorously as the warmth of my thoughts slipped around his. *"One could go mad."*

"Yes." August ran his finger down the curve of my lips. "Though it is different for everyone. This is what an Embrace feels like for *us.*" His mouth hovered against my ear. *"Divine madness."*

CHAPTER TWELVE

I awoke to find dawn creeping over the Triveni Sangam. Everything lay silent around me, except for the river which lazily lapped itself against the shore. A cool breeze drifted in from the water, dispelling the humidity in the air. I rose from the bed we had made upon the sand and saw August with his back toward me, standing in the river with his white garments from the night before shed upon the bank.

He was so beautiful with the early morning rays falling on his skin like honey. I stood and slipped off my dress, letting it fall onto the sand in a silken puddle as I stepped into the river and wrapped my arms around him from behind. The coolness of the water tugged at my skin as August drew his arms around mine. We stood there, watching the brilliant golden fire of the sun crest the horizon.

"I'm glad you are awake." He turned to lift me up against the warmth of him, pulling me deeper into the gentle current, our bodies becoming buoyant. "I wanted to share the sunrise with you."

Drawing my legs around his waist, I surrendered to him as he wordlessly slipped himself inside me. We rocked against each other in the cleansing water, where the three rivers connected as one, our love flowing out, weightless, and unearthed.

From India we headed west into the heart of Africa, with its swollen torpid river, the color of chocolate snaking through the tropical undergrowth of the Congo. We traveled to the rich savannas of Tanzania, teeming with wildlife which hid among the whispering gold of the waving grass, with the delicate arched canopy of the baobab trees, standing like silent observers against the sun-bleached sky.

August had the keen ability to decipher a Giver, a subtle ripple within their energy. Some of the people throughout Africa had chosen to mark themselves, a single red dot hidden behind the nape of hair on the back of their neck. It stood out like a beacon against the beautiful rich color of their skin. Since our night on the ship with Marie, we had begun to prefer the sharing of an Embrace, and there seemed to be no shortage of eager participants. It was a high that always left us feverish afterwards, consuming us with an insatiable hunger for each other.

We lay together on the soft sand. Beads of perspiration trickled down the flush of my skin while the sky shimmered in waves above us. The sound of the colobus monkeys filled my ears as they called out to each other from across the jungle beyond our camp. The day was fading to a rich dusk as the Tanzanian sun dropped its heavy warmth below the savannah. August lazily traced the rivulets of sweat down my chest with his finger.

"*Ha mo ghion ort.*" I whispered in his ear.

He raised his eyebrows at me. "I did not know you spoke Gaelic?"

I smiled, reaching up to brush a lock of hair away from his brow. "It was my mother who taught me."

In that moment, a sudden silence swept over the savanna; the monkeys had stopped their incessant chatter in the trees, and the hush that overcame the jungle left me with an eerie chill. I sat up to look around when I noticed a large shape moving towards us from the tall grass.

"August?" I tried to keep my voice level and calm as the lioness slowly approached. There was a look of hunger within her eyes as she began to close in on the space between us; crouching low, her powerful muscles rippled like water.

"Jezebel. Do not move." His voice was firm as he stood and began to walk carefully towards the lioness.

"What are you doing? Stop!" Panic washed over me he advanced closer. I could hear the deep throaty rumble of the animal as August knelt upon the ground to meet her eyes. They were close enough that if he were to reach his hand out, he could have touched the tawny coat.

"Jezebel, it is okay." August's soothing voice wrapped around my thoughts like liquid.

Seconds passed, my heart hammering in my ears. I watched her tail flick back and forth and then suddenly appeared to relax, sitting back upon her haunches while August continued to gaze into the wild amber eyes. Then the lioness stood, glancing at me once before trotting away and disappearing into the grass once more.

I sat there transfixed as August returned to our blankets, calmly sitting beside me.

"What just happened?" My voice trembled.

"I asked her to leave."

"How?"

"Hypnosis." He looked at me with a steady gaze as my heart rate began to slip back into its normal rhythm.

I stared at him in disbelief, watching as a small smile crept over his face. "You were not aware that your powers of hypnosis stretch beyond humans?"

"No, I was not." I glanced toward the sea of copper and gold, listening to the gentle rustle of the savanna which stretched out before me, endless and filled with the breath of life.

August settled back down beside me. "We are connected to everything around us, and there was a time long ago that humans lived in balance with these creatures as equals. They were each other's teacher, and they spoke the same language. But fear took hold, disconnecting them from one another and therefore from the earth itself." August gestured to the waving grass. "That lion was only doing what she had been taught to do."

"When I took the elixir, you spoke of this. How humans live in disconnect and fear." I gazed out to the horizon, which danced with vibrancy, the earth spilling her majestic watercolors across the sky. "I just don't see how we can help them?"

August rested his hand against mine. "It is not our job to help them. It is our job to offer the tools that will enable them to reconnect with themselves. To live to their fullest potential."

I looked up into his eyes, full of so much love that spilled out and bathed me in all its enormity. Smoothing back my hair, he placed a kiss on my forehead. "And we have been given the precious gift of time. Our job is to take that gift and live as boldly and honestly as possible. When we do eventually relinquish this body, it is only a short journey back home."

We sat in silence for a moment, watching as the last glimmer of the day sunk below the horizon until all that was left was the endless blue ink of the sky scattered with stars.

"You know, Jezebel, you have taught me so much."

I looked over at him, his face obscured by shadows. "I have?"

"Yes. I have spent hundreds of years devouring knowledge, hoping to be a guide for those seeking answers. But in all that time, the knowledge of the heart eluded me." August found my hand in the darkness, squeezing tight. "Until I met you. You have opened a place within me I had been unable to reach before. You have taught me how to love."

"You have never loved?"

He shook his head. "Not like *this*, Jezebel."

I leaned into him as his arms encircled me, his voice a silky whisper between us as his lips brushed against my hair. "You have opened up my soul, giving me the greatest gift one could ever ask for."

His words slipped into my heart, solidifying my own fervent devotion. Our journey had only just begun, and I was filled with elation at the thought of what was to come.

Time blended into weeks, which became months, spinning a luxuriant tapestry of culture and sights that enriched my senses.

From Tanzania we traveled north into Egypt, where the mesmerizing pyramids towered above us, their legends as old as the desert itself, whispering truths within the entombed walls. We journeyed to Morocco, with its clay baked buildings carved from the earth, overlooking the Mediterranean Sea. It was there that we boarded August's ship, and I settled back into the undulant sway as we sailed across the Atlantic to the dense jungles of South America, and into Peru, the land of the Incas.

Settling for a time in Cuzco, a small town nestled among the impressive mountain range of the Andes, we immersed ourselves in the rich landscape of the people who lived there. With their large joyful smiles and colorful clothing, we felt surrounded by an energy teeming with an abundance of spirit.

We decided to spend a few nights up in the mountains. The locals had told us about a sacred abandoned temple by the name of Machu Picchu, and its veiled mysteries beckoned to us from above. Guided by a village goat farmer, we were silently led up a steep trail through lush undergrowth. Bidding us farewell at the entrance, he promised he would return to take us back down in two days' time.

Walking among the sprawling edifices of stone, we marveled in the feeling of ancient power that seemed to emanate from the ground beneath us. "I wonder what happened to these people," I said to August as I sat and leaned against a wall warmed by the sun, the sky stretching above us like an endless blue ocean.

"I suppose the same thing that will happen to everything around us, Jezebel."

I looked up at him in confusion. "What do you mean?"

August gazed out into the distance of the emerald peaks; his hands thrust deep within his pockets as the wind picked up and flirted with his hair. "Countries, cities, towns. They all have a beating heart with a life expectancy. Some will end by the ravages of war, others by disease, but most will end because the purpose of its existence is no longer being honored." He turned to me with a look of sorrow etched across his face. "Sometimes, when I look into the future, I see a world largely consumed by greed and dissociation.

Humans so engulfed in their own discontent that they destroy the very thing that sustains them."

I rose and went over to August. Wrapping my arms around him, I rested my head against his chest. "Is that what you fear will become of this world?"

He shook his head as his fingers reached up to run through the strands of my hair. "That is the thing about the future, Jezebel. It is not yet formed; it is only a path chosen. I can only hope that when the time comes, people will choose to forge a new one."

* * *

That evening, we lay beneath the night sky, watching the stars stretch out in a brilliant magnitude above us. The locals believed that the stars were the spirits of their ancestors, keeping vigil over the ancient sleeping city hidden among the jungle.

"August." I leaned up against his chest, the light of our fire sending shadows dancing across our camp.

He trailed his hand lazily along my arm. "Yes, my love."

I tipped my head back and found the deep blue of his gaze; eyes I knew I would never grow tired of looking into. "I want to make a home with you."

"Here?" he asked, smiling down at me.

I shook my head. "It's beautiful here. But no. I long to be somewhere by the ocean." I closed my eyes and brought up the image that had been following me. A stormy coast, rough seas that battered rocks, an endless expanse of turbulent beauty that called to me with a wild urgency. Though I was enjoying my nomadic journey with August, our travels together like a fragrant dream. I had been a nomad all my life, and I yearned for a place to unpack my bags.

A silence settled over us before August spoke. "There is a new settlement off the coast of the North Atlantic Ocean. The English have established a colony there, fleeing from religious persecution. I have heard that it is a land unfettered and free."

Excitement rose within me, and I turned to him, straddling his lap and running my hands down his chest. "I want to go there."

He pulled me close to him, pressing his lips against my neck, his breath warm on the chill of my skin. "I will go anywhere with you, *Jezebel*."

* * *

I traveled that night, the first occurrence since the Gathering. I lay beneath August, the heat of our bodies radiating off the canvas cloth of our tent as he plunged himself into me. The tingling began just as I slipped into the abyss of our shared pleasure.

"August, it's happening." I gripped his arms as the rush overcame me and a familiar darkness descended upon my vision.

* * *

I was in the field once more, the purple sky above me like spilled paint. Beside me stood a girl with raven hair that fell past her shoulders, her eyes swimming with an intensity I was unaccustomed to seeing in one so young. She turned to me, the dark pool of her gaze piercing into my depths.

"Saint Catherine of Alexandria, you have come to me." Her voice was full of reverence as she fell at my feet, her arms wrapping around my legs in supplication.

I bent down, placing my hand gently upon her head. "No, I am not a Saint. I am only a Traveler."

She looked up at me, her eyes brimming with tears. "But you *must* be her."

I smiled softly, taking her hands, and pulling her to her feet. "What troubles you?"

The girl furrowed her brow, glancing off into the direction of the forest. "There are many things I must do in this life. Voices that speak to me."

I settled myself in the grass, motioning for her to join me. "And tell me, what do these voices say?"

"I must help King Charles. The English are dominating France."

There was something familiar about the words she spoke, sparking a vague memory of reading through old dusty books of history pilfered from the orphanage library as a child. My mind grappled with the realization that I had somehow managed to travel back in time.

I looked at this young girl with her fists clenched tightly in her lap, full of so much fervor it radiated off her with a heavy force. She appeared to be a haunted soul, with thoughts that chased her relentlessly through the tangled brush of her mind, voices like claws reaching out with a strength I knew would propel her somewhere vast and unknown.

"I wish I was a boy, so I could fight alongside my King."

I rested my hand on her shoulder as a warmth hummed in my chest, forming thoughts which spilt forth from my lips like foreign incantations; unrestrained and filled with a power much larger than myself. "You must go to your King then and give to him your support."

She turned to me; her dark eyes wide with wonder. "Go to my King? And what would I say?"

I smiled warmly at her, delicately brushing my hand against her cheek. "You will know what you must do when the time comes. For you have a fire inside you." I took her hands and clasped them tightly as the words continued to flow from me; untethered, and of their own volition. "This tremendous strength that lays within you. It is your shield, your blade, and your compass. You must allow this to guide you and others through adversity. For when one lives by the power of their own fortitude, one will never lose a battle."

As I spoke, my body began its subtle shift once more, drawing me back to the place from which I came. "I believe it is time for me to go now."

"It *is* you." Her hands tightly gripped mine as I felt myself fade away. "Saint Catherine, you *have* come to me."

* * *

When I opened my eyes, the feel of August's breath upon my skin was an anchor as he cradled me against his chest, his voice coiling within my mind like a warm breeze.

"Welcome back, Jezebel."

CHAPTER THIRTEEN

W e stood on the deck of August's ship and watched the faint
outline of the approaching landmass.

"Our new home," August said, sliding his arms around me from
behind as I took in the rocky, wind-battered coastline, reminiscent of
my dreams.

We docked in Massachusetts Bay. Simple structures made of pine
and oak dotted the land with the sound of hammering and wooden
carts creaking past. Women in bleached white caps and grey-colored
cloaks walked among the muddy rutted streets, baskets in hand and
children at their feet. It was mid-spring, and the flowers of the
dogwood trees bloomed along the outskirts of the settlement, a
startling white against the blue of the sky. The energy teemed with
possibilities, an endless vitality that only the breath of freedom could
bring.

* * *

The next day, we traversed the terrain on two gentle horses, guiding
us deep into the hills as we sought a place with flat land and a view of
the ocean on which to build our home. The locals had warned us of
the natives, *savage beasts* they called them, who would skin you in the
night while you slept. But we knew the words they spoke were only
the masks of fear and ignorance, and I longed to meet the people of
this land, with their reverence and song; like steady drumbeats
among the forest calling to me.

Most of the places we surveyed were too densely populated with
trees, and though I loved the forest, I yearned for space and light. The
day began to dwindle as the sun hugged the tree line, and we still had
not found what we were looking for. As we turned to make it back
down to the village, I spotted a reflection of light glinting off a crop of

rocks in the distance. Beyond the trees lay a cliff shrouded in mist where a steep incline rose to a vast level surface.

We stood together on the flat expanse of rock, surrounded by the sea. "*This is it,* August." My words spilled out breathless as I took in the expansive view. I came up behind him, wrapping my arms around his back. "This is where I want to have a child."

He turned towards me, the look in his eyes speaking volumes as he grabbed me with intensity and pulled me to his mouth. My heart swelled, and I fell against him, breathing in his air and all the possibilities that stretched out before us.

* * *

The next morning, we set off to find the native tribe by the name of Wampanoag, following a roughly drawn map of their village that had been given to us by a man who was known to trade with them. We wanted to establish a relationship with the tribe and to request permission to build on the site we had found. Knowing these people were the caretakers of this land, we did not want to encroach upon a sacred place.

Thin trails of smoke curling through the trees alerted us that we had reached their village.

When we approached the clearing and stepped among the rounded birchbark huts with various racks of skins drying beside low burning fires, a sudden silence filled the camp. Children stopped their play and ran to their mothers, burying their faces in the smooth beaded leather of their skirts. The murmur of voices receded, and dark eyes fell sternly upon us. We had quickly learned of the history between the settlers and the natives. It had been one filled with discord and bloodshed, and it made my heart ache, the delicate dance of trust that had been broken long ago.

August slid off his horse and raised his hands up in a gesture of peace. A man approached him, tall and muscular, his gaze upon August was sharp. He wore a headband adorned with a single feather that hung down over the gloss of his ebony hair, which fell long against his back. A necklace of abalone shells and smoothed bone lay upon the rich caramel color of his skin. He spoke in a language that sounded like a song. August crouched down and began to draw pictures in the dirt of our journey by ship and our search for a home. The man watched August silently as the women drew closer. A hand touched my leg, and I looked down to see the smiling face of a child, her amber eyes filled with curiosity.

We sat together among the Wampanoag, communicating through touch and smile, sharing our names like gifts. The women seemed very interested in my hair, running their fingers through it and laughing. The energy of these people was full of joy, and their eyes held a deep wisdom that I had seldom seen in others. August sat beside the man whose name was Namumpum and drew a picture of the cliff we had found. The man shook his head, indicating that it had no meaning for him. August then sketched a house on top and looked to Namumpum, who smiled and nodded, resting his hand upon his shoulder.

The months passed in a flurry of work. Days spent building our home; the consistent rhythmic tone of hammer against nail, working beside the hired help as the cool warmth of spring gave way to the blistering heat of summer. Nights were spent on the ship docked among the harbor, nestled in the quiet sway of the cabin.

We met a woman named Opal, a widow who had lost her two children to sickness on the journey over. She would come to us once a week, wearing the look of someone who had relinquished her life, and while we could not help her regain her spark, we could ease her suffering. When the shadows of dusk fell, she would steal into the ship with her dull eyes and pale skin that was cold to the touch, silently awaiting our Embrace like the dark pull of an opium dream.

I began to travel more frequently, and no longer did my traveling seem to rely on a heightened state of arousal. August believed I had begun to harness it better, though I still had no control over when it occurred. The people I visited all had something in common. They were lost and filled with pain, and I was only a vessel, for the words I shared with them were not my own.

"You are giving the gift of healing, Jezebel." We lay entwined among the bed together with the gentle rocking of the ship beneath us. August ran his hands along my palms, softly kneading the flesh with his thumbs, which had grown sore and calloused from the months of our labor. "You may not think you are helping these people, but I believe you are, on a very deep and profound level that may be beyond our understanding."

"I really hope so." I pulled August on top of me, feeling the weight of him against my body, comforting, solid and consistent. I ran my fingers through his hair, bathing in the warmth of his eyes. "I want nothing more than to have these travels of mine serve a larger purpose in some way."

Our breath now hung in the air like smoke as the icy grip of fall began to cling to the mornings, coating the crisp leaves in the whisper of winter.

Our house was nearly finished.

Upon opening the front door, I stepped inside a small mudroom, a set of stairs on the left, and a room beckoning to the right. As I walked down the hallway, my steps echoed off the polished wood, leading me into a large living room with a brilliant light that spilled from the windows, the view of the ocean stretching out for miles. A large hearth stood in the center while off to the side lay a dining room that spilled into a kitchen where the warmth of a burning stove glowed brightly, keeping a kettle warm for tea. Upstairs was our room, a single expansive space with windows that hugged the floor and double doors leading out to a porch that wrapped around the house, surrounding one in the endless view.

It was there that I stood, feeling the wind play with my hair, my hand resting over my belly, for deep within I now carried life. The sweet and beautiful promise of a child.

The sound of August's footsteps broke my thoughts as he encircled me from behind, running his hand slowly along the swell of my stomach, his breath upon my neck, stirring the embers inside me. I closed my eyes and leaned against him. "I cannot wait to make this our home."

"We can make it our home today if you would like?" August murmured against my neck, his lips teasing the skin.

I turned to look at him as a sensual smile stretched across his face, his eyes harmonizing with the color of the surrounding sea.

"Our bed has arrived. It is waiting for us down by the dock. The rest of the shipment will be here next week."

He ran his finger down my neck, his hand grazing the soft rise of my swollen breasts that peeked out from beneath my dress. My nipples responded to his touch, eagerly pressing against the fabric as he took me in with a look that made me weak with longing.

"But all we really need is a bed, Jezebel."

* * *

The waves crashed against the rocks below us. The soothing sound filtering in through the windows as the soft glow of the flickering lamps surrounded the bed in our new home, reminding me of our wedding Ceremony on the banks of the river in India. I stood above August as he reclined upon the sheets, naked and erect, watching me with a languid hunger as I slipped my robe down below my shoulders and let it fall to the floor. My body aching and heavy as I moved to him.

"*Jezebel.*" His hands slid up past my thighs and cupped his palms against the slope of my belly as his words crept in and softly caressed my thoughts. *"You are so beautiful, it hurts sometimes."*

His eyes were filled with marvel as he pressed his mouth against my skin. I trembled beneath his kiss as his lips drew a lazy path from

197

my navel down to my sex; his tongue lightly teasing my bud. My fingers gripped his hair, pressing him hard against me, my body demanding more as my pleasure surged against him. Just before I was about to lose myself, he pulled away and with a provocative smile, guided me down to my hands and knees upon the bed.

My nipples ached against the fabric of the pillows as he ran the length of himself down the small of my back and hovered below my sex, gently pressing against me. I hungrily pushed myself closer to him, eager to feel him inside me. The frenzy grew within as he lightly stroked himself against my swollen center, tormenting me with my own desire.

August's breath fell labored against me, seeming to relish this slow tease as his hands brushed across my skin, drawing out the pleasure in languid strokes that caused my entire body to tremble.

"August, please." I whimpered, a low growl spilling out of me as I clawed at the sheets, begging him.

"Please, *what*?" August gently flipped me over onto my back, a mischievous glint in his eye as he spread my legs and ran his thumb along my throbbing center. "What is it that you *want*, my dear?"

I reached for him frantically, digging my nails into his arms. "*Enough*," I gasped. "Stop torturing me."

He chuckled, pulling away with a smile and took my hand, guiding it to where I lay wet and eager. His voice was a deep rasp. "I want to watch you let go first."

I moaned in relief as I began to touch myself, fast and feverish as August watched me. His gaze filled with a hungry fire as I cried out to him, lost to the pulse of my own climax.

"You are heaven to me, Jezebel." His voice was a low hiss as he ran his hands lightly along my inner thighs, a look of violent lust in his eyes as I lay there, burning for him. He moved down to trace his tongue slowly against my tender folds, tasting the remnants of my release.

"*August*." My words spilled out in a whispered plea as I desperately writhed beneath him. "I need to feel you inside me now."

He gently pulled me to the edge of the bed, his eyes piercing into my depths as he finally slipped himself inside with a loud groan, the powerful essence of him merging with mine. I frantically grabbed onto him, pulling him closer as a bliss so raw ruptured within, taking me to that sacred place we shared together.

"*God. How you annihilate me.*" August moaned deeply into my ear as another strong wave of pleasure coursed through every fiber of my being, matching the sudden speed of his own. His cries tangled in my hair as he spilled himself into me, reverent and full of so much light.

* * *

That night, entwined in the blissful solace of August's arms, I traveled again; my body slipping silently away as he slept beside me.

When I came to, my hand brushed against something warm and wet and I looked down to find the sheets soaked in blood. The essence of our child, spilling out of me like a river.

August's face was pale as he wrapped me in blankets and rushed me out of the house and to the stable. The chill of the night air gripped my skin, causing me to shake violently as he lifted me up onto the horse and quickly sprinted into the woods. Trees flew past my vision in a darkened blur, and all I could hear was the rhythmic pounding of hooves against the frozen ground.

When we arrived at the village of the Wampanoag, soft hands guided me through the dark and into the dimly lit warmth of the medicine woman's hut. A small fire burned in the center. The thick smell of sweetgrass hung in the air as I was laid down onto furs. August's hand clutched tightly in mine; his eyes filled with fear.

The rhythmic chanting of the medicine woman filled the space with a soothing melody that anchored me as she began to boil herbs in a small bowl upon the fire. The aroma of willow, yarrow, ginger, and black cohosh drifted through the hut. Lifting my head up, she drew the bowl to my lips and motioned for me to drink. I swallowed the bitter, earthy liquid and fell back against the furs, feeling the medicine as it began to swim through in my veins, slowing the flow of blood within me and stimulating contractions.

Pain gripped me as our child slid quickly from my body and onto the furs. The medicine woman gathered up the small child within the palm of her hand, still and breathless, and wrapped her up inside of an animal pelt, placing the bundle against my chest. I folded back the skins to reveal blue veins like a tiny stream underneath translucent skin. Her eyes closed as if asleep, never to open upon this world. August pulled me into his arms, his face streaked with tears as the visceral marrow of our shared loss took hold. We silently rocked together in sorrow through the long night, cradling in our hands the beautiful bud of life never opened.

We named her Karrae, meaning *God's golden Angel*.

As the first rays of morning light rose above the water, bathing the sky in fragile color, we wrapped her in a muslin cloth and placed her body out to sea, allowing the waves of the ocean to cradle her. Forever would she be a part of the endless churning pulse of life.

My womb ached for weeks afterwards, like the phantom pains of the body, mourning the loss of a limb. After that painful night, something in me shifted, for I knew deep in my heart that my traveling had somehow brought on the loss of our child, and I could not bear to lose another. So, I began to drink the tea of Queen Anne's Lace, which I harvested in the woods beside the house, and no longer did we speak of a child.

Winter barreled in with a ferocity that year, blanketing the world around us in ice and snow. The sea became a white mist as we curled into each other, the warmth of the house like a cocoon patiently awaiting rebirth as we began to slowly heal the fragment torn from us.

CHAPTER FOURTEEN

O ur bodies are intrinsically connected to the rhythm of the seasons. The gentle out-breath of winter leads to the fervent inhalation of spring, and the return of warmth felt like sugar upon my tongue. I began to spend my days with my hands deep within the earth. The Wampanoag had returned from their winter longhouses, and I spent much of my time with the village learning the gentle melodic tone of their language. They provided me with seeds for a garden; corn, beans, and squash which I tended to diligently among the poor rocky soil, in awe of nature's steady determination.

Summer's mid-afternoon heat pressed upon my back as I worked outside amid the plants that now brushed against my knees. The wind tossed my hair around as August sat beside me on the grass, gazing out at the sea.

"Do you ever miss Europe?" I asked, settling down next to him.

He reached over and clasped my hand, never taking his eyes off the horizon.

"No. It was never my home." He turned to me, the intensity of his gaze reflecting the endless ocean. "You are my home, Jezebel."

His sincere sentiments never lost their power over me, and my heart fluttered as I leaned into him, resting my lips against his temple. "And you are mine."

The past winter had been hard, but we did not recoil into our own private grief. We sat together beside it like a fire until the wound no longer bled, and we were able to pay homage to the scars.

Sitting with the ocean stretched out before us, I breathed in the powerful, tumbling roar of life as it continuously renewed itself. Our years together had interlaced into a rich plethora of understanding between us. At times we did not even need to speak, for words could only hold so much meaning. It was our souls that spoke more often in these moments, with a delicate, ancient language all its own.

We rarely went into town that summer, except for the few supplies we could not harvest from the land. We spent our days alongside the Wampanoag, immersing ourselves in their culture. They accepted us into their life with warmth and ease. August accompanied the men during their vision quests and drum circles while I would gather shellfish, acorns, and berries with the women. They taught me of the curative herbs hidden within the forest. The immune boosting qualities of goldenseal, the antibacterial agents held inside the crimson sap of the blood root and strengthening tonic of sweet fern.

I fell in love with the connection and the reverence they had to the earth. August often spoke of the kinship he felt with them as well. Their inherent beliefs regarding life so similar to his own.

They called us *Kitcitwawis Pejig.* The Sacred Ones. For they had discovered our gifts of healing, and in return they began to offer themselves up to our Embrace. In doing so, we formed a gentle symbiotic relationship with them, based on the give and take of our energetic resources.

The balmy heat of summer had slowly lifted her skirts to welcome in her squalling child of autumn. The last of the leaves fell in delicate spirals around us as we stood among the Wampanoag and bid farewell, watching them pack up camp once more to begin the journey back to their winter longhouses.

The medicine woman approached me, her face creased from years of laughter, her calm brown eyes gazing into my depths. She took my hand, gently turning my palm up and placing a necklace made of bone inside. "For you. To give strength."

"Kutapatush." I bowed my head, thanking her as I clasped the cool bone in between my fingers.

August stood beside me as we watched them make their slow procession silently through the trees, before disappearing into the woods. A sudden sorrow washed over me as they slipped from my line of sight. Though I knew they would return in the spring, I could not shake the feeling that this was our final goodbye.

August's hand fell on my arm, seeming to sense my unease. "What is it, Jezebel?"

I shook my head, covering up my thoughts before August could slip in. "Oh, nothing. I am just going to miss them."

He furrowed his brow, his eyes searching me, but did not press further as I turned from him and made my way back up the trail.

* * *

That evening as I lay in August's arms with the warmth of the fire at my back, the familiar tingling began its insistent crawl across my body; alerting me to my impending travel as I quickly slipped away from him and into the depths.

* * *

Standing in the field with the deep purple of the sky above, I made out a shape of a man walking towards me. He was tall with dark hair that blew against the wind. As he drew closer, I took in a sharp breath and my heart stilled.

The man standing before me was August.

His face was heavy with a grief as he grabbed me, holding me firmly in his arms. "I have been waiting for you to come to me, Jezebel." His words hovered desperately against my neck.

I pulled back, confusion swimming through me. "What do you mean, August?"

He looked at me with such anguish in his eyes. "You have been gone for a very long time." He cupped my face, tracing his thumbs along my jaw as tears pooled and fell upon his cheeks. "I have missed you so much, *my love.*"

I ran my hands down his chest, rubbing the unfamiliar cloth of his tailored suit in between my fingers.

"August, what happened?"

His voice choked. "They took you away from me, Jezebel."

"Who did?" Panic rose in my throat, and I gripped his arms, willing him to tell me.

August shook his head mournfully, pulling me close to him again. His silence spoke of things I realized I did not want to know.

"*August*." I pulled back for a moment, willing his eyes to meet mine. Within the blue of his gaze, I saw so many years of despair, an overwhelming heaviness inside of him that filled my heart with such sadness, it stifled my breath. I knew that whatever had happened to me had shattered him. "How long have I been gone?"

"It has been centuries now. But I have returned to the home we built together. To find my peace again."

This reality hit me like a heavy blow. But it wasn't the knowledge of my own death that sucked the warmth out of me, it was the crushing weight of August's pain, of all his time spent mourning me. It was a sorrow so large it encompassed all the space between us.

"And have you found peace?"

"I believe so," his voice was a hesitant whisper as he looked up at the sky for a moment, the purple beginning to fade slowly to a pale pink, and the thick desperation of anxiety coiled within me. Throughout my travels to this place of dreams, I had learned this was an indication that my time was soon running out.

August turned to me with a look of tenderness, his face growing soft. "I have met the woman who shares your name. She was the one you visited, the first time you traveled."

My heart began to thump wildly in my chest as I thought back to that young girl with the dark eyes full of loss, and I was suddenly overcome with confliction that pulled at me with sharp claws.

"And this woman, how does she make you feel?" The question tumbled unguarded from my lips.

His gaze penetrated me with a mixture of sorrow colliding against a faint glimmer of hope. "She makes me feel alive again."

The thought of him with another was like trying to swallow a strong tonic. It tasted bitter going down, but I knew he needed this love in order to repair himself. And in that moment, I realized that it was her who held the key to August's healing. That giving her my name had not only been for her benefit, but for August's as well, like a tender thread binding us all together.

"*Good*. You must hold on to that." I placed my hand on his cheek as tears sprung from my eyes. "I do not have much time left."

"No, Jezebel, *please*." He grew desperate as he clutched me, kissing my face with trembling lips.

"You must let me go now."

"I do not think I ever can," he whispered against my cheek.

"August!" I could feel the tingling upon my skin, my body beginning to pull away from him. August's eyes gripped me. This pain that coiled around him was a weight I knew he had to unburden. "*Please*, you have to release me. I cannot bear the thought of you suffering any longer." Reaching up, I tenderly ran my hand through his windblown hair. "I believe that you were destined to meet this woman. Let her give you your life back."

I suddenly felt something small and hard in the palm of my other hand. Looking down I realized that I was clutching a tiny seed. My hands seemed to move on their own accord as I placed the seed into his open palm, closing his fingers delicately around it.

"It is time to start a new life." I pulled him to me tightly as the rush overcome my body.

"Wait!" his voice was frantic and pleading as he grabbed onto my arms. "You can't go yet. What if this fate can be changed?"

"It is too late, for you already exist in a time beyond me," I managed to whisper before I slipped away from him, my body shifting into a translucent mist.

"*Jezebel*." My name on his lips was a mournful goodbye that followed me like an echo as I tumbled back into darkness.

* * *

My eyes opened to a room filled with grey shadows. The fire burned low in the hearth, its embers glowing a deep blood red. August's hand rested softly against my chest, as he so often did whenever I traveled, feeling for the strong steady beat of my heart returning to him.

"Welcome back."

I curled into the warmth of his body, heavy with the realization of what visiting him had meant.

August sensed my unease, and ran his fingers through my hair, placing his lips softly against my cheek. "What is it, Jezebel? Who did you visit this time?"

I shook my head, the truth suffocating me. I could not bring myself to tell him, and for the first time, I drew up a wall between us, shielding my thoughts from his.

"Someone who carried a lot of pain within them. I suppose it took a lot out of me." I smiled weakly as I pulled him close against me. "I need to rest now."

August held me, cradling my back against his chest as he pulled up the blanket and wrapped his arms around me, the warmth of his voice a delicate whisper on my neck. "You get some sleep, my love."

Staring into the fire, the flames flickered and danced before me as silent tears slipped down my cheeks, staining my skin with sorrow.

* * *

For days, I carried this weight, trying to comprehend the meaning of my own fragile fate. It was not death I feared as much as August's pain. So, I buried these thoughts deep within where he would not be able to uncover them. To conceal this hideous truth from him was a secret and a lie, but I did not want whatever precious time we had left together to be tainted with anguish and fear of what had become so clearly inevitable to me now. I took this visceral sorrow of knowledge and wrapped it up tight, releasing it to the wind, hoping it would carry it far from us and give us more time.

CHAPTER FIFTEEN

I sat upon the rocky cliff, gazing out into the expanse of water around me. Within the warm breeze that caressed my skin, I could detect a faint whisper of spring. Lost in the thick liquid of my thoughts, I recalled the centuries of my life, holding each of them with a gentle reverence. For even though so many years had been spent in loneliness and pain, it was my story; my only regret was time, which I now did not have enough of. I had never been able to understand why people consumed so much of their lives running from the only impending certainty of life. But now that my gift had become my own oracle of death, I understood their fears, for my own mortality had now become a ticking clock that watched me with unrelenting eyes.

Throughout the long winter, I knew August could sense my restlessness and unease. He never slipped into my mind to find out why though, and for that I was grateful. It took all the strength I had to bury this knowledge deep enough that his powers of sight could not reach it.

"Spring is coming."

August's voice from behind startled me, pulling me from my contemplation. I turned to him, the hesitant sunlight touching his face, resting on the curve of his full lips. How I longed to curl up forever within the shelter of him. To bathe in the richness of his love, which spilled forth from the depths of his eyes in an endless abundance. My heart trembled, and I choked down the sudden tears that threatened the surface. *How much time did we have left together?*

I took a deep breath of composure and stood. Sweeping dirt from my dress, I entwined my arms around him, breathing in his rich earthy scent. "Yes, I feel it too."

"Jezebel." He leaned down and met my gaze, full of a sudden gravity as his fingers gently brushed across my cheek. "We need to leave this place."

His words hit me like a blow, sucking the oxygen from me. The crushing weight of sorrow gripped me tightly at the thought of what he now knew. "What have you seen, August?" My voice came out in a tangled whisper.

His hands slid up to my shoulders, clutching me with an alarming intensity. "The vision has not been clear to me, which is unusual." He furrowed his brow and gazed out to the expansive sea for a moment, as if grappling for answers. "What I do know is that something grave is impending upon this place."

I stared up at him with the sudden realization that he now shared my knowledge, still obscure and undefined to him, but pressing. Yet, I still could not bring myself to divulge the full weight of this truth, for when I looked into his eyes, there was a strength there, and it was a life raft I desperately clung to. I could not bear the weight of his anguish. I needed to feel as if his strength could save me, even though the voice inside which persisted like a low droning chant, told me it would not. It was all I had left. Illusions of safety tangled among the truth.

August's face grew troubled with apprehension. "I have not wanted to alarm you, and I know you do not want to leave this home that we have made for ourselves, but for your safety, I feel it is imperative that we depart as soon as possible."

"When are we to leave?"

August stared back at our house, the one we had spent so much time building together. The years full of fervent dreams for a new life nestled among the structure of cedar and oak. I nodded as a precipitous thought rushed through me. *Could I have the potential to change my fate?* It was a sudden and tentative bud of hope pressing out against the chill of the snow.

"I will prepare the ship and stock provisions. We will leave in two weeks' time."

The week before we were to set sail, I decided to walk into town. I wanted to take in my last moments with the land in quiet solitude. To breathe in the fresh ocean air and feel the gentle kiss of the sun on my skin as it broke through the clouds and filtered down through the trees, hesitantly bathing the forest floor in a multitude of shimmering fragments. I was going to miss this place. It had an ancient, wild beauty to it that made me feel at home.

I walked through the town streets as people bustled around me, coming back to life once more as the grip of winter loosened its hold. Women passed by, their heads nodding in greeting. Men tipped their hats at me, most of them with a lustful glint in their eye which I had grown accustomed to, the force of their desire like a silent demand. August had always taken it in with slight amusement. He said I exuded a wild sensuality unfamiliar to them, but because of this attention, I was weary of their gaze. Opal had remained the only one we had ever Embraced among the settlers.

I headed in the direction of a shop selling cookery and cloth, the front window neatly displaying the artifacts of domestic essentials. I was seeking to purchase some fabric for a dress when I heard a scuffle, a sudden altercation of angry raised voices pulling my attention away from the store and to the street behind me.

One man was armed with a knife. His blade flashing in the late afternoon sun as he suddenly collided into the other, piercing his flesh. It was a blur of bodies as the wounded man fell to the ground with a guttural cry like that of an animal, a look of betrayal in his eyes as the other man dashed away, blending into the foot traffic.

The man lay there upon the street as a crowd slowly formed, a murmured hush of silent stares. It never failed to surprise me, the way people viewed violence, like a passing storm, uncontrollable but as seemingly natural as the weather.

I rushed over to the man, pushing past people, and dropping down beside him. His dark eyes filled with fear, and his breath labored as he stared up at me in shock. He held his trembling hand over a large open wound in his abdomen, the life within him rapidly pooling out from in-between his fingers, staining the dirt beneath him.

"Help me." His words spilled out in a tangled whisper, his gaze anxious and imploring.

Instinctively and without thinking, I placed my hands upon him, quickly stilling the flow of blood. The warm pulse of my energy merged with his, fusing the wound closed. When I pulled away, a collective gasp rippled around me and my blood ran cold. I knew in that moment, I had made a grave error in judgment. Ignoring the stares upon me, the faint whisperings of the word *witch,* like a weapon aimed at me. I stood up and briskly walked through the crowd.

I took the short-cut back to the house, weaving through the faintly marked hunting trails of the Wampanoag, my heart pounding violently within me. The man's blood stained my hands and cloak like an ominous mark I could not remove.

When I returned home, I found August waiting for me outside. *"Jezebel."* His eyes were full of apprehension as they trailed down to my dress. He grabbed my arms firmly. "Are you okay?"

I nodded, my stomach coiling into tight knots. "Yes, I am. But I think I may have done something reckless."

He grew tense, his gaze dark like the gathering of a storm as he peered into my thoughts, extracting them like liquid. "We need to depart *now.*" His tone was firm and heavy with unease as he quickly ushered me inside. "We will pack what we can carry on the horses, the rest we will have to leave behind."

"August." I stared at him where he stood by the window. The sun was beginning to drop low against the horizon, casting shadows around the room. "Just tell me! What did you see this time?"

He walked over to me, taking my hands in his. "Our gifts must never be exposed like that. People do not understand. What you did was extremely dangerous."

I pulled away from him, a multitude of emotions boiling within. "Don't chastise me, August. What was I supposed to do? Leave him to die in the street?"

He shook his head, his eyes full of sorrow. "I know you are trying to atone for your past indiscretions. But you cannot save everyone. Sometimes you must make a choice."

* * *

We began to gather our essentials, packing only the things we needed into bags which sat waiting by the front door. In a few short hours, we were to depart, taking the long snaking trail of the Wampanoag down into town. Under the cover of darkness, we would embark upon our ship, sailing out of port and into the east waters of the Atlantic towards France.

I stood beside our living room window, staring out at the endless expanse of sea as a heaviness gathered in my chest. August came up behind me and wrapped his arms around my waist, stilling the nervous beating of my heart.

"I will miss this place," he whispered against my neck.

I nodded as tears welled up in my eyes. Everything felt so sudden and final. "Me too."

The sound of horses approaching disrupted the quiet within the house, the beating of hooves upon the ground and the murmured voices of men as they dismounted. August bristled, and released me, quickly striding to the entryway as a violent knock resounded upon the door. The bitter taste of dread swam through me as I followed August into the hallway. Standing in the shadows, I watched as he opened the door to three imposing men who pushed their way forcefully inside.

"Can I help you with something?" August's voice was thick with a controlled anger.

"Going somewhere?" A tall, dark-haired man sneered at him derisively, his eyes scanning over our bags sitting beside the door. His pronounced brows accentuated the air of superiority he carried with him, like the heavy scent of a predator.

August remained silent, his eyes growing dark.

"We are here for your wife." The shorter man standing next to him said, his beady gaze falling on me, thinning hair plastered against his ruddy complexion.

"No. You are not." August spoke in a low warning tone as he moved towards the man.

The rough hands of the third man suddenly grabbed me from where I stood in the hallway. Having slipped himself past August, he locked my arms behind my back. The smell of whisky and unwashed linens assailed my senses as he dragged me to the doorway.

"Get your filthy hands off me, you *bastard!*" I hissed at him, struggling within his strong hold.

"Feisty one, you are." His breath against my neck sent shivers of repulsion throughout my body. His fingers tightened their grip on me, sending a sharp pain through my arms.

The tall man spoke once more to August. "I'm afraid, Sir, that your wife here has been accused of witchcraft. She must come with us now."

August suddenly moved with blinding speed and grabbed the tall man, slamming him roughly up against the wall. "You are not taking my wife anywhere. You will release her this instant. Then you will get back onto your horses and leave. Do you understand me?"

As August spoke, his voice remained eerily calm, and I could see something begin to shift within the man's dark eyes as he pulled him into his powerful gaze of hypnosis. But I knew it was futile. We only had the ability to sway the singular consciousness of another, and we were far outnumbered.

The sound of a metallic click filled the room. The short man stood behind August, pointing a pistol at the back of his head. I stopped struggling. My heart stilled, then began to beat violently within my chest, panic coursing through my limbs.

"I would advise you to release my friend, unless you would like me to put a bullet through your head."

"August, stop! Let him go." He turned to me, his eyes full of sorrow and anger. "*Please,*" I begged.

"It would be wise of you to listen to your wife." The man spoke in a low growl as he pressed the revolver tightly up against August's head. "There are three more of my men waiting outside that would be more than happy to assist me, if I so needed."

August's hands dropped to his sides, and the man slid to the floor, looking dazed. The other two men held me firmly in their grip and ushered me through the door. My name came out a strangled rasp upon August's lips as they pulled me away and onto the waiting horses outside.

Turning around, I frantically called back to him. "It's going to be okay, August!" But I knew deep in my heart, that was a lie. This was my fate, laid out bare and ugly before me, and there was no escaping it now.

CHAPTER SIXTEEN

Within the brick tomb of the prison cell, rain trickled down the walls from cracks in the ceiling above me, punctuating the room with the steady drip of water against stone. The scent of mildew hung in the air, and my skin was chilled and damp, the only light came from the muted glow of a candle down the hall. The faint rustling of straw and an occasional wet cough, stirred the silence around me, alerting me to the fact that I was not alone, that I shared space with another's tangled misfortune. A lonely solidarity born from despair.

My mind traveled to August, and a choked wail spilled out of me. My gut wrenched with the thought of him and his pain, so acute I could feel it as if it were my own. Though we were apart, and our thoughts could not touch, I sensed him reaching to me, beating against the walls of my heart.

Time had begun to take on a different meaning for me now. My breath, I counted like the hands of a clock. I did not know how long I sat there within the cell, whether it was day or night. Occasionally, a guard would come by, the ominous thump of their boots echoing against the brick walls. Swinging open the heavy iron door, they would throw me some food on a tin plate, but they did not want to get too close. I could sense their fear, and it had a pungency to it like the thick taste of metal in my mouth. I did not bother consuming the rations they dispensed, and the weakness that crept over me was not from lack of food.

The sound of voices down the hall jarred me from my thoughts, and I scrambled upright. August's presence was like a warm light illuminating the chill around me, and my heart accelerated in relief at the thought of seeing him. Two men stopped in front of my cell. One was a guard I had never seen before, a flicker of kindness within his eyes. The other wore the dark robes of a priest, and behind them, stood August.

"Your husband has been very insistent on seeing you, and he appears to have some friends in high places." The guard nodded in the direction of the priest by his side as he unlocked the iron door, swinging it open with a loud creak. "You have ten minutes."

The door closed shut behind us with a bang as the sound of footsteps receded down the hallway. August rushed towards me, gathering me up tightly into his arms. My legs buckled beneath me, and we sunk slowly to the floor. The feel of him against me, his scent and presence so solid was an anchor among the turbulent waters of my mind, and I clung to him as if he were my air.

"I am going to get you out of here." His voice was a frantic whisper in my ear. His lips found mine and tenderly kissed away the fear that had been ripping at my flesh.

"Oh, Jezebel." He grasped my face in his hands, pain etched deep within his eyes. "You are in much need of an Embrace."

He ran his finger along my lips before lightly pressing his hand against the back of my head and pulling me close to the warmth of his neck, to the beautiful pulsing beat of his heart. I fell into him with a desperation, our limbs intertwining upon the hard ground. He shuddered and quietly wept against me as I slowly drew out his essence. His devotion like a gift, thick and sweet against my tongue; a bliss I drank deeply of as euphoria coursed through me, enveloping my senses.

As my strength returned, I released him, and August pressed his lips against mine. His kiss was tender and slow, his face streaked with the salt of his tears, the blue of his eyes swimming with sorrow as his breath became my own. My heart began to ache with the realization that this would possibly be our last moments of intimacy together, and a stillness born of poignant grief washed over me.

I finally spoke, breaking the languid spell of my Embrace. "How long have I been in here?"

"Two days." His voice was strained as his hands grasped mine tightly, trying to compose himself. "I persuaded them to move the trial to tomorrow. They seemed content to let you rot away in here, but I managed to pull some strings."

I nodded, but optimism did not flutter within. I knew a trial was only delaying the inevitable. But the look of hope on his face stilled the words that threatened to rush out. How could I tell him that I was going to die, and that there was nothing he could do about it? How could I crush the one thing that was keeping him strong?

"We will fight this." His eyes suddenly grew dark. "And if we cannot, there are other ways to get you out of here."

I recoiled from his suggestion. "No, August. I cannot let you live with that kind of blood on your hands."

He grabbed me by the shoulders. "What other option do I have, Jezebel? I cannot lose you. Everything inside of me is tethered to you." He spoke with such raw desperation in his voice, it frightened me. "I do not care to walk this earth without you beside me."

Hot tears ran down my face, and I took a shuddering breath, trying to find the right words. "August. No matter what happens, you will find happiness again. Trust me. This I know for certain."

"What are you talking about?" His voice was a strangled whisper as he cupped my face in his hands, brushing my tears away with his thumb.

"I traveled to you." My words were cut off by the jolt of the iron gate opening.

When, Jezebel? When did you travel to me?" His thoughts pushed through my mind, sharp and frantic.

"Time's up." The guard walked into the cell and placed his arm upon August, who stared at me in shock. "I'm afraid you need to come with me now, Sir."

August's eyes never left mine as he followed the guard towards the door. "You knew this whole time?"

I nodded, walking to the gate which slammed shut in front of me, separating us once more. His hands wound themselves around the cold metal of the bars and I clasped mine over his. "I couldn't bear the thought of telling you. But yes, I have known this fate of mine for some time now."

"Now, Sir!" The guard's voice next to him was brisk and threatening, and August shot him a searing look.

"Fate can be changed, Jezebel," he said, turning to me, his voice full of determination.

I pressed my lips to his fingers before they slowly slipped from me, and the tall, graceful form of him retreated from my sight, leaving me alone once more.

The small church was packed with the suffocating warmth of bodies. The murmur rose in volume as two men escorted me through the doors and up to the wooden stand. With my legs in shackles and my hands bound in front of me by thick rope, I scanned the faces among the crowd for August. The loud knock of a gavel rang through the air, calming the sea of hysteria that had begun to build within the room. The hisses and jeers like a slap against my skin.

"Silence!" The judge's voice rang out. "We are gathered here today to witness the testimony against Jezebel De Sanguine, who stands before us on trial for witchcraft."

The sound of the door bursting open startled the judge's speech as the imposing figure of August stepped into the room. The harsh clip of his boots rang through the silence as he walked to the front of the pews and took a seat beside the stand where I stood. His eyes were somber and filled with a dark intensity that seemed to bring a chill upon the judge who cleared his throat nervously, appearing to instinctively avoid eye contact with him.

"As I was saying, may the first witness step forward."

A short woman rose from the crowd, her white cap obscuring her face as she walked to the front of the room. "I was there that day in the marketplace, Your Honor. I saw with my own eyes the work of the *devil* upon her."

Voices began to whisper to a frantic crescendo. The judge rapped his gavel against the wood to quiet the room once more.

"Next witness, please."

People filed up, one by one. Tales of witchcraft and sorcery spilled from their mouths like poison. Wives accusing me of seducing their husbands in the streets with nothing more than a mere glance. Then a tall thin man stepped forward, blond curls framed his familiar face, his dark eyes filled with the same fear he held when I had crouched beside him as he lay bleeding upon the street.

"Your Honor, this woman..." He pointed to me with misplaced malice born from the wild frenzy of collective suggestion. "Is the devil! And I have been marked by her."

A chorus of frantic shouting assaulted my ears, fingers pointing at me, faces contorted in fear and anger. The insanity hung so thick in the air I felt as if I were going to choke.

"Enough!" August's voice reverberated through the room, bringing a sudden hush upon the crowd. He turned to the judge, piercing him with his gaze. "Let my wife speak now."

The judge nodded and motioned for me to talk.

I stood tall and looked upon the man standing in front of me. "I saved your life, Sir. What you saw, what all of you saw that day..." I swept my hand across the room for emphasis. "Was not the work of the Devil, nor was it witchcraft. I am neither a devil nor a witch. I am a healer. If I had not been there that day, this man standing before us would be dead... You sit here and want to condemn me for saving a man's life? I ask you this as good Puritans. Which is more important to you, the removal of what you do not understand, or the sanctity of human life? Was Jesus not a healer? Who laid his hands upon the ill? Was he not persecuted as well? Do we want to replicate the sins of our ancestors? Or can we rise above our past and start a new understanding here within this New World."

My words settled across the room, quieting the people around me. Some of them looked down upon their lap in shame, other shifted uncomfortably within their seats. Until the raspy voice of an old woman shouted out.

"Lies! All lies. The devil speaks in tongues!"

And I lost them once more to the cacophony of sound. The judge stood among the chaos, demanding order with his mallet pounding uselessly upon the wood. I met the steady gaze of August, everything else falling away around me. His eyes held mine, full of an unfathomable despair that split me in two, and I knew there was no redemption held for me within these walls.

CHAPTER SEVENTEEN

As the judge called a recess to discuss my verdict, I was roughly escorted back to my cell. My life had suddenly been thrust into the weakened hands of ignorant, fearful men, and I swallowed back my anger which threatened to rise, hot and bitter like bile in my throat.

Pacing the cold, stone floor, my thoughts traveled to my mother, a memory suddenly so vivid, it was as if her rich voice was beside me in the darkness of my cell.

"Jezebel, my dear." She had spoken to me in a hushed whisper. "One day you will begin to change, but you must heed caution with your gifts. For people are full of fear and will not understand them." She had been brushing my long red hair by the fire, the flames crackling and hissing beside us. "For centuries, our kind has been accused. The words thrown upon us will change, but the repercussions remain the same."

I found it strangely fitting in a way, that I should suffer the same fate as my parents. For I knew what the verdict was. I had known before it had even begun. Although August had remained hopeful, his grief shrouding his ability to reach out and see what was written upon the future. I feared this fate of mine could not be altered.

* * *

A heavy silence hung in the air of the court room. The rustling of bodies an ominous whisper as I was led back up to the stand. August sat rigid in the pew, his gaze fixed and unmoving upon me. Hope had drained from him, and his eyes swam with a sorrow that seemed to claw desperately at the space between us. The shroud had been thrown back, and I knew that he now saw my fate clearly as well. We were caught and tumbling in a force beyond our control.

"Upon careful consideration of witness testimonies and evidence against Jezebel De Sanguine, this court has found the defendant guilty on charges of witchcraft. She will be sentenced to death by hanging tomorrow morning."

My gut lurched, and everything around me became still for a moment, as if the veil of time had been lifted, illuminating the rudimentary stage on which life was played out; the cast of characters suspended and awaiting their next line.

The gavel rang out, jarring me back to myself, and the rough hands of the guards pulled me away from the stand among the sudden uproar in the room. August remained still as if frozen in shock, tears falling from his eyes like tiny rivers. I clung to the anchor of his gaze as they escorted me down the hall and out the doors.

* * *

Life is a tender shoot emerging from the heavy weight of the earth. When your body perishes, your soul lives on through the memories of others who will weave your stories until the thread eventually frays, leaving nothing but silence behind. It was these things that bound me to the fragile mortality of others. I was no different. We all shared the same transition from life to death, time really having no relevance in the end. It is only the stories we leave behind that give substance to life.

The priest stood before me, offering me up my last rites, purging me of my appointed sins and casting the weighted hand of their fashioned religion upon me. His robes fell around his tall frame, thin white hair throwing shadows against his face as he murmured his hushed incantations.

"May I see my husband now?"

He looked down at me with pity in his cloudy eyes and nodded solemnly before retreating out of the cell and down the hall. He returned with a guard and August in tow.

"Visiting hours are over, but by request of the priest, you have been granted permission." The guard spoke briskly as he opened the door and let August step through.

"We don't have much time," August whispered as he wrapped me up within his warmth, stroking my hair gently as my tears soaked the rough wool of his coat.

"I'm so sorry." Was all that came out of me as I shook against him.

He ran his hands along my back. "Our love transcends all this." He pulled my head up to look at him, brushing his fingers against my cheek. The deep burn of his gaze held me as his mouth found mine, grazing my lips softly at first, then his kiss grew rough and desperate as he pulled me tighter against him.

A broken moan spilled out of me as I feverishly clung to him, my legs growing weak as this grip of shared sorrow molded us into something primal and grasping. I crumpled to the ground, my trembling hands fumbling with his clothes as my heart silently cried out, tangled and frantic.

"*Oh, Jezebel.*" His voice was a deep sigh filled with longing and a torment that sliced through me, leaving a trail of his tears across my lips as he entered me for what I knew would be the very last time.

I curled around him as he filled me up with aching pleasure. Shuddering emotion spilled out, staining my skin as the burning force of him slammed into the very depths of my being. Consumed by an overwhelming despair that grew lustful and raw, we crashed fast and frantic into each other, hard fevered thrusts that left August crying out to me in tangled, disjointed Latin; until all that was left was bittersweet ecstasy ripping us in two. Everything else faded away as we held onto each other as if the very husk of our bodies could merge into something made of wings, transparent and full of light; and for one sublime moment I grew weightless, transcending the cold dark reality of the cell we lay in together.

Grief is a rough animal, tearing at your flesh, but inevitably one must succumb to the burden of it, allowing the soul to sit with the pain that flails in hopeless desperation. The soft breath of realization is a balm upon the wounds. It is cleansing and purifying, a sacred ritual of release.

We lay together beside this beast of grief, our tears mingling upon the flush of our skin as we allowed the delicate, ragged breath of impermanence to settle over us. August's hands softly stroked my hair, his mouth tasting the tears left upon my cheeks.

"This is not over, Jezebel. *I am not letting you go.*" August's voice was a desperate whisper as he ran his finger along my jaw, forcing me to look at him.

But all I could do was sigh and shake my head, my body tender and worn, ready to relinquish this heavy misfortune. I was too tired to fight the inevitability of it any longer. I wrapped my arms around him tightly as the sound of footsteps drew closer to the cell once more, signaling the end of our time together. The door clanked open as August pressed his lips against mine one last time, soft and full of love. A goodbye spoken through skin, before he was yanked away from me.

I tasted the salt of his tears upon me while I lay in the darkness. My fingers hovered over my lips, tracing the remnants of his touch like the ink of a tattoo while the fragility of my existence counted time, awaiting the cruel and mocking light of morning.

* * *

Sleep did not come, nor did I long for it. I paced my cell, trying to find resolution. The last few hours of my life filtered down to the darkness of my confinement.

The echo of voices drew me from the vanquished state of my mind. The clipped tone of a guard that rang out through the hallway.

"You are not to be here at this hour. Leave at once, Sir!"

There was a momentary scuffle, the sound of a body being thrown against the wall, then the gentle and rhythmic tone of a voice I knew all too well, lulling the guard into a state of complacency.

August appeared like a shadow behind the bars of my cell, holding a key in his hand. I ran to him as the gate squeaked open, throwing myself into his arms.

"August." My words spilled out frantically. "What are you doing? You know they will kill you if they catch you."

"I am getting you out of here." He gripped my face in his hands. "I do not care about anything else."

He enfolded me in his warmth, the strength of his arms like a pulse of life coursing through me. My heart fluttered with the tantalizing possibility of escape like a bright spark of promise as August took my hand and ushered me quickly down the dark hallway. *Perhaps this was not my fate after all? What if my travels to August had only been but a warning?*

These thoughts tumbled fervently within me, filling me with courage as we passed the guard on the floor. He watched us walk past with a calm, glazed look in his eyes as he sat slumped against the wall.

The cool night air wrapped itself around my skin as we stepped past another dazed guard slouched by the entrance and slipped out into the darkened street.

August's voice was a whisper in my ear as he led me through the dense thicket of trees. "The ship is ready and waiting for us at the dock. We will take a shortcut through the woods."

With my hand gripped tightly in his, we weaved at a fast pace through the darkness of the forest. The rhythmic pulse of my heart pounding wildly within my chest. Branches snapped beneath our feet as the dizzying taste of freedom burned upon my lips. The sound of the waves as they crashed against the rocks beyond us, called out to me like a vibrant song of hope.

The trees thinned, and the ocean came into view. Moonlight shimmered over the lapping water. August's boat swayed gently in the port, waiting for us, so close; all that was separating me from my fate was a slope of earth leading down to the shoreline.

The sound of many footsteps behind us made my heart freeze, the icy grip of dread suffocating me as hands suddenly grabbed me around the waist, throwing me violently to the ground.

Closing my eyes in defeat, tears slowly slipped down onto the leaves beneath me as the cold metal of a gun pressed against my temple. A voice hissed maliciously in my ear. "Do not move."

I scrambled for footing upon the soft mulch of the earth as I was pulled to my feet. The faceless man from behind grabbed a handful of my hair, yanking my head back forcefully. My eyes fell to August, who stood there surrounded by three other men, their guns raised at him, the metal gleaming like a vicious light against the darkness.

"Sneaky, sneaky." One man spat at August. "Was it you who put a devil's spell on those guards? Shall we hang you along with your wife tomorrow morning?"

"No!" I called out. "It was me, I did it."

August gaped at me, shaking his head with sorrow in his eyes.

"He had nothing to do with this. Let him go."

One of the guards chuckled maliciously. "Oh, but my dear, you see, your husband has been caught aiding and abetting a criminal. That is a very grave offense, one we don't take lightly around here." The man spoke to the guard who held me in his grip with the muzzle of his pistol pressed firmly against my temple. "Take her back to her cell. We will deal with *him.*"

I struggled within his strong hold as the guard pulled me away, my voice coming out in a choked cry. "August!"

I suddenly felt him inside my mind, his words curling gently around my thoughts like a soothing blanket. *"I will be okay. I love you, Jezebel."*

Morning must have arrived, for the sharp clip of boots upon stone indicated that the guards had come for me. They bound my hands tightly and led me silently through the dark hallway. Dragging my feet, I frantically searched the cells, looking for the form of August within one of them. But they lay empty. *What had they done to him?* My heart flooded with the thick wave of crushing dread.

The light hit me with a force as I walked among the streets and into the center of the town square. I could smell the sweet scent of the mayflower plant in the air, indicating that the first push of spring had finally arrived. Trembling rays of sunlight teased my skin, attempting to warm the damp chill of the early morning. These sensations around me felt brutal and mocking as my body coursed with a rising panic, the visceral instinct of my mind's last grapple for survival.

The men led me up to a tall wooden stand. Below me lay the large crowd which had assembled in the center of town. A closed trap door lay beneath my feet, while above me a long plank of wood traveled up and connected to a noose, slowly swaying in the breeze. I was familiar with this contraption that I stood upon, and the press of bodies around me, silently awaiting my execution with a reckless glint in their wide eager eyes. I knew all too well the history of humanity's insistent need to view death as a form of retribution and entertainment.

I desperately scanned the faces before me when I noticed a figure standing away from the crowd, a dark cloak obscuring his features to everyone but me. My heart soared in relief as I locked eyes with August, the steady silence of his presence anchoring me.

The whisper of his voice gently stroked the space within my mind. *"Do not be afraid, Jezebel. Death is not a vanishing but an expansion. Where you are going is to a place of great beauty, and I will forever love you with the very breath of my being."*

The executioner spoke, but I focused only on August, on the unwavering devotion in his eyes which never left mine. His soft and steady presence caressing away the fear as the sudden and familiar tingle began to travel along my skin. I welcomed it with a blissful relief as the weight of the rope descended over my head.

* * *

I stood one last time among the field with the vibrant purple sky. Below me sat a young child, her legs crossed together in the grass, humming a sweet soft song. She looked up at me with familiar blue eyes and my heart stilled. Her dark wavy hair fell in curls upon her shoulders; she looked so much like August it brought tears to my eyes.

"Hello." Her voice was melodic and full of delight. "What's your name?"

I crouched down next to her and placed my hand upon hers. "My name is Jezebel."

A large joyful smile spread across her face. "That's my mommy's name."

"It is?" I joined her on the ground. "And what is your name?"

She picked a flower, a small daisy, and placed it into the open palm of my hand. "My name is Eva."

"It is a pleasure to meet you, Eva."

She began to pluck flowers from the meadow. "I am making daisy chains." She giggled and pointed to the flowers slowly rising from the ground in their place. "Look! They keep growing back."

I smiled at her, soaking in the essence of August's child. My heart was full of hope, for her presence spoke to me of the resiliently beautiful thread of life.

She began to weave the flowers into a circle, her tiny hands working nimbly as we sat side by side in the meadow. She seemed content, full of a radiance that spilled from her, bathing me in a warm glow.

Eva reached over and placed the crown upon my head. "You look like a princess." She sat back as her face suddenly grew pensive. "But why are you so sad?"

I realized tears were falling down my cheeks, and I slowly brushed them away. "I am not sad Eva, I am happy. Happy that I was able to meet you."

She seemed to ponder this for a moment. "I am happy to meet you." Deep fuchsia reflected in the blue of her eyes as she gazed up and pointed. "Look! The sky is turning pink."

I placed my hand gently upon her head. "Eva, I believe it is time for me to go now, but I want to give you something. It is a gift, and one day it will give you the power to travel through dreams and help others."

She eagerly nodded to me, wonder dancing upon the flush of her cheeks as my hands reached out, gently placing the tips of my fingers against her temples. A surge of energy flowed through me like a brilliant spark of life before my body began to tremble and I slowly slipped away from her.

This time, there was no darkness, only a warmth and a light, and I knew then that my flesh no longer held my spirit, but my story would continue.

AWAKEN

PART 3

Rockport, Maine: 2016

CHAPTER ONE

The sound of the waves drifted through the open window of my office as I stood by my desk clearing out my belongings. Rays of sunlight slanted through the room, brushing its warmth across my skin while I carefully placed papers into a box. My hand lingered over the artifacts of my life, now neatly tucked away like a bittersweet conclusion to a story I had spent so long immersing myself in. I always struggled with goodbyes.

"I'm going to miss you." Jules was beside me, crouched on the floor, going through the customer files in the cabinet. "Though I'm happy you are leaving." She grinned up at me. "Being whisked away to some unknown place by a guy who looks like he came out of some nineteenth-century romance novel. I mean seriously, Jezebel." Jules stood, brushing her auburn hair away from her face. "Where did you find this guy? I didn't think they made them like that anymore." She leaned in close to me with an impish grin on her face. "I bet he's incredible in bed."

I shot her an amused smile; Jules had no idea.

"And you're okay with not knowing where he's taking you?" she asked. "It's all very mysterious." She wiggled her fingers mischievously at me.

"I'm looking forward to the surprise."

I ran my hand along the wood of the desk. So many years spent in front of its oak panels, carving out my own self-reliance upon the faded grain of the surface. I was suddenly overwhelmed with the brisk pace in which my life was unfolding.

When August told me that he wanted me to take a blind leap with him, in the moment there had been no hesitation. But the reality of it all began to hit me with a blunt force. Could I dive so fully into the depths of a life unknown?

"Well, I'm super excited about taking over the business. Though

I'm going to have to change the name you know," Jules called over her shoulder with a wink as she walked into the back.

Jules had always been my strongest employee. She was energetically efficient, personable, and great with numbers. A perfect fit for a business owner, and I had no hesitation in selling the business to her. I lifted the box into my arms and followed her into the storeroom.

"Hey, Jules."

She looked up from the scattered mess of cleaning supplies on the floor.

"I'm going to go. I still have to put the rest of my stuff in storage and run a few errands before I meet August at the airport tonight."

Jules nodded and went to pull me into a hug, the box cradled awkwardly between us. "Have fun out there, okay." Pulling back, she gripped my shoulders tightly. "You know, Jezebel, when I found out what really happened between you and my brother, I was honestly pretty ticked off at first." She tilted her head at me with a small smile that softened the edges of her words. "But I understand that the heart can speak much louder than the mind. And I just want you to know that I'm really happy you've found someone who makes you feel so reckless and alive."

A faint chuckle spilled from my mouth. "You think I'm being reckless?"

"Hell, yes you are!" Jules playfully slapped my arm. "And it's the best way to love if you ask me."

* * *

Driving slowly past the pier on the way back from the storage facility, I spotted Raven's trailer sitting along the wharf, the lazy orange light of dusk glinting off its surface like the glow of a beacon. My heart swelled in anticipation of seeing her again as I parked my car beside her trailer and stepped out, hearing a familiar voice call to me from behind.

"So, you are leaving, huh?"

I turned to see Raven barefoot, walking toward me from the beach, her hair tousled by the warm breeze as streaks of silver reflected the light.

"How did you know?"

She winked, her eyes smiling as she wrapped her arms around me, drawing me into her soothing warmth.

"He finally came back for you." Her voice was soft against my hair and tears began to well up within me. Raven pulled back and cupped her hands against my face. "I knew he would."

I nodded, feeling raw and exposed. All my walls had come tumbling down since August's return, and I was unaccustomed to the lightness. "I'm leaving with him tonight. I just wish I had more time to see you."

Raven's soothing green eyes rested on me. "Don't worry. We will see each other again. This, I know for certain."

I realized in that moment that it was my mother she reminded me of most. The gentleness in her gaze and the wisdom in her words made me want to curl up like a child within her arms; to share with her all the things I never had a chance to speak of to my own mother.

"Do you love him, Jezebel?"

"*Yes*, so much it scares me."

"Good." Raven brushed a stray tear from my cheek. "You are about to embark on a bold new life. No longer are you living within the boundaries of your mind. When you live from your heart, there can be no mistakes, only endless opportunities for growth." She stretched her arm out toward the ocean. "This is my favorite time of day. What do you say we take a walk?"

I nodded as Raven took my hand, leading me down to the beach as the shimmering colors of fading light danced upon the water, bathing our skin in pastel hues of peach and violet. Raven took a deep breath and let it out in one long sigh. "You know, when I was younger, I used to believe that romantic love was only the ego's journey, sent to distract us from really being able to sit with ourselves."

The wind picked up for a moment, blowing her hair wildly about.

"But I realized that it's in fact quite the opposite." Her eyes met mine, filled with a tenderness that wrapped me in a reverent silence. "It is the soul's journey, one that forces you to open yourself up and view the world from a different perspective. Only then, can you truly see yourself."

Biting my lip, I stared out into the ocean. "But what if you don't like what you see sometimes?"

"Ah." She chuckled, stopping to rest her hand on my shoulder. "That is the great challenge of love, and one that most of us run from. But if you learn to face your own reflection in the eyes of another, the debris falls away, and what is left behind is beautiful and filled with infinite possibilities."

My heart fluttered with excitement at the thought of what lay in store for me and August. But at the same time, the pull of insecurity smirked at me from the shadows like a persistent taunt. I only hoped I had the strength to resist it.

We stood along the shore, watching as the soft indentations of our footprints became swallowed up by the endless churning renewal of the sea. A whispered reminder of the delicate impermanence of life.

* * *

My steps echoed against the walls of the empty apartment as I walked to the front door with my bags in hand. It always shocked me to hear that hollow sound with all the emptiness staring back at me. I had poured so much of my life into this space. Now it lay vacant, as if I had never been there at all. I flipped off the light switch, enfolding the room in darkness, and closed the door for the last time.

The taxi took me out through the sleepy streets and onto the long stretch of highway that wound its way beside the water. Rolling my window down, the warm salty breeze of the ocean hit my skin like a soothing caress. I was going to miss this sleepy little town. It had taken me in when I was broken and bruised, nursed me with a calm and steady hand. But now that renewal coursed through my veins with a new life bearing fruit, I was ready to say goodbye.

* * *

The lights of the tarmac blinked their rhythmic code as I stared out the window of Barnstable's tiny airport, my bags sitting by my feet as I waited for August. The room was quiet. Only a few people sat in the faded blue chairs around me, tucked into themselves, their phones illuminating their faces in a soft glow. A murmured hush filled the air, punctuated only by brief announcements over the intercom. There was a rustle of fabric beside me, and August lightly touched my shoulder. "Are you ready, Jezebel?"

I nodded as he grabbed my bags and took my hand, guiding me through the terminal, past the waiting gates, and through a set of double doors that led out to the tarmac.

"Where are we going?" I asked with confusion. "I thought we were getting on a plane?"

"We are," August said, flashing me a wide smile and pointing over to a small jet which sat waiting for us on the runway.

I stared at him incredulously. "Jesus, August. You never told me you had a private plane?"

A playful smirk spread across his face. "Well, you never asked."

With August's hand on the small of my back, I climbed up the steps, my heart fluttering with excitement. "So, what other secrets are you keeping from me?" I asked as I settled into the seat beside him, clipping the seatbelt around my waist.

August shot me a mischievous wink. "You will just have to wait and see."

The plane began to move along the runway, gently gathering speed until it lifted into the air, causing my head to rush with the sudden weightlessness. I gazed out the window, watching as the winking lights of the tiny coastal towns below me grew smaller until there was nothing but an endless stretch of dark-blue sea. I gripped August's hand in mine as my heart swelled with an elation so acute it caused my pulse to race. Wherever he was taking me, I was willing to jump.

* * *

The soft hum of the small plane lulled me into a drifting contentment. August's hand rested on my knee, gently stroking me every so often with his thumb while his other hand turned the pages of the book that was nestled in his lap. I leaned in closer, catching the trace of his alluring scent, which always reminded me of the comforting aroma of pine needles when you rubbed them between your fingers.

"What are you reading?"

He glanced over at me. Dark tendrils of his hair brushed against his forehead. The blue of his eyes never failed to startle me. The luminescent hue of them a vivid contrast against dim lighting.

"The House of The Dead, Siberian Exile Under the Tsars."

I grimaced and playfully poked his arm. "Sounds like a fun read."

He chuckled and shot me a lighthearted smile. "I don't read for entertainment. I read for knowledge." August tucked his book into the front pocket of the seat and pulled me against him.

I leaned my head against his shoulder. "Do I at least get a hint on where you are taking me in this fancy little plane of yours?"

"Hmm..." He twirled my hair between his fingers and pressed his lips against my forehead. "Close your eyes and imagine a place where the richness of a fruit can evoke relaxation."

I looked up at him. "Are we going to a winery?"

He gave me a teasing smile. "Close."

"A vineyard?"

August nodded. "That is all I'm giving you for now."

Through the window of the plane, we watched the sun rise above the curved horizon of the skyline, a brilliant orange spilling out upon a pallet of dark blue sky. The clouds beneath us were like rippled waves, reminding me of the ocean. My eyes began to feel heavy, and I sunk into a dreamless slumber, gliding above the earth on weighted wings.

* * *

The moan of the engine's descent and the sudden shift in altitude jarred me from my sleep. I opened my eyes to find August gazing at me.

"Did you sleep well?" His hand gently caressed my thigh and rested there.

Smiling at him, I moved to stretch my cramped limbs. "As well as I can on a plane."

"We are about to land."

I looked out the window to see a long river snaking its way through green pastures dotted with trees.

"That, down there," August leaned close to me, "is the Tiber river."

I looked at him quizzically as excitement built within my chest. "Where are we?"

The sun streamed in through the window and lit up his eyes. They appeared to shimmer, like light reflecting on water. "We are in Italy, Jezebel."

CHAPTER TWO

I leaned back against the seat of the rental car and watched the bright glow of the moon follow the curve of the road. Suspended against the night sky, I could make out the outline of trees and the dips of valleys in the distance, like brushstrokes against a canvas. I rolled the window down and breathed in the lush scent of the evening, an intoxicating blend of rich soil and fragrant wildflowers.

"We are almost there, *Amore mio.*"

I smiled at the affectionate term August had begun to use with me as his hand slid across the seat and came to rest upon mine, giving it a squeeze. My body hummed with a mixture of exhaustion and elation. After twelve hours of travel, I was just as eager for a bed as I was to find out where he was taking me.

August took a sudden right-hand turn onto a bumpy dirt road. The car bounced over the ruts as we slowly made our way up a steep incline. Through a dense thicket of trees engulfed in bright moonlight, an impressive stone building came into view. Ivy clung to the walls, trailing delicately up to a terra-cotta tiled roof.

He rolled the car to an abrupt stop. The quiet that filtered in through the open window was soothing. Nothing but the ticking of the engine cooling down and the melodic chorus of crickets surrounded me as August stepped out of the car and around to my side, opening the door with a playful flourish.

"Your villa awaits you, my lady." His warm hand grabbed hold of mine, helping me out of the car. Rolling hills surrounded the estate, cradling the large stretch of vineyard below us. A cobbled stone pathway led down to an endless sea of grapevines bathed in vivid moonlight. The view was breathtaking.

"It's so beautiful."

August's arms wrapped around my waist from behind, placing a kiss upon my neck. "This was my family's old vineyard."

I turned to him. "You grew up here?"

He nodded slowly. "Granted, there wasn't much left of the original building when I acquired it almost a century ago, and I have spent the last fifty years coaxing the vineyard back to life. But yes, this is my home." August reached up to brush aside a lock of unruly hair from my face. "And I would love nothing more than for it to be yours as well, Jezebel."

My heart delicately unfurled in disbelief as I took in all that he was offering me. It was almost too much to hold. Tears welled up, threatening to spill down my cheeks as I sought the warmth of his kiss. "You make me feel like Cinderella," I whispered against his lips.

August pulled away with a chuckle and gave me a playful wink. "No more scrubbing floors for you, Princess." He took my hand and proceeded to lead me down an arched walkway where tangled vines hugged the wooden trellises suspended above us. "Let us go inside. You look exhausted." We stopped beside an old oak door, the hinges creaking in protest as he opened it to reveal a spacious room with high vaulted ceilings. August flicked on a switch and the house flooded with light.

My shoes clicked against the marbled floors as I surveyed the space before me. Large, curved, plated glass windows overlooked the vineyards. The living room held a huge stone fireplace, accentuated by a Persian rug of intricate burgundy-hued design. A red velvet couch and two matching chairs faced the hearth. The interior reminded me of a European country cottage, albeit much larger. I stepped toward the windows, pushing my hand upon the glass, and found that it opened without resistance. Night air rushed in, the rich scent of lavender engulfing my senses. "This place is like a dream."

"Come upstairs, I want to show you something," August said, placing his hand against the small of my back. I turned to follow him up a wooden spiral staircase and onto the second floor. A hallway led to three rooms. He opened the last door at the end, standing in the entryway while I stepped into the room. Slanted ceilings met a wall of windows overlooking the vineyard. An empty table and shelves lined the other wall. "I was thinking this would make a great studio for you."

I turned to August and wrapped my arms around him, breathing in his delicious familiar scent; my joy a swift rising emotion longing to take flight.

His hand gently caressed my chin, drawing my face up to his. "You have a gift, Jezebel, and I want to provide you the environment in which you can further cultivate your art."

I ran my hands through his hair, so swept away by his thoughtful gesture and this beautiful place he had brought me to. I was overwhelmed and enchanted; my heart bursting with the bright promise of a life with him.

"Thank you. For everything. *For all of this.*"

* * *

Shadows from the moonlight played upon August's face while he lay on the bed, watching me as I shed my clothes and slipped under the soft white cotton sheets. I drew my body close to his. I was no longer tired as the electric pulse of his bare skin collided against mine, the warmth of his breath in my ear.

"Do you want to know where I was when I left, Jezebel?"

I sought out his eyes among the dancing silhouettes that fluttered across the room. "Yes, I do."

"I was here, grappling with the apparitions of my past. You see, this place does not hold the warmest of memories for me, but no longer do I want to live with these old ghosts beside me. I am ready to relinquish them; to make room for new memories."

I pulled him closer to me. His name tumbled from my lips and rested softly against his skin as his hands trailed through my hair.

"You have breathed new life into the dark spaces within me, *Jezebel.*"

His words moved me, like a beautiful offering laid at my feet. I ran my hands down his chest and then wrapped my leg over his waist, sliding myself on top of him. His lips eagerly responded to my kiss. Gripping my thighs tightly, his desire grew beneath me, and he let out a deep moan as I slid him inside, filling myself up with his heat.

"God, you are so amazing." His words came out in a tangled groan as I began to rock my hips slowly against him. A surge of pleasure consumed me as his hands slid down my back and pulled me closer, thrusting himself deeper inside. I arched my neck and with my hand, drew his mouth against it. I wanted to feel all of him inside me.

"*Embrace me.*"

He hesitated, his teeth lightly grazing across my skin. The tantalizing and familiar sensation of sharpness that gave me goosebumps.

August's voice was a tremble against my neck. "You do know that making love to you while Embracing is almost too much for me to handle?"

"Please." I moaned, moving more frantically against him.

With a soft growl, he sunk his teeth deep into me. The overwhelming orgasm that took hold of my body as he began to draw out my essence was so intense that I must have startled him with my cry. He slowly withdrew for a moment, seeking out my eyes in the darkness.

"Don't stop."

August grabbed me around the waist and suddenly flipped me over onto my back, plunging himself deep into me while his mouth found my neck once more, drawing out my pleasure, and obliterating my senses. His body, possessed by desire, pinned me to the bed as he began to shudder against me, releasing himself as he took my face in his hands. His gaze burned deep into my depths as he climaxed, riding the last feverish wave with me. A sudden powerful silence overcame us in that moment as I fell into the intensity of his gaze, nothing but our labored breath filling the room, our bodies perfectly entangled. A rush of euphoria so strong rose within my chest, and a choking sob spilled out; overcome by him and all the naked beauty he extracted from me.

August pulled me closer to him as emotion consumed me. His voice was a tender whisper in my ear. "*You feel that,* don't you?" His fingers brushed away my tears, and that is when I saw his own, sliding down his cheeks. "This is love, Jezebel."

* * *

Morning caressed my face with its delicate warmth. The sound of birds filled the room as I opened my eyes to a light that bathed my skin in a luminescent glow. August lay beside me, his gaze resting over my body. I placed my hand upon his chest, lightly stroking downward.

"Do you enjoy watching me sleep?"

He smiled and tangled his fingers in my hair. "Yes, very much so. Do you know how often I have watched you sleep? All those times when you would come to me and fill me with such longing." His hand moved to run down the slope of my back, his eyes full of fervor. "How much I yearned for you, Jezebel. It consumed me."

I rolled myself on top of him. My lips found his chest, my tongue teasing his nipple. "Yearned? You speak in past tense."

August pulled me tight against him, a deep chuckle spilling out. "Yearning is the overwhelming desire for something not immediately attainable to you."

I continued my slow journey down his skin. "So, what did you do with all this yearning?"

"You really want to know?" I looked up to find a suggestive look on August's face. "I did what any man would do in my situation."

I raised my eyebrow at him. "Are you saying you would touch yourself?"

"After you would leave, yes. I would touch myself."

The thought of August doing this sent an erotic rush of desire through me. "And you would think of me?"

"Of course," his voice was silky and full of longing.

"Show me." I slid the sheets past his hips and moved his hand down to where he lay erect. "Show me how you would touch yourself."

"Are we feeling salacious this morning?" A seductive smile crept upon his face.

"Yes," I replied breathlessly.

Heat bloomed within me as he began to stroke himself, his hand sliding slowly up and down his length. His eyes burned into me, full of a heavy longing that made me ache inside. His breath grew labored, and a deep moan escaped him as his strokes quickened, all the while never breaking his gaze. My fingers slid up my thighs, parting the coils of my hair and into the slickness of my sex, gently rubbing myself in time with him.

"Oh god, *Jezebel!*" August cried out as his body tensed and contracted in front of me. I watched him as he lost himself to his climax, releasing himself against his hand, his milky seed spilling out in-between his fingers. I was flushed and panting as I slipped my fingers deeper inside, feeling the hot rush of my own orgasm building within, until I collapsed against his chest with a loud moan.

We lay together among the sheets, suspended in stillness as we watched the rays of the sun dance across the vineyard from the open window. A warm breeze filtered in every so often, ruffling my hair.

"I'm so glad that you are here."

I pulled August tighter against me. "So am I."

Trailing his hand softly along my arm, he traced patterns against my skin. "I meant what I said last night."

I looked up at him. "About love?"

"Yes." He leaned in, placing a tender kiss upon my lips. "*I love you*, Jezebel."

My heart soared as his words solidified all that encompassed me. "I love you too."

He ran his finger across my lips, his eyes twinkling. "I know."

Taking his finger into my mouth, I bit down playfully. "Don't get cocky with me, August."

Grinning, he rolled me over onto my back, pulling the sheet up over us. "So, you are a biter? I was not aware of that."

"Must be something we have in common," I said, shooting him an amused look.

"Oh, you're *funny*, Jezebel." August chuckled as he drew me into his arms, encapsulating me in the filaments of soft cotton and muted light that merged with the gentle, hushed rhythm of our breath.

CHAPTER THREE

The car hummed along the road. Warm air rushed in through the open windows as I watched the gentle glide of the hills bend and ripple in the sunlight. The landscape was lush and enveloping, invoking inspiration, and I longed to lose myself in clay once more.

August rested his hand over mine, slipping into my thoughts. "I am taking you to this really wonderful shop in Rome, it has all the art supplies you need."

I turned to him with a soft smile. "And then we can make a day of it."

"Of course." He glanced over at me with a twinkle in his eye. "Rome is your oyster, Jezebel."

* * *

Surrounded by a foreign language, Rome transfixed me with its antique stone and marbled archways as twisted pines towered above us like peculiar, misplaced sentinels. We spent the day walking among the narrow streets. The scent of cannoli and coffee drifted through the open cafes as August showed me around. We stopped by the Trevi fountain, a stunning baroque sculpture which towered above multiple cascading rivers of water, spilling out into a large pool. Its depths glittered with coins. He took me to see the staggering beauty of the Coliseum; its rich history preserved within the ancient limestone. We meandered through Vatican City, where the impressive curvature of St. Peter's Basilica loomed above us. There was a mythical timelessness about Rome, that despite its crowds of hungry tourists armed with cameras; I fell instantly in love.

The sun had slowly sunk beneath the buildings, showering the cobblestones in pastel hues that danced with the lengthened shadows of the day as we walked arm in arm through the streets. Faint notes of music floated through the open doorways.

"This is the time when the city comes alive."

"Really?" I threaded my fingers through his, gazing out toward the Tiber river as the streetlights flickered on, reflecting off the water in bands of shimmering color.

"Yes." August shot me a playful wink. "Romans love to celebrate the night."

I stopped to lean against the railings of a footbridge as the glow of evening slipped over us. Pulling August close to me, I reached up to run my fingers across the light stubble that had begun to grow along his jawline. "Do you feel like dancing tonight?"

He raised an eyebrow at me. "What do you have in mind, Jezebel?"

"I don't know, let's go see what we can find."

Grabbing his hand, I dragged him enthusiastically down the street, weaving through a narrow alleyway. We brushed past a family, a beautiful woman with skin the color of caramel and a baby at her breast. A man walked beside her with two young boys in tow, their youthful squeals of laughter echoing off the bricks. I turned for a moment, watching them as they blended into the city streets and disappeared from my line of sight.

Something churned within me, a longing for a family I realized I may never have. I knew that August was not capable of giving me a child, and I had accepted that. But I still could not push away the sudden ache in my chest. Faint tears hovered just below the surface, and I blinked them back, not wanting to expose the delicate truth which had abruptly tumbled to the surface, unannounced and full of longing. *I wanted to be a mother.*

"Jezebel. What's wrong?" August's hand fell on my back, noticing my sudden shift.

I gave him a small smile, attempting to regain my composure with the gentle sweep of my hand. "Oh, it's just that family we passed. They looked really sweet."

August stopped walking and pulled me closer, cupping my face tenderly in his hands. "I am sorry I am unable to give you that." His eyes searched mine, full of a remorse that curled heavily beneath his gaze. "The last thing I ever want is for you to give up something that is important to you."

I ran my hand down his chest, resting it over the strident beat of his heart. "I'm not. *You* are important to me, August. You are what I want."

August's face was filled with a sudden sorrow. "But is it enough, Jezebel?"

I nodded. "You are already more than I ever thought possible." Locking eyes with him, a silence washed over us, filled with the tangled breath of love's compromise.

"Do you ever think about what it would be like if you hadn't lost your child?" The question crept out of me, cautious and delicate, breaking the stillness between us.

August sighed and glanced up at the darkened sky, which trembled with the faint light of stars above us. "Every day, Jezebel."

I squeezed his hand and drew him close to me, resting my head on his shoulder as we continued walking. The somber mood that had settled over us was broken by the infectious pulse of percussion and horn. My heart stirred in excitement as the familiar sound threaded through an open doorway and I pulled August closer to it.

"Salsa club?" He peered into the dimly lit room, a flicker of reluctance washing over his face as he took in the flashing lights and the forms of bodies moving at a feverish pace across the dance floor.

"Something tells me you're not much of a clubber?" I grinned playfully at him.

Bending down, he placed a kiss upon my neck, lightly nipping at the skin and causing a shiver to slide down my back. "No, I am not. But for you, I will always make an exception."

With his hand at my hip, I led him down the stairs and into the club, my body humming with the rich notes that rolled through me like liquid, igniting that flame in my gut; the one I had not felt in years.

We made our way through the press of moving bodies and over to the bar where I rested my arms against the shiny metal countertop.

"What would you like to drink, *Amore mio?*" His breath was warm in my ear.

"Surprise me."

August nodded and signaled for the bartender, bending over the counter, and speaking to him in Italian.

A tall glass slid toward me, and I took a sip; cool mint glided against my tongue, punctuated by notes of lime. August sat beside me, his fingers trailing over the light condensation on his glass of whiskey as he glanced around, taking in the flashy sequined dresses of the woman as they were whipped across the room by their partners. Moving closer to him, I spoke into his ear. "I take it you've never danced salsa before?"

August shot me a mischievous look. "Oh, I never said that."

He suddenly grabbed me around the waist and swung me onto the dancefloor. His movements were fluid and graceful. My feet struggled to remember the steps and to keep up with him as he twirled me across the room, taking the lead. Eventually, I found my pace, and we glided together; sensual and effortless. It had been so long since I had danced like this.

Laughter bubbled from my mouth, effervescent and full of an energy that made me feel buoyant. "Jesus, August. Is there anything you can't do?"

He slowed his pace for a moment, pulling me tight against him as his hand snaked slowly up my thigh, his fingers teasing my skin through the light fabric of my skirt. "Sing. I happen to be a terrible singer, Jezebel." With a wide grin, he twirled me out before drawing me close once more. "Oh, and I do not know how to ride a bike."

"Can't ride a bike, huh?" I shot him a playful smile. "*That* I have to see."

August chuckled. "I fear it would not end well." His fingers lightly rested against my lips, his eyes pulling me into his depths as the room fell away around me. "And when did you get so good at salsa?"

Memories flooded me as I recalled that young girl fresh out of high school, dropping into classes, hoping to still the restlessness within her. "I took lessons years ago, back when I lived in Boston."

August dipped me slowly, his hands seductively running down the length of my back as his lips trailed up my neck, hovering against my ear. "Well then, we will definitely have to go out dancing more often."

The lights flickered around us as the music grew louder, drowning out our words until all that remained was vibrant rhythmic sound, and the feel of him as he lithely guided me across the floor. I allowed all else to slip away, losing myself to a dance that our bodies both knew; limbs entangled like a language spoken through the heat of our skin.

The days wove themselves into a seamless dream-like state. I spent much of my time outside, tending to the vineyards with August. We would work alongside each other while the insistent ring of cicadas filled the mid-afternoon air, and the hot Mediterranean sun beat against my back; turning my skin a light golden brown. When the heat of the day became too much, I would retreat to the cool shadows of the house and slip upstairs into my studio.

My hands moved across the clay, dipping my fingers every so often into the bowl of water beside me, turning the sensation into silk against my skin. I glanced out the window to see August below, walking among the vineyards with the sloping gait of a dog following behind him like a shadow.

The dog had shown up at the house a few weeks before, a scrawny, timid little thing with wiry hair and a limp in his back leg; his sad brown eyes watching us from the shadows of the foliage in the courtyard. I had begun to leave scraps outside on the front porch for him and within days he was following us around everywhere. We called him Amico, the Italian word for friend.

The sound of the door shutting downstairs jarred me from my focus. The soft muffled tones of August's voice followed by the click of Amico's toenails on the marbled tile filtered in through the floorboards beneath me. I stared at the sculpture I was working on, a woman heavy with child, her arms wrapped around her belly; eyes closed with a look of serenity upon her face. Ever sense our night together in Rome, I had been having dreams of being pregnant, and when I awoke, I was always filled with a foolish sense of hope; as if the very act of dreaming could bring forth a child.

I sighed and stood to stretch my body. From the open window, I looked out to the horizon, growing soft with color. The air smelled sweet as the ripening of grapes on the vine mixed with wet earth enveloped the room around me.

I found August in the kitchen, the rich aroma of sautéed onions filling the room. "What are you making?" I rose on tiptoes to plant a kiss on the back of his neck; he smelled of earth and sunshine. A cold wet nose touched my leg, and I looked down to find Amico standing beside me. Bending down, I rubbed the tawny scruff around his neck.

"Linguini with shrimp." He gave me a warm smile as he tossed some vegetables into the pan.

The loud sizzle startled Amico, causing him to dart suddenly into the living room. I leaned against the counter and watched August. Our days outside had turned his olive complexion a deep shade of brown, and his windblown hair fell in tousled waves against his cheekbones. He had long ago traded his finely pressed suits for casual slacks and linen shirts, which he always wore rolled up, showing the muscular width of his arms, the fine hairs bleached by the sun. He looked rugged and earthy, and I suddenly wanted to skip dinner.

"Why does watching you cook always turn me on?"

August chuckled and shot me a playful wink. "Perhaps it is because you desire a man who knows how to satisfy your appetite."

"In more ways than one," I added with a seductive smile, walking over to the cupboard, and grabbing a wine glass from the top shelf. The deep red cesanese del piglio trickled into my glass, a twenty-year-old vintage wine I had found in the cellar the day before. The lush fragrance of oak and chocolate filled my senses as I took a sip.

"So, I have a business meeting out in New York with the Metropolitan Museum of Art in a few days."

I stared at him. "How is it that I didn't know you worked for them?" It occurred to me that there was so much I still didn't know about August. While he had slowly let me into the intimate spaces of his heart, there were still hidden rooms, places he would go on occasion; times when his eyes would become distant, a million miles away from me.

"I don't work for them so much as I work *with* them," August replied, taking a sip of wine from his glass. "I provide a lot of their arts' funding."

"And all these funds of yours." I swept my arm out toward the window, the gathering dusk obscuring the view. "I can't imagine the vineyard alone makes up for all this money you have."

He gave a small smile and wiped his hands on a dish towel, crossing the room to where I stood and placing his hands on my waist. "Hundreds of years of merchant trade have helped, as well as the invention of the stock market. Money is a dance, and once you learn the moves, it can flow quite effortlessly for you." He placed his lips against my ear, his breath sending tingles along my spine. "Would you like to come with me?"

A part of me did, while another part was itching to finish my sculpture. I felt that if I left the piece half-finished, I would lose my momentum. August looked at me. "You want to stay, don't you?"

I nodded and wrapped my arms around his shoulders. "I love it so much here; I don't want to leave." I smiled up at him teasingly. "Plus, I think I could use some time without distraction."

August leaned down and playfully nipped at my neck, his voice a deep chuckle. "Oh, I'm sorry. Have I become a distraction for you?" His fingers inched themselves up my shirt, lightly grazing my breasts, which felt swollen and ached beneath his touch.

I let out a breathless laugh as his lips trailed down my chest. "A little, yes."

August gently backed me against the counter, his breath hot in my ear while his hands trailed down my stomach and into the waistband of my skirt. "I suppose I will just have to stop distracting you so much then." He teased me with his fingers, which slipped themselves downward and brushed against my underwear, inciting a warm rush of desire to course through me.

"Please don't." I moaned, pulling him closer to me and arching my hips against his hand, wanting more; I always wanted more with him. Suddenly, the faint tinge of smoke filled the air. "*August,*" I gasped as his fingers slipped their way into me. "The food is burning."

Releasing me, he moved to turn off the burner, holding the pan with the charred remains of our dinner. "I hope you weren't terribly hungry?" he asked, walking over to me with a sheepish smile and setting the pan on the counter.

"No," I said, laughing as I pulled him to me. "I wasn't really in the mood for dinner, anyway."

"Oh good," August said with a playful grin as he lifted me up onto the counter, his lips falling against my neck while his hands tangled in my hair.

I stood out in the driveway while August's taxi idled behind us. Early morning dew hovered on the grass and the sky was just beginning to spread her colors across the landscape.

"I'm going to miss you."

August bent down and placed a soft, lingering kiss upon my lips. "I will be back in a few days."

I watched as he disappeared down the slope of the valley, the taxi leaving behind a trail of dust. Looking down, I found Amico standing beside me. "Well, it looks like it's just you and me now, buddy." And with a gentle click of my tongue, he followed me back into the house.

That afternoon, I tried to focus on my sculpture, but a persistent wave of nausea clawed at me. Retreating down to the kitchen to find something to settle my stomach, I wondered what it was I could have eaten the night before? Or if I was possibly coming down with something? Not finding anything helpful in the kitchen, I grabbed the car keys off the counter and headed out the door.

Marcillina was a twenty-minute drive through the open countryside, nestled on the gentle slope of a hill. Lining the quaint, narrow cobblestone streets were small shops tucked into old stone buildings. Parking the car, I ducked into a market looking for ginger. I walked through the produce section, running my hand over the vibrant array of fruit neatly displayed in wicker baskets and placing a few that caught my eye into my cart. As I continued down the aisles, I stopped in front of the feminine products, and a jolt washed over me as I suddenly realized that I had not had my period this month.

I glanced over the narrow boxes of the home pregnancy tests, the optimistic pink script staring at me like a question. Though I knew it couldn't be possible, I found myself placing one into my cart anyway before trailing to the checkout line.

Back at the house, my heart stilled and a rush of disbelief washed over me as I stood in the bathroom and stared down at the white stick suspended on the counter, watching as two faint but decipherable lines appeared.

CHAPTER FOUR

I spent the next few days gulping down copious amounts of ginger tea, trying to quell my morning sickness. The bathroom sink was littered with tests, all of them staring up at me with their various forms of positive results, double lines, plus signs and even a few digital ones with the word 'pregnant' flickering in black letters upon the display.

The same question kept running through my mind on an endless loop. *How is this even possible?* August had clearly explained why I would be unable to have a child with him. The composition of our blood was inherently different, making conception impossible between us. But what if it wasn't so different? Another thought pressed against me, obscure but unrelenting nonetheless; *could this have something to do with his wife?* Had she somehow given me more than just her name?

Full of disbelief, my hand slid down to my belly as I stared at my reflection in the mirror, envisioning myself growing ample with life; with the delicate movement of a child within me. My heart quickened as these thoughts swirled around me like a beautiful, buried dream, suddenly unearthed and full of promise. Filled with an overwhelming wonder, the sharp sting of tears pressed against my eyes.

* * *

The days passed. Suspended in a state of languid elation I eagerly awaited August's return. Though we had spoken on the phone, I wanted to tell him in person. So I carried this secret within me, curled tight like the beautiful bud of a flower, longing to awaken itself to the sun.

Sunlight streamed in through the bedroom window as I placed one of the tests upon August's pillow like a clandestine surprise. The frantic barking of Amico startled me, and I looked out the window to see a car making its way up the steep driveway. My heart leapt, and I rushed down the stairs, my eagerness to greet August like that of a child on Christmas morning.

I watched him as he stepped out of the taxi and turned to pay the driver, chuckling over some shared joke between them as Amico excitedly darted in between his legs. Then his arms were around me, strong and solid, pulling me so effortlessly into the space that belonged to him alone. I breathed in the musk of his skin, his suit smelling of travel, the faint remnants of airports and coffee.

"How was the trip?" I asked, nuzzling against his neck.

August led me into the house, shutting the door behind us. "It was long, but productive." Bending down, he drew me into a heavy kiss, pressing me up against the door. "*God*, how I missed you." His words sent deep brushstrokes of desire sweeping up my limbs as his hands slipped slowly down to my waist, grasping me firmly. That was when I noticed a small purple bruise on his neck. I tentatively reached my fingers up to touch it.

"What's this from?"

August looked down at me, discomfort flickering across his face for a moment. "I believe that knowing the answer to that will not serve you in any way right now."

"What the hell is that supposed to mean?" My voice grew sharp, and I gripped his shoulders tightly.

He pulled himself away, moving to the kitchen to pour himself a glass of water from the tap.

"August. *Tell me.*" I stood rigid in the doorway with my arms crossed, watching him.

"I suppose it was from someone who apparently got a little too carried away during an Embrace."

"You were with a woman on your trip?" My heart began to accelerate, its frantic pulse like a muffled rush in my ears.

The calm look August gave me was unnerving. "Yes. I was with a woman."

His words hit me like a punch to my gut, and a wave of nausea overcame me.

Moving closer to me, his voice grew soft. "I thought I had explained this, Jezebel?" He reached out to cup my face, his thumb slowly stroking down my cheek. "I do not want to risk depleting you, and I want the occasional Embrace to be an intimate part of deepening our connection together, not a necessity I need to fill. I will no longer take from you in that way. You mean so much more to me than that."

I yanked myself away from his touch. Though his words were filled with tenderness, the sharp pang of jealousy curled around me, and venom coated my tongue. "I am very curious as to why you didn't heal that little love bite of yours? Do you get off on flaunting your escapades?"

August sighed, giving me a tired look. "Honestly, I did not know it was there. But even if I did, I would not hide it from you."

"Oh really?" Glaring at him, the space between us suddenly felt heavy and endless. "What about all those times you went into town? Were you just going there to fuck around with women?"

"Jezebel." August's eyes grew steely. "I do not fuck around."

"Bullshit!" I spat at him. "Why can't you just go to a blood bank or something and get your fill there? Why does an Embrace have to be so damn *sexual* with you!"

"Have I not explained the process of how this works clearly enough? It is not the blood I need; it is the energy held within it, which is only accessed through arousal and orgasm." I could detect a wave of frustration flicker across his face as he spoke.

"Can't you find another way? This just feels so sleazy to me."

"Sleazy?" August shot me an amused look. "Well, you certainly didn't seem to think so back when you would come to me."

"*Fuck you.*" My words were like bullets, aiming at him.

He shook his head, his face growing hard while a darkness

255

gathered in his eyes. "Jealousy is not a pretty color on you, Jezebel. The biggest mistake one can make is when they try and shackle love."

"Oh! So, I'm shackling you now! Go to hell!" I whirled away from him and stormed out the door, slamming it behind me. Tears obscured my vision as I stumbled into the vineyard. My emotions vacillated between dejection and anger, and my heart painfully constricted as I realized that there would always be a divide between us. Places I could never go with him, things we would never share together. I sunk down among the grapevines and let the tears flow down my face as the soft mulch of the ground beneath me stained my knees with dirt.

I heard the crunch of twigs and looked up to see August walking toward me, his hands held out in a gesture of defeat. "I am sorry, Jezebel. I am unaccustomed to this."

I snorted, furiously brushing the tears from my cheeks. "Unaccustomed to what, *August*?"

He furrowed his brow, a look of confusion etched deeply upon his face. "To the intensity of these negative emotions between us."

A morose chuckle escaped me, my voice dripping with sarcasm. "It's called having a fight. You're telling me you never had one with your wife?"

August shook his head at me. "No, we never fought." He crouched down and took my hand in his, squeezing softly. "The ceremony of marriage between us involved a sharing of our essence. When one's essence is shared with another, communication and understanding flow freely, and there is no longer any separation between two people."

Tears welled within me once more, and I choked back the lump in my throat. "That's just it. I want that with you."

"I do as well." His hand reached out to wipe a stray tear that had gathered beneath my eye. "The last thing I ever want to do is hurt you, and I know that this reality between us is going to be hard for you to adjust to." His eyes searched mine, the faint glint of tears dancing within. "I believe I may not have handled myself very eloquently back there. This is all new territory for me as well. You see, my wife and I, we always Embraced Givers together."

Glancing up into the bottomless blue of the afternoon sky, I drew in a deep shuddering breath. As much as I had accepted the ghost of his wife who silently sat beside us, it still hurt to hear him speak of her; to know that what they must have shared together transcended anything I could offer him.

"Jezebel." He reached out and softly took my chin, drawing me into the vibrant depths of his gaze. "Please do not go there."

"Reading my mind again?" I smirked.

"No, I am reading your energy." Tangling his fingers into my hair, he drew me close to him. "I do not want insecurity to come between us. You have *all of me.*"

Ensnared in emotions I could barely define; my voice came out breathless. "You promise?"

August placed the warmth of his lips upon my forehead, his voice a soothing whisper against my skin. "I promise." Trailing his fingers down my cheek, he pierced me with a questioning look. "Would it help if you were a part of the Embrace somehow?"

I stared at him in surprise. "What, like a threesome?"

August shook his head. "Not exactly, but I suppose in a way you could call it that, since it would be a sharing of intimacy between multiple people. Do you think that is something you would possibly be open to?"

My mouth pulled itself into an uneasy smile. Although unsure as to what that would entail, being with August had opened my mind to things I had never thought imaginable.

"Maybe. I'll have to think about it."

August nodded as he stood and reached his hand down, lifting me onto my feet and into the warmth of his arms. I clung to him as everything drained from me, the tangled weight of my emotions dissipating into the air around us, leaving a momentary lightness behind.

Tipping my head back, he ran his thumb along my jaw line. His eyes heavy. "I want you to know that you do not shackle me. You deeply fulfill me, in ways I never thought I could feel again, and in ways I have *never felt before.* My love for you engulfs me, Jezebel."

His words surrounded me in warmth as I found his lips. His hands ran down my back, drawing me closer to him, and causing my breath to hitch in my throat as his mouth pressed softly against my neck. "You encompass all my desire, *Amore mio.*" August's voice was a husky growl against my skin, causing a deep burning ache to bloom within me.

I pulled him to the ground. A sudden longing for him taking over as I feverishly unbuttoned his pants, wanting somehow to claim him for my own, to obliterate all the tangled differences that crept between us.

"*Jezebel.*" My name was a soft exhale as August rolled me onto my back with a groan, the cool mud squelching underneath us as his hands devoured my skin.

His eyes flashed with a heat that made my head swim as he plunged himself inside me, bringing forth an impassioned cry that tumbled from my lips. My entire body surged with pleasure as he touched my depths, releasing me from the confinements of myself as we fell against the places hidden, allowing our bodies to articulate all the things unsaid. The rich scent of wet earth clung to our skin as we grappled and collided into each other with an urgent hunger, his thrusts fervent and untamed like a wild animal as the sky spun above us, reckless and untethered.

* * *

We bounded up the stairs and into the bathroom together, peeling off our mud-soaked clothes and stepping into the soothing warmth of the shower. Rivulets of earth ran down my skin and into the drain below. My body was engulfed in steam and in the silky feel of August's hands as he tenderly lathered me with soap, slowly sliding up my curves and gently pulling out bits of dried leaves from my hair. I closed my eyes and rested my head against the shower wall, sinking into the leisurely feel of his touch as he tended to me like something exquisite and treasured.

I was in the bathroom toweling off when August appeared fully clothed in the doorway. In his hand, he held the test I had left on his pillow, a look of confusion and shock written across his face.

"What is this, Jezebel?"

CHAPTER FIVE

I wrapped the towel around me and stepped closer to August. Taking his hand, I placed it onto the soft curve of my belly. "I'm pregnant."

His brow furrowed. "I do not understand how that is possible."

I shook my head. "I don't understand either. But I took about a hundred home pregnancy tests and apparently, I am very much pregnant."

"But what would compel you to buy such a thing?" He looked shellshocked, his hand frozen on my stomach.

"The day you left, I started to feel a little queasy, so I went into town looking for something to settle my stomach. I picked up one on impulse when I realized I hadn't had my period this month."

"Why didn't you tell me this sooner, Jezebel?"

"I wanted to surprise you?" I looked up at him with a tentative smile, drawing him closer. His hands felt stiff as they settled on my back. "We just got a bit derailed when you came home."

"Yes, we did." August's eyes were distant, and I struggled to read the emotion hovering within him as a sharp wave of panic coursed through me.

"August? You don't seem very happy about this."

He stepped away from me, running his hands through his hair. "I'm not quite sure what to feel right now." He shot me a look as a faint sliver of discomfort pierced the depths of his eyes. "Are you absolutely sure it is mine?"

"Jesus Christ, August. Of course, it's yours!" I stared at him in disbelief. This was not going the way I had imagined it. I had envisioned him being elated, a bit shocked, but happy. Instead he just stood there with a wide-eyed glazed look.

He took me by the shoulders, gripping me tightly. "Please forgive me. I need a moment." Releasing me, he walked down the hallway until all I could hear was the steady thump of his feet on the stairs and then the click of the front door closing.

In a state of stunned confusion, I made my way into our bedroom, watching out the window as the form of August came into view. He strode at a fast pace through the vineyards and over the hill, with Amico bounding after him. I lay myself upon the bed. Tears formed at the corners of my eyes once more, slipping in a lazy trail down my cheeks. So many emotions from this afternoon had ripped away at me, leaving me raw and shaky. The blow up in the kitchen, our fevered lovemaking in the vineyard, and now this. Fear coiled in my gut at the thought of him not wanting to have this child with me. Had I been a fool to assume otherwise? How much did I really know about August and the kind of life he wanted?

These questions tore into me with a relentless grip, and I curled myself deep into the blankets, allowing the full force of my tears to consume me. I wept until the heaviness of my own spent emotions finally succumbed to exhaustion, and then to the weightless hold of sleep.

* * *

A gentle hand on my back startled me awake. The room was dark and through the open window, I could hear a chorus of crickets in the distance. August slipped underneath the covers beside me and pulled me close, the warmth of his breath fanning the back of my neck. The cool night air clung to his clothes, chilling my skin as his hand trailed down to my abdomen.

"There is nothing I want more than to have this child with you, Jezebel."

I realized I had been holding my breath, and I released it in one long sigh, turning over to face him in the pale shadowed light of the room. "Then why did you run off like that?"

August sighed and moved to tenderly cup my face. "The night I burned the house, when my wife came to me in that dream. She had placed a tiny seed in my hand." His fingers delicately stroked my temple. "She said it was time to start a new life." August's eyes filled with marvel as his hand trailed back down to my belly, softly running his palm against it. "It is only now that I am fully able to grasp the depth of her gesture."

"So, what are you saying? That you think she had something to do with this?"

"Yes. I believe so. Though the reasoning behind how it is even possible escapes me. This world is mysterious and incomprehensible, and we are only vessels, Jezebel."

I sat up and pulled my legs to my chest, gazing out the window. The full moon had begun her slow ascent into the night sky as if she were heavy with her own child growing within; perfectly round and swollen with light, bathing the hills in an ethereal glow.

"Why didn't you share all of this with me earlier? You just froze on me, August."

His hand reached for mine in the darkness, the warmth of his touch curling between my fingers. "I am sorry. I needed time to process everything. In that moment, the weight and meaning of it overwhelmed me. The idea of a child holds memories of pain for me as well, the heavy grief my wife and I carried together. It is one that never leaves you."

I gave his hand a gentle squeeze, watching as a cool breeze slipped through the windows and played with his hair. I searched out his eyes in the dim light. "I'm so sorry you lost your child."

August pulled me close to him, reaching up and threading his fingers through my tangled strands. "I never thought I would be given this opportunity again." A fervent joy danced within his gaze as his lips pressed against mine, his voice soft and full of reverence. "Such an incredible miracle this is, Jezebel."

I sat in my studio, the hum of summer filtering in through the window. My fingers trailed down the length of the clay, molding the rounded paws of the sculpture I was working on. August rapped gently on the door, waiting for my response before he entered. His warm hands fell upon my shoulders then ran down my back, his touch pulling out the tension within my muscles.

"Is that a bear I see?"

I turned to him, grabbing a cloth from the table, and wiping the clay from my hands. "Yes, it came to me in a dream recently."

August pulled up a stool next to me, taking in the rounded form halfway to completion. "You know the Native Americans believed that when a bear came to you in a dream, it meant that you were to become a healer."

"Really?"

"Yes. Bear medicine is powerful. It represents strength and the ability to transform oneself."

"And what do you dream about?"

He looked at me, the sunlight reflecting on his face, illuminating the haunting blue of his eyes. "I dream of the wild places within myself, tangled jungles- deep canyons and the ocean. A raven is always there, watching me; my dream companion in a way, reminding me of the vastness of thought, I suppose."

Goosebumps ran along my skin as he spoke, remembering the sculpture I had started long ago, before I met him; the raven with the penetrating gaze that had haunted my dreams for weeks.

August stood up and walked to the corner of the room where my work sat displayed on a shelf. He picked up the sculpture of the pregnant woman I had just finished, running his fingers down the swell of her belly. "When was it that you began to sculpt?"

"It was right after my accident. An art teacher of mine thought it would be a good outlet."

August nodded. "Smart teacher."

He held up my sculpture, his face full of wonder. "But does it ever occur to you, Jezebel, that you may in fact be a channeler?"

"What do you mean?"

August walked back to where I sat, cradling the woman in his hands. "You sculpt images that mainly come from your dreams, correct?"

I nodded, my eyes resting on the woman in August's hands.

"Our dreams are more than just our mind's subconscious meanderings. They hold keys to our future as well. When you are able to observe them closely, they can in turn become predictions. We all have this ability within us. You sculpt what you dream, therefore you are putting conscious intent into that energy."

"So, are you saying that my dreams can predict the future? Or that I am able to manifest the future from my dreams?"

August ran his hand up my arm, moving to brush away a strand of hair from my face. "For you, I think it may be a little of both."

My hands fell to where that faint flutter of life swam within me, musing over the potential. "Do you think this child will be born like you?"

August knelt in front of me, cupping the gentle rise of my stomach in his hands, his eyes full of veneration. "I honestly don't know. Only time will give us those answers."

* * *

That evening I found August in the kitchen gazing pensively out the window. Wrapping my arms around him, I rested my head against his back.

"What are you thinking about?"

He turned to me, coiling his fingers deep into my hair as he brushed his lips lightly across mine. "I will be needing to Embrace soon."

His eyes burned into me with the unspoken question that had been hovering between us for days now. I pulled away from him, seeking solace in the darkness outside.

"I don't think I can do it, August. I don't think I can watch you with another woman."

He sighed, a look of disappointment gathering. "I had a feeling you were going to say that."

Moving close to him, I trailed my hand down his arm. "Why can't you just Embrace *me* this time?"

August shook his head as his hand went to rest gently on my stomach. "At this point, I fear it may deplete our child, and I do not want to risk putting any stress on you or the baby."

"You think something would happen to our child if you Embraced me?"

A flicker of sorrow flashed across the surface of his features. "Yes. The child may become weakened, which would potentially compromise this pregnancy." August reached up to cup my face, tenderly running his thumb along my cheek. "I have already lost a child once, and I cannot bear the thought of something happening to this one."

I nodded, understanding the heavy implications as my heart sank and my insecurity gathered like dark clouds upon the horizon of my mind, obscuring the sunlight between us. There was no way around this barricade. I had to find a way to accept this as part of who he was, but I didn't know if I had the fortitude. Tears of frustration welled up inside, and I allowed them to trickle down my cheeks, bathing my skin with the bitterness of my confliction.

"Jezebel." August's words came out choked as he caught my tears with his fingers. "What is it that you fear will happen when I Embrace another?"

"I don't know. I guess the thought of you getting pleasure from someone else..." Taking a deep breath, I fumbled with the buttons on his shirt, trying to find the words. "It makes me feel like I'm losing you somehow."

August gripped my arms, pulling me tightly against him. His voice in my ear was somber and filled with fervent intensity. "The pleasure for me is an arrangement born from necessity. It is only *you* who stir the embers of my desire." His hands cupped my face, his eyes blazing with that fire of his that always managed to burn away my reservations. "You and no one else. You cannot lose me, Jezebel, for my heart is bound to you. How can I make you understand this?" His breath was warm against my cheek as he softly brushed away the remnants of my tears. "Embracing another is not something I choose to do."

"I know." I tangled my fingers in his hair, allowing the heaviness within me to step aside, making room for the tentative footsteps of acceptance to enter.

August pressed his forehead against mine, his eyes pleading. "I want there to be nothing but transparency between us."

My words became a long sigh as he enfolded me in the sincerity of his reassurance. "*Me too.*"

October came, and with it, the crisp autumn mornings which wove themselves around the vineyard, coating the grapes in a fine layer of frost. The leaves in the vineyard had turned a golden russet shade. It was the time of *vendemmia*, the grape harvest. Workers from town would arrive in the early morning, their hands deftly cutting away at the bunches of grapes and placing them into woven baskets. I accompanied them in the vineyards with August. The rich scent of ripe fruit mingled with earth, filling my senses as I cradled the deep purple clusters in my arms.

Sunlight warmed my back as I worked, listening to the melodious cadence of the men speaking in Italian around me. I loved their language, which was filled with such emotion and intensity; it was as if they bared the depths of their souls with every lush syllable.

Dew still clung to the leaves, catching the rays of sun like tiny prisms of light which scattered against my fingertips as August stood beside me, loading grapes into the large basket between us.

"When I was a boy, this place was my refuge." He turned to me as he spoke, his face full of an emotion that appeared tangled and overgrown but longing to be released. "I used to hide here among the vines, allowing myself to disappear until all that was left was the hush of the wind against the leaves, soothing me like a lullaby."

August's words carried a heavy sadness that pulled at me. "What were you hiding from?"

"My father." His eyes grew dark for a moment as he reached out to pluck a strand of grapes, cupping the rip fruit gently in his palm.

I didn't want to press; I knew I was not the only one who stood beside childhood memories that were painful and hard to share. I only hoped in time he would let them out of their locked cage for me. I placed my hand on his arm, rousing him from his thoughts. "I'm sorry you had to hide from your own father."

"We all end up hiding from something at one point in our lives. It is what you find while doing so that makes the experience meaningful."

"And, what did you find?"

A smile pulled at the corners of his mouth, his eyes spilling into me with a warm light. "I found my own peace. A place I could reach for when the world around me grew too loud."

I sighed, allowing his words to settle over me. All the years I spent desperately running from my own pain, only to find that it sat beside me the whole time, quietly waiting for a chance to speak. "I wonder if I have found that place?"

"Yes, I believe so, *Amore mio*" August pulled me to him, resting my back against his chest, his breath like a warm caress in my ear. "It has always been inside you."

The sudden sound of geese overhead cascaded down through the valley, calling out to one another in their wild, sorrowful melody. I tilted my head up and watched the rhythmic movement of their formation glide across the sky. A stillness washed over us as August's hands delicately ran over the swell of my belly, his touch reverent and deep; paying homage to the place where life grew patiently within.

* * *

Sitting beside the warm crackle of the evening fire, my feet rested in August's lap. His hands gently pulled out the tension as my lips hovered over the steam rising from my tea. A soft rap upon the front door jostled the comfortable silence between us.

"Let me get that," August said, shooting me a smile as he rose from the couch and strode over to the door to answer.

"Klyda. It is so good to see you. Please come in."

I turned my head to see a tall woman standing in our doorway. Long black hair framed skin the color of porcelain. She had an enchanting, haunting beauty about her and the way she looked at August made my heart lurch within my chest. They stood there for a moment, hands clasped tightly together, seeming to gaze at one another in a sort of silent reverence, as if they were speaking without words.

"Who is this, August?" My voice broke the intense stillness between them and Klyda's dark, ocher eyes fell on me.

"And this must be Jezebel." She swept past August and crossed the room to where I sat beside the fire. Bending down, she took my hands in hers; they were cool and incredibly soft, like silk. The faint, spicey scent of amber drifted around her. "It is such an honor to meet you at last. August has spoken so deeply of you."

"Jezebel, this is Klyda. She is the midwife we talked about."

Rising from the couch, I gave her a hesitant smile. "It's nice to meet you as well."

Klyda gestured toward the stairs. "Why don't we go upstairs? You can make yourself comfortable, and I can see how that baby of yours is doing."

I nodded as she shot me a look filled with warmth, allowing her to lead me up to the bedroom.

I sat perched against pillows on the bed, while Klyda slowly ran her stethoscope down the taut rise of my stomach, listening for the rhythmic murmur of the heartbeat within.

"The child is strong." Her gaze fell on me. "I do not foresee any complications with this pregnancy."

"How can you tell, just by hearing the heartbeat?" I pulled myself up to a more comfortable sitting position as the child shifted lightly inside me, like a delicate flutter. I had begun to feel these gentle movements more frequently, and they always brought on a profound sense of awe.

"I am a veil lifter, Jezebel. I can see beyond the physical dimensions that separate us. Kind of like a human x-ray." She winked at me.

"How long have you known August?" I tentatively asked, placing my hand over the swell of my belly.

"A very long time." Klyda's eyes flickered with an emotion I could not place as she moved to tuck her stethoscope back into her bag. "I must admit though, I was extremely surprised when he contacted me regarding your pregnancy." Her tone was serious as her eyes pierced mine, seemingly full of questions. "Being able to conceive like this has been historically unheard of."

I glanced down at my fingers as they tentatively ran across the bedspread. A rising defensiveness washed over me as I wondered if she was implying that I was lying about the child being his. "Yes, August has told me all this."

Her hand reached over to rest on my knee, giving it a light squeeze. "Jezebel. I know this child has been created by the love between you two." Her eyes grew soft, distilling my discomfort. "When August's wife traveled to others, she always left a gift of some sort for them. It is no surprise to me that she would leave August with the greatest gift of all, the ability to give you a child."

I looked up to see a smile spreading across her face, filling me with a warmth born from hope and the rich promise of new life.

"Would you like to know the gender?"

"Yes, I would." My words came out in a breathless rush of anticipation.

Klyda's eyes twinkled as she leaned in close to me, speaking in a whisper as if this knowledge were a delicately beautiful secret between the two of us.

"This child will be a girl."

* * *

I lay in bed with August while his lips trailed lazily from the sensitive peak of my nipples, down to the slope of my belly. He suddenly stopped and rose to meet my eyes. "No, Jezebel. Klyda and I were never lovers."

"August!" I slapped his arm playfully. "Stop reading my mind."

He chuckled as he bent down to nibble playfully at my ear. "I am sorry. But I know the question has been eating away at you, though you did not want to ask." His eyes were teasing as he spoke. "Why you insist on tormenting yourself, I will never know."

"So, what is the story between you two then?"

August settled himself beside me, his fingers gently sweeping through the strands of my hair. "We have been close friends for many years. She required my assistance long ago, and in turn, helped me when I needed it the most."

"Well, she's very beautiful." I raised my eyebrow at him. "I'm surprised nothing ever happened between you two?"

"She never stirred my soul, Jezebel."

"Really? And why is that?"

August sighed as his hand slid down and rested gently on the curve of my lower back. "I feel many things for Klyda, respect and admiration being high on the list. But does one ever really know what it is that makes our soul long to dance with another? To feel an emotion that is so raw, it makes you want to weep."

"Like what you felt with your wife?"

August's eyes flashed with a sudden sorrow, and I instantly regretted the question which had tumbled out unguarded from my mouth. I could not seem to shake the notion that I would always be living in the shadow of a woman I knew I could never measure up to. And the familiar claws of insecurity gripped me once more, desperately seeking the validation of his love.

August leveled me with his gaze, his voice becoming a smokey whisper. "It is *you* that overwhelms me with emotion, Jezebel. It is the reason I left, and why I returned." His fingers trailed down my cheek, resting lightly on my lips. "My wife will always have a place in my heart that I carry reverently within me. But there is no comparison. She was a part of my past, while you and this child..." His hand slipped down to cup the taught rise of my stomach, gently tracing over my skin. "You and this child are my future."

August's lips met mine, his kiss like an electric current as he wrapped me up in his arms, stilling my trembling thoughts and caressing the delicate spaces within me. My heart reached out for him, warm and open, ready for whatever the future had waiting for us.

CHAPTER SIX

L ate winter crept across the valley like a wet grey blanket. Through the living room window, the vineyard stood bare below me, rows of tangled limbs shrouded in misty rainfall, tolerantly awaiting spring's verdant growth. The silence that descended upon the land was full of a quiet longing that pulled at me.

I was large and heavy now, my stomach stretched wide and unyielding. Lines traversed along my belly, reminiscent of a road map that no amount of creams helped diminish. The child inside tumbled and kicked, keeping me up at night with her nocturnal ballet. I marveled at her strength and incessant movement, like a tiny boxer enamored with her own limbs.

I shuffled to the couch and eased myself down onto the plush cushions. The sound of rain on the tile roof was a steady and lulling melody. Amico's head suddenly appeared on what was left of my lap, his weepy brown eyes imploring me for a pet. I patted the space next to me, and he eagerly jumped up, circling twice before he curled into himself and settled against me with a contented sigh. I picked up one of the books that lay scattered in front of me on the coffee table, entitled "The Eternal City: The History of Rome." August had introduced me to the world of history and politics. He was an avid reader, and our bookshelves were crammed full of knowledge that I had begun to devour with rapidly growing enthusiasm.

The sound of the front door shutting sent Amico scrambling to greet August, his paws skidding across the marble floor. I looked up from my book, shooting him a wry smile. "Did you enjoy yourself?"

August watched me from the doorway, his hair wet and curling from the rain. "You know I do not do this for my own pleasure."

"Whatever. Just please, go take a shower first." I waved him off with a quick flick of my hand before glancing back down to my book. He stood there for a moment in tense silence, I could feel his eyes resting on me before he turned from the room. The steady sound of his footsteps filled the silence as he retreated up the stairs, followed by the gentle rush of water running through the pipes.

Though I had given August the green light to Embrace others, I found myself growing more reproachful of his frequent trips outside the house. I tried to accept this reality as best I could, knowing that this was just a part of who he was, a small compromise in our strangely unique, but incredibly satisfying relationship together. I wanted to believe that our love was enough to slake the jealous beast within me, but it was stronger than I gave it credit for, and I could not stop the resentment that slipped out whenever he came back from an Embrace.

With a heavy sigh, I pulled myself up from the couch, slowly making my way up the stairs. I paused in the doorway to the spare bedroom which now held a crib, a changing table, and other various implements of childlike delight. Over the crib hung a mobile made of crystal stars I had picked up at a craft fair in town. When it caught the light, it sent a dazzling array of fragmented color across the room.

The door to the bathroom opened, and steam billowed out as August emerged in the hallway with a towel wrapped around his waist, droplets of water running down his bare chest. He looked at me blankly. "Is this better?"

I shook my head and moved toward him. He stared down at me as I reached up to place my hand on his chest. "You know, I never used to consider myself a jealous person."

"Well, Jezebel. You are." His voice was clipped as he stepped past me and into the bedroom.

His words stung, and I grappled around for a retort but could find none. I followed him into the room and eased myself down onto the bed. "You're mad?"

August turned to me, the blue of his eyes flashing. "No, I am not mad, Jezebel. I am just *tired*. Tired of wondering what mood you are going to be in when I get home."

I stared at him as a rush of hot anger coiled around me. "*What mood*? What mood do you expect me to be in? Jesus Christ, I'm carrying your child, and you are off Embracing other women!"

The silence that fell between us felt sharp as pain flickered across his features. August ran his hand roughly through his hair. His voice choked. "Jezebel, *please*. I understand that we are navigating a delicate situation between us. But I did offer for you to be a part of this because I would prefer it if you were. I want nothing more than to be able to share this experience with you, but you declined."

I grabbed his hand as he moved past me, my anger dissipating as quickly as it came. These emotions within me vacillated like waves, pulling me under and spitting me out again. "I know, we discussed this. I'm sorry. I just wish I didn't have to share you with anyone else."

He bent down on the floor beside me, a sudden look of tenderness softening his features. "Do not *ever* be sorry for having feelings that are valid. I want you to know that I am yours, that when I touch another woman, it is only you I am thinking of." August smoothed my hair back, gently tucking a strand behind my ear. "What can I do to make this easier for you?"

The unclothed proximity of him caused a delicate flutter inside me, and I found my eyes trailing downward. "Jezebel." August cupped my chin, a teasing look in his eye. "Focus, please."

"I can't right now." I pulled him onto the bed, and with one stroke of my hand down the length of his back, he responded and grow erect before me. I didn't know if it was the pregnancy, or the fact that he always seemed to possess a potent, carnal energy that radiated off him after an Embrace, but I suddenly needed to reclaim the distance that loomed above us.

"You are deflecting right now, and you know I cannot say no to you," he said with a groan.

"Then don't." My voice came out in a tangled gasp as I slipped off my pants and straddled him. The feel of him inside was an acute shock of pleasure that made my eyes roll back, filling me until there was no room for anything else in my head. I needed him to annihilate all the insecurities that hissed in my ear as if the very act of making love could rectify the barriers between us.

August remained passive underneath me for a moment, regarding me with a measured look. "I think we need to talk about this." He clutched my arms tightly, struggling with his composure as I began to rock slowly against him. "*Jezebel.*" My name spilled out in a disjointed moan as he suddenly gripped my hips and plunged himself deeper into me. "*My God*, you drive me so crazy."

We became lost in one another. A blur of skin, lips, and heavy desire as all the compromises and resolutions we could have spoken fell around us like shattered intentions. There was nothing left but our bodies, the miracle of our child within me, and the soft flush of our souls trembling beneath it all.

It was in these moments with him that everything else slipped away, and my grappling ego retreated as the heavy magnitude of who he was engulfed every fragment of my being. The essence of him spilled into me like an ancient power that I desperately clung to, wrapping me up within the dazzling chords that wove us so intrinsically together.

Spring came hesitantly. The sun teased the hills like a flirtatious kiss as the bloom of life delicately awakened from winter's languid sleep. The first push of the crocus dotted the landscape beneath my feet, peeking itself up through the soil; a vivid purple against the darkness of earth.

I walked among the grape vines with August beside me and Amico joyfully bounding ahead, the white of his tail flashing as he weaved in between the rows.

"So, I know you don't speak about your family very much." My words came out hesitantly. "But I would really like to know the story of this place."

Glancing up at him, I ran my hands over the heavy swell of my belly, feeling the sudden tight clench in my uterus, followed by the faint pulse of a cramp gathering within. These mild contractions had been happening for days; my body gently informing me that labor was close at hand.

August sighed, his eyes flickering with a sadness as he looked out across the meadow. "I suppose my sorrow has not aged in the way I hoped it would. Growing up among the dark shadow of my father's anger and the frigidity of my mother's neglect did not bode well on my psyche. And I was very much still a child when I left this place, never speaking to my parents again. When I heard of their passing over a century ago, that is when I returned to restore the house, with the hopes of flushing out the tangled memories."

"And have you?"

He took my hand, threading his fingers through mine. "I have, though there are many things I wish I could have spoken to them, so many years wasted while they tucked themselves away behind the doors of their own private misery. I only hope they found some peace in the end."

"I'm so sorry, August." I could see the burdensome weight of remorse gathering in his eyes, but the complexity of his past only seemed to solidify that endless strength he carried within him.

"Regret is a bitter medicine, but my parents taught me a valuable lesson."

"And what is that?"

August stopped walking and turned to me, swiping a strand of hair away from my face. "That anger, resentment, and fear is like a prison without a door. As long as you live within those walls, there is no escape, and one will never find redemption within its enclosure."

"Sounds like your parents were as flawed as the rest of us." I smiled wanly at him. "But there are many different types of prisons we enclose ourselves in. Maybe we build these walls so that we can then learn how to tear them down."

August's gaze rested thoughtfully on me, taking in my words as his hands slid up my arms, giving them a light squeeze. "You may be right about that, *Amore mio*. For what is life without challenge?"

A sudden rush of warm water spilled from within me, sliding down my legs and trickling onto the ground beneath my feet. I sucked in a deep breath, filled with surprise as the reality of what was happening settled around me.

"Jezebel?" Concern momentarily flashed across his face. "Are you all right?"

"Yes." I looked up at him, my heart stirring with excitement as the reflection of the sky danced in his eyes. "My water just broke."

* * *

The soft hush of evening light filtered through the windows as I paced around the house, my breath keeping time with the strong grip of contractions that had begun to cascade through my body.

The door opened and Klyda walked in, setting her bag of instruments down on the living room floor. Beside her lay the makeshift bed August had set up for the birth with pillows arranged next to the roaring fire, reminiscent of a cozy nest.

"When did your contractions start, Jezebel?" Klyda's warm hands rested on the flush of my skin, her eyes scanning my belly to determine where the child lay inside.

"They started about an hour ago." I sucked in a deep breath as another wave of pain hit me; this time stronger than the one before, eliciting a low groan from deep within.

"Good. She is anterior. Right where we want her to be." Klyda moved to her bag, retrieved her stethoscope, and placed a sheet over the couch, motioning for me to lie down. The cool metal of the instrument slid down my stomach as she listened to the heartbeat. "The child is doing well, and it appears as if your contractions are about eight minutes apart. So, we may have some time here." Her smile was like a warm, maternal blanket, easing the feeling of anxiety that had begun to creep up on me. Slipping on a pair of gloves, she gently raised my robe. "I'm going to check you for dilation now."

I turned my head and met August's gaze as he sat beside the fire, calmly watching me with a look of adoration in his eyes. The sudden snap of Klyda removing her gloves jarred me from our silent moment.

"You are at about six centimeters, which means you are getting close to active labor." She stood up from the couch and nodded to August. "I will give you two some privacy, but I will be in the other room if you need me."

Time passed in hazy fragments as the contractions grew more intense and closer together. Klyda urged me to walk, so I paced from the kitchen to the living room while Amico trailed behind. His wide eyes full of concern while his soft whimpers filled the silence between my own. When I grew tired of walking, August held me against him while I rocked and moaned beside the fire, sweat gathering on my skin while the gentle press of his hands upon my lower back calmed the tight band of pain ripping through me.

Every so often Klyda would materialize, checking vitals and dilation with a calm and steady hand while August's comforting voice tethered me.

* * *

Klyda bent down beside us, the coolness of her touch like a soothing balm against the heat of my skin. "You are at ten centimeters. I believe it is time."

August smoothed back my damp hair, his eyes full of anticipation as he leaned me against the sturdy hold of his chest and took my hands tightly in his. My entire body shook with a visceral force that stilled my breath and left me trembling as I rode the next contraction. I bared down, feeling the agonizing stretch of my body as it opened up to the violent rush of life inside. Every fiber within me screamed as I collapsed against August, panting, and covered in sweat.

"I can't...." I gasped, my words broken and frantic. "I don't think I can do this." The sharp blade of fear pressed against my throat as I began to panic. The overwhelming magnitude of the pain was so raw, it clawed at the very fiber of my being.

August anchored me with his loving gaze. "You are already doing this," he ardently whispered. "This is only the mind telling you otherwise. Your strength is beside you. I can see it, and it is *so* beautiful." His soft kisses upon my brow became a gentle guide as my body prepared for the next surge within me. I knew I was no longer in control; the pulse of life had taken over.

The light from the fire shimmered across Klyda's face in a dreamlike ripple as she hovered above us. "You are *very close*, Jezebel. Are you ready to meet your child?"

A loud primal wail like that of a wild animal erupted from deep inside me as the next contraction hit with such force it was as if my entire body was going to be split in two. I closed my eyes, surrendering myself to the depths, allowing it to carry me away until there was nothing left but the rigorous beating of my heart.

Suddenly the pain receded, and was replaced by a rush of pleasure so acute it caused me to gasp in shock as the confusing but delicious relief of an orgasm cascaded through me, erasing all my discomfort and replacing it with the sweet kiss of ecstasy. Moaning in abandon, I clung tightly to August, who filled me with his elated smile, his eyes glistening as he spoke in a hushed tone of reverence. *"You are tapping into the divine essence."*

Tears streamed down my face as our child slid out of me and into Klyda's waiting arms, the sharp sound of her tiny cry filling the room with life's fervent gasp.

CHAPTER SEVEN

I gazed down at the beauty of our child in my arms, her eyes a shocking blue against dark coils of wet hair. August cradled me from behind. His hands tenderly stroking her face. Aside from her one cry as she had slipped out of me, she was silent and full of wonder, gazing around the room and then back to our faces as if putting all the pieces of this strange world together with striking clarity.

August wept beside me with an unrestrained joy, moving me to tears as well. I drew the soft bud of her mouth to my breast, a primal pull emanating from deep within me as she latched instantly and began to draw out the milk. Her tiny hands curled themselves into fists as she suckled.

Klyda had quietly let herself out while we laid together among the blankets by the fire. I was suspended in a dream-like state of elation and exhaustion. Nestled against August, I held our sleeping child. I marveled at her perfection, at the beautiful gift of life that we had been given; and so, we named her *Eva*.

Spring lazily stretched herself into the lengthened breath of summer. The air smelled of lavender once more, and dappled sunlight fell upon the grapes ripening on the vines; the lush green of their leaves swaying softly in the breeze. Time was no longer measured by days or months, but by the playful sparkle of Eva's smile, the lively delight of her first laugh, and the brightness of wonder in her eyes. She was a contented, joyful child and seldom cried.

I had taken my sculpting out to the patio while Eva laid on a blanket in the grass beside me. Her face was turned upward as she stared into the blue of the sky, her hands reaching out as if trying to grab the white plume of clouds above her. I was continuously startled by the sharp precision of her gaze. Just like her father, her eyes held a depth that mesmerized me.

August emerged from the vineyards. His skin was warmed from the sun and smelled of earth as he bent down to place a kiss upon my cheek before scooping Eva up into his arms. He began to sing to her in the rich soothing cadence of Italian, which brought forth a toothless smile from Eva. She reached up to wrap her fingers around his hair, pulling him closer to her.

"You're a liar, you know." I grinned at August as he glanced over at me with a questioning look.

"And what exactly have I lied about, Jezebel?"

I waved my hand at him playfully. "You actually can sing."

He chuckled. "I worry your judge of that may be slightly biased, my dear."

"Perhaps a little." Leaning back with a smile, I watched them together. The sun silhouetted their bodies in a cascade of light that spilled out against the backdrop of lush green hills. Everything felt so complete, and my heart swelled as I was suddenly overcome with such intense happiness. I had a family again. The raw beauty of this notion blossomed before me like a delicate dream, one I never imagined could exist, until now.

My thoughts were stirred by the sound of the phone beside me buzzing, and I glanced down to see Raven's name flash upon the screen. August's breath fell against my ear as he leaned in close to me.

"You should take that. I will put Eva down for a nap."

I nodded, brushing my lips against his cheek before moving to answer the phone.

"Jezebel." Raven's chipper voice spilled through the speaker. In the background I could hear the faint call of seagulls and the muted crash of waves in the distance. It pulled forth a heavy nostalgia, and I realized how much I missed the moody expansiveness of the ocean.

"How's motherhood treating you these days?"

"Like a dream. I don't think the hormones have worn off yet."

"Well, ride that wave as long as you can." She let out a laugh. "I do hope I get to meet this girl of yours soon."

"Me too." I smiled languidly as I watched August retreat into the house with Eva nestled against his shoulder, the soft blue of her eyes heavy with sleep. "She's *so* beautiful, Raven."

"I bet she is. I have been meaning to ask you how the labor went? I didn't get a chance last time we spoke."

Slipping off my shoes, I buried my toes into the grass, the sensation like a cool, luxuriant caress against my skin. "It was actually amazing."

"Really?"

"Yes, during labor, right before Eva came out, I had a..." I trailed off for a moment, my cheeks growing warm.

Raven faintly chuckled on the other end. "You had an ecstatic birth, Jezebel."

"Is that what that was?"

"Yes, though uncommon, they are possible when you harness the ability to tap into your life essence."

"My life essence?" I suddenly recalled August saying something related to that during the birth, but I had been in such an elevated state, it hadn't fully registered at the time.

"Yes. I'm sure August has explained this to you on some level. But this essence is what we all come from. Our life begins with an orgasm. And the energy held within one is more powerful than we know. It has the ability to heal and transcend, and it is why we chase after it so fervently, for it is the closest we will ever come to divinity."

My eyes gazed out into the distance, watching as the sunlight bathed the hills in an effervescent glow. "Do you think that's why an Embrace feels so powerful?"

"Yes, I believe so." Raven paused for a moment as if allowing room for my thoughts to settle around me. "You see, an Embrace is not just the sharing of your essence, it is the uncovering of it. A sacred exchange with the incredible potential to transform."

Raven's words stirred the embers within me as I realized the truth of what she spoke. Not only had August pulled forth a love that expanded me, but he had opened a door as well. His Embrace had always been much more to me than a carnal dive into pleasure, and I understood why now. It was a gentle invitation of self-discovery, allowing the quiet whisperings of healing to take root.

* * *

That evening, I stood over Eva's crib, watching her sleep. Moonlight bathed her room in blue tones as her delicate eyelids fluttered to the rhythm of her dreams, her chubby limbs splayed out like a starfish. August came up behind me, wrapping his arms around my waist, his breath warm against my ear. "What do you think she is dreaming about?"

"Probably nursing."

My response caused a deep chuckle from him as he slid his hands up to my breasts, cupping them lightly. His thumb grazed over my nipple, causing a light trickle of milk to seep through my shirt. "Yes, a voracious eater our little Eva is."

"August, do you think something is wrong with her?"

August stopped his exploring hands, letting them fall to my waist. "What do you mean?"

"She never cries." I turned to him; a faint trace of worry caught in my voice. "She's a baby. Babies are supposed to cry."

"Oh, Jezebel." He reached up to cup my cheek, his voice full of tenderness. "There is nothing to worry about. Children of sacred blood very seldom cry."

"Are you saying..."

He nodded. "Yes. I believe she may be a truth holder."

"Why didn't you share this with me before?"

August sighed. "I wasn't sure at first, and I did not want to jump to conclusions, but your observations have solidified this truth for me."

I stared down at Eva, taking in this reality. "Does that mean that she is going to start needing to Embrace?"

"Yes, but not until she reaches sexual maturity, which for us is roughly around the age of sixteen. We have some time."

"What about the aging process for her?" I was suddenly overwhelmed with the implications of what having a child like her meant. How was she going to navigate the world with these gifts?

"Relax." August's hands ran down my back, softly kneading out the tension. "All these things will only begin to shift for her when she reaches her maturity. For now, she is very much a child like any other."

Even though I had sat with the idea of my child being like August, the actuality of it filled me with trepidation, for I now knew there were going to be things about Eva that I would never be able to understand.

The feel of Augusts' hands swept me away from my thoughts, and I closed my eyes, allowing him to take me to the places only his touch could go. A warm relaxation flowed through me as his fingers caressed my back and wandered down the length of my arms.

"Come to bed, *Amore mio*." His voice was a sensuous whisper, filling the space between us.

Summer grew weary and loosened her hold over us as the days slipped slowly into the blush of autumn, the grip of heat softening to a cool breeze. Afternoon sunlight filtered in through the windows of the living room as I sat with Klyda, who had stopped by for my postpartum checkup. Eva's joyful giggles filled the room as she played with Amico on the floor, the dog covering her face with his enthusiastic kisses.

"So, August mentioned that Eva may be a truth holder."

Klyda nodded at me. "Yes, I have noticed that myself. It is in her eyes."

"Her eyes?"

"Children of sacred blood have a calm wisdom in their gaze, they are able to retain the memories from the ones that came before. Therefore, they have an inherent understanding of the world around them." She leaned over and took my hand with a smile. "That is why they do not cry, Jezebel. They have no need to. They possess a comforting knowledge passed down from their ancestors and this inner knowing is what grounds them."

I looked out the window as the last bit of sunlight dipped below the hills, cresting the sky with shades of red and gold that shimmered like fire. "It sometimes feels like she is reading my thoughts."

"In a sense she is, but not in the way you think. It is more like she is tapping into your essence. Actual mind reading will not occur for her until she reaches maturity." Klyda shot me a playful wink. "Puberty is going to be fun."

I laughed as I bent down to pick up Eva, nestling her against my chest. I breathed in her sweet scent, reminiscent of lavender, and ran my fingers through her dark curls. She looked up at me and smiled, filling my heart with a fearsome love. With her piercing blue eyes and honey-colored skin, she was the mirror image of her father.

"Where is August, by the way?"

I raised an eyebrow at her question. "Care to guess?"

"Ah." She regarded me quietly for a moment. "I can see that him needing to Embrace outside of the home has been troubling you for quite some time now." Her hand grasped mine and gave it a gentle squeeze. "It's one of the many reasons we seldom take up intimate relationships with people of your kind... aside from the obvious aging factor that comes into play. There is a need that you will be unable to consistently fulfill for him. This creates a fracture that in time may prove damaging for you both."

I shifted myself on the couch as the sharp and familiar sting of bitterness rose within me. "I know, I try to understand all this... but it just feels like cheating to me."

Klyda nodded, empathy pooling in the depths of her brown eyes. "I understand how it can feel that way, Jezebel. But what August shares with you is incredibly sacred, and what he feels for you is unwavering. It reaches far beyond the flesh and into a place that is deep and eternal for him."

"How do you know? Has he told you this?"

She smiled warmly. "He doesn't have to; I can see it in the way he looks at you. There is only one other woman I have ever seen him look at in that way, and that was his wife."

"You met her?"

"I did once, at a Gathering in Syria. It was so tragic what happened to her." She paused for a moment, her face growing troubled. "And August has not been the same since. That is, until he found you." Klyda reached her hand up to touch my cheek, her eyes full of sentiment. "You have brought him back to life, and for that I thank you, Jezebel."

Winter encapsulated us. The chill of sleet tapped itself against the windows, leaving a lazy trail of ice upon the glass. The gentle notes of August's piano filled the room while I lay beside the crackling warmth of the evening fire with Eva playing next to me. She pushed herself to a standing position and toddled over to August, grabbing onto his pant leg with her chubby fist. "Da Da." Her melodic voice rose above his music and he stopped playing to pick her up, placing a kiss on the top of her head. She leaned against his chest, closing her eyes.

"Someone is sleepy." August stood, cradling Eva in his arms. "I will put her to bed." He gave me a warm smile. "You look far too comfortable right now."

I smiled as he retreated up the stairs with Eva. My eyelids fluttered and then closed as the heat of the fire soothed me into a drowsy inertia.

* * *

August's hand rested on my shoulder, rousing my body from sleep. Turning to him with a drowsy smile, I ran my fingers down his cheek. "How long have I been asleep?"

"An hour or two." August reached up to brush away the wisps of hair from my face.

Pulling him close to me, I nestled my lips against his neck. "I don't know why I've been so tired lately. It's not like Eva keeps me up at night." I ran my hands down his back and slipped them underneath his shirt. All the books I had read during pregnancy in preparation for having a child did not seem to apply to Eva. She slept through the night, teething did not bother her, and she had never once been sick.

"You gave me a perfect child, August."

"No, Jezebel," August said, running his hand down to cup my cheek. "*You* gave *us* a perfect child." His lips fell on mine like a spark of fire, warming every inch of my body.

Time had not dwindled the heat between us, in fact it seemed to grow in intensity as if the act of birthing a child had exposed all the layers of our desire. August's fingers lost themselves in my hair as his kiss grew deeper. I reached up to unbutton his shirt, sliding it down his arms and running my hands over the breadth of his chest. The way the firelight fell against his skin, brought forth a memory of one of our first nights all those years ago; the hesitancy and confliction that swam in his eyes as he had allowed me to touch him for the very first time. Elation coiled fiercely within me as I realized just how far we had come together, how our love had stretched and bloomed into something rich and beautiful.

August deftly released me from the restrictions of my clothes, leaving hot trails of pleasure upon my skin as his mouth slipped down into the waiting warmth of my sex, teasing me with his tongue before he rose up and replaced his kiss with the light stroke of his fingers.

His breath grew heavy as he watched the flush of my arousal spill across my skin. "I long to Embrace you right now."

"Oh god, *yes*." My words tumbled out in a moan as he hovered above me.

His lips trailed across my chest, his voice a deep rasp. "Are you ready?"

"Of course." I arched my neck for him, feeling his teeth grow sharp in response to my arousal as the blissful explosion of his

Embrace cascaded through my body. I cried out against him, frantically digging my nails into the flesh of his arms.

August suddenly pulled away.

"What is it?" I panted, trying to draw him back to me, confused as to why he had stopped.

He shook his head. "You taste different."

"What do you mean?" I looked up at him to see his eyes clouded with worry.

"Something is wrong, Jezebel."

CHAPTER EIGHT

We sat together in one of the many reception rooms within the large community hospital, awaiting the results from the specialist.

The bright fluorescent lights cast a garish hue across my skin. My fingers clenched nervously in my lap, the whites of my knuckles showing until the soothing warmth of August's hand took mine, squeezing tight, centering me. My eyes followed Eva, who tottered around the room, taking in this strange alien landscape around her.

An older woman sitting beside us leaned close to me. "What a striking little girl you have." Eva toddled over to her, flashing a big toothy smile. "Oh my, those eyes. This one is going to steal hearts."

Smiling stiffly, I pulled Eva into my lap and wrapped my arms around her, breathing in her comforting, familiar scent as I tried to still the pounding of my heart. I hated hospitals as the memories they brought back were not ones I wanted to recall. Shifting uncomfortably in my seat, the looming weight of the past week washed over me.

August had been vague as to what could be going on. He had only told me that I needed to get some tests done to rule out possibilities. *It could be something as simple as an infection*, he had said, but his eyes seemed to speak otherwise. We had gone into town and met with a doctor, who after much insistence from August, ran my bloodwork, followed by a lymph node biopsy and a CT scan. I knew why we were here. Nobody was called in regarding a negative test result. I tried to swallow the growing unease which threatened to consume me. I didn't want to think about the pressing reality of it all, and I clung to the faint hope that this was nothing but a mistake.

"Jezebel Plath?"

My name rang out, jarring me from my thoughts as August took Eva from my arms.

"Are you sure you don't want me to come in with you?" he asked, gripping my hand supportively, the blue of his eyes swimming with emotions that I was reluctant to read.

"No, it's okay. You stay here with Eva."

Anxiety coiled tight within my gut as I stood to follow the nurse through the wide double doors and down what seemed like an endless white hallway.

In a small room, I waited for the doctor. My pulse beat frantically, drowning out the sound of the ticking clock above me. The sharp smell of disinfectant hung in the air while my body sat rigid in the black plastic chair that squeaked whenever I moved.

The door opened, and a woman walked in. My eyes darted to her name tag: **Amelia Russo-Head of Oncology**. My breath stilled. There was no escaping this. The symptoms I had pushed away for months came rushing at me. The casual excuses for my gripping fatigue, the nights I awoke drenched in sweat. My body had been telling me something, and I had not been listening.

"Hello, Jezebel. My name is Dr. Russo."

Her voice held a thick Italian accent, her melodic tone coming out slow and soothing as she spoke, an art most likely perfected from years spent speaking to cancer patients. I nodded weakly at her, feeling my vision begin to blur.

"I have the results of your tests." The sound of papers rustling was like an echo against the walls as she sat down at the desk in front of me and opened a folder. "We have bad news and good news." A long pause followed as she waited for me to meet her gaze.

I stared into the proficient composure of her warm brown eyes as a wave of nausea washed over me. "I have cancer, don't I?"

She nodded slowly. "Yes. You have what is called Anaplastic large-cell lymphoma."

The walls suddenly began to tilt and close in around me. "And what's the good news?" My words were dry and bitter tasting like bile in my mouth.

"The good news is, we caught it early. You can thank your husband for being so insistent on getting these tests done when he did. This is a very aggressive, rare type of cancer; had you waited for more symptoms to show up, the prognosis would have been much different. With chemotherapy, the odds are high of beating this."

I closed my eyes, feeling my head begin to spin. I did not want to ask what the statistics were.

"Jezebel?" Her cool hand rested over mine, and I opened my eyes to find her crouched beside me. "Would you like me to bring your family in now? We can go over the treatment protocol together with your husband."

I nodded blankly and watched her rise and slip out the door, closing it softly behind her.

* * *

Rain angrily pelted the windshield as we drove home, the frantic beat of the wipers the only sound in the car as dread clawed at my insides, the haunting echo of the oncologist's words swimming in relentless circles within my mind.

August's jaw was tightly clenched as his hands gripped the steering wheel. From the back seat, I could see Eva's blue eyes staring at us, clearly affected by the leaden energy around her.

August pulled into the driveway and cut the engine, a heavy silence filling the space between us as he slipped his hand in mine, his eyes full of tangled sadness. Opening the car door, my legs shook as my feet sunk into the soft mud of the ground. The cold slap of rain hit my face as I wrapped my coat around me, watching as August strode around to my side of the car, and pressed me tightly against him.

"Jezebel." His voice eased the frantic pounding of my heart as he anchored me in the strength of his arms; warm, consistent, and comforting.

"Can't you heal me?" I choked as tears stung my eyes.

"No. I cannot. My abilities to heal through touch only reach so far. I can repair what is broken, but I am unable to draw out sickness." He gripped me tighter to him, his voice labored. "God, how I wish I could though."

I don't know how long we stood there, holding onto each other with a quiet desperation born of disbelief and sorrow. The steady cascade of rain fell around us, soaking our hair and clothes while Eva sat quietly in the back seat, gazing out the window as drops of water slowly slid down the glass. Eventually, August pulled away and gripped my arms, his face resolute as he looked deep into my eyes. "We will get through this together. I promise."

* * *

I lay curled on the couch with Eva's tiny body nestled against mine, watching the flames from the fireplace leap and flicker before me. Evening had fallen, and the rain continued its incessant patter like a lulling rhythm upon the roof as the tangled thorns of my thoughts swam in my head, incessant and crushing. *What if Eva grows up without a mother?* I knew the burden of this reality, and it was a notion too painful to bear.

August came into the living room, running his hand gently down my back, concern softening the corners of his eyes. "Shall I put her to bed?"

I nodded, my limbs heavy and inert as I placed a lingering kiss on her forehead and slowly released her from my arms. Eva stirred and opened her eyes, the blue of her gaze piercing through my apprehension.

"Beddy?"

I smiled and reached out to stroke her cheek. "Yes, baby girl. It's beddy time."

August headed upstairs with Eva. The faint tone of his deep vibrato spilled through the floorboards as he began to read to her. My eyes flickered over to the coffee table, where the pamphlets from the oncologist lay, a stark reminder of the reality I was too fearful to step into just yet.

I pulled my blanket tighter around me, trying to block out the buzzing in my head. I needed a clear mind to process my diagnosis without the frantic rush of panic consuming me, a panic that no amount of August's calm composure could soothe. The thought of my mortality emerged and faced me beside the fire. I had seen the empty eyes of death before, I knew its unyielding power, but I also knew the strength one could find from facing the possibility of it. I had to be strong, for Eva and August, but most importantly, for myself.

A knock on the door startled me. Bleary eyed, I rose from the couch, my footsteps shuffling as I padded across the marble floor. When I opened the door, a woman stood before me, and I was met with familiar green eyes flecked with light. She pulled me close, the scent of wind and ocean in her hair as she wrapped me up into the warmth of her arms.

"Raven," I spoke into the fabric of her red velvet jacket, cool against my cheek and splattered with drops of rain. "What are you doing here?"

* * *

I sat in the living room with Raven, watching the steam slowly rise from the tea she had made us; fragrant notes of chamomile and lavender drifting around me, soothing my nerves.

"I had a very strong feeling that I needed to come." Raven set her cup down on the coffee table beside the pamphlets and took my hands in hers. "Now I know why."

I nodded as the weight of all my emotions welled up inside. "I'm so glad you're here."

She sat with me in silence for a moment, allowing the space within me to soften as the trickling warmth of my tears rolled down my cheeks.

"You are allowed to be scared, Jezebel." Raven squeezed my hands tight, her eyes full of compassion.

"I can't," I choked out. "I have to be strong."

"You are strong. You are stronger than you know." August's voice startled me, and I turned to find him standing beside us. Leaning down, he cupped my face and placed a deep lingering kiss upon my lips, his thumb gently brushing a tear away. "One of the endless reasons I love you." His breath was soft against my cheek, causing a gentle flutter of warmth to wrap around me, stilling the tremulous feelings whirling within.

August placed his hand on Raven's back. "I am glad you came. It is good to see you after all these years. I just wish it could have been under more pleasant circumstances."

Raven nodded to him, sorrow swimming in the depths of her eyes. "Me too."

* * *

Raven followed me up the stairs and into the art studio. My hands trembled as I moved to pull out the fold-away bed for her. The warmth of her hand on my back stopped me. "Let me do this. You go get some rest; it's been a long day." She drew me close, placing a light kiss on my forehead. "I will be here for as long as you need me."

Tears stung my eyes once more as I sunk into the soothing comfort of her arms. "How am I supposed to get through this?" I whispered.

Raven squeezed my shoulders as she pulled back to look at me, her eyes full of a gentle wisdom I longed to curl up within. "No matter what happens, Jezebel, I know your strength will guide you. Just remember that it is the acceptance of fear, not the removal of it, that gives you strength."

The weight of the day pressed against me, demanding and ominous. *Did I have this strength within me?* I wanted to believe her words, but all the years of my habitual avoidance rushed in with its heavy grip, demanding submission, and stifling my certainty.

With a tense smile, I nodded to her before softly closing the door behind me and slipping out into the hallway. The floorboards gently creaked beneath my feet as the impermanence of life curled around me. None of us were given a guarantee on time. We were all like tiny leaves desperately clinging to the branches of a tree, hoping a sudden gust of wind wouldn't knock us loose and send us tumbling away.

Shutting the door to our room, I found August sitting on the bed with a far-away look in his eyes. I walked over to him, running my fingers through the thick waves of his hair as he clasped me around the waist, drawing his head to rest against my chest. My hands trailed down his back, and I pressed him closer, needing to feel his body against mine, to flush out the noise of my mind; to lose myself in the comforting anchor of him.

"August." My voice came out a tremble. "Make love to me."

He looked up; his eyes faintly obscured by the muted light. "Are you sure this is what you want right now?" His words were hesitant and full of concern.

"Yes." I traced his lips with my finger as my skin flushed with longing, "I don't want to talk. I just need you to make me feel whole again."

August drew me down onto his lap. His mouth was a warm caress against my neck as he gently pulled my shirt over my head and ran his lips softly across my breasts, paying homage to my skin as if it was something fragile and sacred. My hands shook as I reached to unbutton his shirt, his gaze filling me up with an impassioned devotion that stripped away the heavy residue of my thoughts. Rolling me onto my back, he slowly slipped off my pants, and then shed his own upon the floor. The feel of him against me was like coming home from a place of darkness.

"*Jezebel*," he spoke my name in one long, drawn-out, sorrowful sigh against my lips as he slid himself inside me, plunging deep and achingly slow. I gasped as pleasure filled every inch of my body, releasing me from reality. The rain drummed on the roof above us, the steady rhythm drowning out my cries and washing everything away as I clung to the bliss of him within me. All that existed in this moment was him and the intensity of his love, filling me up until I could no longer think.

* * *

Bright moonlight woke me. While I lay sleeping, the rain had finally stopped and through the window the clouds had parted, revealing the brilliance of a full moon. I turned over in bed to discover the space next to me void of his warmth. Pulling on my bathrobe, I tip-toed down the stairs to find August sitting at the kitchen table with a bottle of whisky beside him, his hand tightly clenched around a half empty glass. He turned to me, his eyes bleary and bloodshot, and I realized he had been crying.

I went over to him, placing my hands upon his shoulders. "Come to bed." Leaning down, I placed a kiss on his neck; he smelled strongly of liquor. "Lay with me."

"I cannot sleep, Jezebel." His words came out in a soft slur which startled me. I had never seen him drunk before.

"August." I faced him and grabbed his arms tightly, willing his calm composure to return. "It's going to be okay. Like you said, we will get through this together. You heard what the doctor said, we caught this early, and we have a good chance of fighting this with treatment."

He shook his head slowly, his face full of so much anguish it frightened me. "No, Jezebel. I do not see you winning this battle." The whites of his knuckles showed as he gripped the glass in his hand tightly, his voice a choked whisper. "*And I cannot lose you.*"

His words were like a knife in my gut, and a hot wave of panic washed over me. "What are you talking about?" And then it hit me. How could I have forgotten? *He can see my future.*

August looked up at me, his eyes swimming with tears, and his face a mask of dark turmoil like the gathering of a storm. I sunk down into the chair next to him, my whole body numb as my voice came out in a tremble. "How long have you known this?"

He shook his head slowly. "I only see the future when I look for it, Jezebel. And I have been too terrified to look until now."

"What do you see, August?" The words came out clipped and broken as the reality of my fate slammed into me with a sickening force, sucking the air out of my lungs.

He closed his eyes for a moment, taking a deep breath before he spoke. "Do you remember when you asked me if I was able to change you, and I said no?"

I nodded, nervously threading my fingers together. "Yes, I remember."

"Well, I lied."

"What do you mean *you lied*?" Confusion swam in my gut as I tried to put together the pieces of what he was saying to me.

August regarded me with a look of grave hesitancy. "I mean, there is a way. It is called an Awakening. But it is dangerous and does not always work." He glanced out the window for a moment, lost in the silence of his inner turmoil as the light of the moon cast fragmented shadows over his face.

Leaning across the table, I gripped his hand in mine. "Why is it so dangerous, August?"

"Because," he sighed, his eyes flickering back to me with a somber intensity. "In order for me to Awaken you... you must first face your own death."

CHAPTER NINE

"You want to Awaken her?"

From where I stood on the stairs holding Eva, I could hear Klyda in the kitchen speaking in a low voice to August.

"You know the complications of this. You have mere seconds during the transition. You miss that window. And she will not come back. It's too risky, August."

"This *will* work." he said in a measured tone of confidence. "There is no other option here, and I *cannot* lose her, Klyda."

"He's right." Raven spoke up. "I see this working."

As I walked into the room with Eva, all eyes fell on me, and a thick silence washed over the kitchen.

"Ah, there she is!" Raven's face lit up as she pushed herself out of the kitchen chair and rushed over to where I stood, scooping Eva up into her arms. Eva grasped onto Raven's hair as she twirled her through the kitchen. "Who is the most beautiful little angel?" she cooed in a sing-song voice as Eva broke out into a wide smile.

Klyda turned to me, her face full of concern, and placed her hands on my shoulders. "Are you absolutely sure you want to do this?" Her eyes hesitantly scanned my body. "Because if you are, we don't have much time. I can see the cancer in you, Jezebel, and it is spreading far too quickly. If we wait much longer, your body will become too weak for this transition."

I nodded to Klyda. "Yes. I want to do this." Though a faint trace of fear coiled in my gut, my voice was resolute as I looked at August from across the room. "If I had known this was an option before, I would have done it sooner."

Initially, I had been upset when August confessed to me the night before that he'd kept this truth hidden, but at the same time, I understood why he had. I knew he struggled with the heavy implications of what an awakening entailed. I was struggling as well, knowing that the animal in me would fight this. Death was a fierce opponent, and nobody knew what lay underneath the mask.

But I knew it was the only option, and the lifeline he was offering was worth the surrender. Not only would he be releasing me from this cancer, which was ravaging my body at an alarming rate, but he would be giving me the gift of time. There was a comfort in the knowledge that the things which had separated us would finally fall away. No longer would I have to worry about what would become of us when I began to grow old before him, my skin sagging with the quickening of age. We had never spoken at length of this inevitability between us. Neither of us wanted to focus on the fact that I would eventually die and leave him behind. *"Life is made up of moments,"* he said to me once. *"These moments are lost to us when we spend our lives consumed by a future not yet formed."*

Klyda's eyes held apprehension as she spoke. "And August has explained the process to you?"

I nodded. "Yes, he did." I glanced over at Raven, who hugged Eva close against her chest. The gentle rays of winter's morning sunlight illuminated their faces, causing my heart to swell with urgency. "I just need a few days."

Among the vineyards, against the stark grey light of the late afternoon sky, I walked with Amico at my feet and the solitude of my own mortality beside me. The cool breath of November whispered against my skin as the breeze tossed up my hair and blew around the last of the leaves, which had been eagerly clinging to the vines.

The fragility of the life I knew stared back at me with wide, questioning eyes. *Was I ready to give up whatever time I had left?* Knowing there was a possibility of something going wrong, was I truly prepared to jump blindly into the fire and join August on the other side? The weight of this sacrifice pulled heavily at me as thoughts tumbled around my mind, fervent and pressing. But beneath all this lay a burning ember of determination, I was not just doing this for myself, I was doing this for Eva, and for a love which engulfed every fragment of my being.

The wind picked up, wrapping around my body like a tender embrace that stirred something within me, and I was suddenly overcome with a feeling of hope. This sensation I clung to with an ardent desperation as the frantic noise of my own trepidation faded to a gentle hum, and resolution stood beside me. Quiet and filled with possibilities.

* * *

I found August sitting at the desk in the living room, his brow furrowed in concentration as he scribbled furiously in the large leather book that usually sat tucked away in the top shelf. He looked up at me when I approached.

"Where's Eva?"

"She is napping." August reached out his hand and pulled me onto his lap.

"I've always wondered what you write in this book of yours." I said, tracing the tip of my finger down the soft pages filled with his tightly slanted, Latin script.

"Thoughts that no longer have space in my mind."

A small smile crept across my face as I ran my hands through his hair. "I didn't know you were a writer?"

"I write to solidify my emotions."

I rested my head against his shoulder. "And all your secrets?"

August brushed his fingers down my cheek, lifting my chin to meet the tender burn of his gaze. "I have no more secrets with you, Jezebel."

"You promise."

Nodding, he rested his forehead against mine. "I promise."

I leaned across the desk, flipping through the smooth pages until my eyes fell to a date from four years ago; right after we had met. I gave him a playful smile. "Well, what's this one about then?"

August regarded me with a glint in his eye as he slipped his arm around my waist and began to read.

"*Trembling breath and ebony hair against my skin. Spilling her fragments of beauty onto the rocky soil of my heart. The heat of her tangled limbs calling forth a magnitude of desire I can no longer contain. A sacred chalice filled with possibilities I long to drink deeply of. She sleeps as if she longs to fly, and when she awakens, light swims in her eyes with the reverent hush of a thousand wings taking flight.*"

The eloquence of his words hovered in the air like honey. "Is that about me?"

"Yes."

"It's beautiful."

"*You* are beautiful." August pressed his mouth against my neck, his lips trailing sparks of heat across my skin as his voice dropped to a seductive whisper. "*How I am going to miss the energy of you.*"

I looked down at him. "Are you are saying my energy will be different?"

His gaze grew stoic as he pulled me close to him. "Yes, it will. Your body will resonate on a different vibrational field after an Awakening. It will be a rebirth of sorts, and certain aspects of yourself that no longer serve you will drop away."

"Like what?" A whisper of hesitation coiled around me. All my imperfections had become an intrinsic part of who I was, and I found myself wanting to cling to them.

August's smile was a warmth that enfolded me as he appeared to slip into my thoughts for a moment. "Do not worry, you will not lose yourself. You will only release the things that hold you back from growth."

I ran my hand along his jaw line, touching his full lips with my fingertips, feeling the spark that passed between us whenever our bodies were close. "I'm ready for this, August."

He nodded. "I will summon Klyda then. Raven said she will watch over Eva." A look of hesitancy crept across his face. "Are you absolutely sure you want to do this tonight?"

"Yes, I'm sure." I knew I was running out of time; I could feel it in the quickening of my pulse. My body was losing this battle within. But I had found a glimmer of strength in my long walk out in the vineyard, and I clung to it with a soothing fortitude born of faith.

* * *

I stood beside our bedroom window, holding Eva close to me. Darkness shrouded the landscape below as the gentle rise and fall of Eva's breath against my chest soothed the edges of my nerves, her small body growing limp as she drifted into sleep.

I watched Klyda as she quietly set up a monitor and IV bags next to the bed. My heart accelerated wildly, and my mouth grew dry as the bitter taste of fear washed over me. The gravity of what was about to happen hit me with a sudden intensity. *What if this doesn't work? What if this is the last time I ever hold my little girl?* Unease curled within like a weight against my chest, and I clutched Eva tighter against me.

"Have you done this before?" I asked Klyda in an anxious whisper, careful not to wake Eva.

"Yes, I have. A few times."

"What about August?"

She walked over to me, placing a hand softly on my arm. "Yes. It was *me* in fact that he Awakened centuries ago."

"What? He never told me this?" Shock washed through me as I stared at Klyda in disbelief.

Contemplation swam in the depths of her eyes as she spoke. "I believe he never shared this with you because it wasn't his story to tell. It is mine. You see, I was a Giver when we met, and then I grew ill. But August knew I had much more to do in this world, and so he gave me the gift of time. One I will be forever grateful for." Klyda paused and glanced out the window for a moment, her face flickering with unease. "Though I almost did not survive my Awakening. The invention of modern medicine has made this process far safer than it used to be."

As she spoke, I could see the young woman she once was

reaching out to me, and a tentative thread of connection bloomed between us as we stood in the delicate space between our shared stories.

"So... how does it feel to die?" My words felt like sandpaper, abrasive against my throat as the question tumbled out of me.

"It is different for everyone. For me, it was like coming home to a place within I never knew existed until that moment. You see, it is not so much death itself that is frightening, only our perception of it." She squeezed my shoulder lightly, her voice soft, comforting and filled with a tenderness that stilled the doubt which had woven around me. "You are in good hands, Jezebel. I will be here to closely monitor the entire process, and August will make sure this transition is as comfortable as possible for you. I know this is scary for you, but you must have faith. For faith is the key that opens the door you were meant to walk through."

Raven stepped into the room, holding out her arms to take Eva. I reluctantly released her, leaving a kiss on the soft warmth of her cheek. Raven leaned in close to me, her voice a soothing hum in my ear. "Do not worry, everything will go as planned. I will see you on the other side."

* * *

The whispered shadows of evening stretched across the room. I lay on the bed with August beside me, the warmth of his hand in mine as the soft and steady blinking of the heart monitor attached to me punctuated the stillness between us. A long, thin tube lay connected to his arm, running up the length of the IV bag, and into the vein of my own, tethering us together. August slowly went over the steps with me again, beginning with the Embrace that would still my heart, and then the transfusion of his blood which would Awaken me.

"Are you ready, *Amore mio*?" He cupped my face, running his thumb softly along my cheek as a deep pool of tangled sorrow hovered in his eyes. I knew how hard this was for him, knowing that in order to save my life, he first had to take it from me.

Reaching out, I clasped his hands in mine, realizing he was trembling. "I love you."

The torment I knew he was trying to hide, slipped out through the cracks of his façade, and tears spilled from his eyes. He hastily wiped him away, his voice a choked whisper. "I love you too. *More than you could ever know, Jezebel.*"

My fingers brushed against his cheek, catching a stray tear. "August. I need you to promise me something."

"Anything."

"I already spoke with Raven about this, but if something goes wrong, I want to make sure that she remains a part of Eva's life." My throat constricted as the words tumbled out. "I need to know that she will always have a mother."

"Jezebel. *Stop.*" His tone was thick with desperation as he shook his head. "Nothing is going to happen to you." His face grew dark for a moment. "I will not let it. Losing you is simply not an option."

"Just promise me. *Please.*" My voice became frantic as I gripped his hands tightly. "I need to know she won't grow up without a mom."

August reached over to tenderly sweep my hair out of my face, a look of anguished resolution settling over him. "Of course, I promise."

Leaning back onto the pillows, I pulled the covers up around me, feeling a sudden chill which I knew was not from the cold. I nodded to him somberly. "I'm ready."

Hesitancy flickered across his features. "Are you sure?"

I took a deep breath, summoning courage. A steady flame pulsed within, born of determination and a reliance that felt larger than my fear. "Yes, I'm ready."

"I will be right back." Klyda's hand rested upon my arm, giving me a gentle squeeze before slipping quietly out the door to give us our privacy.

August pressed me close against him. "God, I love you so much, Jezebel," he spoke in a fervent whisper as his fingers tangled in my hair. "*I will see you soon.*"

His lips found mine, soothing me with a long, slow kiss. Warmth cascaded through my limbs, igniting a spark of desire, and softening the sharp intensity of my own apprehension as August's mouth ran down to my neck, his lips lingering against the blush of my skin. With a deep sigh, I drew him closer, guiding his teeth into the vein that throbbed with the rhythm of my quickened pulse.

The walls around me shattered, everything blissfully falling away as I rocked with the pleasure August pulled from within. The endless wave of ecstasy crashed over me and escalated with a sharp intensity as he drew me even deeper into the current of his Embrace, crossing a line I had never neared before.

My limbs became weightless, like I was floating on air. The gentle tendrils of death's lure were surprisingly seductive. I became pacified in its overpowering hold as the room began to blur and fade into a soft, white light. Until there was nothing left but darkness. Warm, silent, and still.

CHAPTER TEN

A loud rhythmic beeping roused me from a place of soft fragmented light, as if my soul had been delicately hovering in the space between dreams.

Voices swirled around in my head, a cacophony of thoughts and feelings not of my own. My eyelids fluttered open to meet with a brightness that burned.

"She's back." Klyda's whisper seemed to echo harshly off the walls. "Turn off the lights, August. She needs to acclimate."

My hands grasped the sheets, the sensation almost abrasive as I felt every fiber against my skin. I opened my eyes once more to a darkness I had never seen before. Void of light, yet each detail and line in the room shimmered with clarity. August's hand clutched mine and squeezed tightly. His eyes were a burning blue and filled with an elated relief. His joy gently tumbled over me like sparks of illumination, dancing against shadows of grey.

"Welcome back, Amore mio." His words became a soothing caress that slipped its way inside my mind.

My limbs buzzed with energy, and a stirring of excitement grew within my chest. "It worked?"

August smiled at me with a warmth that seemed to touch my skin. "What do you feel right now?"

My voice came out in a choked whisper. *"Everything."*

He nodded. "It will take you some time to adjust, all your senses have been heightened."

My body rippled with adrenaline and euphoria, my limbs humming as I moved to sit up. I felt alive in a way I had never experienced before. I longed to move, to dance, to run wildly through the night. Something primal and profound coursed through me, as if I were accessing some energetic power directly from the world around me. My breathing grew labored and my skin flushed with excitement.

"I need to go outside."

Klyda chuckled and glanced at August with an amused look. "She is so high right now."

* * *

I stood under the night sky. The clouds parted above me to reveal the moon, which shone so brilliantly I felt as if I could reach out and touch it. Every sound around me pulsed with a fervent heartbeat. The wind brushing over the blades of grass, the rustle of leaves, and the scurrying of animals rooting through the undergrowth surrounded me in the symbiotic hum of life.

My legs longed to move, and so I found myself running down the gentle slope that led to the vineyards, through the maze of tangled vines and out across the meadow. I marveled at the sudden freedom of my body as if a weight had been sloughed off, revealing a lightness of being within, like wings longing to take flight. Wind streamed against my skin, lifting my hair up into the night sky. Reaching the edge of the vineyards, I gazed out into the endless expanse of hills, like an undulating sea of serpentine before me. My breath came out in short bursts as streams of mist coiled up from the ground, softly rising upward. I could make out the light crunch of footsteps and turned around to see August walking toward me.

"There you are."

"I feel so amazing." I grasped August's arms, my eyes wide with wonder. "You never told me it would feel this good."

August gave me a slow, languid smile. "I suppose for me, this state of being is all I have known." He reached up to run his hands through my tangled, wind-blown hair. "Unlike you, I have nothing to compare it to."

"Will I always feel this incredible?"

"Right now, you are in a state of exaltation. This is your re-birth. In time, your mind will adjust to the changes within you."

He trailed his fingers lightly down my neck, resting against the heavy rise and fall of my chest. His emotions were a sudden palpable force I could feel swirling around him as he drank me in with the heat of his eyes.

"God, you are so exquisite. You remind me of some beautiful, untamed creature."

I looked up at him with a mischievous grin. "Well, if you want me, you have to catch me first."

I darted away from him, laughter filling my lungs as I sped through the meadow, but August was faster than I gave him credit for. Within seconds his arms were around me, snatching me up tightly against him, his breath hot against my neck.

"I got you." His words curled around my mind like a tender touch.

"How are you doing that?" I turned to him; the sharp definition of his features outlined against the ink of the sky.

August's lips curved into a playful smile. "Doing what, Jezebel?"

"Talking to me, inside my head."

August brushed his fingers across my brow, slowly trailing down my cheek. "You now share my blood. This connects us telepathically to one another when we are together."

"Really?" My question hesitantly pressed against his mind, exploring this new concept of communication between us.

"Yes, Amore mio." August stroked against my thoughts like a sensual whisper as he bent down and drew his lips to my skin. Electric sparks of pleasure exploded within, and I leaned my head back, my body surging with a desire that consumed every part of me. In the chill of the night air, I pulled him close to me and reached for the zipper of his pants, cupping the throbbing heat of him in the palm of my hand.

"Jezebel. What are you doing?" His voice was a playful growl against my mouth.

"I want to feel you inside me." I breathlessly moaned.

Suddenly, I was on the ground. The dew on the grass tickled my skin deliciously as he slid my pants down and entered me with such passion and force that I cried out into the night, my body alight and pulsing with bliss.

I didn't think it was possible to feel more with him, but I did. In that moment, something broke open between us and our bodies were no longer separate beings clinging to each other. We had become fluid and raw, transcending skin and bones into an energy I could visually see. I gasped as waves of radiating color washed over our flesh; indigo, purple, and green, shimmering like the northern lights.

I curled around him, shuddering as my body tore open into fierce fragments of ecstasy. August's eyes feverishly bore into me, blue against black, his lips chanting my name as the heat of his devotion spilled deep inside me like a liquid fire, scorching the entirety of my being. Our euphoria merged effortlessly together in the darkness, taking us to that magnificent place that left nothing behind but the raw exposure of our hearts.

* * *

We lay in bed together that evening, watching the sky slip away into the delicate colors of sunrise, bathing our skin a dusty pink. I nestled against the warmth of August's chest as the high of my Awakening slowed down to a gentle rhythmic sway, allowing the vibrant beauty of the evening to wash over me.

"August." I rose to where I could see the blushing light of the sky mirrored in his eyes. "When we were together out in the meadow, I saw these beautiful colors on our skin. Do you know what that was?"

"I believe that was your gift, Jezebel." August ran his finger slowly down my arm. "The colors that you saw back there was the energy between us. Usually after an Awakening, it can take some time for your gift to become apparent. But I am not surprised that it showed itself quickly for you."

I stared at him as the gentle light of the morning spilled across his face. Reaching out, I ran my fingers through his hair. "Why is that not surprising?"

"Well, you were very open to your Awakening. For others, it can be quite frightening at first."

"But what exactly is my gift?"

August smiled, pulling me closer. The deep tenor of his voice sounded in my ear. "I believe that you may be an energy healer. This is a very powerful gift. It gives one the ability to heal deep-rooted emotions within yourself and in others. The colors you see are similar to an aura which allows you to pinpoint where the stagnation or trauma lies hidden within the body."

I sat up, running my fingers down the length of August's chest. "And what about yours?"

August took my hand and placed it upon his heart. "Look closely. What do you see?"

I allowed my mind to settle as a warmth percolated through me. A rosy glow the color of the sunrise washed across his skin, shimmering like light dancing on water.

"I see pink."

Tears suddenly arose and gently trickled down his face, the breadth of his emotion encapsulated within his eyes. "That is the color of healing, Jezebel. Don't you see? You have already helped me repair what has been broken long ago." August coiled his fingers in my hair. "I believe you have always been a healer."

I sank into the warmth of his gaze. The energy between us hovered like particles of color so rich, I felt as if I could reach out and touch them. And I realized that the walls between us had now dissipated, leaving behind a space large enough for us to share.

* * *

I awoke to midafternoon sunlight streaming across our bodies, and the animated sounds of life moving below us. The low voices of Klyda and Raven filtered through the floor, along with the playful lilt of Eva and the gentle padding of Amico's feet.

I quietly slipped out of bed, careful not to wake August, who still lay asleep, his dark hair spilling across the pillow, his body in peaceful repose. The way the light fell on him, hitting the toned definition of his back, he reminded me of a beautiful, bronzed statue, and I suddenly had a longing to sculpt him.

I dressed and made my way downstairs to find Eva seated on the living room floor, an array of toys scattered beside her as her bright blue eyes met mine.

"Mama!"

My heart leapt and tears of gratitude sprung to the surface as she called out and teetered over to me, her dark curls bouncing like a halo around her head. I enfolded her in my arms, feeling the sweet miracle of her skin against mine and the steady and courageous beating of her growing, vibrant heart.

* * *

I sat at the kitchen table with Klyda and Raven, enjoying the overwhelmingly smooth sensation of my cup of coffee. I could suddenly taste every lush undertone within the beans, fragrant layers which I had never experienced before. Through the window, the expanse of hills in the distance beckoned to me with a sharp clarity, like I was viewing the world from a magnifying lens.

Raven leaned across the table, taking my hand in hers. "So, how does it feel to be Awakened, Jezebel?"

I smiled, the ripple of euphoria washing over me as I recalled the night before. "It's incredible. I can feel everything around me now. It's like my whole life was just a tiny fragment of something so much larger that I'm finally able to tap into. I feel like I've been living in a cage this whole time, and I've finally been set free."

"Wow." Raven sat back in her chair, shooting Klyda an enquiring look. "Can I have some of that?"

Klyda chuckled, rising to take her cup over to the sink as August walked into the kitchen with Eva on his hip, his hair tousled from sleep.

"*Good morning, Amore mio.*" From across the counter, August gazed at me lovingly as his words slipped into my mind like a gentle caress.

My heart trembled with the profound joy of this new life, which coursed brilliantly through me as winter's hesitant sunlight filled the room with a rich glow that sparkled like tiny crystals.

CHAPTER ELEVEN

I kissed the top of Eva's head as August and I stood together in the doorway. His arm gently wrapped around my waist, stilling the tangled nerves that had gathered to the surface. Eva bounced in Raven's arms, her pudgy hand splayed out to me in a wave, watching us as August and I made our way out the door and to the car.

The evening held a hint of warmth to it, and I could feel the delicate push of spring in the air. This past week since my Awakening had been filled with so much vibrancy and breathtaking wonder as I took in the world around me with new eyes like that of an awestruck child. But a persistent fatigue like the grip of fever had now settled over my body, and my thoughts were growing disjointed and hard to grasp as if I were suspended underwater. I knew I had to face the reality of what that meant.

"You are nervous, aren't you?" August turned to me, his gaze piercing through the depths of the dim interior of the car.

"A little." My voice came out hesitant as I fiddled with the seatbelt. The idea of Embracing filled me with trepidation, like standing on the edge of a cliff with wings on my back; my mind still struggling with the concept of flight. "I'm not quite sure how all of this is going to go."

His hand found my knee, resting it there for a moment. "You obviously do not have to do anything that you are not comfortable with. Camilla has been a very dependable Giver for me. She is extremely receptive." He leaned in close and brushed his lips against my cheek, his voice warm in my ear. "I no longer want this separation between us, Jezebel."

I nodded, his gentle words soothing me like a warm blanket of refuge. I threaded my fingers in his as he turned the ignition and drove us down the darkened road; the sky awash in stars which followed us in a trail of light, bathing the interior of the car in flickers of illumination.

We passed the sleepy storefronts of Marcillina, with their quaint shop lights winking at us, and parked outside a small cottage at the edge of town. As we stepped out of the car and made our way up the cobblestoned pathway to her house, we were greeted by the melodic tinkle of various wind chimes that hung from her porch.

Before August had a chance to knock, the door opened. A petite woman who looked around my age stood before us with deep hazel eyes and long wavy hair the color of coffee. "Benvenuto." She nodded and motioned for us to come inside. "I'm Camilla, and you must be Jezebel." She clasped her hands in mine. "It's so nice to finally meet you. August talks about you quite a lot." She smiled playfully over at him. "Though it does ruin the fantasy a bit for me, honestly." I found myself laughing at this, whatever insecurity I thought I would have slid off me like water. Camilla shot me a good-humored wink. "A girl is allowed to dream, right?"

I appreciated her candid humor, and it seemed to soften the energy between us.

"No, but seriously," she said, her eyes growing thoughtful. "I only hope one day someone can speak of me the way August does of you."

I smiled at her warmly. "Thanks for being open to this, Camilla."

She nodded, placing her hand on her chest. "No, thank you, I am deeply honored to be your first."

* * *

We sat in her living room, glasses of wine in our hands. Her house had a bohemian flair to it that reminded me of Raven. Long trailing houseplants crowded the corners of the room, accentuated by various buddha statues and brightly colored silk throw pillows. Talk began to grow lazy and languid between us, the energy shifting to a subtle hum of sexual tension.

"Shall we begin then?" Camilla asked with a smile, leaning forward from the couch to rest her wine glass on the coffee table.

August's eyes focused on me with a heavy look of sincerity. "Are you ready, Jezebel?"

313

I smiled nervously. "I guess so."

August rose from the chair beside me and kneeled upon the floor, placing his hands on my knees before slowly running them up my thighs. "Just tell me how you want this to go? You have complete control here."

His touch drew warmth from my core, and I sank into the feel of his hands. "I want you to go first."

"Are you sure?"

"Yes." I ran my fingers through his hair, trying to focus on him and not the quickening of my pulse. "I want to watch you."

I looked up to find Camilla calmly removing her clothes and placing them neatly beside her on the couch. This sudden intimate unveiling startled me for a moment as she lay down upon the pillows, watching us with a look of interest from across the room.

August must have sensed my discomfort, for he threaded his fingers through mine and gave them a reassuring squeeze. "When one takes part in an Embrace, the Giver's energy is best accessed through touch without the barriers of clothing. But if this makes you uncomfortable, Camilla has no problem putting her clothes back on."

My eyes flickered over to her as she lay there and nodded to me in agreement. "Would you prefer me to get dressed, Jezebel?"

I shook my head, taking a deep breath to steady myself. "No, it's okay. I don't mind."

August drew me close to him, running his thumb softly across my cheek. His gaze filtered out the world around us for a moment as he drew me into a deep kiss that spoke of things only shared between us.

August stood and extended his hand. *"I want you closer, Amore mio."* His voice spilled into my thoughts like a rich wine, causing a faint quiver of excitement to suddenly run through me as he led me over to the couch.

Bending down, he placed his hands upon Camilla's legs, his fingers slowly running up the length of her thighs. Her body trembled, already deeply aroused by his touch as he slid past her sex, eliciting a sharp moan from her as he continued up to her breasts, gently teasing them with his thumbs.

"Oh, God." Her words came out breathless upon her lips, causing a gentle flutter inside me as I saw her skin flush and a shimmering purple band of color radiated out from her abdomen, her pleasure like the color of violets.

I was surprised to find that it was not jealousy that coiled within as I watched August touch another woman. It was arousal. His skillful hands on Camilla caused a surprisingly urgent ache to form within me, for I knew exactly how she felt in that moment, almost as if I was feeling it myself. Her pleasure had become my own. She spread her legs, and I knew she longed for him to touch her deeper. Moving closer to August, I took his hand and guided it down below, into the slick warmth of her.

She writhed against him as he stroked her center. I could tell she was close to the edge as August turned to me and pulled me into the heat of his gaze. My limbs hummed with a heavy desire as I lost myself in this erotic moment shared between us. Seeing August bring another woman pleasure only seemed to solidify my own longing for him.

"Please... I'm ready." Her urgent plea pulled his attention back to her as he drew her up against his chest, his lips running across her neck. Camilla clung to him; her eyes heavy with arousal as her gaze met mine.

"Embrace her, August." My words reached out and pressed against his mind.

He sank into her, and a loud cry erupted from her lips as her nails dug into his back, violently climaxing against him. August's hand reached out to me and intertwined his fingers with mine as I watched Camilla with the avid fascination of a voyeur; her head thrown back in unabashed ecstasy as she rode the potent wave of August's Embrace.

Releasing her gently, he laid her back down upon the couch as Camilla turned to me with a playful smile. "Sorry, I think I forgot to mention I can be a bit loud." She breathlessly chuckled as her head rested against the pillows, motioning to me with her hand. "Jezebel, come here."

I sat down beside her, my heart accelerating as she took my hand in hers. "I am ready for you." She gave me a slow, teasing smile. "And I promise not to scream in your ear."

I reached out to run my fingers through her hair. "I don't mind if you do." She looked so beautiful lying there. She had an uninhibited sensual grace that I found to be quite alluring, and a sudden pull towards her drew me closer.

Leaning down, I rested my lips against the delicate flesh of her neck, feeling the race of her pulse and the subtle scent of her perfume, a mixture of jasmine and rose. Camilla let out a soft sigh as my lips touched her skin, eliciting a faint tingling on the upper half of my teeth, her arousal like a pulse of electricity. I drew back, running my tongue over the sudden sharp edges. "It's okay," she said, guiding me close to her once more. "Remember, it doesn't hurt."

Hovering over her neck, I raked my teeth lightly across the skin, the current of her energy beckoning to me like a seductive whisper. "Yes." She moaned, gripping me tighter against her. "Embrace me, Jezebel." Her labored breath was warm in my ear, enticing me, and I was overcome with an unexpected urgency, like a band of tension longing for release.

I plunged in slowly, and an overwhelming rush of euphoria cascaded through my body as I began to draw from her. Her energy merged with mine in a beautiful, symbiotic dance. I could feel her loneliness and her strength, the pain she pressed away and the boundless light she carried within.

Camilla cried out beneath me as August's voice slipped inside my mind like a stimulating caress. *"You know it is time to stop when you feel the intensity of that rush waning."*

I lost myself to the sublime feeling of her. The breathtaking vibrancy of her essence was like a sweet intoxication born from the pulse of life itself, filling me up until August's hand landed gently on my back.

"That is enough, Jezebel."

I released her with a gasp, my entire body coursing with elation. The space around me shifted to a sudden, sharp clarity; my senses heightened once more, reminding me of the night of my Awakening. I looked down at Camilla as she lay there on the couch, eyes half closed with a dreamy expression on her face. Reaching down, I touched the marks left by us, watching as they vanished beneath my fingertips.

* * *

August placed an envelope upon Camilla's coffee table. Her dark hair was splayed across the couch cushions as her lashes fluttered in sleep. I found a blanket hanging over the arm of a chair and went to cover her up, tucking her in, as one would a child.

We let ourselves out quietly, through the hushed night air and into the car. Turning to August, I rested my hand on his knee, squeezing it tightly as my words tumbled out breathless and full of awe. "That was incredible."

He smiled at me, his eyes twinkling as he pulled out of the driveway and back onto the main road. I watched the blur of the countryside going by my window as my body vibrated with a delicious energy.

"Have you ever Embraced a man before, August?"

There was a long pause before he replied. "Yes, I have."

"And did you enjoy it?"

He looked over at me, placing his hand on my thigh. "I have enjoyed every Embrace." He winked at me seductively as his fingers trailed slowly upward. "Despite my obvious preference."

"Which are women?"

"No." His fingers lazily circled the fabric of my skirt, lightly teasing me with his touch. "Which has been you. But in general, an Embrace with a woman is much more potent."

"Really? And why is that?"

"You are life givers. The essence within you is inherently more powerful and refined than that of a man. Yours in particular. The first time I ever Embraced you, I was overwhelmed by the intensity of your essence."

"You were?" I glanced over at him, his eyes swimming with a heavy desire which sent a strong ripple of arousal to course through me as his gaze met mine. "You never told me this before."

August shot me a seductive smile. "Yes, you were quite inebriating, Jezebel."

"I was, huh?" I ran my hand slowly up his arm, feeling the heat between us like a force so heavy it stilled my breath.

"Yes. But it was much more than that. Your soul spoke to mine in a language I have never heard before."

With a sudden jerk of the steering wheel, August pulled the car over to the side of the road, quickly cutting the ignition. "And it still does, Jezebel. You captivate every part of me." With a smoldering look, he grabbed me and kissed me with a rough passion, pressing me against the seat. "I do not think I can wait until we get home." His voice was a thick growl of urgency against my skin.

I unbuckled my seat belt and moved across the console to straddle him, my limbs weak with desire. His breath grew labored and his body shuddered beneath me as his hands impatiently pulled at my clothes.

A powerful blast of pleasure erupted within as August gripped my hips and slid himself inside me, thrusting deep and hard. I cried out, rocking fiercely against him as my fingers dug into his back, slipping into the endless, engulfing bliss of him. The effects of the evening had culminated into this heavy frantic lust, fracturing whatever barriers we had left between us. Colors danced upon our skin, the familiar greens and blues I had seen before, spilling into each other, like waves desperately longing to break shore.

* * *

We tumbled into the house together, our skin flushed from the heat of our arduous lovemaking in the car. The silence was like a cool caress in the darkness as we crept up the stairs, careful not to wake

Raven and Eva. August's hands hungrily grasped at me, his breath like a shiver upon my neck as we slipped into our room and quietly closed the door.

Pushing me gently against the wall, August pierced me with his fiery gaze, devouring my senses as his fingers trailed up my shirt, brushing over the peak of my nipples. His voice was a low, sultry growl in my ear.

"I am not done with you yet, *Amore mio.*"

A deep moan escaped my lips as August removed my clothes, then shed his own upon the floor, his eyes never leaving mine as I led him across the room and over to the bed. I lightly ran my hands down the length of him, teasing him with my touch.

August let out a loud groan and reached for me. *"Come here. I need to be inside you."*

A playful smile spread across my face, enjoying this subtle shift in power between us. "Really?" I whispered, bending down, and grazing my lips against the pulse of his neck. In response to his feverish arousal, the faint tingle began in my teeth, the sharpness pressing against his skin. "What happens if I Embrace you right now?"

He looked up at me, his gaze full of love as he softly drifted into my thoughts. *"Why don't you find out."*

Straddling his hips, I lowered myself down onto him, sucking in a sharp breath as I felt the primal explosion of pleasure within my core as his desire plunged into me again. Bending down, I drew my lips against his neck, gently teasing him with my teeth as I rocked slowly against him, watching as his skin rippled with soft fragments of golden light, the color of joy.

"Oh, God, *Jezebel.*" August moaned, tightly coiling his fingers around the strands of my hair, his words uncharacteristically frantic and pleading. *"Please."*

I sunk deeply into him as he cried out in harsh, fragmented Latin, his arms gripping me tightly. He violently shuddered beneath me as the thick warmth of him spilled into my core with a powerful rush of energy I had never felt before. My body surged and crested against the potency of his release, which collided into me with such force that the room began to spin recklessly around. The blinding torrent of his essence merged with mine, and the threads that tethered me snapped. I exploded into nothing but shattered light, tumbling fiercely into this untamed current of ecstasy with him.

Gasping for breath, I released him and collapsed onto his chest. August's voice was a dreamy caress against my ear. "You just completely *annihilated* me, Jezebel."

My body floated like a weightless vessel as I waited for my head to clear. The racing pulse of August's heart thrummed in my ear, pulling me back to myself. "That was *intense*. You were right."

He slipped his hand down to my neck, gently pulling my chin up to meet his gaze. "Right about what?"

"How making love during an Embrace is almost too much to handle."

A languid smile washed across his face. "Yes. It is called the Completion." August drifted his hand down my back as he spoke, his voice a breathless whisper. "When two points of energy merge as one, it completes the cycle. Drawing forth an abundance of one's own essence, which in turn creates an endless loop. It is beautiful, but also incredibly powerful, and the body can only handle so much before it burns itself out."

I gazed into the depths of his eyes, lost in the moment between us and all the magic that was slowly unveiling itself to me. Like a child full of wonder, I drank it all in, mesmerized by the vibrancy of this world August had brought me into. The achingly exquisite details laid out before me like an endless canvas.

I curled into his arms, watching as moonlight bathed our bodies in a delicate, silvery hue. "So, what *exactly* does it mean to be a Truth Holder?"

"Well, it means that you now have access to the abundance of energy that holds all of existence together. This power comes from the ancient beating heart of the universe itself." He drew me close to him, his lips a gentle murmur against my ear. "The severed chords of your birth have been restored, and no longer is there any separation between you and the endlessness of the stars above."

I turned to look up at him, my reflection caught in the muted light of his eyes. "So, are you saying that we are connected to the stars?"

"Yes, in the same way that everything around us is. Your soul has existed for centuries, but the life you knew before your awakening was only a tiny whisper of possibility. The door is now wide open, Jezebel."

Overwhelmed by the power of his statement, a shiver ran through me, born of excitement and a yearning that stretched me wide open. My fingers reached out to trace over the hypnotic colors that rippled across our skin, in awe of the way our light delicately danced together in the darkness.

CHAPTER TWELVE

"So, what are you going to do with this gift of yours?" Raven asked as we walked among the vineyards together for the last time. Tomorrow morning, she would be flying back to the East Coast.

The day was blustery, but the wind blew warm against our skin, teasing the trees with the promise of spring, their tiny green buds boldly pushing forth.

"I'm trying to figure that out," I said. "I'm still not really sure what being an Energy healer means for me."

Raven's warm hand rested on my back for a moment. "You will in time. When you are ready, the answers will come to you, and when they do, I believe you will help a lot of people."

I turned, pulling her into a tight hug. "I'm so glad you are in my life. I never told you this, but you remind me of my mother."

Raven placed her hand on my cheek tenderly as tears formed in the corners of her eyes, her voice wavering as she spoke. "And you remind me of my daughter."

"You never told me you have a daughter."

She nodded, sadness pulling at her features. That is when I noticed a wave of dark blue shimmering against her chest, the energy of her own trauma held within her.

"I *had* a daughter. But I lost her years ago." Raven glanced up at the sky as if trying to pull forth her own fortitude from the endless depths of blue. "But I am beginning to understand that the people we have loved and lost, they don't truly leave us. The mark they imprint upon this world becomes an essence that resides in others." She grasped her hands in mine, squeezing hard. "We are all connected by these invisible chords, and that is what makes this life so incredibly beautiful."

August and I stood in the airport together as Raven held Eva in her arms, showering her pudgy face with kisses. "I'm going to miss you guys," she said, putting Eva down onto the floor where she immediately began to inspect Raven's suitcase, unzipping the pockets and pushing her hands inside.

"You know, you could always just move here and live with us?" I said with a playful smile as I wrapped my arms around her tightly, not wanting to let go of the woman who had become such a solid force in my life.

Raven laughed. "Careful now. I just might take you up on that offer." She shot August a teasing wink as she went to pull him into a hug.

Raven turned and took my hands in hers, her face growing serious and full of tenderness. "I see a long wonderful road ahead, and many beautiful things for the four of you."

"The four of us?"

"Yes, Jezebel." She smiled warmly. "One day, you will have another child."

Raven picked up her suitcase and gave us a nod that spoke of the quiet truth unspoken between us. Words were not needed, we were family now. We watched as she blended into the sea of bodies waiting in the security line, her long flowing hair and bright red jacket slowly fading from sight as she proceeded through the terminal.

Stepping out of the shower, sunlight cascaded through the bathroom window as I grabbed a towel. The melodic sound of Eva's giggles from downstairs filtered through the floorboards. Glancing down, colors washed over my skin, faint shades of grey and dark blue, rippling across the scars of my thighs. I took a deep breath and touched them hesitantly as a swift visceral memory overcame me.

Blood on my hands and the piercing sound of my own screams.

Yanking my fingers back, the image faded as quickly as it had come.

My pulse whooshed violently in my ears as I began to tremble, suddenly terrified of my own body and what it held within. My deep-rooted memories were no longer dead and buried to me, but very much alive and clawing at the surface. A piercing sob escaped me as I slid to the floor.

The door opened and August rushed in, his face tense and full of concern. Kneeling beside me, he drew me into his arms. "What is it? What is wrong?"

Tears spilled onto his shirt as I clung to him. "I am seeing things I don't ever want to see again."

"Oh, Jezebel." He pulled my chin up to meet his warm empathetic gaze, instantly calming my rapid heart. "You know that this is your body healing itself."

I shook my head. "I can't... I can't go back there."

"You can. The only way you will be able to truly heal is if you face the pain of your past." August gently brushed away the tears from my cheek with the pad of his thumb. "Believe me, I am all too familiar with this truth. I have spent many years running from my own."

I knew he was right, but I wasn't prepared for the intensity of my memories to flood in so vividly, as if I had been propelled back in time and forced to relive them all over again. At this moment, the gift I'd been given felt like a torment.

August's strong arms lifted me off the floor. Wrapping the towel around me, he threaded his fingers softly through my hair. "All you have to do is face the pain. You owe yourself that."

I walked into the bedroom on shaky legs and collapsed down upon the bed. The colors still rippled across my flesh like a dull ache, demanding my attention as August sat beside me, his eyes a deep well of concern.

I knew that my trauma was the ghost that haunted me. So many years I had spent hiding from the past like it was an ugly secret concealed in a dark room with no air. It was time to face this shadow of loss and give it closure. Only then would I be able to fully release the pain and allow healing to take root.

"I think I need to do this alone."

"Are you sure?"

This was my wound, and something within me knew I needed the fortitude to confront it without the comfort of August's steady guidance blanketing me. I had spent too many years avoiding this. I nodded slowly and reached my hand out to him. August clasped it tightly in his, and drew me into a tender kiss, his lips against mine dulling the edge of my trepidation.

"I understand. I will be right here if you need me," he said in a whisper, before turning and closing the door softly behind him.

A heavy silence filled the room as I laid down on the bed, curling myself into a fetal position. I braced myself with slow, deep breaths as my fingers reached down and made contact once more with my scars.

* * *

Rain pelted the car windows. The reflection from the streetlights cast an orange glow upon the streaks of water cascading down the glass. The rhythmic thump of the wipers drowned out my mom, who sat in the front with my dad, humming along to the radio. I sat hunched in the backseat pouting, my arms crossed in adolescent defiance, angry at them for telling me I couldn't go to my friend's party that weekend.

My mom turned around in the seat to face me, her long blond hair shimmering a copper color from the taillights in front of us. "Chickpea," she said imploringly. "Please don't be cross."

"Stop calling me that!" I shot back at her.

She threaded her hand in between the seats and rested it on my knee for a moment. "Don't worry, you will have plenty of time to hang out with cute boys unsupervised, but I need you this weekend, okay?"

"God...Mom!" I moved away from her and turned my eyes toward the window. She softly chuckled, and I jutted my chin out in annoyance. "I don't understand why I have to be there for the stupid baby shower."

"Because, Sara," my mom said, sighing, her hand coming up to rest on the large swell of her belly. "I would really like for you to be a part of this. It will be fun."

"Please don't give your mom a hard time, Sara." My dad spoke softly

from the driver's seat, flipping on his blinker to navigate around a truck. His warm brown eyes met mine from the rear-view mirror. "You know how difficult this pregnancy has been, and now that your mother's feeling better, I think it would be really nice if you could celebrate with her."

We had rolled to a stop at a red light, and I watched as my mom slipped her hand into my father's. He turned to her, a look passing between them, causing me to roll my eyes.

"Dad, hello... the light's green!"

My Dad chuckled as he pressed upon the gas pedal. "You know, Sara..."

But his words were cut off by bright lights filling his side window, the screeching of tires on the wet road and the sudden sound of metal crashing against our car.

Drops of rain splashed across my face as my eyes fluttered open. Somebody was shouting from far away, and something warm and wet covered my thighs. I reached my hands down to my lap and they came up obscured in the thickness of blood. Panic coursed through me. I tried to move, but my legs were stuck. That's when I recalled where I was. The windshield was cracked like a shattered spider web. In the crumpled front seat lay my mother, her head bent at an odd angle, eyes blank and staring. My father slumped motionless against the steering wheel.

"Mom...Dad." My voice came out a hoarse whisper, like when I was a young child stuck in a nightmare from which I could not awaken. But this was not a dream, and the screams that spilled out of me were loud, shrill, and full of a choking fear.

* * *

The screaming faded as I was jolted back to the present, my face damp with tears, and the bedspread soaked with my perspiration. My body shook with a heavy fatigue as I sat up, gently pulling on the threads that connected me to the solid reality of my life. A life I loved with so much ferocity, and one I abruptly realized would not exist for me if it had not been for that one night that shattered the person I was. A sudden lucidity washed over me as I recalled what Jezebel had said to me in my dream all those years ago...

"We each have a story, Sara. One that we carry within our own compartment of pain. But hidden beneath the sorrow lies such raw beauty. One day when you begin to unravel your own story, you will see this, and you will understand why these trials were handed to you."

A lightness washed over me, a sharp clarity I had never felt before. I knew this journey to healing was not over, it was just beginning. But for the first time in my life, I felt ready to face it. Glancing down at my scars, I brushed over them lightly with my fingertips to find the swirling blue-grey replaced with a light pink that shimmered like the sunrise, and then dwindled away; leaving nothing behind but the shocking purity of smooth skin.

Spring was not shy this year. It burst forth with the vibrancy of life, the landscape shivering with color and filled with the euphony of birds unbridled song. Like a tender bud unfurling its own gentle renewal, my scars had now become a memory, tucked away within the tender archives of my past. I carried this healing reverently inside, paying homage to my repair, and alight with all the potential this gift had given me.

I stood in the kitchen making breakfast for Eva. Her big blue eyes watched me quietly from the table as August walked in from outside with Amico, who skittered at his heels, bouncing around and shaking the morning dew from his coat.

"Mama." Eva giggled, pointing at Amico. "Mico's dancing."

I smiled as August came up to me from behind and left a lingering kiss upon my neck. He smelled of rain and earth, and in his hand he held a bouquet of wildflowers, which he pressed softly against my chest.

"For you, *Amore mio*." His breath was a tender whisper in my ear.

I took the flowers, marveling at the vivid blues against delicate petals of poppies. "These are so beautiful," I responded, placing a kiss on his cheek. "What's the occasion?" August just stood there with a warm smile, watching me while I reached into a cupboard to grab a vase. As I went to fill it with water, a glint of silver flickered against the stems, and my fingers brushed against a ring which was nestled discreetly in amongst the flowers. Elegant bands of white gold entwined against intricately sculpted vines with a beautiful amethyst stone resting in the middle. My breath stilled.

"I want to spend the rest of my life honoring you, Jezebel." August's lips fell against my cheek as he slipped his hands around my waist.

My heart fluttered, and I turned to find his eyes full of a fervent emotion that enclosed the space around me. I swept back the dark strands of hair that fell across his forehead. "Are you asking me to marry you, August?"

He smiled warmly. "You can call it whatever you would like. The concept of marriage is only a formality that reflects the heart's intention." He took my hand in his, slipping the band over my finger. Sunlight caught the stone in shimmering prisms of light. "All I know is that you reach the places inside of me I thought had been forever closed. You touch every part of my soul, and I never want to stop dancing with you."

Tears welled up within me as I wrapped my arms around him. "Well, I've been wondering when you were going to ask."

"Mommy, Daddy. Huggies!"

Eva's crisp, joyous voice rang out as she climbed out of her booster seat and toddled over to us. Reaching down, I lifted her up and placed a kiss on the top of her head as August enfolded us both in his arms. The morning sun spilled through the windows, bathing us in a golden light that filled me with the tender sweetness of a joy unfettered.

Eva wiggled out of our arms and bounded across the floor after Amico, her rich laughter filling the room. August's lips found mine, backing me against the counter and drawing me into a long, languid kiss that sent a deep rush of longing through me.

"You make me so *incredibly* happy, Jezebel." His words were impassioned and breathless as he tangled his hands in my hair, piercing me with his fiery gaze that never failed to obliterate my senses. "I am not frightened to look into the future anymore. For when I look forward, all I see is endless beauty."

I gripped his arms as an immense emotion born of gratitude and a boundless love spilled out, running a path down my cheeks. "My God, how did I ever find you?"

August reached out to softly brush away a tear. "You didn't, *Amore mio*. I found you, remember."

CHAPTER THIRTEEN

A warm spring breeze filtered in through the windows, bringing with it the sound of exuberant laughter. The hills were bathed in a rosy glow as the last rays of the sun sunk below the horizon. I rested my hand on the soft swell of my belly, August's ring catching the fading light as I reached for the platter of food on the counter.

A commotion burst through the kitchen as Eva ran through with Amico excitedly barking at her heels.

"Mommy, Mommy! When are the big fireworks going to start?" She bounced on her toes; her face flushed from outside.

I ruffled her hair. "Soon, Eva."

She gazed up at me. "Did you know that me and Rome almost have the same birthday."

"Yes, you do. Though Rome is much older than you," I said with a smile.

"I'm old," Eva stated with brassy vivacity as she bounded out the door, calling over her shoulder. "I'm almost five."

Amico stood beside me panting, and I chuckled, bending down to stroke his head where traces of grey had begun to form. "You can't keep up with her these days, can you, boy?"

I walked out onto the patio where I was met with the familiar faces of Raven and Klyda. They stood talking with a few others gathered around the table, which was spread with an assortment of food. The neighbor down the hill from us stood talking to August, an older man with smiling eyes who would let Eva run among his flock of docile sheep, tangling her fingers through their soft wool. The vineyard workers and their families were there as well, with their children's laughter weaving in between the adults.

In the grass overlooking the gentle darkness stood Camilla. She was wrapped up in a loving embrace with a man who looked at her with such tender affection as he brushed a strand of hair from her face and leaned in to kiss her. Life swelled around me with abundance, while down below the pale green buds of the grapes awaited sunlight's eager caress, transforming a season of growth into the rich sweetness of wine.

A distant explosion of color collided with the sky, showering the hills with crackling sparks of light. Eva entwined her hand in mine, her face filled with awe. "It's so pretty mommy."

I pulled her close, breathing in the scent of lavender which always seemed to encompass her. "It is, isn't it?"

August appeared from behind, slipping his arm around me and gently running his hand across the rise of my belly. Leaning back, I rested my head against his chest, watching as the fireworks reflected off our skin in a vibrant, trembling blush of color.

* * *

The evening grew quiet, leaving a blanket of stars strewn across the sky as our guests slowly filtered out. Raven stood beside me in the kitchen, helping me clean up.

"So, I found a little apartment in the city." A delicate beam of light from the moon spilled over her face as Raven wiped down the folding tables we had brought from outside. "I think it would be a great place for me to set up shop." She winked at me.

"Are you serious?" I turned to her with a large smile. "You're really moving here?"

"For the time being, yes." Raven moved toward the window to gaze out upon the landscape dusted with moonlight. "This place suits me."

Walking over to where she stood, I placed my hand on her shoulder. "You don't know how happy I am to hear that."

Raven draped an arm over my shoulder, drawing me close against her. "How are the classes going these days?"

My heart swelled as it always did when I thought about the pottery classes I taught in the city to troubled youth and kids in the foster care system. They would show up with the bright red colors of tension curling around them, wearing the closed off look of children who had seen too much and spoken too little. By the end of our four-week sessions together, they left clutching their sculptures close to them like talismans with a warm, rose colored glow pulsing within their chests and a lightness in their eyes; a beautiful reminder of their own inherent strength growing inside them.

"They have been amazing. Words cannot express what it feels like to help these children through art."

A commotion from above startled me as Eva bounded down the stairs and rushed into the kitchen, wrapping her arms around the back of my legs. August followed behind her, a look of amusement flickering across his face.

"I cannot get this wild child to bed. Too much excitement for her this evening."

Eva giggled as he picked her up and placed her on top of his shoulders.

"Mommy, we are going to say goodnight to the stars. Come with us!"

I stood out amid the cool evening air, the gentle breeze running over my skin as I watched August and Eva chased each other through the grass, shrieks of laughter rising into the dark ink of the sky. While above us the stars winked softly, like tiny beacons guiding us steadily onward.

Darkened hours passed into an early morning light that danced over my skin. I awoke to the feel of August's arms gently wrapped around me in sleep. Turning over in bed, I pressed my lips against his. His eyelids fluttered open, meeting my gaze.

"Jesus, Jezebel. You are so beautiful."

His voice was a lustful whisper as he pulled me close to him and rested his forehead against mine. His fingers began to lightly trail across my swollen breasts, teasing the nipples, and drawing out that deep endless ache from within me.

Suddenly the door flew open and Eva bounced onto the bed, her long curly hair flying wildly around her face. She nestled in between us, burrowing into our blankets, her feet chilly from the wood floor.

August chuckled sleepily. "Good morning, Eva."

"I had a dream last night."

"Really, Chickpea? And what was your dream about?" I asked, running my hands through her mass of dark tangles.

"I was in a meadow and the sky was really purple. There was a woman there, and she had the same name as you, Mommy."

I turned to August, who reached for my hand under the covers, squeezing it softly.

"She gave me something."

"Really? What did she give you, love?" August's voice held a faint tremble of emotion as he spoke.

"She said that one day I will be able to travel into other people's dreams and help them."

A silence settled over us for a moment as we both took in the meaning of what this meant. Eva had been visited by Jezebel. Our child would one day have the gift of dream travel. This truth stirred the embers of revelation as I ran my hands across my belly, wondering what gift the little boy that grew within me would possess. Would he be a seer like his father, or an energy healer like me? Or would he become something else entirely? Something rare and vibrant, like an undiscovered gem.

"Mommy, can you make me pancakes?" Eva broke the stillness between us, her imploring blue eyes peeking out from beneath the covers; vibrant and filled with such breathtaking innocence

"I will make them for you, sweetie. Let your mom rest for a little while longer." August gathered himself out of bed, leaning over to place a kiss upon my lips as Eva bounded down the stairs.

"Are you okay?" My question gently pressed up against his mind. Knowing this was stirring up emotions for him. I placed my hand on his chest for a moment, my fingers tracing over the faint colors; ripples of blue and pink that flowed from his heart.

He nodded, and a lightness gathered in his eyes. "I always

wondered where she went right before she died." He ran his hands tenderly through my hair. "And now I know. She was with Eva."

As August walked from the room to join Eva downstairs, a feeling of profound marvel washed over me like a whisper of serenity entwined among the ties that connected us to this delicately beautiful world. I rolled over in bed, cradling my arms around the life growing inside me. "Elias," I whispered to the child within, bestowing upon him the name of my brother who I had never been given the chance to know. I now realized the truth Raven had delivered to me all those years ago in the vineyard.

Those we lose never really leave us. They are caught and held against the beauty of a sunrise, within the joy of laughter, and in the love that we boldly weave throughout this glorious canvas we call life.

FINEM

CPSIA information can be obtained
at www.ICGtesting.com
Printed in the USA
LVHW020346241121
704332LV00006B/312

9 781087 915821